Highland Chances

Emma Baird

VINCI
BOOKS

Vinci Books

vinci-books.com

Published by Vinci Books Ltd in 2026

1

A CIP catalogue record for this book is available from the British Library.
Paperback ISBN: 9781036711214
The EU GPSR authorised representative is Logos Europe, 9 rue Nicolas Poussion, 17000 La Rochelle, France contact@logoseurope.eu

By Emma Baird

The Highland Books

List of Characters

Gaby
A graphic designer of some talent and a woman who staked her future on moving to a small village in Scotland.

Jack
Gaby's very recent husband. Mean, moody, magnificent. He bears a striking resemblance to Jamie Fraser or rather, the actor who plays him, Sam Heughan. Gaby might occasionally suggest he's the actor's much better looking and younger brother.

Mildred
Their fabulous, and fabulously spoiled cat.

Ashley
The owner of the Lochside Welcome in Lochalshie, where you will find one of the world's most Instagrammable toilets, and a man desperate for business.

Caitlin Cartier
A 'self-made' reality TV star who achieved billionaire status at the age of 21, thanks to the beauty company she set up. Some of you might think she is based on a real-life person. The author refers you to the front of her book, where she tells you everything in this book is fiction and any resemblance to real-life characters coincidental. Entirely. Especially any bits that might be read as libellous.

Dr McLatchie aka Caroline aka Psychic Josie
Jack's mum, a GP who has embraced a side hustle as a psychic, one she freely admits is a complete fraud.

Mhari
A 'friend' of Gaby's and to date the nosiest woman in the world. Complicated love life, see asterisk one and two below.

Hyun-Ki
A hyper-talented South Korean graphic designer. Loves cats. Dates Mhari the modern way by conducting all communication via the medium of mobiles and exchanging Tik Tok lip-syncing tips.

Xavier
A French Canadian. Definitely oui-oui.

Katya
Gaby's best friend, a freelance writer, Pilates aficionado and talker of much sense. Bluntly, a lot of the time

Dexter

Her boyfriend, an American too fond of hyperbole and long working hours.

Jolene
A New Zealander ex-pat and new mum with a weird taste in boyfriends.

Stewart
Boyfriend of the above. Worshipper of all things porridge. If boring people ever becomes an Olympic sport, Stewart will take gold for Scotland.

Tamar
Their adorable child.

Mandy
Gaby's mum and owner of an unreliable Ford Fiesta.

Nanna Cooper
Gaby's grandmother. A woman with a wise saying for every occasion.

Zac
Posh, blonde. Unspeakable, according to Gaby.

Miles
Posh, blonde and the owner of a flash car.

Tindra
Posh, blonde. Mummy and daddy wangled her an internship and bunged her money, so she didn't need to worry about trivialities such as getting paid.

Big Donnie
A man with a fondness for the rules.

Lachlan
An on-off boyfriend of Mhari. Upon reflection, he prefers the 'off' status.

Lucas
The owner of a terrible orange wig.

Laney Haggerty
Just always in these books, okay?

Chapter One

"Happy six-month anniversary, hon! Here's to you!"

A raised champagne glass came toward me on the screen, contents gently fizzing. I clinked back; my own glass filled with sparkling apple juice instead. It was, after all, early Tuesday afternoon, and I was supposed to be working.

"And you! Can you believe we've been married this long... Seems like only yesterday that I was Gabrielle Amelia Richardson, spinster of Great Yarmouth, weeping and wailing and wondering if I would ever meet the man of my dreams?"

Slight sarcasm there, but it flew over my fellow cele-brant's head. "Oh, same! Y'know, Gaby honey, the best advice I ever received was..."

The story made me smile. I'd heard it countless times—the meeting that changed two people's lives, bringing bliss to one and a tonne of money to the other.

"... and now you're Gabrielle Amelia McAllan and sooooooo happy waking up beside the man of your dreams every single day..."

I snapped back to attention. Slight sarcasm there too? And every single day was an exaggeration. This week, for example, I woke up to him four days ago and no sign of him since. Phone calls and FaceTime are all very well but in person works best for me.

That is what happens when you marry someone who works in the tourist industry. It was June, though you might not know it from the temperature outside, and Jack was ferrying people to and from various scenic destinations. Thanks to the resemblance he bore to a particular red-headed fictional Scottish character, he ran Outlander themed tours. They took in Doune Castle, Skye, Clava Cairns and Glencoe.

Earlier this year, he'd employed an assistant to help lessen the amount of time he was away. Sadly, it didn't work out, and we were back to situation typical—prolonged absences and him exhausted and grumpy when he returned to the house at the end of each tour.

And if anyone had the right to be exhausted and grumpy just now, it was me. But best face forward for the boss and all that.

"Yes," I sipped my apple juice. "Soooooooo happy. What are you doing for the rest of the week?"

A huge sigh. "Filming today, Wednesday, Thursday and Friday. A date night late Friday with Donal to celebrate our six-month anniversary. Then, off on a promotional tour to South Korea for five days, plus an interview with Women's Health to launch my new fitness app, and I need to do a work-out with Pop Sugar to highlight that, and then at the end of the month, I'll be—"

Do not ask a world-famous reality TV star/'self'-made billionaire about her schedule. Her busyness was insane. It was 5 in the morning in LA, the only break in her day she could take. I often wondered why Caitlin Cartier chose me as her occasional confidant, but she went on and on about how the best thing in her life—Donal—was thanks to little ol' me.

I married Jack the day before her wedding. She then borrowed my 'proper' wedding day, my venue and all my guests and decided this bonded us together. We were 'besties' even if my real 'bestie' objected strongly to Caitlin's claim to the title.

"Doesn't mean anything, Katya!" I told her when she'd brought this up recently. "Caitlin has more than 700 'besties'. You're one of them too!"

Katya wrote Caitlin's 'autobiography' qualifying her for close status to the famous one—hence their friendship. And she too was a frequent recipient of the Caitlin 5am in LA Skype calls. Caitlin was also 'besties' with a lot of other famous people who might need their autobiography written by someone who knew how to spell and where to place commas and apostrophes, so when her laptop vibrated as a call came through on Skype, Katya plastered a smile on her face.

"My mom wants me to try for a baby," Caitlin said, fiddling with the stem of her glass, making me inhale sharply. Timely. Was Caitlin able to see anything…?

"Your mum?" I asked, screwing my face up. "But that's…"

"She says it'll push the show's rankings up again."

Keeping up with Caitlin was an offshoot programme of the original show, which featured all the Cartiers. The original show idea came from Caitlin's mother, a woman so Botoxed her eyebrows haven't moved in decades. Caitlin had been in the show most of her life until she decided to go her own way. She still appeared in the family show occasionally, which wasn't as popular these days. Adrienne Cartier must have reckoned lots of hints about Caitlin, and her sex life would win *At Home with the Cartiers* more viewers. Especially if she *did* conceive.

"What does Donal say to that?"

Caitlin's husband point blank refused to appear on either show, though you often heard him speaking to Caitlin in the background. His witticisms had earned him fan forums, all dissecting every remark. He did his best to give his in-laws a wide-body swerve.

Caitlin grimaced. "He says it's up to us and my mom can shove her rankings where the sun don't shine."

She put on a Northern Irish accent to mimic Donal, making me laugh. It must be hard living with a famous person when you don't like attention. I rubbed my belly in sympathy.

Caitlin gestured her glass towards me. "How are you, anyway, hon? Y'know if we got pregnant at the same time, it would be absolutely amazing, right?"

The apple juice went down the wrong way—or rather, that's what I told Caitlin as I went off on a massive coughing fit.

"Er…yes. Amazing. Anyway, I'll let you get on. Talk again soon?"

Caitlin had never worked out 'I'll let you get on' is British-speak for 'seriously, leave me alone. Do not talk to me a second longer'. Luckily for me. But I did need to do my own work. Jack always put his fingers in air quotes when he asked me about my working day. Because I had wangled a deal where I worked from home, he thought I spent all my time taking personal calls and watching cat videos on YouTube.

But so far this week, I'd only managed to see Cat Man

Chris, Kitten Lady's latest litter rescued from a dumpster and the Vet Ranch's operation to save a cat injured in a car accident. And another five I'd had to put on my list to watch later.

A woman entered the room behind Caitlin tapping her wrist. Caitlin screwed her face up once more—her assistant also wanting her to end the call. "Bye-bye bestie," she called out before the screen went blank. Behind me, in the not-so-glamorous Gaby world, a cat yowled. Lunch had only been two hours ago, and it was time for Mildred's afternoon snack.

I got to my feet, hands going to the small of my back so I could stretch. These days, it only took a few hours of sitting down for me to became uncomfortable. Maybe I needed to invest in one of those Swiss ball chairs perching on top of half of a beach ball to work.

"Okay, okay," I told Mildred as we made for the kitchen. "The finest Felix coming up."

Another yowl. Possibly a protest. Mildred worked out a long time ago that I was a pushover. We'd been trying to persuade her Felix cat food was delicious. Not so when you were used to organic venison and lightly poached chicken breast. I opened the packet, its off-fishy tang making me grimace.

Mildred fed, I wandered back into the living room, trying to motivate myself to design amazing web pages that made people want to spend too much money on fake tans, glow serums, false eyelashes and eyebrow shapers.

My phone pinged. A message from Jack. *"Hey, gorgeous. How are you…?"*

Always a tell-tale sign. As a Scotsman, Jack kept the soppy stuff to a minimum unless he had at least three pints in him. I discounted tipsiness. The greeting was meant to soften me up.

"I'll be back Friday, not Thursday as the tourists want to squeeze in a whisky trip to Speyside. Think of the extra money!"

Huh.

There was a knock on the door. I didn't get to it before the door swung open and my mother-in-law bustled in, loaded with shopping bags she dumped on the floor. "Broccoli. It was on special offer in Tesco's!"

She straightened up and put her hands on her hips. "How're ye, Gaby? Sit doon, sit doon, and I'll make ye a tea!"

One of these days I was going to insist Jack took the front door key she had to our house off her. A month earlier, she barged in when Jack and I had decided to spend a Sunday afternoon finding out if a roaring fire lent itself to… let your imagination fill in the blanks. I was on top too, all the better to eyeball her in horror when she burst in. "Was that nipple piercing no' awfy sore, Gaby? Mind, ye'll need tae take it out seven months fae now."

Privacy issues aside, the key thing had its advantages. Such as now when answering the door zapped energy from me.

"D'ye want some shortbread wi' it?" Caroline called through from the kitchen.

Yes. No. At this rate, I'd never fit into my favourite jeans again. I could hear Caroline talking to Mildred, telling her off for her impatience. She scraped out wooden pellets from the litter box, sending wafts of pee through to the living room. I did my best not to heave, the smell of it overwhelming.

Urgh. I stumbled to my feet and lumbered upstairs, making it to the bathroom just in time. Up came this morning's Special K, the fizzy apple juice and the beans on toast I'd eaten an hour ago. I flushed the toilet and rinsed my mouth out.

By the time I managed to get back downstairs, Caroline was in the living room once more. She handed me a glass of water and made me sit down.

"Still bein' sick, then?" She took my hand, turning my wrist over and glancing at her watch so she could take my pulse. "You poor wee thing. But that's the cat litter cleaned out for the day, so ye dinnae need to worry about that. Drink your water, and I'll fetch ye another glass. When's Jack home?"

"Friday."

"Och, that's too bad. I thought he promised you he'd no' work so hard this year?"

She didn't let me reply. Just as well because it would turn into a bitch-fest. "Anyway, I better go. I've got five patients booked in the surgery this afternoon. And then I'm meeting wi' that whisky company about this year's sponsorship o' the Highland Games. See you tomorrow."

With that, she was off, a car engine starting up a few minutes later despite the GP surgery only being four doors away.

My iMac screen had blacked out—sleep mode activated. I'd been too long not using it when I should have been working. Those glow serum product pages weren't going to create themselves. Still, the big boss was to blame. Caitlin insisted on phoning me while I was doing my best to work for her company, Blissful Beauty—currently the most successful start-up make-up company in the world, ever. It was the only beauty brand that had managed to crack the South Korea market—a country where people viewed skincare as a religion.

I was their second-in-charge graphic designer for the company's UK operation, allowed to work remotely and under a super-understanding boss.

On cue, his name flashed up on my phone. I hit the FaceTime button.

"Hyun-Ki! How is the most marvellous designer and boss in the whole wide world?"

"Magnificent!" I'd done my best teach my South Korean boss the English language's most excellent words. He came up with a different variation every time I asked him how he was. "How is the nine hundred and thirty-first best designer and eight hundredth best employee in the whole wide world?"

I blew him a ginormous raspberry. Good job he wasn't a formal kind of guy.

"I have big news, Gaby," he said, face solemn. "I wanted to tell you first."

"Oh, that's a co-incidence I've-—" But my words were cut off by Mildred who miaowed in the background.

Hyun-Ki broke off to blow her kisses. Always, always choose a boss who loves cats.

"The LA office wants me to work on a brand-new campaign," he said, giving me thumbs up with both hands. "And I'm going to be heading over there next month. If it goes well, I might end up the creative director for Blissful Beauty, Gaby!"

Oooooohhhhhh. Unlike me, Hyun-Ki ate ambition and the need to over-achieve for breakfast. When I first met him last year, he was a mere 22 and had already been promoted twice. In his spare time, he favoured self-improvement on a grand scale, signing up for advanced coding courses and working on improving his already excellent English.

He wasn't a hideous person to work for if you forgave

him the 7am starts and the nit-picking perfectionism. But how on earth would I cope with a new boss? One who might, whisper it, not want to spend the first half-hour of the day comparing notes on the cat videos we'd watched on YouTube?

As I pondered the awfulness of this, Hyun-Ki's voice broke through. "… so, as it's a temporary secondment, I've recommended you for my position in the interim. What do you think?"

My jaw dropped open. "What?! Are you kidding? They'll never let me do that job remotely, and I'm not working in London again. It's hideous."

The thought of it made me shudder. I'd spent three months there at the end of last year. Sometimes I woke up from nightmares where I'd dreamt about being on the Tube in rush hour, squashed up against a stranger's sweaty armpit.

Hyun-Ki smiled. "I knew you'd say that. You'd only need to come to London once a month. And look at that fantastic job you did for the Tantastic launch earlier this year. The launch broke all records for a beauty product."

Tantastic was a sponge on/sponge off fake tan ridiculously easy to apply and remove. The streaks and patchy bits that came with your usual fake tan? Not the case with Tantastic. Determined to get it right, I'd worked 16-hour days on the campaign for a week. I created an anime figure website that Blissful Beauty's social media followers could customise with their own faces, which then became avatars, demonstrating themselves applying the fake tan. It took Instagram by storm.

Then, as Tantastic was deliberately put on limited release, every time stores or the website restocked it, the product sold out in seconds.

Hmm. My imagination took over. Gaby McAllan, international jet-setter, hopping on a plane in Glasgow, waking 45 minutes later in London (Stansted), drifting into work, phone glued to ear as I negotiated critical work-related things before sitting at a desk while minions scurried around me.

"Here, Gaby—we got you a coffee. Black, no sugar, right? Do you want a doughnut?"

That happened when you were the big boss, right?

Blissful Beauty's HQ in central London included a flat. Katya stayed there most of the time with her significant other, Dexter, the head of marketing for the company's European, Middle East and African market. Might be nice to catch up with them once a month.

Be serious, Gaby.

I shook my head, making my earrings jangle. "I don't think I'm boss material. "Literally. Today, I was half-dressed. FaceTime and Skype let a caller see only the top half of your body, so I'd kept on my pyjama bottoms. International jet-setters, with their phones glued to their ears, while yelling at people about the design for the fake tan's summer advert, was wrong, wrong, wrong, did not wear their pyjamas to work.

Bosses also had to deal with budgets. Last year's planning for the wedding fiasco had convinced me that budgetary control wasn't within my skill set.

Hyun-Ki pressed his face closer to the screen, dark hair flopping forward. "Will you think about it? It's only for nine months."

"Okay. I'll give the idea serious consideration," I said, waving him goodbye, and saying, "Absolutely not!" out loud as soon as he'd gone.

Much as the idea of Gaby Boss had its merits, one

crucial point stood in its way. I rubbed my stomach again, the tiny bump that made my jeans too tight but was for the time being discreet enough for no-one to notice.

Why would Blissful Beauty want a head designer who was planning to start extended maternity leave in five months?

Chapter Two

"Why am I doing this?" Jack waggled the nail varnish bottle. The bonus of working for a make-up and skincare company was that I always had plenty of free samples. Earlier this year, Blissful Beauty brought out a new range of iridescent varnishes, this one a gorgeous sea-green with sparkly silver bits.

I swung my legs around and put a bare foot on his lap. "To make me feel better," I said. "When you're done, I'm going to slide my feet into my lovely cork wedge sandals and hope they distract Mhari from staring pointedly at my stomach."

"Will that work?" He stroked my foot, thumb kneading the pad of flesh under my big toe and making me arch my back in pleasure. I leant back against the sofa arm and let out a sigh.

"I doubt it. Last week, she snatched my glass off me, took a sip and announced it was only tonic water, to every-one. She then demanded to know if I was not drinking for the usual reason women my age suddenly start saying no to alcohol."

Jolene had taken the glass from her, swigged it down and said, "That's a G&T, Mhari. Shut up." She winked at me afterwards, and I sent her silent grateful thanks. Of all my friends in the village, Jolene was the most discreet. If she had guessed, she would keep her mouth shut. I was now past the 12-week mark—just—but my plan was to hold out making my condition public for as long as my body lets me.

"Tell her you're doing a detox. A health thing where you..." His voice petered out when I shook my head. The health excuse did not work when your well-known order of choice in the pub was a four-cheese pizza and chips, and you were regularly seen buying industrial quantities of pickled onion Monster Munch in the shop.

"Nice dress, by the way," Jack added, as he shook the bottle and opened it, applying precise strokes to my toenails. He painted in the winter months when he wasn't ferrying tourists around, so his pedicure skills far excelled mine.

The 'nice dress' was an empire line smock close in colour to the nail varnish. It skimmed my stomach and hid the small bump. So long as I didn't stand side-on in front of Mhari, I ought to be okay.

"Wait until it's tacky," I said, admiring the neatly applied colour on my toenails, "and then apply another coat."

"Your wish is my command, oh about-to-be mother of my child. How's your week been?"

I ought to bring up the job offer if only to promise Jack I'd lied when I told Hyun-Ki I'd consider it. I settled for how I felt right now.

"Knackering. Yours?"

"Same. Can we skip the pub quiz and..."? He paused,

finger and thumb, gripping the tiny brush and glanced up to catch my eye, dirty grin in place. His other hand slid up my bare leg, fingers sure and warm.

When we got married, I wondered if that would kill lust stone dead. Didn't couples moan all the time that the wedding ring acted as a chastity belt? In a previous job, my colleagues and I once stumbled on our boss's online calendar, the one she'd not made as private as she should. Sunday mornings 8-8.30am were highlighted—SEX WITH GREG. She'd added a 15-minute-in-advance text alert too. Josh, the guy I worked with, changed the day to Tuesdays and shortened the time slot to ten minutes. Not sure how that worked out for them.

But my own Highlander still made my heart flutter and my body tingle. Auburn hair that touched his shoulders, the evening summer sun picking out the gleaming gold bits in it. Dark eyes that glittered and a body made hard and muscular thanks to the prep he put in for the Highland Games every year. Tonight, he wore a T-shirt, which moulded to his torso, and dark jeans. I flirted with the idea of getting him to dress up in a kilt for me. Jack's knees did powerful things to my libido, and a kilt made access to the exciting bits further up dead easy. His hand continued its slow, lazy progress upwards, gripping my thigh.

"Love to." I let out a sigh. "But Ashley kind of relies on that quiz these days."

The landlord of our local pub, the Lochside Welcome, was finding business tough. He missed out on a lot of passing trade thanks to the Royal George at the other end of Lochalshie. The hotel had been taken over by a small chain which promised they were no threat to local businesses as they concentrated on the boutique mini-breaks market. It turned out, though, that coach trips, tourists doing the North West 500 and others saw the George and made straight for it.

The Lochside Welcome ran a weekly pub quiz every Friday that attracted mostly locals, but visitors often poked their head around the door and decided to stay too. Then, there were the professional quizzers—competitive types who drove all over the Highlands seeking out pub quizzes where they could show off superior knowledge and swoop up the prizes.

We always bought food beforehand as did most of the quizzers. Nowadays, Friday nights propped up the Lochside Welcome's income.

"I s'pose," the hand slid back down again. "But as soon as it's finished, we sneak out o' there as quickly as possible? Those newly painted toes put me in mind of something I might—"

Whisper, whisper, whisper. Dear heaven. I wasn't sure I was that flexible, but it would be fun to find out.

Nails painted and feet slipped into wedge sandals, I held my hand out so Jack could haul me up. What on earth would I be like by the time I got past six months? Caroline promised me most women found the first trimester exhausting. Growing a baby in the early stages took everything out of you. "But when ye get ower that bit, Gaby," she said. "Ye'll get a wee surge o' energy. It's the nest-building stage. Your hoose will be the cleanest it's ever been!"

Jack squinted at me when I told him that. We were a modern couple; in that, I did next to nothing housework-wise. Once upon a time, I moved into a neat and tidy home. Within days, my clothing covered the floor in the upstairs bedroom, the bathroom sported a layer of fine powder thanks to my make-up and printouts of designs covered the coffee table in the living room.

He said at the time he didn't mind.

We headed out, Jack shutting the front door behind us. His house was at the far end of the village on a street that overlooked the loch. As it was June, the sun sat high in the skies, its rays bouncing off the grey-blue water. I spotted Stewart walking his west highland terrier, Scottie, at the far side and waved. His house was close by so he must be on his way home.

Jack took my hand. "What kind of pizza do you want?" It disappointed him that I hadn't developed any weird cravings. He always asked the question wistfully, perhaps hoping I might say something bonkers like cheese, charcoal and pickled onions, please. Or, worse, a ham and pineapple one.

No, my only craving was tonnes and tonnes and tonnes of food. Most days, I battled the so-called morning sickness that lasted until two o'clock. By the time late afternoon came around, I was ravenous.

"A sixteen-inch," I said. "Four cheese. Two portions of chips. Mayo to dip them in. Garlic bread and a side of macaroni cheese."

"It's a myth, ye ken, Gaby," my mother-in-law's voice started up in my head. *"That eating for two thing."* Maybe, but what would you prefer to believe? That the baby growing in you needed plentiful food or only a measly 300 extra calories a day, which worked out, when I googled it, as one and a half slices of thinly buttered toast.

Inside the Lochside Welcome, every table was taken. Jack made his way to the bar and bought us both drinks, stopping there to order food. Lachlan, Jack's best friend, leapt up as soon as he spotted me, gallantly pulling out his chair. Or it might have been to escape Mhari, his on-off girlfriend, glued as ever to her phone. She put it down as I lowered myself onto the seat and pointed at my feet.

"Is that one o' Blissful Beauty's Christmas collections?"

No-one knew nail varnish better than Mhari. She wore inch-long talons year-round. An impediment to constant mobile phone use you might think, but not as it turned out. Ha. My distraction technique had worked a treat.

"That's an awfy loose dress." She plucked at the material, making me cross my arms protectively over my stomach. "And what's that you're drinking?"

I knocked back a massive glug of liquid and faked an unconvincing burp. "A brandy and lemonade. *Totally* delicious!"

She stared at me. "You dinnae drink brandy. That's no' even the right colour. Here, let me hae a drink o' it."

Food ordered Jack sat down, promising me it would not take long. I signalled 'rescue me!' vibes.

"Did ye hear, Mhari," he said, resting his forearm in front of my glass so she couldn't lift it up and try it for herself. "That Caitlin told Gaby her ma wants her to get pregnant because it will help the show's ratings?"

"No!" Mhari exclaimed, hand reaching once more for her phone. "Mind, you can see how that would work. Aw they folk who are bored of the Cartiers and their non-stop moaning because some eejit got a bigger limo than them."

Unseen by Mhari, I grinned at my husband. He shielded his face with his hand, waggled an eyebrow and made a point of looking at my feet. Ah yes. That super-flexible move he'd spoken about earlier. I nodded, and the corners of his mouth turned upwards.

"Mebbe I could be the official wean photographer," Mhari added, clicking out of an app on her phone before I could see what she was doing. My conscience stirred. Should Jack have made that conversation public via the world's biggest mouth? On the other hand, did she have any influence beyond Lochalshie?

"How's the college course going?" I asked. Mhari was taking an online photography diploma, a qualification she hoped would lead to bigger and better things than Lloyds Pharmacy, Lochalshie.

"Aye, fine. Look at this."

She opened the gallery on her phone, showing me an impressive selection of local landscapes. "Course when you're out and about taking pictures, sometimes you see folks in places they shouldnae be." She tapped her nose and grinned.

Heaven help anyone in Lochalshie embarking on an illicit affair.

My stomach rumbled. Fingers crossed my order was not far away. If Mhari dared nick any of it, I'd deck her. Jolene joined us, borrowing a chair from the next table. "How you doing, Gaby? That's a great dress? Matches your nail varnish?" Her New Zealand accent made everything sound like a question. Once upon a time, back-packing Jolene landed in Lochalshie and went to a ceilidh where she encountered the man of her dreams (ahem) and decided to make the place her home.

"Is Stewart looking after Tamar?"

Jolene's little boy was coming up for a year old. Once my pregnancy was official, I planned to bombard Jolene with questions about pregnancy, labour, and what looking after a tiny baby involved. Much more than I was ready for, I suspected.

Ashley, grey-faced and weary, appeared, arms laden with food.

"He can come back here anytime if he wants," he told

Jolene. "Doesnae need tae drink. He could have a coffee or orange juice."

Much to the astonishment of everyone in Lochalshie, Stewart had given up drinking four months ago. His bairn, he said, needed to grow up with positive influences. Sober Stewart was a strange creature; all of us unfamiliar with him. Before, he could bore for Scotland about porridge, coding and the superpower qualities of the midge, Scotland's mosquito. No-one else in the entire world has ever decided midges have redeeming qualities. These days…

"I know it's awfy wicked of me," Jack said, "but if he promises me once more that me and everyone else I know is an alcoholic in the making while we're supping a pint, I'll punch him."

It's telling that Jolene chose to escape their house as often as she could.

"I'll pass that on," she said to Ashley. "But he says the pub's a trigger and he needs to steer clear of it for six months?"

Privately, I wondered if Stewart's teetotalism contributed to the current state of the hotel's finances. The pub had been his second home. Ashley sighed and began unloading plates. He shifted from foot to foot. I'd noticed he was limping these days, badly, though he always dismissed questions about it. "D'ye need anything else, Gaby?"

Before me, a pizza took up most of the space on the table, our friends needing to whisk away glasses to allow Ashley to put down chips, garlic mayonnaise and a bowl of macaroni cheese.

I opened my mouth about to ask for dough balls when I clocked the look on everyone's faces—incredulous disbelief.

"That cannae be just for you!" Mhari said, prodding the bowl of macaroni cheese and narrowing her eyes as she stared at my stomach. I did my best to keep my expression neutral.

"I haven't eaten anything all day," I protested. "No, thank you, Ashley. But I'll have some of your Chocolate Decadence dessert afterwards, and if you nick any more of my chips, Mhari, I will kill you. No, even better, I'll nab your phone and lob it in the loch."

She pulled her hand back, poking her tongue out. As it turned out, my Nanna Cooper's favourite saying (she had many), 'eyes bigger than your belly' proved right. Half-way through the pizza and only one helping of chips down, I gave up pushing the remains towards Jack. This was now an established pattern, so he never bothered ordering anything for himself these days. His diet was 90 percent leftovers now. Just as well he had no objections to lukewarm/cold food.

The 'brandy' and lemonade (a bottle of Appetiser) pressed hard on my bladder, frequent toilet trips my new normality. As I got up to go to the loo, I passed the bar, Ashley deep in conversation with Caroline.

"... aye so, ye only need to say the word, Ashley. Ye don't even need tae come to the surgery. We could do the test here. Only takes seconds, ye ken."

Ashley topped a pint of Guinness with a fluffy white head and pushed it to her. "Mebbe. Have to be next week, though."

They clammed up when they saw me, alerting my Spidey senses. An over-the-top curiosity in other people's affairs was among my weaknesses these days—blame it on living in Lochalshie for too long—but unlike Mhari, I knew where to draw the line. I pretended not to have noticed or heard anything and squeezed past the tables to get to the loos.

Once upon a time, one of the world's most famous bottoms parked itself on the toilet in the Lochside Welcome's Ladies. For 12 months, that toilet became the most Instagrammable one in the UK as Caitlin Cartier fans queued up to take photos of it. The odd one even included pictures of them using it. I know: eww. But the hotel's fame as a Caitlin toilet stop had worn off. Yet another contribution to Ashley's plunging profits?

I got back to our table in time for the start of the pub quiz, as Big Donnie, the quiz master began rustling his sheets and calling for silence. The chatter petered out gradually, and he glared in our direction.

"It has come to my attention," he said, voice booming, "that there has been some cheating in this quiz the past few weeks."

He pointed at Mhari, her phone now hidden. At our table, the other occupants sucked in air, dismayed.

"Hand it over, and you are marked down twenty points."

"What?!" "But that's not—"

Our protests were drowned out by a chorus of boos. The weekly pub quiz was a serious undertaking. Those who resorted to their phones were despicable sorts. But our team had only ever been good when Katya was part of it. Thanks to her freelance career researching and writing about anything and everything, she was a font of knowledge. This week's quiz would need to rely on me, Mhari, Jack and Jolene's combined brainpower and memory alone.

"We'll start with the Scottish history round," Donnie's voice boomed out. "What was Macbeth's full name in Medieval Gaelic…?"

Chapter Three

"Do you need a hand weez 'er?"

Xavier gestured towards Mhari, her arm slung over my shoulders and head hanging down. It might be shame. Without access to the gods of Google, we'd managed a paltry ten points out of a possible hundred, and that was before the twenty-point deduction.

On the other hand, I hadn't allowed her any more of my chips. My mistake. The nosey one hadn't bothered with any dinner and had knocked back one cider too many. Five minutes ago, she'd slumped against my shoulder. I thought about torturing her by confiding some bit of juicy gossip. *Guess what, Mhari? I'm pregnant…* Ho, ho, ho! Tomorrow, I would fake regret about opening my big mouth and enjoy her dismay when she realised she couldn't remember anything.

"I'm sure Lachlan can…" I told Xavier as I scanned the room for him. Where was Lachlan? None of us was able to work out Mhari's relationship status with the village's man of dubious reputation and when it was on or off. Was it off because he had decided a drunk Mhari wasn't his responsibility? Jack had disappeared when Ashley asked if he could have a word with him.

"Is that okay?" I asked Xavier, referring to his offer to help me escort Mhari home. "Are you finished for the night?"

Xavier was Ashley's new barman and Jack's once upon a time assistant. Xavier was a Canadian and in the middle of a gap year between university and a career in corporate law. He'd stumbled onto the village while doing his bit of touring. The countryside appealed to him, so he decided to make Lochalshie his base for a while, asking around about job possibilities.

Jack snatched him up. The Highland Tourers loved him —French accent, Scottish roots and male model looks. For the two weeks he was with Jack, everyone leaving TripAdvisor reviews on the Outlander-themed tours made comments such as, *"Phwoarrrr. Hard to pick who's the best-looking guide. Highland Handsome Tours, for sure."*

Also, for that fortnight, Jack worked hours closer to nine to five. Just as well, since that was in the early stages of pregnancy. I was prone to bursting into tears about anything and everything; cancer charity adverts on the TV, running out of toilet roll; everyday life became a mine field, and I spent my days wishing my mum lived closer.

"Cat litter," Caroline warned me when we told her at the six-week mark, eyes solemn. "Awfy stuff. Causes toxoplasmosis infections in pregnant women. That might lead tae miscarriage or a stillborn."

Your first pregnancy. Just what you want to hear. Jack took on cat poo and pee cleaning duties. Caroline had to step in when his work swallowed up his time once more.

To be fair to Xavier, he did not leave us willingly.

Shonagh, Ashley's long-term barwoman, moved to Glasgow to care for her mum who had dementia. Lochalshie, being a wee place, didn't have many choices for employers. Xavier had worked his fair share of bar tendering as a student. He also knew how to knock up a mean pizza. When Ashley begged Jack to let him be Xavier's boss instead, how could Jack refuse? It helped too that Xavier was so easy on the eye. Ashley probably hoped such an attractive member of staff would pull in the punters.

Xavier nodded now, bending so he could put an arm around Mhari and haul her to her feet.

"Eet's the flat five doors from here, right?"

I nodded. Between us, we got Mhari out of the pub and along the main road, progress slow as she kept forgetting that the crucial part of walking involved putting one foot in front of the other.

A car streaked past us, making me blow out air. Xavier raised an enquiring eyebrow over the top of Mhari's head. "I don't like cars driving too fast down the High Street," I explained. "Someone killed my last cat that way."

"Fils de pute!"

Quite. The car—a moss-green jaguar—pulled into the Royal George's car park and stopped at a jaunty angle. Two loud posh voices started up, distinct enough for us to hear every word.

"Oh! We're here much earlier than I expected, Angeline. Enough time to get a whisky at the bar before they call last orders."

A peal of laughter.

"Last orders don't apply, Lois, when you're the owner. Do they?"

Urgh. "Les putains," I told Xavier. "Nous les detestons."

I don't normally slut-shame, but those two deserved it. And funny how the only bits of schoolgirl French I remembered were the swear words.

We'd reached Mhari's flat. Five minutes of fumbling where I tried to get her keys out of her jeans pocket—*"Gerrofff me, Gaby! You're no' ma type"*—and Xavier took over the job of hoisting her up the stairs, dumping her on the couch. I found her 15-tog duvet (needed in Scotland even in the summer) and covered her. I returned from the kitchen with a glass of water, Xavier had lifted her head to put a cushion under and was carefully moving her hair out of her eyes.

He stopped as soon as he saw me. Hmm. Double hmm.

He stood up. "I better help Ashley lock up."

"Yes, I'll make Mhari drink all this water and then head off myself. Thanks, Xavier."

He smiled, sketched me a wave and let himself out of the flat.

Mhari mumbled something indistinct. "Drink this and hurry up," I said. "I need my beauty sleep."

Mhari's eyes pinged open, stirred into consciousness once more. "Too right, you do. Better sch-tay asleep fae the rest o' the month." Mhari was not your typical gal pal. Kind comments were not her thing.

She rolled onto her side, thrusting aside my attempts to drape the duvet over her, and sat up swaying from side to side.

"Oh dear. Are you going to—"

"No. I'm okay," the words come out slow and slurred, but she'd stopped swaying, blinking instead at me.

"Gaby, d'ye think…" She burst into tears, startling me.

"Mhari! What on earth's the matter?"

I'd known her for more than two years and never seen

her cry. Not even that one time when she dropped her phone down the toilet. Good job I was only sitting on the sofa arm, allowing me to lumber to my feet again and find toilet roll. My eyes prickled themselves, crying is the one thing I now did relentlessly.

"Here," I said, pressing a wad of toilet paper to her.

"Why are you greetin'? What's wrong wi' you?""

"Oh, hormones making me weepy, the preg—nothing! Period due! Want to tell me why you're so upset?"

The problem upsetting her came out in fits and bursts, not helped by her stumbling over words and repeating herself several times. The gist was Mhari and Lachlan were no more. Definite this time. He'd met someone else—how, how, how and why hadn't he confided in Jack, swearing him to secrecy so that then Jack could then tell me… oh. That was why.

"And the other boyfriend's off tae LA 'n nae even a sniff o' an invite for me, Gaby."

Had I misjudged their relationship, thinking it mainly conducted online and not that serious?

I pointed out LA's population was more than four times the size of Glasgow. Mhari hated cities.

"Oh shu'-up! He still shoulda asked, shou'nt he? I wan' a proper boyfriend!"

News to me. Katya, who'd also lived with Mhari once upon a time, reckoned she preferred other people's love lives to her own. All that opportunity to ask personal questions and not bother with the complicated bits yourself.

"What about Xavier? He's nice, isn't he?"

A big sniff. "Dinnae be daft. He's no' gonnae stay here. When we leave the EU, he'll need tae go back tae Canada."

"Canada isn't in Europe, Mhari."

She gulped down water. "Is it no'? Anyway, he's loads younger than me."

Four years. The same age gap as Mhari and Hyun-Ki. I referred to this. A drunken explanation that this was precisely why she wasnae going to waste her time on younger men. Shallow. Totes immature. She ended the last statement with a loud fart, which made the two of us giggle for ages.

I checked the time discreetly, desperate to go to bed myself. "Can you drink your water? Will you be okay if I go home?"

Too late. Mhari was fast asleep. I put the water beside her, found a bucket under the kitchen sink and stuck it next to her just in case, and set off for home.

Punters were still spilling out of the Lochside Welcome as I walked by, snatches of lively conversations drifting over the top of my head. A woman standing outside Jamal's General Store flicked her blonde hair, making me do a double-take. Not Katya, surely? But then she turned, phone pressed to her ear. My age. No, a bit younger.

"Miles, it's perfect," she said. "Great location for filming, busy and—*get this!*—loads of gorgeous men. You should come take a look. How about next Friday?"

She listened to the reply, head bobbing up and down in agreement.

"See you then."

I watched as she turned and let herself into the house next to Jamal's store. Jamal hadn't said anything about new neighbours. Nor, more importantly, had Mhari noticed any newbies in the village and she knew everything and everyone. Often far better than they would like.

Great location for filming, Ms Mystery had said. A-may-zing. It must mean Starz the TV company, the makers of Outlander, had finally decided to film an episode in Lochalshie. Most of the 'American' locations in the series were Scottish. Perhaps they wanted our village to double up as an 18th century one in North Carolina.

About time too!

Chapter Four

"I've stocked up on pickled onions if ye want some, Gaby?" Jamal unfolded from his habitual leaning on the counter pose and pointed at one of the shelves in front of him when I popped in the next morning to stock up. As his shop was the only one for miles around, he jam-packed every available space with food, drink, toiletries, sun hats, welly boots and midge repellent.

"No thanks," I said, dumping a packet of organic venison for Mildred (I know, I know…) on the counter. "But if you've got any pickled onion monster munch, I'll take those."

He reached behind him and put a six-pack on the counter. "Or what about these?" A packet of potato scones was dangled in front of me. "Wi' fried bacon and a dollop o' ice-cream on top? I got some Irn-Bru flavoured stuff in 'specially."

What?

"For your cravings? When Enisa was pregnant wi' her

last yin, she swore by gherkin and jam sandwiches. Hud to be raspberry. The one 'afore that was the Irn-Bru ice cream on fried chicken."

Cravings for bonkers food combinations... How did he know?

Duh, Gaby.

I pulled my phone out of my pocket. Sure enough, the Lochalshie WhatsApp group had 26 notifications unspotted by me as I'd turned off the alerts months ago to save my sanity. Understandable what the subject was—me and my pregnancy. I flashed back to the night before and cursed. Why on earth had I thought Mhari would not notice me admitting to feeling hormonal and put two and two together? Stop her taking in a piece of gossip and being the first to spread it around?

I fired off a hasty message to her, *Thanks very much for telling everyone my news!!!!!!!!*

The reply: *No, bother! You're welcome.*

Cheeky cow. Oh well. I was more than 12 weeks pregnant, and any second now, my boobs and belly would make the announcement for me. Up until a week ago, I was congratulating myself for having a celebrity pregnancy—i.e. one where it doesn't show for months and then ends up a small, neat bump. I was now wearing yet another new bra, and all my jeans and tops refused point-blank to fasten.

"You've heard I'm pregnant then?" I asked, and Jamal nodded. Enisa appeared from behind him, a smile lighting up her face. She wore a short-sleeve tunic over her sari, the logo *Enisa's Mobile Beauty* emblazoned on her chest.

"Congratulations, Gaby. Have ye heard I do this mum-to-be pampering package where I come to your home and massage ye from top to bottom? I also offer a wee deal on waxing so that when ye go to the hospital, your bush is as neat as—"

Argh. Make it stop.

"I don't have any cravings," I burst out. Jamal looked crushed. "Apart from pickled onion Monster Munch, which is definitely not hormone-related. I've been mainlining those things forever."

Thanks to my hen party last year, the glamorous superstar Caitlin Cartier adored them too. She had to order from a specialist Brit food supplies website, StewNDumplings, to get them delivered to her in LA. I kept telling her monster munch was the gateway drug to Marmite. She refused to believe me, screwing her nose up in disgust.

"What's your accumulated score on the pub quiz now," Jamal asked with a sly grin as I paid for my food, adding in a packet of Rennies to help with the ghastly indigestion Baba McAllan had foisted on me.

"I'm not sure."

The accumulated score was a sore point. Ashley's weekly pub quiz kept a running total and every six months, the team with the highest score got their photo on the Lochside Welcome's website and Facebook page. There was no prize except for the acclaim, where people congratulated you/wished they were that brainy. Thanks to the massive deduction in our points, we were now at the bottom of the list.

Jamal's team—these days Caroline, her husband Ranald and their secret weapon Laney Haggerty who knew everything—were current quiz champs. We'd taken the title from them the odd week, mainly thanks to Google help. Not any more now we'd been rumbled.

He put all my shopping in the bag for life I'd brought

with me. "I'm a bit worried about Ashley mind." Enisa nodded.

"Oh?"

"He doesnae seem well these days. I saw him on the High Street this morning, and he didnae even say 'Awfy nice day, Jamal' the way he usually does."

"Yeah!" A voice piped up behind me. "I've just walked past the pub,, and he hasn't put the sign out about today's specials yet? Congratulations, by the way, Gaby. Maybe your kid will end up dating mine, and we'll end up in-laws."

Jolene, *very* forward-thinking. I nodded an acknowledgement; her smile told me she'd known my news an age ago. Thank heavens, some people knew the value of discretion. She dumped pots of baby food on the counter and pulled a canvas shopping tote out of her handbag.

"He's got that specials sign out way before lunchtime usually. Build anticipation and attract new customers."

"D'you think we should drop by?" I asked.

Jolene agreed readily. Stewart was busy coding for a business client and far too eager to share every riveting second of his work in progress. We set off for the Lochside Welcome, Jolene asking me when I was due and how I was.

"Fine," I said. "Well, flat-out exhausted, weepy and throwing up most of the time. But other than that, tickety-boo."

She shook her head. "Y'know, when I rule the world, men will be the ones who get pregnant."

"I second that."

Outside the Lochside Welcome, there was no chalk-board sign promising flavour of the month pizza (rocket and ham seeing as it was the summer) or pulled pork macaroni cheese (lush). Snatches of loud conversations from the beer garden reached us. Nothing much could be wrong if the hotel had customers.

Inside, every table was taken up. Ashley's two hired for the summer waiters dashed between them delivering trays of drinks and pizzas. Xavier was in the middle of pouring what looked like an epic round of craft lagers. He caught sight of us and mouthed, "Help!"

"You alright, mate?" Jolene asked once we pushed our way through the too crowded tables to the bar.

"Rushed off my feet! Ashley est malade, I mean not feeling well. Er... could either of you 'elp out? Gaby, you've worked behind this bar before, n'est ce pas? Congratulations, by the way."

The pregnancy was public knowledge for sure then. Two of the regulars who parked themselves at the bar and drank their way slowly and steadily through pints every day echoed him, raising their glasses to me.

The ruddiest-faced of them, Terry, shook his head. "Dinnae let her anywhere near plates and glasses, son. She's awfy clumsy. Ye'll lose all your glasses!"

One blasted time. I'd offered to help Ashley clear tables on a Friday night when he was short of staff. One hour later, he begged me to stop.

"What's wrong with Ashley?" Jolene asked.

In all my time in Lochalshie, I'd never known him to take a day off during peak tourist season. From the look of the crowds around me, people had flocked here fresh from a day's walking. The twin hills behind the loch—affectionately christened Maggie Broon's Boobs by the locals—were popular. Corbetts rather than Munros and therefore not as high, they presented enough of an achievement for people to feel they deserved a giant pizza, chocolate cake and a glass of wine to wash it down afterwards. The place reeked of waxed jackets, Kendall mint cake and the faint undertone of sweat.

Xavier gave an elaborate shrug, shoulders touching the lobes of his ears. "'E sleeps. Exhausted."

"I'll help," Jolene said, handing me her canvas tote bag and pulling her dark hair up in a high ponytail. "Can you take the baby food to Stewart, Gaby?" She rummaged in the bag, removing one jar, baby oatmeal, and tucking it in her handbag. Wise. Stewart had a thing about porridge. He'd take the hump if I handed over pre-made stuff, whereas Jolene could sneak it in later and feed it to Tamar without him realising.

Back in our house—baby food delivered and me managing to escape after only half-an-hour of cording/benefits of sobriety/congratulations on being pregnant and I should tell Jack to talk to him for an expert knowledge of fatherhood chat—I sent Jack a quick message. "Ashley ill this afternoon."

Jack was taking tourists to Inverary. (Loch, castle and decent fish and chip shop—what more could they want?) A cryptic reply pinged back. "He said something to me last week. Asked me a wee favour."

With the after-pub quiz disappearance where I had to help cart Mhari back to her flat, I'd forgotten that Ashley had wanted to speak to Jack, and my husband hadn't mentioned it when he let himself back into the house last night. Neither had I passed on that I'd seen Les Putains.

Had Ashley confided in Jack and told him about—gulp —a life-threatening illness? About to hit a Google search for *what does sleeping in the afternoon mean*, I changed my mind. As much as my mother-in-law was often the voice of gloom and doom when it came to a person's health and the many things that threaten it, she counselled against googling symptoms. If I looked up exhaustion online, I'd end up convinced *I* was the one with a terminal condition. It would just have to wait.

"When will you be home?" I pinged Jack a message via WhatsApp.

"5pm. Promise. Plenty of time to talk. X"

Chapter Five

Jack took my hand as we walked to the Lochside Welcome the following Friday night.

"I forgot to tell you," I said, pointing towards the Royal George as we left the house. "When Xavier and I were hauling Mhari's sorry carcass back to her flat last week, I spotted the Evil Twins at the George."

He screwed up his face, getting the reference straight away. "What, those witches from London?"

"Yes. Up to visit their investment, no doubt, and suggest other ways they can undermine the best pub in the village. Oh! And what was it you wanted to say to me, that message the other day?"

He'd been as good as his word last Saturday, turning up bang on the dot at 5pm. I'd been so overjoyed to see him I'd spent an hour babbling about my job—the trouble with working from home was the lack of chat—and then we'd shared a shower that turned X-rated in record time.

Retaining information demanded far more skills than I had these days.

By this point, we were at the pub door, nods and hellos from others going in. Jolene called out a cheery 'Hello!', rushing up as Jack opened the door. His fingers gripped mine, and he whispered the words, "Tell you later."

"Is Ashley any better?" I asked. Jolene had finished the lunchtime shift last Saturday, and Xavier begged her to come back that evening just in case Ashley was still in bed, which he was. Tonight, the man we spotted behind the bar looked as if it had taken every ounce of will power he possessed to drag him from there. Jolene took one look at him and vaulted over the gate across the bar. She rolled up her sleeves. "What do you want me to do?"

Jack nudged me. "I'll get drinks. Go sit down."

I parked myself at our usual table where Mhari waited, eyes flicking up quickly and then returning to her screen. She'd nabbed the best seat—a thickly-padded armchair. "Can I sit there?" I asked, pointing at it. "In deference to my pregnant status."

"No. You're only expectin' no' ill. In the olden days, women used tae be out pickin' tatties right up until they gave birth. Then they'd just squat, pop one oot, swaddle it under their shawls and get back on wi' it."

I glared at her. She didn't shift, so I settled for kicking her chair as I took the stool opposite. Jack, a pint in hand and a soda and lime for me, returned from the bar, corners of his mouth twitching. I waited for him to forcibly shift Mhari. In vain.

"Please can we join your team?"

It was the woman I'd seen a week ago and mistaken for Katya. The brief conversation I'd overheard I had forgotten all about. *Duh, Gaby!* When I'd listened to her last week, I'd been convinced a film crew was about to descend on the village. I'd got totally excited, and then, I'd gone home, fallen fast asleep and forgotten about it until now.

"*Awfy common, Gaby!*" My mother-in-law's voice, the warning she'd given me some weeks ago. "*For your heid tae turn tae mush in the early stages. Your body's busy makin' a human being. It's got nae time for thinkin'.*"

So, the woman I'd initially mistaken for Katya was still in Lochalshie then. She stood in front of our table and smiled winningly. The man next to her pocketed his phone, his gaze appraising. If asked, I would have compared it to how a big cat eyes up a baby gazelle. His eyes swept over Jack several times, gaze finally lingering on his collar bone just visible above the open-necked shirt Jack wore.

Now I looked again. Whoever this woman was, she did not resemble Katya that closely. Same height, hair colour and style but thinner. A few years younger than me, although Mr Predatory was older. Early 30s, maybe, tightly curled sandy hair that was starting to edge back from his forehead and dressed in chinos and a Diesel T-shirt. He said nothing, but his eyes fixed on Jack.

"I'm Tindra," Katya's not quite double said, her accent posh English. She stuck her hand out. "And this is Miles. We're visiting the area."

Mhari yanked her chair to the side and pulled up another one. "Oh, aye? What for? Are you tourists?"

A benefit of friendship with the unashamedly nosey one was that you got to be curious vicariously, though I thought she must be losing her touch if she hadn't noticed them before. Jack and I tipped our heads to the side, also waiting for the reply. I nudged his thigh with mine.

Tindra's accent… didn't lots of well-spoken, privately educated people work in TV/media? They were here because of Outlander for sure. Miles fascination with Jack proved it, surely?

Tindra opened her mouth to say something, stopping when Miles put his hand on top of her arm. "Scotland's wonderful, isn't it?" he cut in. "Particularly the Highlands. An old school friend of mine told me we should visit Lochalshie."

"Who?" Mhari scanned the pub as if picking out prospective friends of Miles. "I dinnae see anyone in here who looks like a friend o' yours."

I tittered nervously. Our straight-talking friend sometimes came across as… outright rude and tactless. Who liked confrontation? Not me.

Miles gave another half-smile and a shrug, apparently unbothered. "I'm amazed at how beautiful the scenery is. We caught the sunrise this morning above the loch. Incredible."

"What friend?"

Next to me, Jack's thigh pressed back against mine. I didn't dare look at him for fear giggles might start up. Those who hadn't met Mhari often underestimated how difficult she was to put off.

Jolene weaved her way towards us, pizza and two bowls of chips balanced in her hands. Silence as she put down the food and a welcome break from the Miles-Mhari stand-off. He turned towards Jolene. "Oh—can we try the food? I don't suppose you have anything for vegans…?"

Jolene rolled her eyes. "Yes, mate. There's a vegan pizza? Roasted veggies and cashew nut cheese. The Lochside Welcome is the number one spot for vegan pizzas here?"

The only place, more like.

"Ah! Well, we'll have that. One 12-inch should be enough for the two of us, Tindra?"

It wasn't a question. Tindra looked as if she wanted to object. Order taken, Jolene retreated.

"Who's your friend?" Mhari, who ignored my hand slap when she reached for one of my fries, managing to snatch the prize few that were mostly covered in cheese. "You havenae told me yet."

The man took a fortifying gulp of his craft beer. "You won't know him. He doesn't live here. He visited some time ago."

Mhari helped herself to more of my chips. I gave in, mindful of what had happened last week.

"When? And why did he like it so much?"

Jack cleared his throat. "Mhari, the sign at the entry to the village says, 'Welcome to Lochalshie'. Maybe ease off the interrogation?"

Miles sent him a grateful smile. His eyes lingered on my husband. If I were to guess his thoughts, I'd go with, yum yum yum. Was he attracted to Jack? I wouldn't blame him. Tonight, Jack's newly washed hair gleamed as locks of it caught the overhead lights, and the firelight next to us picked out the planes of his face. He got stared at a lot. Luckily for me, he didn't notice it nor allow the constant adulation to make him big-headed.

Mhari muttered something indistinct and picked up her phone. If software existed that allowed a person to take a discreet picture of a stranger, upload it and then find out all their deepest, darkest secrets, Mhari would know about and use it.

Jolene returned with the vegan pizza. Its size pathetically small next to the one I had. Tindra noticed the discrepancy too, eyes darting from their pizza to mine. I pushed the remains of my chips towards her. I'd read about boyfriends who policed their girlfriends' food portions; domestic abuse in my book. She picked up one, bit it and closed her eyes briefly. My internal promise to her: *I'll do my best to leave you some of my pizza but don't bet on it.*

As it happened, our team was one woman down, Jolene too busy pouring pints for demanding customers.

"How are your general knowledge skills?" Jack asked. "Seeing as you're now part of our pub quiz team. Gaby here is our celebrity gossip specialist, as is Mhari. I'm history, geography and sport. There are a lot of gaps."

Miles finished his slice of pizza and wiped his mouth on a paper napkin. "Music, TV and films."

"Books," Tindra piped up. We were covered then. And their knowledge further proof that my theory was right. A TV crew, here in the village to check out Outlander filming potential. Sworn to secrecy by the boss.

Big Donnie tapped his gavel on the bar counter.

"Silence please, ladies and gentlemen! Mhari Colquhoun—come here at once and hand your phone over." She grumbled but got up, disposing of her mobile in the glass bowl that sat on the bar, used to stop people googling the answers. Big Donnie waited until she returned to her seat. "We'll begin with the sports round."

Time to regain our pub quiz honour.

Our new teammates were exceptional. Not only did they know everything about music, TV, films and books, but they also filled in all the gaps in our supposed knowledge of celebrities, history, geography and sport. Tindra came up with the name of the winner of *Love Island* and knew who was lined up for the next series. Miles got the exact date for Culloden. Something Jack ought to have known since he took tourists to the battlefield on a weekly basis.

When we were announced the outright winners, there were only a few catcalls of 'Cheats!', Mhari agreeing to a pat-down to prove she had put her phone in the bowl. (In previous weeks, we'd relied on her burner phone.)

As the grand prize was a voucher for food, Jack handed it over to Miles and Tindra. They'd won it fair and square. As they went to collect their prize, there was a sudden clatter behind the bar and a shriek from Jolene.

"Ashley!"

She dropped down, vanishing from our sight. Jack leapt to his feet and hurried over as did Caroline, pushing her way through the crowds yelling, "Oot ma way! I'm a doctor!"

Mhari got up too. I yanked her sleeve. "Give the man some peace, Mhari!"

She scowled but sat down again. Someone turned the jukebox off, the quiet a weird contrast to the pub's usual nosiness. Most people muttered the same things I'd been thinking—*hasnae looked well for a while, lost a wee bittie o' weight, sleepin' during the afternoon.*

Jolene stood up slowly, grim-faced, and I turned cold, fear making me shake. Was it a heart attack? My Papa Cooper had died suddenly, leaving my nanna a widow aged only 42. One night they'd been leaving the cinema arguing about Sharon Stone and whether she was handy with an ice-pick or not (and Papa's admiration for *that* leg-crossing scene). Next, pfft he was gone. Nanna never went to the cinema again.

Caroline straightened up, face pinched. I steeled myself for the worst. "Can someone phone an ambulance?"

Relief. Dead men didn't need ambulances. Jack came out from behind the bar and fished his phone out of the glass bowl. He stabbed in the numbers 999 and pressed it to his ear, a further hush descending. "Fifty minutes!" His mother shook her head. "But that's too long... oh? Aye, alright then."

He hung up. "An ambulance can't get here for another fifty minutes and then it's another hour to the nearest A&E. Someone'll need to take him there."

"I will!" "Me!" "I can dae it!"

"How much have you all had to drink?" Miles' home county tones cut through the clamour. "You're all over the limit."

He gestured to his right. "Tindra? I'll let you borrow my car. You can do it."

To her credit, the dismay that flashed across her face was momentary. She replaced it with a sturdy smile. "No, I haven't had anything to drink. I can drive him."

So could I, seeing as pregnancy stole all the fun bits out of life. But it also meant 60 minutes away from a toilet. My bladder wasn't up to the challenge, and as I wouldn't get home for another few hours after that, I'd be in danger of falling asleep on the way back.

"I'll come too," Caroline said, telling Tindra she was the village's GP, qualified to get Ashley in and out of the car safely and be on hand if anything went hideously wrong. Bless my mother-in-law but having lived through years of colds, twisted ankles and the odd case of piles and/or gastric flu, this year had proved terribly exciting so far; a pregnancy and whatever Ashley had. She was in her element. Orders sternly issued for how to lift him, Jack and Xavier took the now conscious Ashley under each arm and staggered outside while Tindra fetched Miles' car.

Miles owned a dark blue Toyota Supra, its lack of space and comfort compensated by speed. A crowd gathered outside the Lochside Welcome to watch as it left, the 30mph speed limit ignored. Jack wrapped an arm around me. I tipped my head to lean into him. "What happened?" I asked. "I thought it was a heart attack and that he mi-mi-might be…" I sniffed. Jack did too, hastily rubbing his free hand against his eye. He didn't have my hormones gone haywire excuse.

"Mum reckons type 2 diabetes," he said. "She's been nagging him to get tested for a while now—sudden weight loss, exhaustion, fearsome hunger and thirst, and needing to go to the loo all the time."

"What if he's the first medical miracle—a male pregnancy?" I said, remembering Jolene's comment from the other week.

"Weight loss," Mhari dug a not gentle enough elbow in my side. "Did ye miss that bit? No' developing a double chin."

"Thank you, Mhari. Yet again, you've scored a big fat zero in the Supportive Friends test."

"Saying too many nice things makes a person awfy big-heided."

"Too many?" I countered. "How about just one thing?"

A two-fingered response. Rude laughter followed our departure, but Jack and I were not in the mood for post-mortems in the pub. Especially when that post-mortem might have been literal. We walked home along the High Street, the wind picking up and making me shiver. I spotted Miles unlocking the door to the house next to Jamal's general store. "Weird," I said to Jack. "Do you think they've moved here?"

Jack shook his head. "That's one of Big Donnie's properties—an Airbnb place. Mhari's cousin's friend's wife does the cleaning for it. She should be able to find out more. I don't buy that 'we're just visiting' line."

"Me neither! I think that they are—"

An earlier WhatsApp message I'd forgotten resurfaced. We'd reached our house, Mildred mewling at us behind the window in protest at a long evening of neglect.

"You," I said, prodding Jack's chest with a pointed finger, "were meant to tell me what Ashley wanted to talk to you about last week."

A flash of something passed across Jack's face. When I first met him, I found him impossible to read. Two plus years on, not so much, but always a bit of a challenge. I ran through various options before deciding the 'something' was shifty. A guy weighing up his options. *How am I going to present Gaby with a fait accompli…?*

He unlocked the door whistling *Flower of Scotland*—a tune he'd taught Mildred to associate with being fed. She wove her way around our legs, purring her head off before bolting in the direction of the kitchen, a loud miaow ticking us off for our tardiness.

Jack hastened after her.

"Hubby-dubby donuts!" I called after him. (Revolting phrase I know and one I'd never admit in public, but couples… right?) "You've got stuff to tell me! As soon as you've fed Mildred, I demand to know!"

Chapter Six

"But, but, but what will you do with Highland Tours! No, not Highland Tours. Highland Handsome Tours, remember? Best Outlander experience in Scotland. You, number three on 'the man my partner would give me a free pass to sleep with' list and I don't even mind!"

"How about some toast, Gaby? Lavishly spread with butter and Marmite? Made by my own fair hand. Or shortbread, the batch I knocked up this evening? I used a new kind of butter—hand-rolled between virgin's thighs while nymphs and shepherds inserted flakes of Himalayan sea salt. Sugar reaped under the Caribbean sun and harvested by the dictates of a bio-dynamic moon. Flour extracted from—"

"McAllan! Spare me."

Jack, knelt before me with his hands on my knees, kept fluttering his eyelashes and doing his best to smile winningly. Persuasively. Last week after the pub quiz while I was busy ferrying Mhari home, he'd confessed, Ashley put a proposal to him. Ashley had taken over the Lochside Welcome more than twenty years ago and built it up from a naff, outdated village pub to a successful hotel/pub/restaurant. Well, until the Royal George decided Lochalshie offered opportunity a-plenty and muscled in on the delightful pubs in far-out places market.

He was exhausted, he told Jack, tired of never having a social life or time to visit his sisters and their families. He missed Shonagh, he added, a wistful look in his eyes. It would be nice to have the time to pop down to Glasgow and ask if she fancied a coffee, or more perhaps… Work had left him no time to find himself a girlfriend or a wife, and he was fed up of it.

How would Jack like to take over management of the place for the summer? The summer included the Highland Games, the most prominent and busiest event in the village.

Jack shook his head. "Ashley, I'm sorry. I don't think I can. What wi' the baby coming and everything."

Echoes of what I'd said to Hyun-Ki when he put the head designer idea to me; the difference being, I dismissed the idea out of hand. He brought it up every time we spoke, dangling enticements in front of me. "Gaby. I'll mentor you. Did I mention the salary?"

Gosh. What a lot of money. Next year, my old high school Caister Academy was having a ten-year reunion. When I'd told Katya about it, she grimaced. "No way! You only go to school reunions if you're now the CEO of a multi-million-pound company so you can lord it over everyone else. And anyway, aren't you in regular contact with the only former school friend you like?"

We'd been friends since primary school. When I pointed out how successful she was thanks to the money she'd made writing Caitlin's 'autobiography' and the subsequent writing gigs she'd landed; as a result, she still pooh-poohed the idea.

"The trouble with ghost-writing, Gaby, is that you sign contracts promising not to tell anyone the celebrity who can't string two words together did not, in fact, write their life story."

Difficult to resist picturing myself at the said reunion, though. "Gaby, hi!" My nemesis. Tina Bitch-face. "Brave dress choice! D'you know I'd always put you on the top ten list of people who'd never leave Great Yarmouth, ha-ha! What are you doing now?"

"Tina, hi! I'm the head designer for Blissful Beauty's EMEA operation. Me and Caitlin Cartier have regular Skype chats. Amazing, huh?"

Clang! Forgive the name drop, even if I've only done it in my imagination, but some people deserve to have their faces rubbed in your status as a friend to the rich and famous.

I brought myself back to the present. Ashley's request of Jack last week had gained urgency now that he'd been whisked off to the hospital. The Lochside Welcome had many positive associations in Jack's mind. He listed them for me. It was where his mother had gone for her first date with his stepfather Ranald, starting what was to be a long period of stability and happiness after a tumultuous childhood. He and his friends had spent their late teens/early 20s in there playing pool and chatting up the best-looking tourists, and—

"The public bar is where you and I shared our first bowl of chips!" I burst in, just in case that collection of lovely memories skipped the most significant one.

"Mmm. Did we share them? I thought you grabbed the bowl off me, scooped up everything in it and crammed them into your mouth. I should have realised then how ma life would work out if I stuck with you. Destined to never eat all my own chips ever again."

Huh. I slapped his hand lightly. He grinned, face turning severe again a second later.

"But you see why I can't stand by while the hotel goes to rack and ruin?"

Why had Ashley approached him, I asked. Experience, Jack replied. He knew what the tourist industry entailed thanks to his years running Highland Tours, and—crucially —he was used to handling budgets. And if I thought about it, the voice turned persuasive, wasn't the situation better than the present? He'd be close by all the time, instead of spending nights away here and there because of the tours.

I put his hand on my stomach. Mhari's announcement of my news appeared to have given my bump permission to explode—the size of it disproportionately huge. When we felt a tiny fluttering, Jack and I stared at each other, taken aback.

"Was that…?"

"I dunno," I said. "I thought movements weren't supposed to be noticeable until you were at least four months. I'm only 14 weeks. But anyway, what happens come the end of November? We'd worked it all out."

Jack's birthday present had been my pregnancy announcement. I'd only been a few weeks gone at the time, but we'd discussed what we would do. The pregnancy timing was ideal. I'd work until the end of November and then take six months off. Jack wouldn't be working because the tourist season was over by October and the tours finished. We would have lots of lovely time together to welcome the new addition to our world come December.

(And work on persuading Mildred she had nothing to

fear. Plentiful food and love would continue to be sent her way.)

"Lachlan could take over at that point, and Ashley said he only wanted a six-month break. It would just be until the New Year."

Did Ashley have any choice in the matter now that he'd been taken ill? I shifted on the sofa so I could put my legs up —another Caroline warning— *"Aye, Gaby. You need to watch out for varicose veins. Lucky you're no' a man. Did ye ken they can get them in the scrotum? Put your legs up as much as ye can."*

"Lachlan? I've never seen him as mine host."

Jack flapped a hand. "He's got plenty of management skills."

Best not to ask. Jack's best friend and on-off and now permanently off partner of Mhari ran all kinds of illegal operations—from poaching to number plate switches, stolen vehicles and everything else. Life in the grey area of right and wrong must equip you with lightning wits and an ability to juggle things—the perfect candidate for hotel management.

"Did you discuss it with him first? Before me?" I narrowed my eyes; the fait accompli suspicion confirmed.

"No. Promise." His eyes met mine. "I've been mulling the idea over—figuring out how it might work."

"I'll never see you!" I said. Evenings and weekends were out the window. Thursday, Friday and Saturdays and Sundays till mid-afternoon were the Lochside Welcome's busiest times. Fair enough, Jack worked long hours taking people on trips, but we always had one to two days to ourselves every week.

He opened his mouth to say something, his phone's ring tone interrupting us. "It's Mum," he said, checking the screen. "I'd better take it."

He put the phone on speaker mode, Caroline's voice booming out as she struggled to be heard above the din of A&E. Her diagnosis was right—type 2 diabetes. Ashley had been seen by one of the doctors and moved to a ward. He would see a specialist in the morning as the A&E doctor didn't like the look of the ulcer on his right foot. But before the porter wheeled him away, he'd asked Caroline to beg Jack to visit him as soon as possible.

Jack could hardly refuse. I knew what was coming.

He sat opposite me, tossing his phone from hand to hand and his eyes observing my expression.

Responsibility for the Lochside Welcome. Goofy and impulsive as I often was, it still felt too much. But a deep attachment to the local hub where he'd been so happy and a request from a seriously ill man stacked the odds against Jack saying no.

I let out a sigh. "You have to take over management of the hotel."

His face tilted upwards, dark eyes grateful. "Yes. We can make this work, Gaby."

The last sentence seemed to be aimed at convincing him more than me. I rubbed my stomach and pushed myself to my feet.

Jack stood too, encircling me in a tight hug. He rested his chin on top of my head. "I promise Gaby."

"I know you'll be brilliant." Just as well he couldn't see my face. My expression would have given away how unsure I was.

"Thank you, thank you, thank you."

His arms moved, hands sliding down to my bottom. "Any chance we could end our evening with me unbuttoning your shirt, unhooking your trousers and kissing my way down until I reach the fun bits?"

I smiled despite myself. "Oh, alright then. But promise you won't be offended if I fall asleep half-way through?"

Chapter Seven

"Wrong ward, love!" The nurse called out cheerfully as we pushed open the door. He was stationed behind a desk at the start of a long corridor, rooms to the left and right.

"Oh, but we were told…"

"You probably heard it wrong. Ward eight not eighteen is the one you're looking for." He picked up a clipboard and gestured towards my stomach with a pen. "Bet you can't wait to meet him or her."

Huh. He thought I needed the maternity ward, equating the size of my girth with someone nine months as opposed to just over three pregnant. That dress I'd ordered from Amazon the other day had been a mistake. Specialist maternity wear made you look huge. I'd gone from looking not pregnant to nine months' gone overnight. Tomorrow, I was straight back to loose shirts or sweaters worn over joggers.

"No, no," Jack threw in hurriedly, too aware of the vast number of things that made me cry these days. "We're here to see someone."

It was Monday afternoon, the soonest we'd been able to make it through to the hospital in Lochgilphead, me using flexitime and Jack tourist-free. The nurse forgot to add an apology for his mistake as he directed us to the room two doors down. In it were four beds, all of them surrounded by flowers, cards and balloons.

Ashley's appearance took me aback. He seemed to have shrunk drastically, the head and shoulders sticking out the top of the blanket and sheets much smaller than I remembered. At the bottom of the bed, a frame held the blanket above a heavily bandaged foot, the skin there an inflamed, mottled purple colour.

"Have you bought food," he whispered, one eye on the nurses pulling the curtains around the bed opposite. "They gave me porridge this morning that could hae doubled up as wallpaper paste. Nae sugar because of the diabetes, nae salt because of the stroke risk and nae cream as my cholesterol levels are sky-high. Made with water. Water! I've never tasted anything so flavourless in ma whole life!"

"Er… we've got tangerines?" I said, holding up the bag. Caroline had warned us beforehand that Ashley would beg for food. "And he's got tae change his diet," she warned. "Otherwise, diabetes will kill him within five years!"

He let out a huge sigh, holding out a hand to take them. "Better than nothing, I s'pose. Have a seat."

Jack pulled me up a chair and got himself one, so we could sit either side of Ashley.

"How are you feeling?" I asked. "Must be a relief to have a diagnosis."

Ashley sighed. "Aye, I guess so. But Caroline's already read me the riot act—nae sugar, nae salt, low-carb this and that, lots o' exercise and sleep and she wants me to start meditating. Meditating! I'm no' sitting on the floor cross-legged saying 'um' all day."

Quite. I'd been given the meditating line too when I told her I was pregnant. According to Caroline, it would help me relax and in turn, produce a more placid baby. I made Jack try it with me, the two of us sitting opposite each other on the floor and concentrating on our breath. We lasted 30 seconds before I flicked my eyes open only to discover him doing his best not to snort with laughter. When I read that mindlessness was the new mindfulness, I cheered. See? Justification for watching too much of *The Real Housewives of New York* and/or *Love Island*.

"And as for that yin," Ashley gestured towards a harassed-looking doctor walking past us in the corridor outside trailed by two students. "He came in this morning, took one look at my right foot and started muttering things about maggots. Maggots! This hospital is trying out a new treatment where they put wee beasties on ulcers to eat away aw' the dead tissue. Have ye ever heard the like? Wee white things wrigglin' all ower ye, and—"

The details were far too graphic for me. I heaved myself up and bolted for the bathroom, a shout of "Hey, that's patients only!" ringing out after me. Up came that morning's breakfast and last night's supper. If nothing else, pregnancy had given me a close acquaintance with toilet bowls, the feel of cold porcelain against the cheeks hugely comforting in such circumstances.

"Are you okay?" Jack tapped lightly on the door. "The nurse has gone to fetch you some water."

I unpeeled myself and attempted standing. Oh, this was ridiculous. I wasn't that far advanced. Getting up should not be this tricky. A further minute of undignified lurching and unbalancing convinced me it was.

"Er—can you give me a hand?" Thankfully, in my haste to escape Ashley and his far-too-graphic maggot description, I hadn't locked the door. Jack tried and failed to hide a grin as he took in the sight of me, sprawled on the floor.

"Not funny," I said. "This," I pointed at my belly, "is entirely your fault. A ten-second contribution and that's you! All over and done with the grow-a-baby process."

He took the hand I held out and bent over to kiss it, mischievous eyes flickering to mine. "Ten seconds, Gaby? Please."

"I looked it up! The average length of time it takes a man to—y'know."

He stroked my cheek. "That bit, maybe. But if I could refer you to this morning and how late I made you for work…?"

The heat in my cheeks migrated southwards, re-kindling the fire in my belly. "Mmph. But it doesn't cancel out the totally unequal division of work when it comes to baby-making and what I'm putting up with. Ashley better not have anything more to say about… those things."

"I promise he won't. Put your other hand on the floor beside you, and I'll haul you up."

The nurse was waiting at the door when we opened it, a glass of water in hand and warning us that we both needed to use the hand sanitiser before going back to sit with Ashley. He apologised profusely, adding the by-now-familiar question people kept asking me. "I thought morning sickness wasnae meant to last beyond 12 weeks?" And my too-often repeated reply through gritted teeth, "It's not."

"Oh well," he said, patting the chair next to his bed. "You're in good company. Didn't the Duchess of Cambridge have awfy bad morning sickness wi' all her weans?"

A great comfort. Not.

He moved on from maggots to the real reason we were here.

"Have ye thought any more about what I asked ye, Jack?" Behind the question, I heard desperation. When we'd driven here earlier, I'd run through all kinds of improbable scenarios in my head. A miraculous recovery, where doctors put Ashley on medication, and he met us at the hospital doors raring to go. Or a long-lost rela-tive/friend who'd suddenly turned up and happened to have years of experience in the hotel trade. *"So lucky! And what timing. I've always wanted to move to a remote part of Scotland where it rains 95 percent of the time!"*

(Actually, 72.3 percent last year, but that's what it felt like.)

No, there was only one solution, and my husband was it.

Jack glanced at me, eyes asking permission for some-thing I'd agreed to the minute we entered the room. I closed my eyes briefly and nodded. When I opened them again, Jack blew me a kiss.

"It's fine, Ashley," he said. "I'll take it on. If Xavier can manage for a few days, I can sort out the arrangements for Highland Tours. There is a freelancer I've used before for the guided tours of the castles, and he said he would be happy to take it over for the rest of the summer season."

Ashley gripped his hand, tears in his eyes.

"Jack, ye've nae idea how much better that makes me feel."

He twisted so he could look at me. "And you, Gaby. Thanks too. I know it's bad timing, what wi' the bairn coming and all, but that doctor says I cannae work for eight weeks if not longer as I need to keep the weight off my foot until it heals."

He and Jack settled down to a discussion of what the day-to-day stuff management of the Lochside Welcome would entail. As he'd lived in Lochalshie most of his life and spent so much time in the pub, Jack knew what went on and which were its busiest days. But viewing it as a punter was much different from running the place. And he'd have the challenge of running the Lochside Welcome at the village's busiest time of the year—July, August and September. Not to mention the Highland Games, now only six weeks away…

When I realised I was pregnant, the one incredibly sensible thing I'd done was resign from the Highland Games committee. I'd been on it for two years—an incredible feat given the committee expected blood, sweat and tears. It wasn't enough to offer to show people where to park their cars on the day or agree to take bookings for Psychic Josie (Adviser to the Stars).

No, no you got roped into arrangements for exhibitors, organising the entertainment and programme for the day, sorting out the licence for the beer tent, traditionally provided by the Lochside Welcome, and running around like a blue-arsed fly on the day.

"Two years' dedicated service," I told Caroline, the head of the committee, back in March. "And don't forget what I did the first year…"

As if she could. Thanks to an administrative cock-up in London, Dexter was left with the Blissful Beauty company launch and no venue. I pretended insider knowledge of what millennials wanted, which was not your old-fashioned, boring event to propel a new make-up company into the stratosphere. A presentation and freebies at a top hotel in London? Yawn, yawn, triple yawn.

"No," I said at the time, faking super confidence, "what we want is something entirely different."

To travel to the far end of the UK, for instance, witness their heroine Caitlin Cartier open the Highland Games and launch her lipsticks, powders and paints in a tiny village.

It was a triumph.

That Caitlin chose to spring a surprise on everyone by opening the Highland Games Lady Godiva style was neither here nor there. Make-up and skincare so good you don't need to cover up. The village raked in hundreds of thousands of pounds, thanks to business in the Lochside Welcome, people staying in the B&B and Airbnb properties, and visitor spend in the small shops and at the Games.

No matter what I did afterwards, I'd never top that. Best, my Nanna Cooper always said, to quit while you're ahead. The year later, I proposed to Jack at the afore-mentioned Highland Games. A fantastic move, life-choices wise, but if you take one thing from my story—NEVER EVER PROPOSE TO SOMEONE IN PUBLIC.

Ashley began to talk about money, budgets and licensing —Jack would need approval by the local licensing board to serve alcohol—and I zoned out. Maybe this would be much better for us, Jack nearby all the time ready to come to the rescue if another falling-down-unable-to-stand-up situation arose. Or when I went into labour and needed taking to the hospital asap.

Free pizzas. Double servings of chips while I waited, gratis... ooh! Bonus!

The nurse tapped her watch, signalling visiting hours had come to an end. Now the nausea had passed, I was ravenous once more. Close to the hospital was a terrifically good coffee shop that did amazing home-made soup and filled rolls. Cheese and pickle or ham and mustard? Both perhaps along with a double helping of spicy lentil soup followed by some of their banoffee pie with extra whipped cream…

"I forgot to ask!" Ashley called out, catching us just before we stepped out into the corridor. "Who was that young lassie who took me to the hospital last night?"

Jack turned back. "Tindra, she said her name was. She and her boyfriend Miles are visiting the area. They're staying at that house next to Jamal's store—the Airbnb place?"

Were they really a couple? I still hadn't told Jack about the phone call I'd overheard (pregnancy brain for real) and my theory about scouting for Outlander locations. Miles and Tindra didn't have the boyfriend-girlfriend vibe to them. If she was dating him, I would question her life choices. A man who monitored your food and bossed you around? No. Thank. You.

"Mind you gie them a free meal," Ashley said. "And a few drinks as a thank-you."

Jack nodded.

"They're vegans," I said. "They've exhausted the menu already."

Ashley's expression changed to alarm. He propped himself up on his elbows. "Vegans? That's a trick they do. The UK's Best Restaurants folks. Order something awkward off the menu to see if you're any good."

The Lochside Welcome had a prized UK's Best Restaurants Taste of Scotland award. A sign proudly proclaiming the status hung on its front door.

"They'll have gone up the road to the Royal George afterwards," Ashley continued, his words coming out in laboured gasps. "That place has three vegan dishes on the menu these days. My award will be taken off me, and those wankers will end up with it instead."

The occupants of the other beds looked up, disapproval radiating off the face of one.

"And every time, visitors research places to visit in the Highlands, they'll see the Royal George wi' its award and the Lochside Welcome wi' none. I'm ruined. Ruined!"

And with those words ringing in our ears, he fell back against the pillow.

"They're not restaurant critics," I said to Jack as we got into my car.

After Ashley's hysterical reaction, we'd hastened back to his bedside. No, no, no. The Lochside Welcome's vegan pizza was a marvellous thing, I said. Didn't people rave about it on TripAdvisor? He had nothing, repeat *nothing*, to worry about.

"I kept meaning to tell you about this conversation I overheard the other week," I pulled the seatbelt over my belly. "Tindra was on the phone to someone talking about how Lochalshie would be an amazing place to film."

I checked the mirrors and drove out of the car park. "I think they're scouts. Here to check out the village for a film or TV. Maybe even... Outlander. You could be Jamie Fraser's double in it."

Though I would veto any Jamie naked scenes, obvs.

Jack shook his head. "I don't think so. Ashley might be right. That Toyota was parked in the Royal George's car park this morning. I spotted it when I went out for milk."

Blast it. According to our spies—on principle Jack and I never set foot in the Royal George—their menu was all small portions, slate plates, foams and expensive seafood. The sort of thing food critics liked.

"But filming…" I said, remembering Tindra's insistence.

"Could mean anything—oh, watch that car!"

Jack wasn't a great passenger. Because he drove all the time for work, he tended to sit next to me, foot slamming down all too frequently on an imaginary brake.

"It's miles off!" I said, ignoring the Honda's driver who gestured furiously at me.

"The filming could be anything," Jack said. "I think they televise the UK's Best Restaurants annual awards these days. Maybe she was assessing the Lochside Welcome for that."

Perhaps. For the sake of both our blood pressures, I returned to concentrating on the road, and we arrived back in Lochalshie with no further questioning of my driving abilities. The Lochside Welcome was the first building after the village sign, and Jack signalled to me to pull over outside it.

"I need to get back to work," I bleated. "I've missed so much time today!"

"You were on flexi-time," Jack growled. "Taking back some of those excess hours you put in last week. Nine o'clock finishes, remember?"

"Yes, but Trish in the office wants my advice on… Oh, alright then."

He was right, Blissful Beauty demanded blood from their employees. I followed him into the Lochside Welcome. We'd agreed the announcement of his temporary management of the hotel should wait until the arrangements for

Highland Tours were in place. And to stop speculation reaching the Royal George. If the hotel management knew the hotel was missing its manager, they would up the ante pushing out special offers left, right and centre.

"Your new place of work," I said as Jack pushed the door to the Lochside Welcome open.

The change made me look at the hotel with fresh eyes, trying to imagine how Jack might develop it further. The hotel was beautiful, a white-washed old stone building with broad wooden beams and a large garden at the front just before the loch.

Upstairs, there weren't that many rooms—seven—but all of them offered views of either the lochs or the hills. Inside, most people chose to sit in the public bar rather than the lounge bar, which was more like a dining room. Jack had always said the two spaces didn't make sense to him and would be better off as one large area.

The late afternoon crowd inside included plenty of Lochalshie regulars who all greeted us with, "How's Ashley?"

"Fine," Jack said. "Recovering well. Should be back here in a few days."

Mhari slid off her stool at the bar and scooted up to me straight away. "Is that so? Only I heard his foot needs chopping off as it's there's this rot set in, and he's got gangrene goin' all the way—ow! What was that for?"

"Slip of the foot," I said, dropping my voice to hiss at her. "And stop spreading nasty rumours. I'll tell you what's really happening if you promise to keep your extremely enormous mouth shut!"

Said big gob opened to protest and then closed. "You better."

Xavier, busy pulling pints while two women eyed him

hungrily, caught sight of us. He pointed at the door behind the bar. We made our way over, Xavier closing the door behind us. In the kitchen, he checked the temperature of the wood-fired oven and began rolling out pizza dough.

"What ees going on?"

Jack related what had happened during our visit, skipping the embarrassing emergency dash to the toilet to throw up bit. Ashley wanted Jack to take overall charge of the Lochside Welcome, but the day-to-day responsibility of running the pub and food side of the business would be Xavier's. Would he be able to manage by himself for a few days until Jack offloaded Highland Tours to the freelancer he'd lined up? Ashley had passed on the name of an agency that supplied temporary waiters and chefs, and Xavier would be able to call on them if necessary.

Xavier nodded. "Okay, we could use another pair of hands. I think the Eenglish school holidays start in the middle of this month and eet will get busier?"

Eenglish, beezier… a French accent made words so delicious. Honestly, Mhari needed her head examined resisting this one. I memo-ed myself. Point out Xavier's charms to the nosey one at every opportunity. Suggest she could do much, much worse.

"And are you okay to stay here until the end of the year?" Jack asked. Xavier's gap year had already lasted ten months, his absence from Canada coming up for its 12-month anniversary at the beginning of September. Xavier might not have noticed, but Jack's voice had a pleading note to it. How on earth would he find someone so capable (and er… cheap) otherwise?

"Sure. I like eet here."

Jack blew out a long breath, leaning back against the wall. "Thank you. I'll just have a word wi' Jolene."

I'd spotted her waiting tables when we came in. In the car on the way back, I'd suggested Jack offer her a permanent arrangement. Once upon a time, she'd worked as a classroom assistant but thanks to cutbacks in the council budget, the job had disappeared. If her hours were super flexible, she'd be able to fit bar work around Tamar as Stewart did most of his coding work from home. Money and absence from Stewart would sweeten the deal.

Alone with Xavier, I admired his cookery skills. He was able to do that thing where chefs toss dough in the air and stretch it out by hand. A stint in a top Italian restaurant as a teenager, he told me—the technique made for super-thin, crispy pizza bases.

"I'm glad you like it in Lochalshie," I helped myself to a stray bit of cheese. "Anyone—I mean, thing—in particular? Can't be the sunshine."

"Ah, the weather's not so bad. You try winters with temperatures of minus 10 for days on end, your 'ands and feet freezing every day. You were an outsider too, n'est-ce pas?"

I found myself a seat as standing up for any longer than five minutes was beyond me these days. "Oof, that's better. Yes, and look how wonderfully it all worked out for me. I followed in the footsteps of Jolene. A fine tradition of people who move to Lochalshie, meet the love of their lives and have babies with them!"

Xavier's eyebrows shot up, framing his expression. Horrified panic.

"I'm only 22! I do not want babies!"

He backed away from me as if I had some hitherto unknown power to make people go forth and reproduce.

"Oh no, no, no!"

Whoops. Misjudged that badly.

"I didn't mean to suggest that that you—"

"Gaby?" Back in the kitchen, my other half took in the scene. "Please don't frighten Xavier. I'm going to be relying on him over the next few months."

Sincere apologies murmured and reassurances that no-one wanted to put him out for stud, Xavier returned to stretching out pizza dough, and we left. Jolene gave me a cheery wave, obviously pleased at the prospect of future paid work behind the bar. A group of walkers argued among themselves over who had bagged the most Munros to date and what pizzas they should eat to build up their energy levels.

"The four-cheese one!" I called out, earning thumbs-up from everyone. "It's amazing."

"What did you say to Xavier?" Jack asked as we stepped out onto the main road. The sun doing its best to peek between the clouds—rays dappling the top of the hills and picking out the white crests of the waves on the loch.

About to answer, 'hook Xavier up with Mhari', I decided against it. Jack's ex—the girlfriend immediately before me—was a YouTube star who called herself the Dating Guru where she offered dodgy 'fool-proof' ways for the modern woman to find herself a partner. Reminders of her tended to make him growl. My clumsy efforts with Xavier were too close to what she offered.

"Nothing!" I said airily, my phone providing a welcome distraction as the Messenger app beeped. "Better check my messages in case I've missed anything work-related." The app showed multiple replies, most people answering with heart emojis, hands clapping and drinks. We'd reached our front door, Mildred bounding out from behind a bush and yowling angrily in protest at the hours of neglect.

"'Save the date'," I read, "because... oh bummer, bummer, bummer!"

"What's wrong?" Jack asked as he bent to tickle the top of Mildred's head.

"An invite. One of those appalling ones where you really can't say no."

Chapter Eight

"Can't you plead pregnancy?" Jack asked as he made tea. Mildred scoffed a helping of gourmet, hand-cooked beef casserole flavoured cat food almost as expensive as the organic fresh meat she'd grown accustomed to.

I shook my head. "Not this time."

Growing a baby, I reflected, ought to be a woman's fool-proof excuse to get out of everything. But the company was way ahead of me there. I'd let HR know about my pregnancy last week. The Messenger app invite included links to airline policies on flying when with child. Apparently, I was still at the stage where air stewards would not take one panicked look at me and point-blank refuse to let me on the plane.

And, as Blissful Beauty prided itself on its drive towards minimal business air miles (Caitlin, the owner of a private helicopter and jet, very much the exception to that rule), why didn't I travel down on the sleeper the night before…?

Hyun-Ki's leaving party was to take place on a Friday. No harm to my boss, a most excellent example of the species as already indicated by the committed watching of YouTube cat videos. But work parties and informal get-togethers with your colleagues? Name one person who liked them, and I'd call them a liar.

The invite had come from the company, rather than my boss. If he had sent it himself, I'd have rung him up and begged for a virtual party. He was sure to know of a game where Gen Y folks got to enjoy all the excitement of a big club night without having to leave their home. I'd set myself up with a super-glamorous (thin) avatar, drink everyone under the table, dance like a maniac, stay up all night and, best of all, do it from the comfort of my bed.

A company invite though… Even if I did have the official sanction of Caitlin Cartier to work from home thanks to our joint(ish) wedding and my vital part in her rescue from a gunman (that everyone else claimed was much exaggerated), Blissful Beauty's real bosses muttered things from time to time.

"When was the last time you touched base here, Gaby?" Marcia in Personnel, an immaculately dressed Texan, drawled on any conference calls we had. Or she dropped heavy hints about how the work/life balance wasn't meant to be tipped so far to the life side.

I had no choice. Party it was. With any luck, that would be my last trip to London until the end of my maternity leave.

Post the unpleasant Messenger revelation, another surprise awaited me. The doorbell went half-an-hour later, just as Jack finished dishing up bowls of butternut squash curry and rice, the smell of coconut, lemongrass and coriander drifting from the kitchen.

"I'll see who it is." At some point, in the none too

distant future, my days of getting up from the armchair without a winch were going to grind to a halt.

The door opened to reveal Mhari. "I dinnae want to intrude…"

One of her much-used sentences and a lie every time. I sighed and swung the door back so she could come in.

"Oh, are youse about to eat your dinner?"

"Would you like some, Mhari?"

Someone once told me that the difference between the east and the west coast of Scotland was that west coasters opened the door, asking the question, "Come in! Have ye had your tea?" Whereas Scottish east coasters made it a statement. "Ye'll have had yer tea."

Lochalshie was on the west.

Mhari scraped her feet on the mat. "Very kind of you tae offer."

Jack handed her a bowl, and she joined me on the couch, poking the chunks of squash and asking where the chicken bits were. When Katya lived with her, she said Mhari had no idea what most vegetables looked like. But it proved no barrier to mooching a free dinner.

"How are ye getting to Hyun-Ki's party, Gaby?"

I paused, fork half-way to mouth. "By sleeper?"

"Fine. I dinnae like aeroplanes. Are we goin' down on the Thursday night, then?"

A snort from the kitchen. Jack in super-supportive mode. A party in London I didn't want to attend plus undiluted Mhari for 72 hours.

"I thought… I didn't know you were…"

The company Messenger invite had gone out to all and sundry. I hadn't noticed who else was on it. Otherwise, I might have been prepared.

"I'm his girlfriend. 'Course I've got to go. And you need

lookin' after. When my cousin's wife fell pregnant the first time, her heid went to mush. Couldnae mind the day o' the week. You'll get tae London and realise you've nae money, nae party clothes, nae make-up and dinnae know the way to the office."

Jack took the armchair opposite us and nodded sagely. "You are a bit forgetful these days, Gaby."

The look I sent him promised revenge of a torturous, drawn-out for ages infliction of pain later. He shrugged and poured us all water.

Once Thursday night came around, and we arrived in Inverness ready to catch the train, I got out of the car and suggested Mhari carry my rucksack, to which she suggested where I stick it. So much for the help, she'd promised.

But apart from the massive shunt when two separate trains joined at Edinburgh at one in the morning, the sleeper proved surprisingly comfortable. The cocoon-like feel of the tiny room and narrow bed made for a peaceful night's sleep. I'd taken the bottom bunk to aid frequent toilet trips and only needed to get up twice. Result.

It arrived in London just before seven, but we were allowed plenty of time to disembark. I pulled on the Highland Tours hoodie, a T-shirt and jeans, leaving the top buttons undone and admired the effect. Much, much more slimming than the awful maternity clothes I'd bought.

Katya was waiting for us at Euston, a grease-stained paper bag in hand. "Mhari! I wasn't expecting you as well."

She did her best to make the surprise sound like a delightful one and thrust the packet of almond croissants at me. "Breakfast."

"Where's mine?"

"I only buy meals for besties, Mhari." She rummaged in

her handbag. "If you're starving, you can have this plant-based protein bar."

Mhari scowled and stalked off to Burger King, returning five minutes later with a double cheeseburger. I turned down her offer of limp gherkin slices to go with my croissants. Yet another person who believed in the myth of pregnancy and bonkers food cravings.

"Who's going to carry my rucksack for me?" I asked as we followed the signs for the Tube.

"No' me," Mhari said through a too-large mouthful of hamburger. She'd accidentally bought the vegan one, Katya whispered to me and was yet to notice. "Carry it yoursel'."

Katya held her hand out for it. "I'll take it, seeing as I'm Gaby's favourite friend. All you are is an extremely poor second-best."

Finished burger wrapper dumped in a bin, Mhari smiled slyly at her.

"Oh aye? She hasnae telt you her news yet, though, has she? Why d'ye think she needs someone to carry her bag for her? Or why I want tae know if she'd like gherkins wi' that fancy pastry thing she's eating?"

Ah. And arrrrrgggghhhhhhhh.

Katya stopped, brow wrinkled and mouth hanging open.

"Gaby! Are you pregnant?"

Some months ago, Katya did what she called a Hard Whexit—where she left WhatsApp, fed of non-stop notifications and the splinter factions that broke away from the many groups she was already a member of.

"I can't keep up with it all, Gaby," she told me. "It's exhausting."

So, she hadn't seen Mhari's handy little update where she told everyone I was pregnant for me. Jack and I had wanted to keep our news quiet until I passed the 12-week mark, although we'd mentioned it to our families. Nevertheless, the secrecy had made me squirm every time Katya, and I spoke on the phone. I'd always shared everything with Katya.

Crowds surged around us at the top of the escalators, London's rush hour kicking in. Katya, arms folded, Mhari pretending innocence.

"Thanks, Mhari. I'm mega-sorry, Katya. Yes, I am. You —and only you," dagger looks at the trouble stirrer to my left— "will be my child's godmother. And this will do nothing, nothing to change our friendship."

Katya rolled her eyes. "They all say that."

"Aye," Mhari piped up, ignoring the glares she got as people bustled past, offended at the breach of London Tube etiquette (move, move, all the time!) "My cousin's wife turned into this woman who only talked about her baby's poop for months. All her friends ran for the hills, screamin'."

On that happy note, me swearing on the life of everyone I knew that my future conversations would not revolve around faeces, we got on the Tube.

"Pregnant lady!" Katya bellowed at the passengers already sitting down, all of whom ignored her. The Highland Tours hoodie and jeans combo must hide the pregnancy well enough to convince commuters I was not enceinte or maybe London citizens were as hard-hearted as the stories said.

"I can't believe you managed to keep it quiet for so long," Katya added, eyes hard.

Neither could I. You try living in a village where nosiness is an art form. I had a reputation for spilling all too. I would have made the world's worst spy.

"Um," I said stalling. If I said I'd promised Jack we wouldn't tell anyone until I reached the 12-week mark, I drew a line in the sand. The one that stated loud and clear —*my most significant loyalty is Jack, not you.* But much as I loved Jack, Katya and I had been friends for years.

"I wanted to know everything was okay," I settled for and squeezed her hand. "And then events took over, and I didn't get around to telling you. Sorry."

"How do you reconcile your decision to breed with how over-populated and at breaking point the world is already?" Over the years, Katya had always made her feelings about having children clear. No, no, and 300 hundred times more no.

"Thanks, Katya."

A massive sigh. "Sorry. Congratulations. I'm thrilled for you."

Chapter Nine

By the time we'd reached the Blissful Beauty company flat —conveniently located above its UK HQ—she had thawed, conceding that yes, it was best to keep the news to yourself until you felt more confident. And in deference to my pregnant state she didn't make us walk up the stairs to the flat either, as she usually did, Katya a big believer in exercise.

We had five hours to fill before the party started. I was in no hurry. The traffic noise didn't startle me having stayed in the flat for three months last year, but it surprised Mhari. It was a reminder of why I disliked London so much. Triple glazing didn't temper it at all.

Now Katya and her partner Dexter were the London flat's only and most permanent residents, she'd given the place a makeover. When I'd lived there, it was all magnolia walls, thickly carpeted bedrooms and hardwood flooring, the décor and furniture complementing each other. Katya had added floor to ceiling bookcases in the living room, their contents stuffed tightly in. A photo wall decorated the hallway, me squealing in recognition when I spotted the old pictures of Katya and me at school.

Mhari studied them carefully, head to one side. Her detective skills honed through years of nosiness, she pointed at one picture, triumphant grin in place. "Is that your auld boyfriend, Gaby? The Ryan yin?"

"Why have you got that one up?" I asked Katya aghast.

Katya swung around to face me. "I love that photo! You and Ryan visited my house that night. We'd fallen out the week before, remember?"

Ah. Katya and I had only had a bust-up twice in our long friendship. The first time not long after I got together with Ryan and Katya made her thoughts on him clear. (I should have listened.) The second? A year and a bit ago when I realised she'd known more about Hammerstone Hotel's plans for the Royal George and kept it quiet... Her eyes sought out mine, both of us remembering. Her thinking, 'Oh, I kept a big secret too'?

Mhari curled her top lip. She didn't do soppy stuff. And had no idea about the back story behind the picture. "What did ye argue about? Too much honesty ower Gaby's awfy haircut?"

Not only was it a picture of Ryan and me, arms wrapped around each other but one of the Unfortunate Hairstyle. No-one knows what best suits them when they are 16, do they? Katya and I had ventured all the way from Great Yarmouth into Norwich, determined to visit the salon rumoured to be owned by the guy favoured by Norfolk's celebrities. All two of them.

Turned out Starcutz by Penny, the mobile service my mum used for spring, summer and winter visits to our home for years, knew what suited my hair and face shape far better than Mr Fancy Hair Salon Charges Ten Times More for It.

A short fringe, jaw-length, dyed black bob might work well on a tall, skinny, heart-shaped face person. It was disastrous on me. Mhari peered at the photo again, shaking her head. This was the woman with thick, wavy, down to her waist auburn locks. What did she know about bad hair days?

The much bigger photo of Jack and me on our wedding day cheered me up; especially since in it my light brown hair was swept back in a ponytail and threaded with a few flowers. Much more flattering.

Katya pinched my arm lightly. I smiled at her. In the wee sma' hours (as they say in Scotland), no-one would notice if a pregnant lady got out of bed, sneaked along the hallway to the photo wall and whipped that picture of Ryan and me off it and tore it into tiny pieces, right?

Katya steered us both into the flat's kitchen, the room equipped with equipment so top of the range it was straight out of a catalogue. Such as the coffee machine promising lattes, espressos, cappuccinos and everything in between.

I shook my head when Katya pointed at it, strong caffeinated drinks yet another of the pregnancy no-nos. Katya made a coffee for her and Mhari and held up a herbal tea bag for me.

"As long as it's not camomile."

Drinks made Katya suggested we sit in the living room. Her computer sat in the corner—the brand-new iMac proof of how well she was doing these days. The Caitlin autobiography had paid extremely generously and led to other jobs.

"What are you working on?" I asked.

She rolled her eyes. "Promise you won't laugh." A quick glance at Mhari. "Or tell anyone who the real author is?"

We both nodded solemnly.

"Caitlin is branching into romance novels to expand her billion-pound empire. I'm the one writing them."

"Why is that funny?" I asked. It wasn't that much of a change in direction for Caitlin either. Katya moaned to me that the only new 'authors' who were given book deals in today's world were celebrities, and most of them didn't write a single word of their so-called novels. The Caitlin empire already included make-up, a fitness app and exercise wear. Hardly surprising she'd decided to apply the Caitlin magic to something else.

"They're about… about… No, I can't say it out loud. Here."

Katya reached behind her, pulling up a sheet of paper lying on her desk and handing it to me.

The sheet—it's top stamped with red, capital letters that said 'strictly confidential'—was entitled *High Heels and Pink Glitter*. There followed a lengthy description of characters, chapters and what needed to happen when and where. The tag line under the title stated, *Genre: female billionaire clean romance.*

"Clean romance—what does that mean?"

People who washed extensively before embarking on a kiss? Couples who only considered contact if they were wearing hazmat suits and surgical gloves?

Mhari, reading over my shoulder, sat back down again. "Nae dirty bits?"

Katya nodded. "Nope. And this from the woman who was the subject of a 'leaked' sex tape of her and her then rapper boyfriend featuring an extended session with rubber toys and a table tennis paddle three years ago."

A collective wince. You should have seen the colour of that man's butt cheeks afterwards. I started to snigger, Mhari and Katya joining in. "Le-le-let me read you the main ch-ch-character description!" Katya said between splutters of laughter. "LeAnna D'Arcey has successfully built her bi-billion-dollar bra business, Storm in a D Cup, from scr-scratch."

"Huh!" Me. Much easier to build a billion-dollar business when you were bonkers rich and a celebrity already, right?

"... but along the way, she has sacrificed love and friendship and spends what little free time she has alone in her huge mansion in the Hollywood hills."

More spluttered laughter from Mhari and me, Katya miming herself playing the world's smallest violin.

"...ca-ca-can her new chauffeur stroke bodyguard, the mysterious Daniel, prove able to provide her with the love and affection she so ba-ba-badly craves?"

She gave up, descending into full-blown hysteria so infectious it spread to Mhari and me. When she pretended to act out the first encounter with the chauffeur/handyman, I almost wet myself. (Incontinence, my mother-in-law told me, was one more thing to look forward to, postbirth.)

"What's so funny?"

Katya whipped around, tucking the sheet behind her back. Strictly speaking, she shouldn't have said a word to us about her new project. Okay, so the guy asking the question was Dexter but as he was also employed by Caitlin to market her make-up and skincare, who knew what he might think of our unprofessionalism?

"Nothing!" Katya sang out. "You're home early!"

True. When we'd both worked there, I'd never witnessed

Dexter leave the office before 7pm. It wasn't even lunchtime yet.

"Yeah, I wanna grab a shower," he said, leaning across to peck Katya on the lips. "Before the party starts."

Liquid chocolate was how I described Dexter's voice. He was a Texan native, accent still fully intact after two years along with a complete aversion to British weather.

"They've brought forward the time it starts," he added, heading for the bathroom. The sound of water gushing from the showerhead started up. "Two pm, not four."

I cheered silently. The sooner the party started, the sooner it ended. Or rather, the earlier I could employ the French exit—the one where you go to the toilet and beat a hasty retreat without saying goodbye to anyone—and tuck myself up in the spare bed way before midnight.

"What are you planning to wear?" Katya looked me up and down. The hoodie top sported its usual coating of cat hairs, and although I'd packed the maternity dress, I dreaded putting it on.

"Er…"

"On your feet, Richardson!" My best friend was never going to get used to calling me McAllan. "Luckily for you, I have connections everywhere."

———

She was as good as her word. Katya's chums in useful places included a nearby west end London boutique she'd written website copy for a few months ago whose lines included party maternity wear.

In the window at Mouki Miche, pouty mannequins their feet hidden by a sea of multi-coloured polystyrene baubles modelled beautifully cut dresses, jeans and blazers. All super tight.

"I'm not sure…" I said, receiving a light push to my back.

"Trust me."

A pink-haired woman greeted us, eyes alighting on us one by one. Her eyes slid off me, finally settling on Katya.

"Hey, Katya! Great to see you. Are you after something special?"

"My friend," Katya pointed at me, "is pregnant and needs a party dress, Mariel."

"No problem!" Mariel made her way towards the rails at the back of the shop returning to us seconds later, dark brown fabric draped over her hand.

"This! It's a discontinued line, and it's in the sale. The boss isn't around so if you're incredibly careful with it, I'll take it back tomorrow."

Katya took the dress from her, the sales tag revealing that even cut-price that dress was way beyond my means. "Mariel, you're a star."

Back to the flat again, we got changed in Katya's bedroom. The cocoa-coloured outfit featured a bodice made of stretch soft floral lace with sheer sleeves, a fitted skirt in soft jersey and a satin sash in a darker chocolate colour that created more definition between my bump and boobs.

I put it on and looked at myself, tears coming to my eyes. Mhari, stripping off herself so she could pull on her best sequinned blouse and skinny jeans combo, tutted. "Dinnae mind her, Katya. She started greeting on the train last night when this old guy said goodbye to his girlfriend and her dog. Totes emosh all the time."

I hugged Katya anyway. "Thank you, thank you, thank you!"

"What has happened to your boobs?" Katya said as she tied the sash in a neat knot underneath my bust. As pre-adolescent girls I'd watched with envy as she outgrew first the B-cup, then a C, D and eventually landed on the letter F. The last bra I had to buy raced past all those letters.

"Gross, aren't they?" Mhari. Once more picking up the first prize for Best Supportive Friend Act.

Katya peered at my cleavage and wrinkled her nose. "That blue vein thing."

Mhari, joined on the podium by Katya, also picking up the same award. But they made it up to me by forcing me to sit in front of the massive mirror on top of the antique dressing room table in the room, its surfaces covered with Blissful Beauty skincare and make-up. Dating the company's head of marketing made Katya super popular with all her friends. She got far more freebies than I did.

Mhari, a dab hand with tongs, piled my hair up and pulled down the tendrils, so they framed my face. At the same time, Katya dabbed on glow serum, bronzer, high-lighters and contouring powder, making me resemble my pre-pregnancy self before the fat padded itself all over me.

Dexter whistled when the three of us emerged. No slacker in the style stakes himself, he'd changed out of his suit into a pointed collar animal-print shirt and high-waisted flares that moulded to his thighs. He took my hands in his, eyes shining.

"Gaby, you look so… like, super amazing."

Behind me, I sensed Katya shift from foot to foot. Dexter eyed my stomach hungrily, glance suddenly alighting on his girlfriend. Oh-oh.

But I welcomed Dexter's admiration. Weeks of feeling

like a puffed-up slug made you drink the stuff in. Even Mhari managed a compliment, hers the tempered variety. "Aye, you look alright for once." She took my photo, and I sent it to Jack. Might as well remind him of the glamorous Gaby, long since disappeared under shapeless clothes, messy hair and extra padding.

"Right," Katya said. "Time to party. Let's do this thing!"

Chapter Ten

As this was Hyun-Ki, the party had to take place in the office. He was far too busy preparing extensive handover notes to allow for time out to travel to a venue.

"Hyun-Ki doesnae like surprises," Mhari said as we took the lift down to the next floor, me preening myself in the mirror in there before panicking that my look was borderline drag queen. Fancy dress, make-up, hair... Katya's velvet jeans and a camisole top, and Mhari's silk blouse over leggings were far more understated.

"Am I over-dressed?" I asked, Dexter, hastening to reassure me fecundity made me 'super-gorgeous', the hint making Katya scowl. The lift door opened, where we met the rest of Blissful Beauty's UK employees who'd sneaked away from their desks. They must have tarted themselves up in the toilets, as outfits matched mine in formality. Different perfumes competed for air space. Blissful Beauty's Jewel—similar to dousing yourself in a vat of vanilla and cinnamon—dominated.

Marcia from Personnel held a vast cake covered in

fondant icing, an edible photo of LA superimposed-on top. We all followed her through to the central office area where Hyun-Ki sat, attention glued to his screen, noise-cancelling headphones hiding our stifled giggles.

"He really doesnae like surprises," Mhari threw in, the sound drowned out by everyone else's shout of "SURPRISE!"

The headphones didn't have a £450 price tag for nothing… Dexter had to lean over and lift one of the over-ear cushions up, so we could yell once more. Hyun-Ki whirled around his chair, face a mix of astonishment and dismay. He needed to be dragged from his iMac. When he protested that he wanted to make one further change to the new blog template, Dexter shrugged.

"Don't worry, man. Just put it in a format we can edit."

Behind Dexter, I grimaced. That sentence was one we graphic designers included in the top ten of things never to say to a designer. However, once Hyun-Ki had recovered, he threw himself into the proceedings. This being Blissful Beauty, the company had hired top-rate caterers who glided in, bearing trays of South Korean specialities and Goju shots. Someone dimmed the lighting, and a DJ mixed K-pop hits. The playroom where stressed-out employees went to play table tennis and use the space hoppers was opened out. Bouncing on those things was ten times more fun after a drink, though it looked far more dangerous. I steered well clear.

Promising me we'd catch up later, Hyun-Ki was swallowed up in a crowd of people I didn't recognise. The invite must have extended to those outside the company. Mhari wangled herself in with Lucy, the head of PR, the two of them comparing photos on their phones.

Katya grabbed a plate of food, scrutinising it for pregnancy unfriendly items such as pate and prawns, and steered us into the boardroom. Thankfully, no-one else had commandeered the space, but she kept the lighting low, so we weren't easy to see.

Katya divided canapés between two plates, handing one to me. "I was thinking of coming back to Lochalshie for a few weeks," she said and bit into a tiny spring roll dipped in chilli sauce.

I copied her. How many canapés made up a meal? Twenty? More?

"That would be wonderful," I said. Your best friend is someone best kept close by.

Outside the boardroom, someone had started up a conga line. Amazingly, Hyun-Ki was in the middle of it, face beaming at me every time it sailed past the board room.

"It might help me write Caitlin's billionaire romance book," she explained. "Peace, quiet and rotten Wi-Fi reception so no social media distraction."

I helped myself to three more of the spring rolls; four down, 16 to go. "Lochalshie has almost total Wi-Fi coverage now. Not like the good ol' days."

That set me off on a nostalgia fest. When I first arrived in Lochalshie, having convinced my then boss I'd be able to work remotely, I discovered the village's Wi-Fi and mobile signal reception was patchy and unreliable. When I asked around, the local GP (Dr McLatchie, my now mother-in-law) suggested I borrow Jack's house. He wasn't in it most of the time, she explained, and the reception at his home was awfy good.

The rest, as they say, is history.

"Come in, Richardson, Richardson, come in! You were

back remembering those first few encounters you had with Jack, weren't you?"

"Maybe. What about Dexter?" I asked.

"He won't effin' notice!"

Oh dear. "Be lovely to have you nearby again, though. We can spend our evenings in the Lochside Welcome too, keeping Jack company as he works behind the—"

"What?"

Out it all came. Ashley's original request and then why it became urgent post his collapse and admittance into the hospital. Jack's strong ties to the place. Mine too. How neither of us could bear it if the Royal George ended up the only hotel in Lochalshie.

Katya knocked back a Goju shot and took another one. The conga line snaked past us again, Dexter bringing up the rear and Mhari giving us a cheery wave. No sign of sulking from her at the loss of her one-time boyfriend.

"He's taking over the Lochside Welcome? Are you two bonkers? And why are you only telling me now? Is the pregnancy affecting your brain? You keep forgetting about it (and to tell me) and everything else at the same time?"

I blinked. Her comments were too much for my hormonally challenged head to take.

Katya put down her glass and took my hand. "Sorry. That was mean."

"I am forgetful these days. Mhari said pregnancy turned her cousin's head to mush."

"I know it's not an illness and years ago women squatted in fields, gave birth and carried on with whatever they were doing," Katya added. How come everyone else knew so much more about pregnancy in ye olden days than I did? "But is this a case of taking on far too much?"

A tight crush of my fingers. Brusque as my bestie could

be, we'd been friends for years. She knew me better than anyone, possibly even Jack. And everything she said was what I'd thought from the outset.

"He won't be away on overnights all the time," I said. "And he's already factored in time off when the baby is due. And won't it be fun, running the pub where all our friends spend so much time?"

Katya raised her eyebrows. "Maybe. I know I'm harking on about it, but aren't babies hard work in those first few months? Waking up all hours of the night, etcetera?"

"Tamar's okay."

Katya muttered Jolene and Stewart had landed themselves an exceptional infant. One who slept right through the night from the start. He'd breastfed beautifully, transitioned to solid food smoothly and ticked off every box on the midwife/health visitor/GP checks when he should.

"Have you ever looked after Tamar?"

Ah. No. Partly this was because all Jolene's former teaching assistant colleagues queued up to babysit for her. She'd once told me if she took up all their offers, she could go out any weekend she wanted. But Katya was right. As my older brother Dylan was a committed commitment-phobe and Jack an only child, we had no nieces or nephews to practise on. We needed to borrow Tamar for an afternoon or evening and find out more.

Cat care, much as it was demanding in Mildred's case, did not count as parent training. Pity.

Katya placed another tray of canapés in front of me—crispy-fried chicken wings. She added a stack of paper napkins. The dress was meant to go back to the shop. Best we didn't return it covered in greasy stains.

"And perfect timing too," she flicked a hand at the screen. "The tiny boss…" Caitlin was a mere one metre forty tall and proof positive celebrities were always much shorter and thinner than they looked on screen. "...is just waking up in LA and wants to wish the designer who once saved her life..."

"I did too!" I piped up. Katya sent me her best 'c'mon' look. Strictly speaking, Hyun-Ki was the one who disarmed the gunman that time a stalker burst into the office and begged Caitlin to marry him. But me grabbing his weapon and impersonating an American gunslinger as I told him to drop to the floor clinched it.

"... all the best running her empire in LA and ensuring it keeps bringing her in millions of dollars."

On cue, the conga line came to a halt outside, everyone piling into the board room. Dexter flicked the remote at the screen and Caitlin beamed at us. "Hey, guys!"

"Hey!" We all chorused back.

As usual, there was nothing business-like about the background. Caitlin's mansion was right on the beach, a vast living room with French windows that opened out onto a deck with views of the ocean, white-tipped waves rolling and crashing on the shore behind her.

Despite it being early, she was immaculate—super shiny hair, the no make-up look I knew was foundation, bronzer, contouring powder, highlighter, mascara and lip gloss expertly applied, and dressed in a designer T-shirt and shorts.

"I just wanted to say, 'Good Luck' times a billion to Hyun-Ki, the most a-may-zing designer in the world!"

Hyun-Ki stood up and took a bow to a chorus of cheers. The caterers came in behind us, champagne bottles popping. "Vintage stuff," Katya whispered to me. "Seventy-five pounds a bottle, Dexter told me. Make sure you say yes to a glass, and I'll drink yours."

"Gaby, are you here?" she asked, and I heaved myself to my feet. "Cute dress! Hon, we're so pleased you came down for the party."

Were they?

"So a-may-zing to have you here! The perfect time to ask you…"

Oh-oh again. Out of the corner of my eye, I spotted Hyun-Ki edge closer to Dexter, the two of them exchanging conspiratorial glances.

"… why not take over the UK head designer role temporarily? We love your work so much, Gaby!"

She puckered her lips and blew me kisses. Much as I thought Caitlin was surprisingly okay for someone who'd always been incredibly well-off and famous all her life and lived in a world where no-one said no to her.

Talk about being put in an awkward position. At the door of the board room, Marcia from Personnel rolled her eyes and pursed her lips. I was not her favourite person. Oh well, she'd back every excuse I came up with to refuse.

I fake-laughed. "Wow, what an honour. Um, but I guess this is the perfect time to share my news with you…" I turned side-on and pulled the dress tightly to my stomach.

Caitlin's hands went to her mouth. "Oh, hon! That is so super-amazing. I'm stoked for you. When is your baby due?"

"The second week in December," I said, "and I wanted my maternity leave to st—"

She didn't let me finish. "Hey, I pride myself on how I support women, right, Dexter?"

Dexter nodded. "Oh yeah. We're such a modern company we never let pregnancy stand in the way of a career progression. We're in the running for the UK's

Female-Friendly Workplace of the Year, and boy we want that prize."

Ah. An ulterior motive then. At the start of the year, Caitlin and her sisters were slagged off in the press and on many of the social media sites for promoting old-fashioned attitudes towards women by dressing and acting the way they did. Then, a story surfaced where it was revealed one of the sisters' clothing lines used a sweatshop factory staffed by women and children in India. Were they giving me this job partly to prove the Cartiers were decent sorts who bent over backwards to support women?

To the right of me, Mhari's thumbs moved frantically over her phone screen. Great. Another update to the Lochalshie WhatsApp group where people got to know the full story as soon as it happened. Fingers crossed Jack was somewhere out of mobile range.

"The Lochside Welcome!" Katya hissed. "You've got that as well!"

"London," I said. "I can't work—"

"That's not an issue," Caitlin waved a hand. "We're super modern. You can video conference your team. You'd only need to travel to London once every two months."

She must have spoken with Hyun-Ki. When he'd tried to persuade me, he said once a month.

"And you've been mentoring Trish, haven't you?" Hyun-Ki said, gesturing behind him where Trish nodded agreement. I wouldn't have called it mentoring. Blissful Beauty was her first proper job out of art school, and she liked to bombard me with questions. I made suggestions and—

Oh. Maybe it was mentoring, after all.

"We want you to be our UK head designer sooooooo much, Gaby!" Lots of kisses blown my way. A chant was taken up by everyone in the room apart from Marcia and

Katya, who apparently still thought it was the daftest idea they'd ever heard. As did I.

"Do it, do it, do it!"

A little known fact about me—*oh be honest with yourself, Richardson* as my friend Katya would say… Okay, a *well-known* fact about me is that I'm just a girl who can't say no. Pushy people recognised this quickly and forced me into corners I couldn't then back out of.

The 'do it, do it, do its' got louder, Caitlin adding impact by clapping her hands and joining in. Hyun-Ki nodded furiously at me, hands in front of him with his thumbs up.

Dexter flung his arms out. "Well, Gaby—what's it to be? D'you wanna join us as Blissful Beauty's UK's acting head of design and help make us even more super-awesome?"

"I'll need to talk to Jack!" I bleated.

The 'talk to Jack' bit was drowned out by cheers and the pop of several more vintage champagne bottles opening, as I continued to mutter about not having said yes. Caitlin blew me kisses, wished Hyun-Ki *"all the very, very, very best in the whole wide world!"* again and went back to advanced crystal light yoga followed by smashed avocado on kale toast or however else she spent her mornings.

"I didn't agree!" I said, accepting one of the glasses of champagne to give it to Katya. I took a gulp, anyway, appalled at the situation which had spiralled out of control.

Katya accepted the half-empty glass I gave her and sighed. "No, but everyone in this blasted company seems to think it's such an amazing honour to work here."

Ooh. Eyes narrowed as she looked at Dexter. Every so

often, Katya phoned me to complain about her boyfriend's workaholism. Perhaps the writer's retreat suggestion had another point to it, where she let him miss her.

Mhari sidled over, two champagne flutes held aloft. "The Lochalshie WhatsApp group says congratulations. And they want tae know how much more money you're gonnae get? I've also uploaded your story to the official Blissful Beauty Instagram account. Got 326 likes already."

Another unfathomable Blissful Beauty company decision, allowing Mhari access to its social media profiles. Ever since she'd taken the pictures for Caitlin's wedding, her own account had taken off, meaning Mhari was considered a micro-influencer. "Much better," she said to me, "than a big influencer, so Dexter says. Folks trust ye more."

Whatever. But yes, Mhari got to upload updates to the official account from time to time. They even bunged her a bit of money for it. Who better to be part of the vast Blissful Beauty social media team than someone who spent 95 percent of her waking hours staring at a phone screen?

She showed me the slide show she'd created, a picture of me and the create your own anime, with avatar me, sponging fake tan all over my bump. 'Meet Gaby, our new UK Head of Design!!!!!! #blissfulbeauty #womenpower #womenfirst #pregnantpositive.' My first (unworthy) thought, *Wow, that dress! Thank heavens, I don't look like a whale. And a super-cute avatar.* My second, *OH CRAPPING HELL, what's Jack going to think? I haven't even discussed this with him yet, please, please, please let him be out of range!*

"Your phone's ringing, Gaby. D'ye think that's Jack? Want me to answer it for you?" Mhari, face faux innocent concern.

"No thank you, Mhari. I can do it." Then, as she made to follow me out of the boardroom. "By myself!"

Katya sucked her teeth as I walked past her, people clapping me on the back. I slipped into Dexter's office—him being so important he didn't have to put up with the open-plan schtick ordinary folk had to endure. His seat was an ergonomically designed one and massively uncomfortable thanks to it having been adjusted to his six-foot-two skinny frame, rather than a five-foot-four pregnant woman.

"Jack!"

"Gaby. Got anything to tell me? Another of those little things you forgot to discuss with me?" Emphasis on the 'little'.

I entered full-blown 'It'll be fine!' mode. Goodness me, companies were so progressive these days they promoted you, allowed you to work from home and cared not a tick-ety-boo if a small body was about to burst out of your own… No, no, no, no! Six months' maternity leave coming up where Jack and I would enjoy weeks of bliss while we got to know McAllan Junior.

"Anyway, didn't you accept the challenge of taking on the management of the Lochside Welcome after minimal discussion with me?"

A silence his end, punctuated by him blowing out air. "I s'pose."

I threw in the money. And the benefits package. Blissful Beauty offered its staff private healthcare. If we wanted, perhaps McAllan Junior would make his or her way into the world via the Portland, the hospital where the Royals went to give birth. We might bump into the Duchess of Cambridge there, giving birth to her fifth child or whatever number she was up to now.

"The NHS is fine," Jack said. "My mother would never forgive us if we didn't go that route."

Fair enough, even if I'd sneakily looked up private

healthcare maternity hospitals when I first heard of Blissful Beauty's benefits. Double beds! Rooms to yourself! Massages! Hot and cold running consultants!

Another pause, allowing me to take in the background noise. Low chatter. Someone putting glasses in a dishwasher. A person asking him a question in French-accented English.

"Are you in the Lochside Welcome?"

"Yeesssss?"

"Working behind the bar?"

"Er, yeeessss?"

"Jack! I thought you weren't starting there until you'd handed over responsibility for Highland Tours?"

There followed a long explanation. He'd only had a day trip with tourers today, which meant he got back to Lochalshie for six pm, allowing him to put in the evening shift at the Lochside Welcome on the busiest night of the week. The place was ram-packed, thanks to a rumour that had started up online about Sam Heughan's younger brother, or possibly Sam Heughan himself aka Jamie Fraser on TV's Outlander was working behind the bar at this hotel in a wee village in the Highlands…

Mhari? The Lochalshie WhatsApp group? Ashley himself? Someone somewhere had planted that rumour out there and let it run…

"Pint o' that Heineken Zero, Jack!"

The request cut through the background noise. Sentences I never thought to hear in my lifetime—Stewart in the Lochside Welcome asking for a pint of alcohol-free lager. He must have decided the place was no longer triggering for him.

"I better go, Gaby. There's a rush on for pizzas. How are you feeling anyway?"

"Much better." It struck me this had been the first

morning in weeks where I hadn't battled nausea. The irony —exposure to London's filthy, toxic air, and I felt fit as a fiddle. Now that we came to mention it, my nipples and groin tightened. Ooh, this must be the fabled randy pregnant woman stage, a welcome return of my libido, but rotten timing.

"What are you dressed in," I whispered. "Are you in your kilt? What about that shirt you wear with it…? Tell me it isn't fastened all the way up, and your throat's on show, the vein there pulsing. What have you got on underneath your kilt? I hope you've honoured proper Scots tradition and there are no boxers so that if I was there, I'd be able to drop to my knees and…"

Behind me, someone coughed. I spun around, feeling the flush start on my chest and make its way upwards.

"Hey, Dexter! Just telling Jack all about my promotion, and how I have to crawl on my hands and knees most of the time these days to get anywhere because this blasted bump gets in the way all the time ha ha ha!"

At the other end of the phone, Jack spluttered with laughter and told me he couldn't wait to hear the rest. "See you, Monday!" He dropped his voice. "Oh—bring that dress home with you. I've got some ideas for what we might do wi' that ribbon."

Dang. I had to return that dress. My stirred-up libido roared. Monday couldn't come quickly enough.

Chapter Eleven

Katya insisted on a full programme of cultural events on Saturday, determined we country bumpkins pack in as much as possible.

London in the summer was impossibly hot, worse when you were carting around an internal hot water bottle. As soon as we reached Hyde Park and the outdoor theatre thing she promised was worth the effort, I collapsed on the rug she'd bought and made her set off in search of ice-cream and a freezing temperature fizzy drink.

Mhari lay beside me. Around us, others did the same. One group nearby had cushions, hampers and ice-boxes—the men removing their tops and the women stripping down to bikinis. The air stank of coconut sun cream and sweat.

"What did Hyun-Ki say to you before he left?" I asked, curious to know how they'd finished their on-off mostly screen time only romance.

"Says he'll pay for me to visit him in LA if I want."

"Do you?"

"No. Why would I? I dinnae know anyone out there.

Dexter telt me he caught you and Jack talkin' dirty to each other last night. Said he didnae know where to look. Does that help youse keep the romance alive, seein' as you've now been together forever?"

I'd kill Dexter. Slowly and as painfully as possible. And Jack and I together forever? Hardly. A mere two and a half years. I was spared answering by Katya's return, ice-cream already dripping from the cone.

She sat beside us. "Mhari, I'm thinking about returning to Lochalshie for a few months."

Sticky-sweet cream dripping down my hand, I caught her eye over the top of Mhari's head. Last night, I'd over-heard parts of a muffled conversation through the walls of her bedroom—two people hissing angrily at each other. Katya's idea to spend some weeks in Lochalshie not a welcome one then?

Mhari sat up and reached for her phone. "Aye? Want tae share a flat with me again? Rent's awfy expensive on your own."

Her eyes narrowed, the implication finally hitting her. "Are you an' Dexter having problems? Takin' a break from each other?"

"No, no and no. I'd be returning there so I can write in peace and quiet. There's the caravan park on the other side of the loch. I'll splash out on one of those static caravans. The perfect writer's retreat."

In front of us, five people on a makeshift stage and all dressed in what looked like red tents clapped their hands, promising us the performance was about to begin. I stifled a yawn. It was bound to be avant-garde and meant to improve our minds. All my 'heid turned to mush' brain could manage these days were repeats of *Love Island*.

"You'll get peace," Mhari said, firing off yet another

update to the WhatsApp group. "I'm at work in the chemist's all day. You willnae even need tae upgrade your Netflix account as it's still—"

She put her phone down and clammed up suddenly.

"Mhari, have you been logging in to my account?" Katya demanded. "Did you upgrade my subscription to multiple devices?"

"No! Aye, well, mebbe. No' my fault you didnae check. And it was only a few extra quid."

Katya snatched the second ice-cream back off her. "Oh, for heaven's sakes!"

That settled it then. Katya needed to move back to Lochalshie and in with Mhari, if only to keep a close eye on her and check she didn't try out Katya's passwords anywhere else, seeing as most people only bothered with one or two of them for multiple accounts.

The play started. The other groups around about shushed us. One of the tented women stepped forward and began to speak, the words indecipherable. Katya's outdoors in London kit included a rug and one cushion. I nabbed it, tucking it behind me so I could lie back, the sun hot on my face.

"Will you be writing full-time Katya? Every hour of the day... and the night?"

She stretched out beside me. "I'm not sure I can churn out female billionaire romance words for more than three or four hours a day. Any more and my creativity grinds to a halt."

"Perfect," I said. "All the better for seeking out alternatives to refresh your mind via the medium of menial bar work to help out your dearest friends."

She poked her elbow in my side. "I'm not returning to Lochalshie just to be an unpaid skivvy working for Jack!"

"Why no'?" Mhari asked. "Jack's gottae make the Lochside Welcome succeed. Otherwise, that awfy Royal George place will get aw the business in the area. And that smug git, Zac Cavanagh, will return there and think he's won. Mind him, do you, Katya? The one who once diddled you under the table in that restaurant we were in eating our fish and chips? Did it that secretly none of us noticed. 'Cept me. Could nae help it. That noise you made when you—"

"Mhari!" Katya sat up, triggering a fresh round of 'shushes' from all those people trying to watch the theatre production. Although a good few of them had been diverted, too enthralled by Mhari's storytelling of dirty goings-on in wee places. The hampers/icebox/bikini group stared at us, aghast. Or maybe it was envy. One woman was drop-jawed in awe, eyes darting about. ~Perhaps she hoped Zac, the mystery diddler, might suddenly appear.

"So, that's settled, eh?" Mhari pinched my cushion and lay back, phone held up as she squinted at the screen. "You, me and Gaby on that train tomorrow. We can share a bunk, Katya. Leave Miss I Need Tae Pee Every Five Seconds to hersel'. I'm going on top."

Chapter Twelve

If Jack was surprised when he picked up three people at Inverness train station and not two on Monday morning, he didn't let on. He opened the door to the minibus, heaving our bags in and grinned at her.

"Come to try your hand at bar work, Katya?"

She rolled her eyes. "Your wife's already done her best to persuade me my real vocation is pulling pints and been told where to shove her ideas. I'm here to take advantage of the peace and quiet. All the better to mine the creative depths of my imagination and invent improbable scenarios where lonely billionaires suddenly fall for the hidden charms of their chauffeur stroke handyman."

Jack wrinkled his forehead. "What?"

"Never mind," she sighed. "It's a long story. Or rather, not that a long one. I'm told female billionaire romances aren't supposed to exceed 50,000 words. So that you don't run out of words for book two. And then numbers three, four and five in the series."

"And nae shagging in any o' them," Mhari threw in.

Jack flashed me a look. One of those—'please, please save me from this' expressions I recognised so well. I clapped my hands. "Shall we get this show on the road?" I beamed at everyone, the saying one my Nanna Cooper used all the time. Everyone else was impressed with my bossiness —if they chose to show their admiration with poker faces and no comments. My husband let out a sigh, and opened the front door, beckoning me to the seat beside me. "Gaby, in you come! Let's get out of here before rush hour sets in."

'Rush hour' in the Highlands was a relative term. A delay of ten minutes or so while you waited to get off the dual carriageway to the B-road taking you to Lochalshie. The occasional stop while a farmer took his cows or sheep from one field to the next. But it meant Katya and Mhari were relegated to the seats behind us, bickering about who got to choose what they watched on Netflix that night already, Katya voting for a vegan documentary, Mhari requesting anything but. Argument unresolved, they both put on headphones and ignored each other.

"What's going on with Katya and Dexter?" Jack said, sotto voce.

I shrugged. "Who knows? I got the usual moans—he works too hard, blah blah. I have a nasty feeling she's hoping she might run into you know who if he returns to the Royal George. Unfinished business and all that."

He screwed his face up. "What, so him working for the opposition, having told her all those lies a few years ago and then getting me locked up for the night hasn't put her off?"

Apparently not. I was always going to root for Team Dexter, but my best friend often proved tricky to understand. Whatever her real motive for returning was, she didn't believe in openness the way I did.

By the time we got back to Lochalshie, it was nine am.

We dropped Katya and Mhari off at Mhari's flat, Katya having discovered that the nearby holiday park had no static caravans to spare thanks to it being peak summer holiday time. As Jack reversed the minibus into the tiny driveway in front of our house, another car drew up. A man jumped out and waved at us.

"Who's that? And what's that on his head?"

The thing on his head was a dreadful orange wig.

"Lucas," Jack squinted at him. He's my replacement— the freelancer who's going to run Highland Tours for the next few months. That's an attempt to look like Jamie Fraser I think."

A terrible one. Lucas topped the orange wig with a tartan bunnet, similar to the ones Jamal sold in his store. All he needed to do now was break into "Och aye the noo," and a poor impersonation of a Scot would be complete.

Jack pulled the gear stick into neutral. "He's early. My plans for today included getting you to put that dress on, and then I untie the bow, unthread that ribbon and use it to hae my wicked way wi' you."

Darn it. That little scenario tied in precisely with what I had in mind. Even if that dress was back on the sales rail of Mouki Miche.

"Later," I said, pushing down the door handle and jumping out as agile as a 15-weeks pregnant woman was able to do so. "And we'll need to improvise the ribbon. I'm off to buy milk and bread."

Tindra and I bumped into each other in Jamal's shop, wire baskets clashing as we knocked against each other. Thankfully, mine wasn't full of pickled onion monster munch. Explaining peculiar crisp habits to others embarrassed me.

"Tindra, hi!"

"Gaby!"

Ten out of ten for remembering my name; I'd have pegged her for one of those people who wouldn't. I hadn't seen her since the night she'd taken Ashley to hospital but why was she back in the village if not to scout its potential for filming possibilities…?

"How's Ashley?"

"Amazing!" I said, mindful of Ashley's warning she and Miles worked for the UK's Best Restaurants people even if Jack and I didn't think that was the case. It wouldn't take that long to assess a hotel and decide whether it was worthy of an award.

"Recovering super-fast and ready to return to the Lochside Welcome very soon, welcoming in visitors and tourists from around the world who flock to the place all the time because it's the one hotel in the whole of the High—"

Tindra tipped her head to the side, puzzled. "Caroline said he'd been diagnosed with type 2 diabetes, and that the ulcers on his foot are so bad, he might need to have it amputated. I drove her back to Lochalshie after I took them both to the hospital?"

Curses.

Jamal, following our conversation closely, nodded. "Aye, nasty business type 2 diabetes. Runs in my family y'know. Two brothers wi' it. My father deid at the age of 56 because of a diabetes-related heart attack."

My discreet *shut up now, Jamal* signalling bumped into its target and crashed to the ground, ignored. More musings from Jamal on the dreadful things diabetes did to a person.

Tindra picked up a bottle of suntan lotion and replaced it almost immediately. Wishful thinking on her part.

I put my basket on the counter. Jamal waggled the two-litre bottle of diet lemonade I'd placed in there. "Are ye awfy thirsty, Gaby? Mebbe you've got gestational diabetes. From the size of your stomach now, certainly looks like it. You're enormous!"

"Thank you, Jamal. My mother-in-law has tested me for it. I do *not* have gestational diabetes."

And on that note, Tindra and I left the shop.

"You've been here a while now," I said. "You must really be enjoying those sunrises."

Hint, hint. It was more than a week since Ashley's emergency hospital dash. If they were tourists as they claimed (and by now I was sure they were not), they would be the types who made Lochalshie their base, climbed a different Munro every day, took tonnes of pics to prove their adventurous, right-on credentials to all their friends and then sodded off on their real holiday to somewhere hot, far-flung and exotic a few months later.

Tindra's expression changed to shifty. "Yes. Scotland's, like, so peaceful. And everyone in the village is so friendly."

Tactful of her. Nosey might be closer to the truth.

She hovered in front of the door to the Airbnb house next to Jamal's. They were still using that as their base then.

"It would be a great place to do some filming," I tried. "The sunrises, the hills, the local people…"

Subtle, right?

She gulped, eyes widening and mouth dropping open. "What do you know? I haven't told anyone anything about what we're filming. Oh God, Miles will kill me!"

"Nothing, nothing! You haven't told me anything. I just

thought that's what you were here for. Aren't you from that company Starz?"

Knew it, I told myself triumphantly. They need Jack to double up as Jamie Fraser, and they're going to turn the Lochside Welcome into ye oldie ancient pub. Máybe I could be an extra too. A barmaid pouring pints of mead or whatever it was they drank in the olden days and slagging off the evil English?

I got a puzzled stare in response.

"Y'know. The ones who make Outlander?"

"What? No, no, we don't work for Starz. Why did you think that?"

In the cold light of day when someone sounds so astonished by your thought processes, you do reassess yourself and wonder if it is time to rein that overactive imagination in.

"Er… well, my husband, Jack looks exactly like—"

"Jack's your *husband*?" Astonishment changed to incredulous disbelief. Yes, I didn't look my best at present as ably pointed out by Jamal, but on a good, non-pregnant day, a guy wouldn't push me out of his bed for farting.

"He is indeed and about take over the management of the Lochside Welcome seeing as Ashley is on extended sick leave."

I didn't suppose it mattered now if she knew. Ahead of us, Lucas—bad wig and bunnet half on half off his head— came out of our front door, Jack following him. They shook hands in front of the minibus. Lucas got in it and drove off, sounding the horn in a cheery beep as he left.

The minibus's departure made me oddly tearful. Part-pregnancy weepiness, I guessed, that and the many happy memories I associated with that minibus. The time before we started dating when I travelled with Jack and a load of

American tourists to Doune Castle, one of them making us pretend to be Jamie and Claire, staring from the ramparts.

I pulled myself together. "Jack will be starting there today."

I'd lost my audience. Tindra had walked to the other side of the street where the mobile reception was much better, phone pressed to her ear. "Miles! Brilliant news!"

It was? Life in Lochalshie had taught me specific things. Number one lesson—never be embarrassed by blatant nosiness. I walked straight up to her; she turned away; I planted myself in front of her again; another quarter turn, me scooting round too.

"Jack," she said, "the red-head in the pub the other week? He's the new manager of the Lochside Welcome, and you said, didn't you…?"

The wind had picked up, making it too difficult for me to hear the rest of the conversation. But when Tindra hung up, the friendliness ratcheted up 100 percent.

"Hey, Gaby, let me help you," she said, taking my shopping bag from me. "And can Miles and I have a chat with you and Jack, please?"

We got to the house just before Jack shut the door. Miles suddenly appeared from the Royal George's car park. He waved at us and trotted over.

"Miles and Tindra want to talk to you," I said to Jack.

Miles had come to a halt next to Tindra. He tucked his phone back in his pocket and smiled at us—at least that's what I think it was. Maybe those muscles did not get enough practise for it to seem convincing.

"Okay," Jack shrugged. "But can we do it down there?"

He pointed towards the benches on the other side of the street that faced the loch. "I've been cooped up inside for too long today. I need some fresh air."

Tindra's face registered dismay. Southerners had difficulty adjusting to what people in Scotland called summer temperatures. Today, the minibus's temperature gauge had shown 19 degrees, which counted as a heatwave, even if the accompanying wind made it feel much lower.

Jack noticed too. He vanished inside and emerged with one of the Highland Tours fleece blankets he kept for tourists. When they stood in front of the viewing rail at Glencoe marvelling at the elements, it was far more pleasant to do so when wrapped up well against howling gales.

Tindra allowed her fingers to brush too long against Jack's as she took it from him. I resisted the urge to clear my throat. A good job I'd grown used to invisibility when I was with Jack, women and men's eyes bypassing me as they drank him in.

There was a small, sheltered area surrounded by stone walls near the loch. Once upon a time, Jack kissed me for the first time there. Cheered, I noticed him glance at the exact same spot I did. We exchanged small smiles before sitting down on the picnic bench. As the rain had eased off, the dog walkers were out in force, most of them horrifying Tindra by allowing their wet, muddy pets to jump up on her. White jeans never work in Scotland.

The ice cream van that took up an almost permanent position on the loch's shores in the summertime and belted out its tinny version of Greens Sleeves. Gareth, the owner, popped his head out of the hatch, eyes scanning the shores for prospective customers.

"Can I buy you an ice-cream?" Miles asked Jack, gesturing towards it.

Jack shook his head, but I nodded. Gareth's van specialised in ice-cream made from local dairy farms' organic milk and cream. The prices reflected this. I only ever had one if someone else was paying.

"Double chocolate chip please, no, scrap that. The Millionaire's Shortbread version," I said. "Three scoops, not two."

"Tindra, can you get them?" Miles ordered her. "See if he does a sorbet for me. And get whatever you want yourself."

Tindra opened her mouth and then shut it, wandering off in the direction of the van, blanket tightly wrapped around her. Miles hadn't given her any money. If I ever got her on her own, my advice would be of the 'dump that bossy mean git now' variety.

"How are you finding Lochalshie?" I asked Miles. "I didn't think you'd be staying this long."

"A charming little place," Miles said, his gaze unwavering as he stared at Jack who squirmed under the scrutiny. His thigh pushed against mine.

Tindra returned, raspberry sorbet for Miles, Millionaire Shortbread ice-creams for me and a tiny Mr Whippy (about three pounds cheaper) for herself. I took mine, ignoring the rule that you're not supposed to start eating until everyone has been served. Gareth had added an extra sprinkle of white chocolate to mine. That stuff needed eating fast.

"I own a small production company," Miles said as he accepted his ice-cream. "Kudos Media. Have you heard of it?"

Knew it, knew it, knew it. My thigh nudged back against Jack's, him returning the gesture. Good news, too, that they weren't from the UK's Best Restaurant. The Lochside

Welcome's award wasn't at risk. Kudos Media, though. Not Starz.

Miles frowned when we both shook our heads, then remembered that he wanted to ask us something and that half-smile half grimace returned.

"Well, you probably haven't. Our programmes though we're responsible for…"

He listed several reality TV titles, mainly series set in hospitals where overworked junior doctors dealt with whatever Accident & Emergency brought them or midwives coached screaming women through labour. (Nowadays, for obvious reasons, if I accidentally stumbled on screaming women programmes, I changed sides immediately.)

"This year, though, I wanted to move away from the hospital angle. It is a saturated market and not of much interest beyond the UK. We've pitched an idea to Netflix, and they are *very* keen on it." His tone changed, the diffidence becoming something far more fevered.

"But Outlander's on Amazon!" I burst out, and Miles and Tindra stared at me, puzzled.

"Aren't you here to film the village and Jack, and the place will double up as 18th century North Caro…"

The incredulous stares continued. *Okay, Gaby. Barking up the super wrong tree.*

Miles shook himself and picked up where he'd left off. "Research by the Campaign for Real Ale has shown that there has been a decline in the number of pubs in the UK by 10,500 in the past 20 years.

"We've come up this idea where we follow the fortune of a pub or hotel for several months, capturing the highs and the lows. We are particularly interested in venues that attract the locals and are at the heart of communities.

When we visited the Lochside Welcome, we thought it would make a fascinating subject for a documentary."

"Netflix you said?" Jack asked.

"That's the plan. We haven't got the go-ahead yet, but we want to put together a detailed proposal and a small film that demonstrates the potential. I've got a few other streaming services interested, but I want to try Netflix first."

Netflix—not only a British audience then, but an international one; imagine the free publicity that would give the Lochside Welcome. As the Royal George was part of a chain, it could afford fancy things such as inclusion in the back pages of glossy magazines and social media campaigns using photos that did the impossible—made it look as if Lochalshie enjoyed year-round sunshine and blue skies.

"And you are taking over management of the hotel?" That gleam was back in Miles' eyes; the predatory look I'd seen when he first encountered Jack. Now, I knew what it meant—a TV guy checking someone out and saying to themselves, *"Hmm. You will be perfect on the screen. Everyone will tune in just to watch you."*

"Yes," Jack said. "But just temporarily until Ashley's back on his feet and then you'll be able to film him. What a storyteller he is! Wait until he tells you about the time Caitlin Cartier used the toilet in the Lochside Welcome. Or when she got married there. And then there's—"

"I'm meeting with Netflix UK's Head of Originals Acquisitions and Productions on Monday. If we get the go-ahead, we'll only be filming for six months," Miles cut in, "so it's unlikely we'll be around by the time Ashley returns. Christmas, didn't you say? But I'm sure we can do a lot in that time with you."

"You get the best views from the Lochside Welcome," Jack said, eyes panicky. He pointed in its direction where the sun picked out the people sitting in the beer garden in silhouette. "And there's plenty of great local characters you can film—lots of folks who've been going in there for years and years. Then, there's the Highland Games in August. People flock to it. So fascinating!"

Ah. Jack had recognised the gleam too and imagined a camera that spent all its time focussing on him. Once upon a time, Jack's ex, the so-called Dating Guru used to take pictures of him all the time #hunk #handsomehighlander. It drove him mad, and everyone in Lochalshie ripped the piss out of him. Every time he walked into the Lochside Welcome, catcalls would start up, people pouting or flexing their biceps. You can get away with many things in Scotland, but if people think you've developed an over-inflated opinion of yourself, it ranks among the worst crimes possible to commit.

"Sure," Miles said. He'd taken out his tablet and was busily adding notes. When I glanced at it as discreetly as I could manage, the list appeared to be a long to-do list for Tindra. Their relationship confirmed then. She worked for him, and he was nowhere near as sweet a boss as Hyun-Ki. I bet their working day never started with them both cooing over YouTube cat videos. She saw me checking the list and rolled her eyes.

"So, how does this work?" Jack asked. "Xavier's in charge of the Lochside Welcome for the moment. Why no' film him in there tomorrow? He's awfy good at pizzas. Throws them up in the air and everything."

Still desperately trying to divert Miles' attention.

Miles shook his head. "No, I need to return to London tomorrow ahead of that meeting. But I'll be in touch. What's your mobile number?"

Contact details exchanged, he stood up. "Tindra? We'd better make a move."

They walked off; Tindra wrapped in the blanket. Those things were made from lambs' wool and not cheap. I hoped she remembered to return it. Washed and dried too.

"That will please Ashley," I said. Jack sat on the bench, elbows on knees and his head held in his hands.

I wriggled to try and ease my hurting back. Jack pulled me into a hug against him. The wind had dropped, and the sun warmed my stomach and knees. I shifted, so I faced the Lochside Welcome, its car park nowhere near as full as the Royal George's.

"Yeah, mebbe," his dark eyes solemn, "but why do I get the feeling I've just bitten off far more than I can chew?"

One thing for sure, I decided as the two of us sat in silence watching a dog at the far side charging to and fro as its owner threw sticks. I hadn't signed anything official where I agreed to be Hyun-Ki's temporary replacement. I would tell the company I'd changed my mind. How could I take on a new role as the boss when all this was going on?

Chapter Thirteen

"One thousandth and forty-second best designer in the world! Why have you not signed that contract yet?"

Behind Hyun-Ki, the LA office made Blissful Beauty's London operation look like a teeny-tiny operation 20 years out of date. He was in a break-out area in what looked like a hollowed-out Rubik's cube, his Mac book balanced on his knees.

"Hyun-Ki," I said, grateful that I'd lost the habit of accidentally calling him Hunky. The nickname suited him. If he hadn't decided that graphic design was his calling, modelling could have been it. As it was, he often wore outrageous outfits your average British bloke would never get away with. Today was another perfect example—a lace blouse and green PVC trousers.

"You know I never actually said yes when I was asked. I can't be a boss. Imagine if I had to tell someone off? I'd be rubbish at it."

Confrontation had never been my strong suit. I fast-forwarded to a scenario where I had to reprimand an employee for spending too much time on YouTube instead of coming up with brilliant visual ideas to sell lipstick. Much of my working day was taken up by YouTube. Hypocritical of me to pull someone else up for it.

"I'll mentor you," he said. "I've been on lots of How to be the Boss courses."

Obviously, he had. What little free time Hyun-Ki had, he spent on self-improvement. From advanced Pilates to coding, programming, English grammar and film editing skills, Hyun-Ki found a teacher and added hours of homework to his schedule. I never shared with him what I did at weekends, too scared he would think me a lazy slacker. True. These days, it mainly involved slumping on the sofa, and binge-watching box sets with Mildred curled up beside me.

"The British operation design team is only you and three others. And I'll be the overall gaffer—gaffer, is that the right word? I'm still working on my British English slang."

"Yes, along with tosser, wanker, psychopath and utter cockwomble. That's how most people I know refer to their bosses."

He faked hurt. "Do you call me those names?"

"No. But from time to time, I tell myself you are a delicious dictator."

Oops. The words came out before I could stop them. Last year, Hyun-Ki and I snogged after the traumatic and emotionally charged rescue of a cat from the perils of a busy London road. Afterwards, we both decided we had no chemistry whatsoever. Handy, as I was engaged to be married at the time. But to this day, I tried to steer conversations clear of potential minefields. Moving on...

"And Jack's taking up a new role," I added. "He's now

the manager of the Lochside Welcome because Ashley isn't very well."

Hyun-Ki had visited Lochalshie and the Lochside Welcome when he attended Caitlin's wedding. He nodded thoughtfully. "New directions for you both."

"I haven't said yes! This is bullying, Hyun-Ki!"

He grinned. "No, it's not. It's me trying to get you to accept more money. Caitlin wants to launch a pharmaceutical skincare range in the UK in time for Christmas. If you work on that campaign on top of everything else, it will be brilliant for your portfolio."

Hyun-Ki showed far more interest in my portfolio than I ever did.

"What is pharmaceutical skincare.?"

"Serums and creams that are ten times the price of others because they are stuffed full of acids or something. Supposed to be prescription-strength. Doesn't that make you excited? You in charge of creating beautiful visuals for a brand-new campaign?"

Frankly, no. Much as Hyun-Ki and I bonded over our love for cats, he lived for work. I didn't. And the new campaign would mean close cooperation with Dexter, a nightmare person to work with. Whenever I showed him anything, he would praise me to the skies.

"Wow, Gaby. That is super awesome! What an incredible job you've done on those visuals. Wow, wow, wow…"

Then, he would start up with his suggestions. What if I move that over there and this over here? Could the tag line for the serum be made bigger and bolder? What about those colours; was it possible to make them 'pop' more? And then yet another of those sentences you should never utter to a designer—Can you use Photo-Shop to do that?

So, I would change everything. He would make more

suggestions—another round of revisions. I presented him with a totally different look, we did the same again, and then he decided he preferred the first version after all. By which point, I wanted to throttle him, the boyfriend of my best friend or not.

(Status currently unknown? Katya button-lipped about it.)

Hyun-Ki checked behind him and leant forward, dropping his voice. "Gabs, don't tell anyone this but…"

Ominous.

"If you don't accept that job, there is a chance your role will end up contracted out."

"What?"

He shushed me as two LA employees, huge coffee cups in hand, drifted by.

"Blissful Beauty is considering moving most of their British-based staff to contract work instead of full-time employment. Lawson Kramer's idea. He's worked with a lot of businesses and has a reputation for leanness."

"Leanness?" From what I could remember of the terrifyingly intimidating man in charge of Blissful Beauty's Europe, Middle East and Africa operation, he was indeed on the thin side. Why was that relevant?

Hyun-Ki smiled. "Did you read that book I recommended the other day? *Business Management in the 21st Century and How it Applies to You?*"

"No."

As. If.

"Leanness is scaling back a company, so there is no wastage. It is far cheaper to run people on six-month contracts than employing them. No sick leave, no pensions, no national insurance and no maternity benefits."

"But Caitlin says…"

Get a grip, Gaby! I told myself. *You know she has no say.* Caitlin was like the Queen, nominally in charge while the real bods (white, middle-aged men in the main) ruled the roost.

"But if you were the head of design in the UK, your job would be safe. They plan to contract out all roles apart from a small core team."

"You said the position was temporary while you were seconded."

He squirmed, eyes flashing away and back again. "I'm not coming back—LA's too big an opportunity for me. I'd like to take charge of the South Korea team at some point. Then I could go home."

McAllan Junior chose that moment to make my heart burn—an 'Oi, Mum! I'm going to be super, super expensive. Remember?' reminder. Katya had sent me a link to an article the other day—*How Much Money Your Child Will Cost You By The Time it Gets to 18*. And some suggestions of what she would rather spend those hundreds of thousands of pounds on.

Then, there was our house. Jack was self-employed. Banks and building societies turned their noses up at him. Property was way, way cheaper in Lochalshie than it was in most of the UK, especially down south. My brother often told my poor put-upon mother there was no way he was getting on the property ladder until he was 40, which meant she was stuck with him in her house paying minimal rent and having all his washing done for another ten years.

But the cheapness of Lochalshie aside, we'd struggle to persuade any of those banks and building societies to part with their pennies for an increased mortgage if or when we wanted to move to a new house. The second bedroom in Jack's end terrace house was little more than a box room.

McAllan Junior might need a more significant place at some point. It would be simpler to convince money lenders of our abilities to make monthly mortgage payments if one of us was in a stable job. Also, as we were to be parents all too soon, grown-up life decisions were all part of the fun.

Fun, Katya kept promising me, was something I could wave goodbye to come December.

"I'll sign it," I said. Hyun-Ki punched the air and gave me a thumbs-up.

"Awesome, Gaby. Do you want me to break the good news to your team?"

My team… oh, good grief. What I kept forgetting was that 'head of design' didn't just mean more decisions and, the only good bit, a salary increase. It entailed managing people; four of them—Logan, the web developer, Ali, the Mac op, Marty, the digital coordinator, and Trish, the newbie.

What about, urgh, disciplining people? Marty wandered into the office most days at 10am. He was six foot four, about half as wide and sported one of those Pirate beards that added to the Hell's Angels effect. As a joke two months ago, he'd taken the film Leanne had of me pointing a (fake) gun at the stalker who'd burst into our office determined to persuade Caitlin to marry him.

When I yelled, *on your knees mother*******, at the gunman —hey, wouldn't you? Blame too many action films from my childhood thanks to a brother who hero-worshipped them —my voice made an accent detour where it started off Samuel L Jackson and veered wildly via Dublin and Mumbai.

Marty created a gif of me repeating it endlessly that he arranged to be playing when I dialled in for a conference call. Everyone else at the meeting laughed like drains for a good five minutes, and this was the man I now had to dish out orders to and tick off for tardiness.

The door in our living room opened, and Mildred padded through, leaping onto the space next to my keyboard. Once he got back to Seoul and found himself a flat, Hyun-Ki promised, he was going to get a cat. Then we could have conference calls where our cats 'chatted' to each other. Mildred flicked her tail, indication that she much preferred to be the only cat in the room, even if the other one was thousands of miles away.

"Yes please," I said, referring to his offer to tell the team. "Oh… er, say to them we'll do a conference call on Monday at 9am to… um, discuss our plans for the next few months and the pharmaceuticals thingie."

What initiative, eh? Arranging a meeting and making it for 9am to show Marty I meant business and was not a person to be trifled with.

"Will do," Hyun-Ki replied, hands filling the screen as he moved his hands in circles as a goodbye. "You won't regret it, Gaby!"

Fingers crossed I didn't. And anyway, I was not that far off maternity leave. Nothing could possibly go wrong in the space of 20 short weeks, could it?

Chapter Fourteen

"He's run off his feet, Gaby hen. If you're looking for a wee smooch behind the bar, you're oot o' luck!"

Stewart, who was heading back in as I entered the Lochside Welcome with Tamar fast asleep in the baby carrier wrapped tightly around his chest and belly. It was Friday night; the first weekend with Jack in charge, and I'd come to see how he was getting on, oddly nervous. *Please, please, please let this evening be a success.*

When I pushed the lounge bar's door open, the numbers cheered me. A positive sign if people knew the regular landlord was not here but showed their support anyway. The usual regulars sat at the bar, and the groups of folks who came for the weekly pub quiz took up the tables and booths.

Far more cars and coaches parked up outside the Royal George. I told my brain off for disloyalty, even if I couldn't change what I'd seen.

We hadn't heard anything further from Miles—an over-excited conversation, say, where he told us the bosses at

Netflix jumped for joy when he told them his idea and ordered him back to the village to film something pronto.

Tindra, however, had popped into the pub on Thursday evening and asked Jack if he would mind if she organised some filming on Friday night that they would use as part of a package selling Miles' idea. Jack, his mind-boggled by all the things his new job involved, nodded a distracted 'yes' at the time, suddenly remembered it on Friday morning and groaned. "It's not as if I've got enough to do, what wi' taking over a business and makin' sure all the tourists are happy."

A sure sign he was stressed. His Scottish accent always got that little bit stronger. Secretly, I loved it, but those hyper-rolled Rs and missing consonants were terrible for his blood pressure. I rubbed his back as he stood in the kitchen, waiting for our old toaster to brown the bread. "I'm sure it will be okay."

I said those words so often these days it had turned into my catchphrase.

There were signs up all over the Lochside Welcome, warning us that film cameras would be present for tonight's quiz. On a table at the front lay a pile of leaflets outlining why the cameras were there and consent forms. I flicked one over, Kudos Media logo on top (someone desperately needed the services of a better graphic designer) and general blurb. *"We are in your village filming for a prospective, yet to be confirmed TV show. Please give your permission for us to film you by signing a consent form."*

Those too shy to appear on film were offered badges to wear so the editor could pixelate them out afterwards. Lochalshie people, it turned out, were not shy. No-one in the room had picked up any of the sticky red labels.

I spotted Tindra standing next to a woman holding a camera. She waved and gave me a thumbs up.

"I came here to escape the trappings of fame!" Katya, who'd sneaked up behind me.

I grinned. "'Fraid not. Remember, this is the village where Caitlin Cartier launched Blissful Beauty in the UK and then made it where she tied the knot. We are a people now used to film cameras, flashes and Instagram influencers knowing our names."

"If you insist."

She dumped her bag on the booth behind and slid in. I took the seat opposite her, scanning the room for my other half. Jolene wandered over with a mobile ordering system in hand. This was the first change Jack had put in place in the Lochside Welcome since taking over management two days ago. The handheld system linked straight to the inventory, so he always knew how much or how little to order.

"I mean to tighten up the profit margins, Gaby," he'd said to me. Confession: there was yet something else that gave me a frisson of excitement. Business talk: Him determined, in charge and sounding exactly like a highflier... What was not to like?

The mogul himself waved at me from behind the bar, using the opportunity to escape Stewart's clutches. He had reclaimed his favourite barstool and occupation—boring people full-time on the wonders of coding while his dog slept under the stool, but now he drank alcohol-free lager. Snatches of conversation drifted over. I heard the words Stack Overflow and JavaScript and cringed on Jack's behalf.

"How's the writing going?" I asked Katya, triggering an exaggerated eye roll. She put her head in her hands, hair falling forward.

"Ten thousand words down, only another 40,000 to go," Katya said, grabbing a menu. That had been spruced up too, Jack telling Xavier he had free rein to add any other specialities he fancied. Now, the food on offer at the Lochside Welcome included pea and ham soup and a sponge cake drenched in maple syrup served with ice-cream. Best of all, Quebec Poutine. Chips slathered in gravy and cheese. Lush. The dishes reminded him of home, Xavier said. He was mulling over the possibilities of Scots/French-Canadian fusion—a first for the Highlands if not the whole of the UK.

"I'll have the vegan pizza," Katya told Jolene, my friend, an on-off vegan depending on her state of mind, "with blue cheese on top." The writing must be taking it out of her. I sympathised. Had the billionaire bra company owner kissed the chauffeur/handyman yet?

She shook her head. "No, they're not allowed to until the last chapter. He's just accidentally touched her cheek though. It's been burning hot for two days ever since."

I chortled. "She needs Blissful Beauty's complexion perfection cream for excessive redness."

Katya groaned. "Please don't joke about it! Dexter has already suggested I weave in tonnes of plugs for Blissful Beauty products— 'LeAnna awoke in her king-sized bed, her skin clear and radiant thanks to her generous application of Blissful Beauty's Glow Serum the night before...' This ruddy book already counts as the worst thing I have ever had the misfortune to write. A story with promotions for make-up and skincare every second page will mean no-one will ever take me seriously."

She knocked back half of her vodka and diet coke and put her head in her hands.

"But you're a ghost-writer. Your name won't be in the book."

"I negotiated for 'Edited by Katya Bukowski' in big letters underneath Caitlin's name. Everyone in publishing will know what that means. I might renegotiate. Under no circumstances put my name anywhere near this steaming pile of dung."

Xavier emerged from the kitchen to have a quick word with Jack behind the bar. "Who's he?" Katya gasped, attention well and truly diverted. I filled her in, adding that I thought he and Mhari would make a perfect couple if only I could persuade her to see past her unreasonable age prejudice and him not to worry. I expected him to get down to baby-making as soon as he and Mhari paired up thanks to one of my stupid comments.

"And where is your flatmate anyway?" I asked, it being unusual for Mhari not to follow Katya to the pub worried she might otherwise miss out on top-quality gossip.

"Reading a book," Katya said.

I stared. Mhari read nothing but her phone.

"In return for me promising her some of the money—okay, a lot of the money—I get for this writing job, she has to read the billionaire romance book and tell me what she thinks. I left her a list of questions to answer. It doesn't count if she just says, 'pish'."

The ridiculous list of things that made my eyes water added another item to the bottom.

"Wh-wh-why didn't you ask me? I wo-wo-wouldn't have asked for any money either!"

It came out far louder than I intended, attracting stares from nearby. I cursed as the camera I hadn't noticed up until now zoomed in on us. Probably counted as local drama in the village pub. I'd lifted one of those red badges, keen to avoid being caught on film looking so… big. Even if that footage was going nowhere.

Katya, her face stricken, reached for my hand. "Mhari wasn't joking about the totes emosh thing, was she? Okay, sorry, sorry! You're welcome to read it if you want. I was trying to spare you unless you need it because you've got a bad case of insomnia and need help dropping off at night?"

"One vegan pizza with blue cheese, macaroni, chips and aioli?" Jolene put the plates down, the smell of garlic overwhelming. She sat down next to Katya, waving her hand in the direction of the bar. "The new boss? He says we need regular breaks. If I hang out at the bar area, Stewart will talk to me? I'm gonna stay here for a few minutes."

Fair enough.

Tindra and her camera-wielding colleague conferred briefly, and the camerawoman drifted off, making her way around the crowded tables and chairs.

Around us, men and women whipped out compact mirrors, applied face powder and checked their hair. Everyone swung around to face the woman, who returned the stares bemused. She hadn't even switched her camera on.

Tindra joined her, clapping her hands. "Hi everyone! Thanks for agreeing to be part of our documentary. Nina is only looking for general wide shots this evening so please just act naturally."

If 'act naturally' translated to stare straight at the camera, raise your voice and talk as loudly, clearly and slowly as possible, she'd got her wish. I suspected it didn't. Still, Nina wove her way in and out of the tables and booths smiling in a non-committal way when people asked her to make sure she got their best side. The camera returned again and again to Jack, catching him as he reached high above him to pull down a bottle of 30-year-old single malt for Big Donnie, the quiz master. His T-shirt edged up as he did so, revealing taut abs, and a glimpse of that delightful thin line of red hair that ran from his chest to his groin.

"She was here this afternoon," Jolene said, indicating Tindra, "asking heaps of questions. I said I was happy to answer them, seeing as the guys were busy." She pursed her lips. "But she insisted on speaking to Jack. Took up two hours of his time!"

Huh.

Katya, half-way through her pizza, paused mid-chew. "What did you say this programme is called? *Highland Hunky Hotties? Barmen I'd Bonk in Scotland?* And get off, that's mine!"

Mhari withdrew her hand, snatching it back and muttering that share and share alike was an acceptable saying to live by. She'd snuck in without us noticing and shuffled her bottom along the bench, putting her opposite me. I pulled my bowl of chips closer and crammed as many of them into my mouth as I could. Katya helped me out, dipping the remaining crusts of her pizza into the aioli and closing her eyes, expression blissful.

"Awesome!" Tindra clapped her hands. "Nina got all that on film. We can use it to demonstrate how much people love the food here!"

Katya's expression changed from bliss to horror. No doubt she was remembering the time two years ago she was photographed eating someone else's food, and the picture made the centre spread of a glossy Sunday supplement. She was yet to live it down.

"Red badge!" I called out. "Remember to pixelate me out!"

But they'd moved off, Nina returning once more to the bar and Jack.

"Have you finished your homework?" Katya asked Mhari.

"Aye. Didnae take me long because I kept skipping pages to find the dirty bits. There werenae any."

Katya glared at her. "You knew that! I told you I was writing clean billionaire romance."

"I thought you were only joking," Mhari answered, attention half on Katya the rest on her phone. "Or that you would sneak in the dirty bits wi' codewords. Y'ken, the chauffeur's flagpole dipped hard in her honeypot. Naebody reads the clean stuff, do they?"

I did my best to hide a smirk. Not well enough, as Katya kicked me under the table. Not as hard, though, as she kicked Mhari who responded with a loud 'ouch'.

Her break finished, Jolene got up as people waiting at the bar were now two-deep. Big Donnie banged his glass and announced it was time for this week's quiz to begin. I squeezed Katya's hand. "I'm glad you're here. Our team's been relegated to Third Division ever since you left. Now we stand a chance of not coming last."

"Second last," Mhari said as she returned from the bar vodka diet cokes in hand two hours later, mine an orange juice and soda. "I thought you were brainy, Katya? You use an awfy lot of big words in that soppy romance thing you're writing."

Katya took her drink and reached for her phone. "Okay. Scrap the big words," she typed into the phone's memo app. "Caitlin's publisher told me not to use too many of them. Wrong audience. I'd better go back to the book and change that. Anyway, second last is better than last. And you got the question about who died in Episode 3, Season 5 of Game of Thrones wrong."

I blew a kiss at Jack, one he failed to notice. To be fair, he hadn't stopped all night. The pub quiz must count as an enormous success. The food and drink orders had come through fast and furious up until 9pm when the quiz started.

Then, and again this was a Jack-led change, he'd allowed food to be served right up until 10pm. Jolene looked knackered. They would need to hire extra staff through that agency Ashley had mentioned. As it was, Jack came out from behind the bar and began collecting plates and glasses himself, stacking up plates along his arm like a pro. Nina's camera, its lens magnetically attached to him, filmed as he leant over to listen to his mum, red hair hanging forward and two sets of almost identical dark brown eyes close together.

"Will it take you long to clear up?" I asked when he finally reached our table—more in hope than expectation. On a Friday night, the pub was licenced until 1am, and it was now just gone 11. Too many chips and a Thursday night sleep that broke the Trades Descriptions Act calling itself rest had kicked in. My PJs, duvet and that memory foam mattress that I sank into beckoned.

"I'll be back home when we close," he said, bending over to kiss my forehead. "I promise I'll sneak in as quietly as possible."

As Katya and I got up to leave, Mhari said she wanted to stay, joining Stewart at the bar. Xavier wandered over at once, asking her if she wanted more ice in her drink. I nudged Katya. "You see? I'm a natural match-maker."

"Whatever. Come on then, I'll walk you home."

That was the thing with being pregnant, it made everyone ridiculously over-protective. Our house was only a five-minute walk from the Lochside Welcome. Nothing would happen to me in the time I took to walk (well, shuffle) there apart from the risk of stepping in dog poo, but my friends insisted on treating me with kid gloves. On the other hand, I enjoyed it. Fingers crossed, I'd be able to eke out special treatment way into the baby's first year and beyond.

"When do you start your new job as the boss?" Katya asked once we got outside. The fresh air was a relief after the stuffy, overcrowded bar. Thanks to my stint in London, I never took air quality for granted these days. We walked along the shore, the air scented with the tang of muddy seaweed and the full moon giving us enough visibility.

"Monday. A conference call led by me, at bang on 9am where I show Marty who's boss."

Katya squinted at me. "Alright then, that sounds prom—"

She stopped abruptly. "Look."

That moss-green jaguar again, driving far too fast towards the Royal George. Two people in it again. Someone different in the passenger seat this time though. A flash of blonde hair and a profile I recognised at once.

"Is that…?" I asked. *Please don't let it be that guy.*

"I don't know," my friend said, her expression unreadable. But she kept her eyes glued to the car as we watched it pull into the car park. The doors slammed, and the voices of its occupants reached us. "The forecast is terrific for tomorrow, by the way. I checked."

Voice one. Evil Twin.

"That will help. We'll need all the space in the beer garden to cope with all those guests. The biggest wedding we've hosted so far isn't that right?"

Voice two. Despicable, lying, murdering git.

Oh-oh.

Chapter Fifteen

Day one with me as the boss started with a Zoom conference call that was supposed to begin at 9am. I'd come up with an agenda and even written a little speech, telling 'my' team how much I was looking forward to working with them and praising their talents to the skies.

Katya's idea. She'd visited the house on Sunday, ostensibly to have lunch with me but mostly to discuss the reappearance of the dastardly lying git, Zac Cavanagh. 'Biggest wedding we've hosted so far.' Huh, huh, double huh.

"Did you tell Jack that Zac is back at the helm of the Royal George?" she asked when I handed her a cup of green tea.

"Yes," I said, "but he didn't seem to be too fussed. Too busy worrying about the Highland Games and how he's going to cope. I was the one with my knickers in a twist, pointing out what a rotten, lying, murderous git he is."

Katya pursed her lips. "Well, he didn't really... oh, nothing. What about that wedding though?"

That blasted wedding the day before *had* bothered Jack.

No harm to the happy couple but a thousand curses on them for choosing to cement their union in the Royal George when they could have whooped it up in the Lochside Welcome. All-day Saturday, I'd watched cars and minibuses drive past our house, glamourous and raucous guests spilling out.

After Caitlin married in the Lochside Welcome last year, Ashley had told us he'd been booked up for weddings for three years. There had been some in April, May and June, but when Jack took over, he checked the books. A few in October. Not one until then. He'd been half relieved—who wanted the headache of weddings to add to first-time hotel management—half worried. Why wasn't the Lochside Welcome more popular? We'd mulled it over again this morning, wondering why couples were so attracted to the Royal George.

I handed Katya a bowl of mushroom risotto, which she'd sensibly made herself and brought with her, knowing my cookery skills amounted to zilch. The first few mouthfuls swallowed, she admitted to having run out of ideas for the billionaire romance book. The chauffeur/handyman, she said, was now so incredibly attractive, kind and generous no sane single hetero woman would hold back.

"Can't you make him seem untrustworthy, so poor LeAnna is not sure if he wants her or just her wealth?" I suggested. "That would fill a few chapters, wouldn't it?"

Katya let out one of those drawn-out sighs. "Nope. Caitlin hasn't had much say-so in the development of this book, but she did insist the chauffeur/handyman be gorgeous and super-nice. He's modelled on Donal."

Ah. Stumbling block. Caitlin's real-life husband and a 'nice chap'—Nanna Cooper's ultimate compliment. Katya had invented a backstory for the chauffeur/handyman where he didn't want any of LeAnna's money because he'd grown up the son of a wealthy billionaire himself and hated what it had done to his family.

To take her mind off plot problem-solving, I gave Katya a real issue to think about: how to be a boss.

She finished her helping of mushroom risotto. "Go for it."

I handed her my agenda for the meeting with ideas of what to say to my team. She ripped it up. "No, no and no. Luckily for you, my copywriting work a few years ago included a client who did leadership coaching. Want to know her suggestions for how to be a brilliant boss?"

Of course. Number one: appear super-interested in your team members, find the one skill they excel at and go on and on about it. "That makes people feel valued and therefore more likely to jump when you say so," Katya said. "Let me write something for you. We'll start with…"

By the time she finished, I had stirring words in front of me. Bound to inspire anyone. More instructions. "Speak slowly, Gaby. And look your team members in the eye one by one."

I rehearsed my little speech, again and again. I woke up in a cold sweat two or three times during the night where I appeared in a dream on a stage in front of an audience of thousands and forgot everything I was meant to say, and the usual anxiety one, where I walked out and realised I was as naked.

(Worse. No-one noticed.)

Monday morning dawned. Jack told me to "Go get 'em, Tiger!" before dashing out the door to deal with the delivery from the brewery. The rain lashed down—an ominous sign. I'd often noticed that stormy weather affected the Wi-Fi signal, making connections intermittent. When I logged onto Zoom, the system booted me out after five seconds, unable to hook me up with my London colleagues.

One hour later and the meeting started, 30 minutes behind schedule. I apologised profusely, pointing at the window behind me where dark grey skies clouded out what remained of the natural light.

Katya's advice via the leadership coach? As a boss, never explain, never complain. Do not over-apologise. *Failed already, Gaby,* I told myself. Five minutes into the role.

Three people, not four sat in the small sound-proof studio Blissful Beauty used for team conference calls.

"Morning team!" I overdid the cheeriness. "Where's Marty?"

"Not in yet!" Trish announced. "At the dentist, he said."

An appointment, he'd 'forgotten' to tell me about when I sent the meeting invite around. I made a note to myself to ask Katya's advice on what her leadership coach said about dealing with outright insubordination.

First on the agenda: YouTube cat videos. Not, strictly speaking, Katya's tips for ways to begin business meetings but bonding, right? And straight from the school of team management a la Hyun-Ki. Had anyone seen the latest upload from Kitten Lady, I asked, where she rescued this tiny thing from the back of the shopping mall where it had mewed piteously from its little brown bag until…

Silence.

I repeated myself. The connection wasn't great thanks to the weather, Wi-Fi being disagreeable to wind and rain. They couldn't have heard me.

More silence.

Ali cleared his throat. "We're, like, not cat people?"

Beside him, Logan nodded. "I don't like animals. Dirty things."

Mildred sat in the window, thoughtfully licking her front paw. With any luck, she hadn't heard herself (incorrectly) described.

"I thought you were a vegan, Trish?"

That implied love of animals, right? I confined my meat consumption to bacon these days and felt vastly guilty when eating it every time.

Trish shook her head. "Yeah, for the planet? So the baby you're about to give birth to gets to be an adult before global warming, like, kills us all?"

Moving swiftly on… Had Logan set up the landing page for Blissful Beauty's Halloween range? Was Ali on top of the Photoshop work for the lipsticks? Then there were Blissful Beauty's plans to unleash their pharmaceutical-grade skincare on the UK market. The US launch was scheduled for two months, and already there was a waiting list for every product in the range.

"I've got the brand bible here," I said, waving the sheets of paper I'd printed out courtesy of the LA design team and marketing experts. "But we're allowed a little freedom. According to Dexter, as Brits don't respond to the same marketing messages and images as Americans do."

Thanks, he said, to our nation's deeply inbuilt bulls*** detector and hatred of exaggeration, a random person filmed holding a cream yelling, "This is the best, no, THE GREATEST thing I have ever used on my skin, like EVER!!!!!!" was out the window. Pity, because the graphics for that sounded dead easy.

"Have you all read it?"

My team nodded. Well done you. I'd skimmed the first and last pages, too exhausted last night to keep my eyes open for longer than the instruction on what colours, fonts and messaging we needed to use.

"Great, so you know that Pantone—"

"They've decided to move the launch," Logan said.

"Wait, what?"

"Yeah, Dexter swung by earlier. Told us to tell you it's a staggered release. The exfoliating pads with prescription-grade glycolic acid need to come out in September, not December. He wants to match the US launch date. There's some change in the law about acceptable levels of acids in skincare products. If the pads come out three months earlier, they won't qualify."

I stared at him, aghast. Firstly, why was this the first time I was hearing such important news? Secondly, my schedule for the next few months. The new skincare range had to be fitted in on top of loads of other campaigns. Sunscreen, back to school/college, Halloween, winter, Christmas—there was a make-up and skincare product for every occasion. As well as the day to day stuff where we churned out web pages, social media campaigns, videos, graphics, leaflets, product packaging and more. They all needed care and attention.

The work on the pharmaceutical skincare range would need to pass the Dexter hyper-picky test way before it got signed off by head office.

"Okay," I said. "I'll talk to Dexter. Thanks, Logan."

He smiled. I tried not to read too much into it. Smugness, say. A man telling herself, *You know what? Blissful Beauty should have made me the boss, not this flaky incompetent idiot.* Did I say, 'Talk to Dexter'? Scream blue murder at him, more like. Team Dexter? Not anymore, pal, I told him in my head. If your girlfriend decides to finish with you because she's sick of living with a workaholic, I will cheer. Loudly.

Back to the meeting. "I want you all to come up with six

or seven ideas for what we can use to accompany the exfoliating pads launch, by the end of play tomorrow."

Oof. Channelling Hyun-Ki levels of employee demand there.

"Um, if that's okay...? I mean if you've got time, and you're don't need to leave early as it's your nanna's 75th birthday and she's desperate to have all her family nearby when she blows out all those candles..."

I stopped myself. That had been a Marty excuse two months ago. Come to think of it, hadn't he claimed a Nanna 75th birthday as a reason for leaving early four times already?

Ali, Trish and Logan's faces expressed... derision? Scepticism? Glee as they anticipated how much of a pushover I was going to be?

I blew them kisses, cringing inwardly as Katya's horrified expression appeared in front of me. *Richardson! Do NOT be over-familiar and friendly with your staff. Tip number 4!*

Next up, a phone call to Dexter. The one where I told him exactly what I thought of him informing my team about bringing the launch forward before he thought to share it with me. It rang out, as it did the ten times I tried again afterwards.

The rest of the day was spent writing lists of everything that needed to be done and working my way slowly through it, trying my best not to cry. When I spotted the email Dexter sent me later that afternoon, I called him names that would have made a sailor blush. The c-word might even have surfaced.

"We're thinking of a super-amazing launch for the skincare range starting with the exfoliating pads AND the retinol, then moving onto the sheet face masks. Can you and your team come up with all the beyond awesome graphics and landing pages? We need for both by Friday so I can ask the American team what they think."

At the bottom, he'd added a plaintive plea. "Hey, Gabs! Is Katya okay? I can't seem to get hold of her."

I took back the c-word. And fired off a message to Katya. "Call Dexter. Please."

No reply, but not something I could afford to add to my already towering pile of worries.

I opened InDesign and tried to summon up creative energy. *Come to me, come to me, oh brilliant ideas!* No reply whatsoever.

League, way out of, Gaby, I told myself—*rearrange those words until they form a common saying and force yourself to learn the importance of, like your husband, not biting off far more than you can chew.*

———

"How was your first day as the woman with all the power?"

Jack needed to shake me awake for the answer on Monday night. I'd dozed off on the sofa awaiting his return, the TV still blaring, and Mildred stretched out next to me. These days, she had to cling precariously to her spot on the couch, me and my bump taking up much more room than previously.

"Wassa time?" I muttered, swinging my legs around and sitting up. Last time I'd looked it had been…

"Half eleven. Sorry. I wouldn't have disturbed you," Jack said, holding out his hand so he could help me to my feet. "But I thought you might wake up with a sore neck later. And I wanted to ask about how work was. You really need a good night's sleep. Come on."

Upstairs, I changed into my pyjamas and got into bed, patting the space beside me. Jack stripped off, every movement emphasising bone-tiredness thanks to the effort it took just to get undressed. He got down to his T-shirt and boxers, and gave up, collapsing on the bed.

"I thought you'd agreed with Xavier that he would close up this evening?"

Mondays to Thursdays, the Lochside Welcome's licence to serve alcohol ran till 11pm. Years ago, I'm told, lock-ins were commonplace. Trusted locals were granted the privilege of continuing to drink to oblivion way beyond official closing time. Ashley locked the door to prevent passers-by coming in, dimmed the lights so any nearby police car saw nothing, and swapped his side of the bar for theirs. Nowadays, a combination of lack of demand and far stricter licensing laws made that a no-no.

Still, Jack had promised he and Xavier would divvy up shutting shop at night. Tonight was supposed to have been Xavier's turn. Made possible by it being a Monday. Not your traditional riotous night out for most people.

"Blasted minibus tour," Jack said, eyes closed. "Lucas, my Highland Tours replacement thought he was doing me a favour bringing them to the Lochside Welcome at 8pm. Awfy kind, but they all insisted on trying all the single malts to figure out which one went best with pizza. And singing *Flower of Scotland* that I had to find on the karaoke machine after disappointing everyone by saying no-one in Scotland knows the words beyond the first verse."

"Angus does," I said, referring to the Lochside Welcome's part-time bouncer and a member of the local rugby team. When Scotland managed to beat England in a Six Nations game last year, he sang that song on repeat all night.

"No, no' even him. He just hums it after the 'tae think again' bit."

"Oh, okay then. But I suppose you appreciated the extra customers after that wedding at the Royal George on Sunday?"

"Aye, s'pose so. Tell me what it's like to be Blissful Beauty's big boss?"

"Well, my day was…"

Too late. My audience had gone out like the proverbial light, breaths coming in deep inhales and sighs, his arm slung across me. Sleep ironed out his face, shaggy red hair desperately in need of a wash settling around it. The summer sunshine, limited as it was, had dusted a crop of tiny dark auburn freckles across his nose and cheeks.

I got out of bed and found one of the Highland Tours blankets to put on top of him, seeing as he'd fallen asleep on top of the duvet, and snuggled next to him. At least this meant he was in no danger of being woken up by my snoring.

Yes, another glamorous pregnancy side effect. Jack told me I "snorted like a wee baby pig" while sleeping. When I protested, he kissed the top of my head. "Cute animals, piglets. And it doesn't put me off *too* much."

Even if I did lie on my side, stomach supported by one of those bolster pillows, the snoring happened anyway.

I lumbered downstairs to the loo—Jolene had warned me the toilet trips during the night in pregnancy were a total pain—and returned, now wide awake and resentful. My day had finished late too, me finally putting the iMac to sleep just before 9pm, having started it up 12 and a half hours earlier.

Jack might have no experience of working in offices. He always shuddered when I mentioned all the elements it involved. Office politics. The hours spent in front of a computer. But I enjoyed running my day past him, and I longed to talk over the problems I'd encountered with a sympathetic listener.

Back in bed again, Mildred leapt up, shoogling her way into the space between Jack and me, a favourite spot thanks to its warmth potential. "How about you, Mildred, coochy-coo? Would it thrill you to hear all about my day?"

She answered by promptly falling asleep too. I'd just need to mull it over all by myself and come up with my own solutions.

Chapter Sixteen

When Caroline opened the front door—still in possession of that wretched key—at the end of the week, the distraction was a relief. I'd spent most of Tuesday wrestling with various ideas for the launch ably assisted by Trish, Logan and Ali. Marty, meanwhile, was yet to surface in the office before 11am.

"How're ye, Gaby?" she asked, scooting into the kitchen. I heard the rattling as she picked up the industrial size bag of cat litter. "In charge o' the whole of that wee Caitlin's company now, aren't ye? Me and your mum were WhatsApping each other about it the other day. We're both awfy proud of ye."

Argh. Lovely though it was that my mum and Jack's now had their own modern-day version of the in-law to in-law relationship, it did mean that the truth often ended up warped. I'd phoned my mum to tell her about my promotion. Evidently, she'd heard the word, 'head' and decided for herself what it meant.

"I'm not…"

Sod it. Let them think what they wanted.

Cat litter changed—Mildred celebrating the occasion with a poop in the fresh litter—Caroline sat down in the armchair, handing me a cup of herbal tea. I swung my chair around to face her.

"Now, me and your mum are worried that you're takin' too much on. Are you still sufferin' wi' the morning sickness?"

I smiled, sitting as upright as possible and doing my best to look the picture of health.

"No! No, it's fine, Caroline!"

Half the truth. Ever since I'd returned from London, I hadn't thrown up once. Until this morning when my heightened sense of smell caught a whiff of the bin lorry trundling passed our house when I opened the back door.

Caroline rummaged in her overstuffed handbag, pulling out a small plastic bag and handing it over.

"What's that?"

"Ginger. Grate it and steep it in boiling water for five minutes then drink it. Awfy good for nausea. When d'ye start your maternity leave?"

"End of November," I said. "When I will take a whole six months off. No work whatsoever."

Hopefully. Marcia had already emailed me to tell me about something called keeping in touch days, where I regularly 'touched base' with my team and my line manager. "Essential," Marcia's email read, "for keeping in the loop with everything Blissful Beauty does in your absence". Presumably, so I didn't return to work having forgotten my job, title or name even.

Caroline nodded, tipping her head to one side. "Aye, well. I can look after the wean three days a week when ye go back if ye want?"

Circumstances—a bad first marriage and then later hooking up with Ranald who was unable to have children—meant Caroline had missed out on the number of kids she would have really wanted. I knew she already babysat for Tamar occasionally. McAllan Junior was likely to see a lot of his/her gran.

"Thanks, Caroline," I said. What was my mum going to say? Much as she and Caroline enjoyed their regular WhatsApp exchanges, wouldn't the knowledge that Caroline was doing so much childcare sew the ugly green seeds of jealousy? Problems to consider another day.

As Katya wasn't around to ask for tips on what her leadership coach might say, I ran the Marty issue past Caroline, who didn't look as if she was in any hurry to leave. Last year, she needed to deal with a receptionist who kept 'forgetting' when her part-time shifts were meant to be. Caroline had been forced to run her surgeries with one eye on the door when people came in for their appointments. How had my mother-in-law solved the problem?

"Easy! Yon woman didnae know about my sideline as Psychic Josie."

How, how, how? The Highland's worst-kept secret. Had the woman been hiding under a rock?

"So," she said, putting her coffee cup down on the table and helping herself to the biscuits she'd put out on a saucer. "When she turned up at a Highland Games gathering in Oban I was booked for, and didnae realise it was me, I said I was channelling her late, lamented mother. Who was awfy disappointed her daughter didnae use the lovely Scottish pictures calendar hangin' in her kitchen she'd given her tae fill in aw' her appointments for the week."

"What happened?"

"Worked a treat, Gaby! I've never had any problems wi' her turning up for work since."

Good grief. But desperate times… "Um, d'you think if I arranged…?"

"Aye, of course! Tell me when your next team meeting is and put me as Psychic Josie on the agenda. I'll channel yon man's grandmother and pretend she's shocked at him for no' working hard enough."

With that, she was out of her seat and off, leaving me wondering if 'Using Your Mother-In-Law as a Fake Psychic to Improve Attendance at Work' was a chapter in any book on management. And weren't all Marty's grandmothers alive and kicking, judging by the number of 75th birthday parties for them he'd attended? A great-grandmother might have to do instead.

By the time I switched my iMac off, a powerful headache had taken up residence in my temples, the thumpity-thump of it, made much worse by the knowledge that all I could take for it was low-dose paracetamol, rather than super-strength ibuprofen. I forced myself out of the house and took a walk along the shores of the loch, the fresh air and the light spit of rain working its magic. As a bonus, I spotted two otters near to one of the old, wrecked fishing boats, their little heads ducking in and out of sight.

Back home, I made myself a late dinner Mildred was only too happy to help me finish. A tuna salad for the baby's developing brain and five slices of bread and butter for the much-needed carbs. After that, the sofa whispered tempting things to me—*stretch out and watch some TV… You'll manage to stay awake long enough to get up in an hour and make your way to the Lochside Welcome in time for the weekly pub quiz…*

The sofa fibbed. At nine o'clock, my phone woke me up. Several messages from Katya and Mhari. "Where are you?????????? Pub quiz, pub quiz, pub quiz!" and other ones asking if I was okay.

"I'm fine," I typed back. "Just too knackered. Sorry." I sent the same text to Jack, apologising profusely and hoping he didn't think my no-show was disloyal. Unable to face talking to people who might phone to persuade me to leave the house—Mhari—I went to switch my mobile off, attention grabbed by a message from my mum.

"See you tomorrow, love! Can't wait."

What?! I sat up tiredness banished in a tidal wave of panic. Pregnancy brain once more. How could I have forgotten that conversation? And no offence to my mother, but...

Oh no. Times 300.

"...and when your nanna said to me, 'Mandy, let's visit Gaby. We haven't seen 'er since she got married,' I thought, 'what a great idea, Mum!'"

Phone pushed to my ear, I groaned to myself. As soon as I'd seen that message, I'd phoned my mum back praying she'd made a mistake and meant, *Speak to you tomorrow, love!* From this angle on the sofa, close inspection of the carpet made me cringe. Housework, however substandard it had been up until recently, had now dropped off the schedule. Neither Jack nor I bothered at all. Sheets of paper littered the living room. Dirty dishes were stacked high in the sink, and the soap scum in the shower had taken on its own life form.

So much for the nesting/cleaning stage, Caroline had promised. Tidying up for a visit from your mum was the rule, right?

My mum had been in Norwich with my nanna earlier, she told me. Picking up a few baby things in the Jarrolds' summer sale to bring with her. Had I missed the bit where I asked her to come and visit, I asked. There was nothing in my calendar...

"Oh no, love! Your nanna said to me, 'Let's surprise our Gaby! We can drive up there on Saturday and stay for a few days.'"

Luckily for me, my mother wasn't FaceTiming; otherwise, she might have spotted how horrified I looked. Thank the universe she'd re-thought the surprise element and given me 24 hours' notice. Imagine if I'd answered the door to them both on Saturday afternoon not having expected them...

I shuddered. Mildred, in one of her favourite positions draped across my lap, got up and stalked off.

Don't get me wrong. I loved my mum and missed living close to her. But her landing on us with Nanna Cooper in 24 hours was far from ideal. This morning, I'd got up at 6am and typed up yet another a to-do list that took me half an hour. By the time I'd dealt with all my emails—was this same for everyone who was a boss?—it was 9am.

Tomorrow, Saturday, promised to be a busy day in the Lochside Welcome as you might expect, but Jack had promised if I popped by at lunchtime, he'd take his break at the same time, and we could sit outside and catch up. Two weeks into his management of the Lochside Welcome, he was a shadow of a man who drifted in and out of the house only to sleep. How were we going to entertain Mum and Nanna when both of us were barely able to grunt at each other?

"Wouldn't it be far better for you to come once I've had the baby? Or for me to pop down for a weekend at the end of September?" I asked, even if the possibility of time off before I went on maternity leave seemed remote.

"We're going to do that too, of course we are. Your nanna's dead excited about becoming a great-grandma. Everyone in her circle is already one, and she feels left out. Says it's her turn to bore them all to tears while she shows them the hundreds of pictures on her phone."

Lucky them. Though the Nannas of Norwich had nothing to fear. My nanna's phone wasn't high spec and her storage titchy. She'd be lucky to manage 10 pics.

"Is she the size of a beached whale yet?" My brother in the background, my mother shushing him. "Dylan sends his love, by the way!"

I raised my voice. "Ask him what kind of saddo guy, who isn't even 30 yet, stays in with his mum on a Friday night?"

"Saturday then!" my mum continued brightly; having told Dylan, I sent my love back.

"Er… sure. But we're so busy…"

Mum guilt-tripped me into it, pointing out that she and Nanna hadn't seen me since Christmas, life having gotten seriously in the way since then. When Nanna phoned me immediately afterwards and added to the pressure, I gave in wearily.

Phone switched off, I settled for scribbling a note to Jack. "Mum and Nanna coming tomorrow for a 'surprise' visit. Tried and failed to put them off. Mega, mega sorry!!!!!!!! XXX." And then hauled myself upstairs, hoping I was fast asleep by the time he came in and read it.

Chapter Seventeen

Sun streamed in through the curtains, waking me up at nine and I relished how relaxed I felt, having slept solidly ever since my head hit the pillow the night before. A nine o'clock lie-in. What a luxury. Even better—my husband was in bed beside me, body pressed up behind me. Maybe we could squeeze in—

Argh. Mum! Nanna! The state of this house, our bedroom the perfect demonstration of how much needed doing. The sunlight picked out all the dust.

"Stop wriggling," Jack muttered, nestling in closer, so there was no mistaking his intentions. "I just need another few minutes to wake up and then I promise you'll get my full, undivided attention. And I dinnae need to go into the hotel until early evening, so I'm all yours all day."

Double argh. I'd placed my note on the coffee table in the living room, but if he'd come in last night and gone straight upstairs, he wouldn't have seen it. I turned over, kissed his nose and slid downwards—the duvet muffling the words, "My mum, nanna, surprise visit!" Or it might have been where my mouth landed that stopped him hearing the joyous news. Whatever, but once I'd made him groan and then grin, promising me the same favour in return, I sat up and repeated myself.

The grin disappeared. He put his hands over his eyes and gave another groan, this one far unhappier.

"I see lots of your mum," I said, "compared to how much you see of mine."

His fingers spread, allowing him to peek at me through them, eyes meeting mine.

"Gaby, I'm fine with your mum and grandmother, I really am." A hint of over-emphasis there.

"But right now? Why didn't they both decide to visit when the baby is here—when we're not working and in need of people to do the housework for us and cook us food?"

Arguably, we needed that now. "They're coming then too. For a month."

His eyes widened in horror. "Oh, fu—I mean, what fun."

"And staying with your mum and Ranald."

Palpable relief on his part. He sat up, thrusting the duvet aside. "S'pose we better tidy the house up a bit."

I lay where I was. Our house was a bomb site, but it wouldn't take that long to clean it if we shoved everything into cupboards, vacuumed and washed up.

"McAllan," I sat up myself and pointed at him. "You promised me a return of the favour."

A return of the grin, tongue flicking out at me. "What ma lady commands, ma lady gets." He rolled to one side, pressing me back down against the pillows, and hovered above me, eyes sparkling. "But only if she begs first."

Ooh… he'd gone all Jamie Fraser on me too!

Travelling to Lochalshie was not easy, mainly because it involved coming from one place that was a bit out of the way to another that was extremely far out of the way. Mum and Nanna had set off at six am, according to the text they'd sent earlier.

Clean-up completed I spent the rest of the day nervously switching on the radio where I fully expected the travel news section to include an item about a crash involving two women in an old Fiesta. Their progress updates were infrequent—the one when they'd left first thing, then another when they stopped at Southwaite Services around lunchtime complete with a moan from my nanna about how much they'd charged for egg and cress sandwiches. My phone beeped once more when they drove over the border.

After that, nothing.

By the time, I opened the door late on Saturday afternoon, my nerves a jangled wreck, I met two fractious people.

"It is time that your grandmother gave up driving!" my mother said, throwing her arms open and enveloping me in a cloud of Nina Ricci's L'Air du Temps, the perfume she always wore. "Tell her, Gaby. Hello, Jack, love! I swear you get better looking every time I see you."

Following behind her, Nanna Cooper grimaced at me and stuck her tongue out at her daughter, which made me smile. Mum's Fiesta should have been put out to grass a long time ago. The gear stick needed delicate handling; something that was difficult to gauge if you didn't drive the car all the time.

Jack took their bags. "So lovely to see you, Mandy and Lillian!"

He managed a smile that almost met his eyes. Returning to the hallway, having dumped the bags in the spare room, he apologised and told us he needed to go. He and his team were discussing the Highland Games and what they needed to order ahead of it. Huh. Hadn't early evening been the time he'd promised me before I dropped the Mum/Nanna visit bombshell?

We all waved him goodbye, my mum standing in the doorway and pointing out to my nanna all the people she now knew thanks to her visits here. Nanna nodded and stamped her feet. "Can we shut the door now?"

Scotland's summer came as an unpleasant shock to Nanna. Last time she'd visited had been December when it was reasonable to expect cold temperatures. Nanna had worn thermal vests, thick tights, a padded coat and scarf. This time, she was dressed in jeans and a tight-fitting turquoise cardigan over a blouse, making me sigh with envy. Would I ever wear fit into my jeans again?

The irony… Me, a late twenty-something envious of my grandmother's sartorial style.

"Mandy! Mrs Cooper!"

The shout stopped us before I closed the door. Katya. I'd enlisted her help with entertaining Mum and Nanna. She'd agreed all too readily, leading me to suspect progress on the billionaire romance novel had ground to a halt once more. I'd given her what I thought was a brilliant idea for a scene the other day, where the heroine consulted with one of her over-worked, underpaid employees to ask what poor people bought for their loved ones, so she didn't overwhelm the chauffeur handyman love interest with a gift that was far too expensive. Even that hadn't helped her get back on track.

"Hello, gorgeous!"

If I'd been paranoid, I might have found Nanna Cooper's greeting of my best friend far more enthusiastic than the one I'd received. Nanna flung her arms around Katya. "Don't call me Mrs Cooper, Katya love! It's Lillian."

Like my mum, Nanna had a strong Norfolk accent. Doan Cuup'r. Mine was starting to disappear, the edges of it gobbled up by Scottishness. I didn't say Aye, or mebbe yet, but I used 'wee' frequently. Such as now. "Come in, everyone! And I'll get us all a wee cup of tea."

In the hastily cleaned living room, Mildred and Nanna locked eyes. In cat years, Mildred was the same age as Nanna. My grandmother, unfortunately, was no fan of moggies.

"What are you going to do with that thing when the baby comes along?" Nanna said, making me suck in air. Mildred was not a 'thing'. Yes, cats didn't understand the words, but I often wondered if Mildred picked up on disdain or dislike. She narrowed her eyes and made her way over to me, lifting her chin up for a rub.

"Er, adapt?" I said, and Nanna Cooper rolled her blue-mascara-ed eyes. "You say that Gaby, but years ago I remember this woman I knew whose cat jumped on top of her baby while he was sleeping in his cot and the little boy suffocated to death!"

No wonder Nanna Cooper and my mother-in-law got on so well with their taste for worst-case scenarios. Even so, the story made me gulp. Mildred was licking a paw, delicate tongue flicks over the right one that then went behind her ear and back again, the picture of feline innocence. Even so, it was possible to summon up a hideous picture where she climbed into a cot and settled down on top of my baby and… oooohhhhh.

Katya cleared her throat. "Lillian, Gaby has thought about all of this."

I had?

"And prepared."

Ditto the last question.

"In the lead up to the birth, she needs to expose Mildred to babies, which she will do through regularly inviting Jolene and baby Tamar to visit. Then, she has to put out the baby's cot, so the cat knows the new furniture is part of the house. If she lines the cot with tinfoil, when Mildred jumps in, she will find that unpleasant. She'll dissociate herself from it."

I didn't have a private sightline to Katya, one where I could signal furiously with my eyes, *"Is this for real?"*. But her advice sounded stellar. Cats hated change, so gradually introducing new furniture helped them adjust. They also objected to nasty rustling noises and the feel of tinfoil.

The Tamar thing too… hadn't I thought that myself? Apart from anything else, Jack and I needed the practice. We had no idea how babies worked. As soon as possible, I'd suggest to Jolene that we babysit while she and Stewart… urgh, the inner censor stepped in unwilling to continue with thoughts that might lead to me imagining Stewart naked.

"Then, she buys herself some organic, paraben-free, yummy mummy brand baby lotion and starts slathering it all over herself every day," Katya continued, "so that when the baby comes along and Gaby rubs that stuff into him/her/them/it, Mildred recognises the smell."

Nanna Cooper, my mum and I stared at her. "I had no idea," I said, "that—"

You needed to do this much to get a cat used to a new baby? Or that your best friend would do a tonne of research to find out what needed to be done? And that she would know you would do Sweet Fanny Adams about it… the last the most likely.

Another note to self: google organic, paraben-free, yummy mummy brand baby lotions and order the cheapest one. Or, and this was way out there, suggest to Caitlin that her business move into organic, paraben-free, yummy-mummy baby skincare and offer to test-drive them.

Tea downed, Nanna started asking questions about food. She ate her last meal of the day at six pm, convinced that doing so any later gave you violent indigestion and made you pile on the weight.

"Let's go and see Jack!" I announced. "Where we shall be served the best food in Scotland."

My mum and Nanna jumped to their feet. "Hallelujah!" Nanna Cooper. "We were worried you were gonna make us eat your food."

Family loyalty. Always there when you ask for it.

Katya and Nanna went ahead, Katya discussing the plot of her book with Nanna, a Mills and Boon devotee who'd have ideas a-plenty. "This is what you should do, Katya," she told my friend. "Put in a car crash, so the chauffeur chap has to take the unconscious LeAnna in his arms and carry her to the side of the highway while they wait for an ambulance. Add in some light bleeding but no nasty injuries."

My mum threaded her arm through mine. "How are you doing, Gaby? You look awfully stressed. Have you taken on too much?"

"No, not at all!" I trilled. If I confessed all—Jack and I are worked off our feet, and honestly, I have no idea if we can be parents at all!—she'd insist on phoning me all the time. She might even decide to up sticks and move to Lochalshie for the foreseeable future.

Distraction techniques needed, I called out for Katya and Nanna to wait up. "I forgot to tell you, Nanna," I said when we reached them just before they got to the Lochside Welcome. "A filming company wants to make a docu-series about the pub. And put it on Netflix. Imagine that!"

Far from being excited, Nanna glared at me. "Now she tells us! I haven't got my best dress on, and I'm gonna look terrible on the TV! That does it. We need to go back to our house right this instant, young lady. You'll need to get changed too. Your hairstyle's a disgrace!"

And with that, she marched off, leaving me opening and shutting my mouth like the proverbial goldfish.

***

"The Netflix docu-series is not confirmed yet, Nanna," I said when she came downstairs stylish jeans and cardigan swapped for... oh heck. The dress she'd worn for my wedding seven months ago—a blue 50s rockabilly satin number. Sixty-five pounds well spent but totally unsuited for a summer Saturday evening in a rural pub.

Nanna fluffed her hair out, removing Velcro rollers one by one. To keep her quiet, I'd agreed to do something with my hair sweeping it up in a chignon and adding lipstick, bronzer and face powder. My best friend, as usual, was understated glamorous and in no need of tarting up. Nonetheless, she'd hidden a smile when Nanna made her reappearance.

"Lovely dress, Lillian, but I'm—"

"I can't wait to tell all my friends I am going to be on the Netflix. We're all big fans of that Frankie and Bennie's programme. I used to do Jane Fonda's workouts years ago, you know."

"Netflix, Nanna," I said, "no need for 'the'. And it's Grace and Frankie. Besides, the cameras aren't there right now."

We hadn't heard anything further from Miles and Tindra. Nor had I seen either of them. But Jack had received a detailed email from Miles, outlining what filming the docu-series would involve. He read it and told me he hoped the idea would fall through. "It's too much work, Gaby. I cannae run a pub at the peak of the tourist season and cope wi' filming demands at the same time."

I made 'there, there' type noises, gently suggesting that such an opportunity offered brilliant free publicity. He grunted in response.

"We can't be taking chances," Nanna said, as we left the house once more. Despite the ferocious heat blasting out of the Lochside Welcome, Mum and Nanna Cooper insisted we sit inside instead of in the beer garden where I could have enjoyed the light breeze.

"No cameras. See!" I said. My grandmother announced that it was because they were waiting for her to arrive. I rolled my eyes. Trust Nanna to take an idea and run with it.

Katya smirked. "I'll be your agent, Lillian. TV people are sharks. We'll need to make sure you get the recognition you deserve."

"Don't encourage her," I hissed. Nanna was once interviewed for BBC Look East. We had to watch the clip endlessly, Nanna pointing out how many questions the reporter asked her and how brilliant her grasp of European politics was.

Nanna smiled in the direction of the (invisible) camera and sucked in her cheeks. "They say the camera adds an extra stone, don't they, Katya? If Kathleen Miller sees me looking fat, she'll crow. We have our weekly competition, you know."

Nanna and her best friend Kathleen Miller had competitively dieted throughout the 40 years they'd known each other. On the day of her third marriage, Kathleen Miller insisted on them both weighing themselves that morning just so she would know she was lighter than her bridesmaid on the day.

Jolene greeted my relatives cheerily, handing over menus and squeezing us into a table near the roaring fire. Outside, the Highland Tours minibus was in place once more, Lucas having dropped off tourists at what he promised them was the best venue in the Highlands.

He gave me a cheery wave from the bar where he was deep in conversation with Xavier. Lucas spoke French—nice for Xavier to be able to converse with someone in his own language. All everyone else ever managed was "Bonjour, Xavier!"

"Can I look after Tamar some time? Whenever you want a night out?" I asked Jolene, congratulating myself for managing to remember something.

Jolene grinned. "Getting ready for the big day? Yeah, why not? Me and Stewart have got our anniversary of the first time we met coming up in a few weeks." She wandered off, a group outside looking for table service for their drinks.

Nanna picked up the menu—the new one I'd made for Jack when he decided to add additional items to what was on offer, including Xavier's French Canadian-Scottish fusion dishes. A risk for sure. Ashley had built up a reputation for fabulous pizzas and chocolate cake. The Lochside Welcome had achieved a status for its food, mainly because it was one of the few places in rural Scotland where you were able to get decent grub. Many places relied on 60s staples such as prawn cocktails, and scampi and chips. All of them coming ready-made and straight from the freezer. The only chef skill most people needed in those places was the ability to programme a microwave.

That was then; this was now. The food at the Royal George had gained its formidable fame. Earlier this year, Zac had appeared on the BBC's Landward programme waxing lyrical about his use of local, seasonal produce. We watched, dismayed, as cars flocked to the car park of the George for weeks afterwards.

Would the Lochside Welcome's regulars welcome a change in direction? The hotel didn't want to compete for fine dining customers—cheese and gravy chips on the menu ably demonstrated that—but what about an extension of incredibly-made comfort food?

Fears of camera-added fat looks didn't deter Nanna from ordering the biggest pizza she could when Jolene returned. "Cheese and tomato, please. And I'd like some of that garlic dip for the crusts, please."

"Mandy! Mrs Cooper! Awfy nice to see you back in our wee village!"

Katya kicked me under the table. Too much to hope that Mhari wouldn't notice there were strange folks in the pub, and she'd wander in and wangle herself an invite. She took hold of the back of a chair and dragged it over. "Oh? Are youse eating? I dinnae want to intrude."

She was the queen of the free food scrounge. I sighed. I'd need to pay for her food. My mum had offered to pay for our meal, but that was when it was just Katya, Nanna and I. Mhari's greediness matched mine. The bill, family discount for me as the manager's wife notwithstanding, would be too much for Mum.

Across the room, I spotted Tindra, her eyes meeting mine at the same time. Blast, blast, double blast. They'd returned then after that first bit of filming and the meetings in London. She smiled and made her way over. Just what I needed.

"Katya, Mum, Nanna," I said as Tindra drew up another seat. "This is Tindra. She works for that TV company I told you about."

Nanna preened. "Aren't you glad I made you do your hair, Gaby?"

She and Mhari proceeded to bombard Tindra with questions. Visiting the area, Mhari reminded Tindra referring to the first meeting weeks ago. She'd known all along that was a crock. But what famous folks had she filmed and what programmes had Kudos Media made? Her sneer made it apparent she didn't rate any of Kudos Media's previous productions, though Nanna confessed she loved the A&E dramas. She patted her hair and applied another coating of lipstick.

"I am a TV regular," she told Tindra, "I've been interviewed by Look East. Twice, in fact."

How had I managed to forget the first time when she'd whacked a man who attempted to grab her handbag outside the shopping centre? It was caught on CCTV and went viral. A reporter tracked her down, and the piece was billed as 'Have-A-Go-Granny Hammers Hooligan'. Just like now, she crow-barred it into most conversations.

"Look what?" Tindra asked, someone unfamiliar with local BBC stations. Our generation thing. No-one our age watched regular TV unless we stumbled on it by accident.

"I know," Nanna continued, undaunted, "that people must speak slowly when they are being interviewed."

Then, in case Tindra hadn't got the point, "and, They. Muuuust. Pronounce. Their. Worrrrrds Carrefully."

"Too. Rrrrright," Mhari threw in. Unhelpfully. "I havenae been on telly, but there are loads o' YouTube videos you can see me in."

Katya's questions were more direct.

So… Were Kudos Media pitching a docu-series idea to Netflix? How far along the process were they? Didn't Netflix prefer experienced producers and directors? When would filming begin?

These were the questions I wanted answering too. Tindra shrugged. "I don't know. Miles has all that information."

She gestured vaguely behind her, but there was no sign of Miles.

"Do you mind if I do a bit of filming myself this evening? Just on my phone?" She waved the latest iPhone in front of us. "I'm trying to put more ideas together for Miles. Pitching him what I think would work. You won't even notice I'm here. What about if I get your reaction to the new menu?"

My nanna sucked her cheeks in once more. Darn it. Now, I was obliged to have something off it instead of my usual four-cheese pizza choice, be filmed in my beached whale state and praising whatever to the skies, so the pub looked good.

"No problem," I said, and Tindra clapped her hands. "Awesome! I'll tell Jack he needs to be the one to deliver the food."

That would go down like a lead balloon; bang in the middle of a Saturday night and Jack needing to act as a waiter when Jolene or the agency staff could do the job much better. Tindra disappeared anyway, returning a few minutes later.

"Just act naturally," she called out, aiming her phone at us. "I'll film you talking. Don't look directly at the phone. Just at each other or me."

"What a splendid place this is! I love it," Nanna Cooper using her best Queen's English, the 'I' coming out like 'Ay'. Katya's lips twitched, and my mother shook her head.

"I've come all the way from Great Yarmouth to sample the amazing food that is on offer here." Words slowed, she stared at the phone's camera enclosure the whole time.

"Marvellous! Here is our food. I cannot wait to eat it!"

That bit did look authentic. Two of Xavier's creations were placed before us—a Tourtiere pie and Ragoût de Boulettes, accompanied by the smell of gravy, spices and flaky pastry. Tindra switched the phone from Nanna to Jack, who refused to look in her direction. Nanna exaggerated her reaction as she tucked in before realising she didn't need to, fake ecstasy transforming to reality as soon as she swallowed the first mouthful.

My turn to overdo the theatrics, wittering on about how much I and my baby-to-be loved French/Canadian cuisine given a Scottish twist.

Mhari's fork hovered above my plate, and forgetting about the camera, I told her to where to go (not as politely as that). Tindra lowered her phone and grinned at me. "Food that good, eh?" She reached over with a fork, helping herself to a meatball.

"Wow—they are amazing, aren't they?!"

Food finished, Jack allowed himself five minutes off to come over and talk to us. He eyed Tindra warily, but she'd put her phone down, too busy tucking into the chips covered in cheese and gravy.

"You're awfully busy, Jack," my mum said. Now I looked properly, I saw she was right. Saturday night and every table taken. A large party commandeered the outdoor space, Jolene out there delivering yet more trays of drinks.

"A coach party from New Zealand," he said, pointing at the group. "One of them walked in, heard Jolene's accent, and that was enough to bring them all in."

We watched as Jolene stopped to chat, a broad smile lighting up her face. She didn't encounter that many of her fellow countrymen and women living this far north in the UK. I hoped it didn't make her too homesick.

Jack stirred himself, perhaps realising he better pretend an interest in Tindra's filming efforts—the key to massive publicity for the Lochside Welcome.

"Did you, ah, get what you needed, Tindra?"

She nodded. "Loads! What an amazing place this is." Her hands spread out, taking in the room. "And the village, so scenic, so real," she glanced towards Nanna Copper, not an actual villager, "so full of life! D'you think," the words hyper-casual, "I could get some footage of you behind the bar pouring pints?"

Jack sighed. "Aye, okay then. If you think it will help."

She leapt up so fast, our table tilted to its side, and the empty plates slid towards the floor. Lightning quick, Jack caught them all—Mhari holding her own phone up, triumphant smile in place. "I got that on film," she sang out. "you can add that tae yours, Tindra. Awfy impressive move. I'm a camerawoman too."

Tindra blinked. Maybe she hadn't expected so much TV and film expertise in one tiny place. Jack, saved plates in hand and a sigh in my direction, headed to the bar, Tindra racing after him.

"Well," Nanna declared. "Safe to say Tinder"—Nanna

often got her words muddled up—— "and her TV company will be filming here. And the programme will be viewed by millions. Don't you think?"

———————

Fuelled by one Prosecco too many, my mum decided to remain in the Lochside Welcome when I yawned for the tenth time and said I needed to go to bed.

My nanna, now in conversation with Jolene and expressing New Zealand knowledge I never realised she possessed, said she would stay too.

Katya got up. "I'd better head back too. That billionaire romance isn't going to write itself."

The High Street was deserted, though chatter from the Royal George's beer garden was clearly audible. Once again, it appeared far busier than the Lochside Welcome.

We set off in the direction of my house, Katya insistent I needed to be escorted home. "Dexter says TV companies make all sorts of prom—"

She froze, raising a finger to her mouth and grabbing my arm so she could push us both behind the tree in front of us. We were opposite Jamal's shop. The door to the neighbouring house—the Airbnb property—opened and one figure came into view.

He turned, a hand running through blonde hair and pushing it back from his face, so the streetlight showed him clearly.

Zac. In Lochalshie for sure then.

Katya's eyes narrowed. She nudged me. I elbowed her back, both of us wide-eyed. Behind Zac, I spotted Miles in the doorway, arms folded, and mouth pursed in a thin line.

Zac had left Lochalshie when Katya realised what a

lying, murderous, two-timing creep he was—wise enough to know the Royal George would never flourish with him in charge. Since then, he'd popped up a few times like one of those nasty Jack in the Boxes you see in horror films.

Thanks to a mix-up about where Jack and I would be getting married at the end of last year, Katya had to phone the Royal George and cancel at short notice. Zac marched straight into the local police station the next day and told them he'd been the victim of an assault back in September when Jack punched him, calling him an 'English wanker' at the same time. If he'd stuck to 'wanker', getting him off those charges would have been much more straightforward. Thanks to the E word, the police decided it counted as a racially aggravated offence and much more severe.

The accusation threw a considerable spanner in our wedding works even though Zac did drop the charges after Katya used all her powers of persuasion on him.

But the brass neck of him. Appearing here after the trouble he'd caused. Hammerstone Hotels circulated their chefs and hospitality staff to keep them 'fresh'. This must be one of those occasions.

"What a nerve he's got!" Katya said. I tried to make sense of the way she stared at him. Was it favourably or nastily? "I know," I whispered back. "And er... why is he talking to Miles?"

She shushed me.

"They aren't pleased." Zac's words drifted towards us, his plummy accent carrying clearly through the air.

I flashed back to when Jack and I had spoken to Miles and Tindra a couple of weeks ago. Miles had wandered out of the Royal George car park at the time. I'd thought it a coincidence. Hadn't he told Mhari he was in Lochalshie because a friend of his had told him how brilliant the village was? Was Zac the friend?

Katya pressed her finger to her mouth again, furiously gesturing that I stand behind her to keep us out of sight. Miles started to speak. A dog walker passed them—Laney Haggerty, her two enormous Alsatians straining at their leashes. She said an automatic hello, realised who it was, and stomped off. In my pocket, my phone beeped loudly. No doubt Laney updating the Lochalshie WhatsApp group.

"What's that?" Zac spun around, staring out over the loch. Katya and I huddled in closer behind the tree, her muttering "Why on earth don't you put your phone on silent after 9pm?"

There was another loud beep, but this time from where Miles and Zac stood. Zac dug in his back pocket, pulling out his own phone. "Speak of the devils."

They huddled over it, staring at whatever the screen said.

"Read it out loud!" Katya urged them, the wind hiding the sound.

"Does that date suit?" Zac said, glancing up at Miles. "Y'know they've got a lot of money they could invest elsewhere? Like a—"

Loud barking drowned out the rest of the sentence. Laney's dogs passing my house, I guessed. Mildred was smart enough to stay inside whenever she sensed dogs nearby. Didn't stop her taunting them, though. Hissing and spitting at the window, secure in the knowledge she was perfectly safe behind it.

"It's my decision, Zac. I never promised anything. But Monday is fine," Miles said, extending his hand. Zac ignored it, pulling Miles in for a man hug instead. The back-slapping made it seem threatening, despite the smiles.

He walked back towards the George, Miles also following him with his eyes. Katya and I waited until Miles closed his door until we emerged from behind the tree.

"What was that about then?" I asked. Katya didn't answer me, her eyes fixed on the George.

"Hello! Look, Mum! Gaby and Katya waited up for us! Isn't that nice?"

Mum and Nanna, picking their way back to our house along the loch shores, the former very unsteady on her feet. Thanks to recent epic rainfall, the sand underfoot wasn't the steadiest ground to place a foot on. I shouted a warning. Too late. My mother tipped over, face first.

"I told her not to start on that second bottle of Prosecco, Gaby!"

I about-turned, closely followed by Katya ready to haul my mum back on her feet. "I don't know, Gaby," Katya said. "But it doesn't sound good."

Oh. I'd wanted her to say, "It's nothing to worry about, Gaby! Just relax."

No such luck.

Chapter Eighteen

"What shops are there in Oban, love?"

My mum and nanna decided the next morning they'd had enough of the charms of Lochalshie, having visited a couple of times before. Walks around the loch, visits to Jamal's store where he kept them chatting for a long time, having remembered the existence of a branch of his father's family who'd settled in the Norfolk area, and coffees in the beer garden at the Lochside Welcome only kept a person entertained for a short time.

I tried suggesting a hike up Maggie Broon's Boobs—Mum and Nanna were members of a local walking group—but they took one look at them and shuddered. Just as well, perhaps. The local mountain rescue volunteers would think me irresponsible if I sent a 70-plus woman up there. Also, Mum's hangover was brutal. She was on her fourth cup of coffee already, and it showed no sign of abating.

I popped slices of wholemeal bread under the grill, promising her I'd make us something to eat. "Well, there's an antique place, a specialist chocolate shop, an art gallery, a smokehouse, a boutique and a Tesco's."

Mum put the kettle on again. Jack had disappeared an hour ago, muttering about needing to visit the cash and carry, a round trip that would take two precious hours out of his day. Perhaps I should have made him take Mum and Nanna with him. They could have helped load and unload the van.

"There's the fish and chip place too—where we went after Jack, and I got married."

Nanna's voice drifted through from the living room. "Ooh! That place was lovely. Best fish and chips I ever had, and you don't think to say that when you lived next to the sea for 40 years."

Mum took the teas through. "I thought I might buy you some baby stuff, love. You don't seem to be very well prepared."

Nanna nodded. "It may seem as if you have plenty of time, Gaby, but it will pass in a flash, and before you know it, the baby will be here and no high chair, no changing mat, no nappies or anything."

I buttered toast and found Marmite and jam, adding it to a tray. Breakfast of champions. "But I don't need anything! We've got an old cot from Laney, and Jolene's promised me all Tamar's clothes."

Mum and Nanna exchanged meaningful looks. "Does that mean you know…?"

The million-dollar question. But there were a few more weeks to go until the scan that would be able to tell Jack and me the sex of the baby we were expecting. If we chose to find out. Then, we could do a gender-reveal party where we made a cake, a little piece of paper with the info on it baked inside. D'nah! It's a boy. D'nah! It's a girl. Oh, wow—it's a cat. Part of me was tempted to do that just to see the look on everyone's face.

"We don't know yet," I said, flapping a hand. "Jack and I are Gen Y, remember? We refuse to let binary gender stereotypes such as boys must wear blue and girls pink influence our decisions. Anyway, most of what Tamar wears are neutral colours."

Mum gripped her cup of tea and pursed her lips. "Oh! But they have such beautiful things for little girls in all the shops. Asda's stuff is amazing! All those princess romper suits."

Nanna helped herself to toast and jam. "I thought you were millenniums? Yellow will clash something horrible with your baby's red hair."

"Same thing, Nanna. Gen Y. Millennials. And perhaps my offspring will take after me and be a brunette."

She shook her head, sending me a pitying look. "Oh no, love. Everyone knows how dominant ginger gene is. Everyone will know Jack is your child's father. 'E or she won't look like you at all."

How supportive. Not.

"If you really want to buy me something, there's the boutique shop along the seafront in Oban," I said. If they both bought me a white hat or a pair of booties for the baby, that would suit us all. Me, because I wouldn't feel guilty about them spending money they didn't have. Mum and Nanna because that satisfied the requirement to buy their grandchild/great-grandchild something new.

An argument about who did the driving started up. "Not you," Mum said, pointing at my belly. "And definitely not you," looking at Nanna. "You'll be a total menace on those twisty country roads. And what about those farmers taking their sheep or cattle across the road? You'll run over a sheep."

Nanna disputed this as I locked the door to the house, arguing that the Nannas of Norwich had made her the trusted driver for their weekly pensioners' bingo outings.

"I'll drive," I said, opening the door to my car. "Mum, you're still over the limit."

That elicited a smug smile from Nanna, who got in beside me, leaving the back seat to Mum. I crossed my fingers it wouldn't make her puke.

Oban was busy as the sun had brought out the tourists. It was one of those towns that looks much nicer in the sunshine. Don't they all? But it was particularly true here. You got a clear coastal view for a start. The sun's rays picked out the pretty ice-cream scoop colours of the houses and shops along the seafront and highlighted the pale gold of the sand. McCaig's Tower looked out over the town and the sea, today offering perfect views of the surrounding area thanks to the clear skies.

Plenty of people came up here from Glasgow on a sunny day as the train ride was so scenic. Tradition had it, they wandered the streets of Oban, shopped, ate ice-cream, drank a few beers and then went home again, via the local Tesco's where they bought a carry-out for the train, making the scenic journey back blurry.

I parked in the car park, Mum and Nanna marvelling at the lack of charges—there were few towns left in England that let you park for free—and we set off towards the town centre.

"If we go to Daisy Doo's first," I said, pointing at the boutique two numbers down from the chocolate shop, "then let's visit the antique shop. Jack has a few paintings in there.

Then how about an ice-cream or some chocolate after that?"

I knew I'd made a mistake as soon as we walked into the boutique. Daisy Doo's smelled overwhelmingly of wool, tweed and lavender. Scottish music played softly in the background, and an entire display was set up at the back in tribute to all things Outlander; books, a so-called Fraser tartan pashmina, fake dirks, crystals promising mysterious stone-like benefits to the buyers and VisitScotland guides to all the Scottish locations used in the TV series.

Everything in the shop would be expensive. Scarves that cost £80 because they were made with lambswool and hand-knitted. In theory, I agreed that those who used their skills to create quality goods should receive a decent reward, but not so much when I was trying to find something cheap for my relatives to buy.

"Ah, no baby stuff here," I announced as Nanna shut the door behind us. "Pity. Let's go somewhere else."

A woman pounced, long brown curly hair drawn back and a tweed skirt and jacket I guessed was supposed to make her look like Outlander 1960s Claire in series 3.

She held out a hand, fingers tightening around my forearm. "I'm Daisy, the owner," she said. "And we have lots of baby stuff over here." She pointed behind her at a table heaped with intricate lacy shawls, mini kilts made from wool and hand-knitted tiny socks. No sign of any price tags.

Delaying tactics. "Goodness, such lovely stuff," I said, wandering over and picking up one of the shawls as if I was genuinely interested. The tag dangled loose, making me wince. Imagine what you could buy with that in Asda's kids' clothes department.

I clapped my hand to my heart. "But I don't think I can!

It's jinxing fate, isn't it? To buy anything for the baby before he or she is born because you know…"

I put my heart and soul into that subtle bit of acting. From the way, my mum's mouth twitched, perhaps it wasn't an Oscar-winning performance after all.

"Investment pieces," Daisy pressed on. "A lot of people choose to buy cheap baby clothes these days. At Asda. Dumping things into their baskets while they pop in for their bread and milk." The curl of the top lip revealed what she thought of them.

"A false economy, I always say. Do you know what they're made of? Nasty, cheap material that irritates a baby's sensitive skin and is made by five-year-olds in China. They come back here afterwards, those mothers. Once they've had endless nights of a screaming child because the poor little thing is sore and itchy. 'Daisy,' they say to me, 'you were right. Please, please can I buy your—"

"I'll take it!" I burst out if only to stop the ghastly sales spiel. And yes, the sweatshop point had hit its mark. "The shawl. Yes, this one. Thank you."

Mum and I had a brief tussle at the counter where she tried to insist on paying half for it. I refused. Her GP receptionist job didn't pay well, and her and Nanna Copper had already splashed out a small fortune in fuel driving to Lochalshie. The money they'd need to cough up again when the baby finally made an appearance.

Daisy tried to persuade me cashmere socks were worth adding too. A baby's feet, she said, were even more sensitive and deserved cradling in super-soft wool. To everyone's astonishment, Nanna whipped out a credit card and handed it over. "I'll buy the socks," she declared grandly. "Two pairs."

"Nanna, are you sure? You don't need to."

"No, no, Gaby! Kathleen Miller spent a fortune in Jarrolds when her first grandchild was due. And didn't I hear about it for weeks on end!"

Our packages neatly wrapped in tissue paper and placed in a paper bag with a satin ribbon handle, we staggered out.

"Far, far, far too much money," I said, "and as for that rubbish she—"

"Gaby?"

I stopped, dismay replacing surprise when I worked out who'd just called my name.

Dear oh dear, oh dear.

Jack McAllan, Senior. My husband's father, and the man who'd caused a furious row between us a mere ten months ago.

I'd only met him the once, but Jack's father knew who I was anyway, disproving my theory I was now unrecognisable thanks to the hamster cheeks and inflated belly. (And a big fat raspberry to that.)

The smile that lit up his features when he recognised me reminded me so much of Jack, it made the hairs on the back of my neck stand up. It was as if I'd fast-forwarded 30 or so years, the man in front of me my husband, the much older man. Fingers crossed the years would be as kind to me.

The last time I'd seen his father, I thought him a faded version of Jack. Now, those additional months of abstinence had given him bright eyes, and even skin. And apart from a tiny bit of recession at each corner of his forehead, he had all his hair. A genetic blessing I must remember to point out to Jack.

The resemblance obvious, my mum and Nanna worked out the connection instantly. My mum's none-too-discreet elbow nudge either not noticed or ignored by Jack's father. She'd heard all about him—the man who'd assaulted Caroline numerous times while married to her, and on one occasion four years ago.

Jack and I had run into him before our wedding. He was, he told us then, a recovering alcoholic and on the 12-step programme. He wanted to make amends.

I've always been a sucker for a heartfelt apology. A bit much of me, though, to expect Jack to forget those frightening early childhood years. Him and his mum, awaiting the return of McAllan Senior from the pub, not knowing what state or mood he'd be in. And the later attack on Caroline was unforgivable. I invited him to the wedding anyway, except that I sent the text message to the wrong Jack. Cue a shouting match they probably heard in the next village.

Later, Jack said he might think about getting in touch. Perhaps they could try to repair their relationship slowly. Life got in the way. The wedding, Christmas, me getting pregnant so quickly, work... He never did.

"Nae need to ask how you are!" He beamed at me. "Blooming! You cannae hae long to go now."

My mum cleared her throat.

"Not until mid-December, actually," I said. "Very big baby. This is my mum, Mandy, by the way, and my grandmother, Lillian."

He held out his hand and my mum shook it. My nanna pursed her mouth and looked him up and down. We all pretended not to notice.

"Can I buy you all an ice-cream?" Jack Senior gestured

behind him. "I ken where they make the best yins in Oban."

As did I. A small harbour-front place that sold the same organic, delicious stuff Gareth in his ice-cream van punted out. Already, I could feel sweet, icy cream sliding down my throat... But, dilemma. This counted as disloyalty. Was there any way for me to discreetly message Jack, say, 'Help! We've just run into your father in Oban, do I let him buy us all ice-creams,' wait for a reply and then ask for my ice-cream? No, probably not.

"Very kind of you," I said. "But so sorry! We need to get back to Lochalshie because..."

Too late, Katya's words for 'how to be a boss' popped up. "Don't apologise. Don't explain." I racked my brain for an excuse. Nothing obliging popped up.

"Aye, aye," Jack Senior said. "Must be awfy exhausting for ye."

I threw him a grateful look—a dignified exit for all of us. "Yes," I faked a yawn that quickly turned into a real one. "Ever so tiring this baby-building business!"

Jack Senior smiled at me, the move so my Jack-like, I did a double-take. "Of course! Gaby, would ye... mind telling ma son I wouldnae mind talking to him? Say to him I havenae had a drink in a long time, and I'm awfy sorry for everything I did tae him and his mum."

I nodded. "Yes, yes! I'll pass that on."

He doffed an imaginary hat and walked off.

Mum, Nanna and I hurried back to the car park, full by now as it was lunchtime and visitors flocked in for fish and chips, or doorstep sandwiches they could eat on the seafront.

I waited until we were out of sight to slow down.

"Well?"

"He sounded sincere to me, love," Mum said, as Nanna tutted.

"Don't you let him near my great-grandchild, Gaby. The proof is very much in the pudding, be it chocolate, an apple tart or a spotted dick."

Mum started to laugh, hastily turning it into a cough. I struggled, splutters of laughter working their way up from my stomach and threatening to explode out of me in a most undignified way. I wasn't sure if Nanna realised what she'd said. Yes or no, it was pure genius. Katya would laugh like a drain.

I yanked the door open, fed up of my zig-zagging emotions. One minute, sympathy for Jack's father, the next wishing I didn't have to deal with this further complication to our lives. Fathers were personas non gratis in our household. My own hadn't been in touch ever since I'd moved to Scotland.

Nanna and Mum were wise enough to wait a good ten minutes before throwing their tuppence in. We'd just rounded a particularly hair-raising bend when my mum piped up, "Well! I thought he seemed to have turned over a new leaf," at the same time as Nanna said, "Once a violent man, always a violent man!"

Mum sniffed. "It might be nice for your child to have *one* grandfather around. I did let yours know you were pregnant, Gaby."

And guess what? He hadn't been in touch.

"Why you ever married that absolute dust-bag, Mandy, I will never know."

Nanna Cooper from the back seat. Not 100 percent au fait with modern slang. Mum, who agreed with her about my father's status, argued back anyway, this being the default way they interacted.

"There's Ranald," I said. "Jack calls Ranald Dad, and you should see him with Tamar. He's a natural with babies."

The Welcome to Lochalshie sign loomed into view.

"What are you going to tell Jack, love?" Mum asked, swivelling in her seat so she could look at me. She'd told Nanna there was no way on earth she'd manage the journey back unless she was in the front seat on the way back.

"The truth," I said. But when Jack asked my opinion— *what d'you think, Gaby? Do you want our child to have a relationship with his grandfather/a grandfather*, what was I going to say?

"Are you going to get in touch with him?" I asked. "He seemed anxious to talk to you."

We were curled up together on the sofa, having waved goodbye to Mum and Nanna earlier in the day. Bless 'em, they'd done their best to stay out of my way when I was working, but exaggerated tip-toeing around the sitting room rarely works.

The four days meant I had to watch a lot of soaps too, Nanna desperate not miss the goings-on of everyone in EastEnders, Coronation Street and Emmerdale. She even stumbled on the Scottish one, River City which only went out north of the border and declared herself hooked.

Jack caught hold of my fingers, whisking them away from my belly. The skin on my stomach had started to itch like mad, the combination my mother-in-law told me, of skin stretching and prickly heat. The other night, I'd attacked the area just above my groin so hard I'd drawn blood.

"I don't know. And I've no energy left to mull it over."

What I'd thought. Following on from our argument last

year, I wasn't prepared to offer any advice on how Jack dealt with his father.

Mildred wandered in and yowled, an instruction often meaning shift yourself humans and adjust your laps so I may sit there. As Jack shuffled up, so his knees were in plain sight, I repeated Katya's advice on getting your cat ready for a baby.

"Wouldn't it be easier to…" He shut up, my sharp intake of breath sounding like a warning. No. We would NOT be ridding ourselves of Mildred. Unaware of his treacherous thoughts, she curled up on his lap anyway, and he stroked her under her chin.

"I'm sure she'll be fine. Anyway, big day tomorrow, Gaby-sketch."

Tomorrow, we were going to the hospital at Lochgilphead for the 21-week scan. The scan where we could, if we chose, find out if our little home was about to become even more gender imbalanced than it already was—me and Mildred versus Jack. His hand returned to my belly, hand rubbing lightly to relieve the itchiness but careful not to use his nails.

"Mmm-hmm. Do you think…?"

… there is actually a baby inside me, and this huge bump hasn't just been caused by too many pizzas and an excess of shortbread? Did every first-time pregnant woman watch her body explode and worry like mad that what was inside them wasn't an actual human being? Jack had once made me watch Alien with him. There ought to be a warning before that film starts—Please note. If you ever intend to get pregnant in the future, viewing this film is not advised.

Or, and I squirmed uncomfortably, what if the baby wasn't… y'know. Okay?

Jack tipped Mildred off his lap and pulled me in close,

dropping a kiss on the top of my head. The scan would tell us if the baby were developing as it should. After that first hint of a flutter we decided afterwards had only been our imagination, there had been no movement at all. My working week had thrown up tonnes of problems, not least Marty's continued lateness, and I'd woken up most nights at 3am, hideous thoughts pinging around in my head.

Heaven knew how I would manage sleeping tonight.

Chapter Nineteen

The hospital visit began didn't start well, thanks to us arriving half an hour behind schedule.

The NHS prefers you to arrive on time and then wait two hours while they run late, rather than the other way around. The receptionist in the maternity clinic tutted when we got there, panting at her desk, me apologising profusely and blaming the traffic—a lame excuse when you live somewhere where the rush hour lasts 60 seconds tops.

She cast her eyes upwards at the clock. "Take a seat. There is no guarantee when you'll be seen."

The waiting room's occupants greeted us cheerily—a woman announcing loudly, "Dinnae mind her, hen. Someone must ha' shat on her cornflakes this morning," which made the receptionist send her a death stare.

The woman, who looked a few years younger than me, patted the seat beside her and introduced herself as Britney. Yes, named after the pop star. She was going to follow the family tradition and call her wean Taylor if the baby was a girl and Justin for a boy.

"What about Lady Gaga?" I threw in. "Be unusual in the playground."

Britney nodded thoughtfully. "Aye, I like that. Or mebbe Blac Chyna. Goes better wi' Birnie, ma second name."

By the time we were called through 45 minutes later, I'd heard her entire life story up to and including all the intimate details of her baby's conception. Proof, Britney said, that lassies should not believe that old wives' tale about not getting pregnant if your man took you up against a wall.

"Repeat offender," the nurse who led us along the corridor, whispered. "Baby number five that one and her only 24."

The sonographer beamed at us when we walked in, my eyes immediately drawn to the bed next to a large computer screen.

"Gabrielle McAllan?" she said, consulting the notes she held.

"Call me Gaby." I shook her hand. Her name badge said Sheila Murdoch. Maybe she preferred formality, but I was going to use her first name, seeing as she was about to touch my stomach and stare at my insides.

"And you're"—a quick glance at my stomach—"only 21 weeks. Goodness me. You are showing big, aren't you?"

"Genetic," I snapped. "My mother was the same with me and my brother."

Next to me, Jack shifted from foot to foot. "Sorry," I said. "Everyone keeps telling me how huge I am."

Sheila nodded. "You tell them to eff off from now on. Get up on the bed, and I'll get ye scanned and checked."

My already jangling nerves intensified—heart thudding so loudly everyone must be able to hear it. Jack had listened to Britney while we waited as he had no choice. But he leant in when she told us how every scan she'd had over the years had never shown anything wrong. The words must have comforted him. As I swung my legs up onto the bed and lay back, he took the chair next to me and gripped my hand—eyes darting between the sonographer and her screen.

"Right, Gaby hen," Sheila said. "Undo your trousers and raise your T-shirt to your chest. This might be a wee bittie cold."

Hands tucked under my arms as I held up my T-shirt, I yelped as she applied gel, making Jack smile. Did they store that stuff in a freezer?

"D'ye want to know the sex?" Sheila asked, probe hovering above my stomach. "Mind, I cannae be 100 percent accurate."

Ah. The all-important question. We'd discussed it last night, having decided at the start no, we don't care. Jack asked me again last night and this morning. Which led to endless back and forths. *No, I'm okay not knowing. But we can if you want*, both of us trying to second-guess what the other felt deep down.

In the end, we settled it by tossing a coin. I know. Serious life decisions shouldn't be made this way. But when the 10p landed heads up—not knowing—Jack's grin matched mine, the right choice then.

Sheila pulled up the chair opposite Jack and turned the screen to face her. She ran the probe over my stomach, the pressure of it making me faintly queasy. In my head, the probe had zig-zagged a few times before the sonographer turned to me and said, "Everything is fine!"

Instead, Sheila moved it super-slowly. The screen in front of her flickered, but nothing appeared. Jack tightened his grip. I battled panic. Then, there it was—a triangular image and an active, steady whup-whup noise that slowly began to make sense. Sure, Sheila had to explain most of it to us—ah, so that was the head—but I felt as if I was finally grasping the reality of giving birth to an actual baby in 25 weeks.

"You're no' 21 weeks, by the way," Sheila threw in. "Closer to 23, I reckon. Explains that showing big thing a bit better, eh?"

Oh. And Oh. I recalculated my maternity leave, figured it didn't make that much difference and exchanged panicky looks with Jack. Okay then. We weren't prepared for a due date of mid-December. Now it had been fast-forwarded. Argh…

Checks made and a pass on them all, she asked if we wanted a picture. One that would not reveal the baby's sex.

I said no at the same time as Jack said yes. We might as well, he said, clutching my hand. His mother would be champing at the bit to see it. As would mine.

"You can always put it on Instagram," he added, winking. (That too had been a discussion where I'd argued that people who posted their scan pics were the pits.)

We passed Britney on the way out, standing in the car park and on her phone. From the conversation I overheard, she was ordering her boyfriend to make his way to the local Tesco's and shoplift pregnancy vitamins for her, and to throw in a tray of Krispy Kreme donuts while he was at it to help with her cravings. Not sure that would be as easy to nick.

"How do you feel?" Jack asked, the photo held tightly, as we sat in the car.

"Weirded out," I said, "but at least when yet another person remarks on how big I am, I can tell them I'm more advanced than we thought."

He nodded. "Are you in a hurry to get back?"

It wasn't a great day, weather-wise. Grey clouds blocked out most of the sun, but at least it was dry.

"No," I said. Blissful Beauty got their pounds-worth of flesh out of me every day. Sod them and their dumb pharmaceutical strength skincare. "You?"

Ditto Jack and the Lochside Welcome. Sod the tourists, the locals and their demands for drinks, food, and a place to sleep for the night.

"Good," he said, turning the key. "I packed you some overnight stuff and asked Mum to look after Mildred for us. Let's escape."

We headed for Plockton—the A82 quieter than usual thanks to a less than sunny day. "Promise me you haven't booked us a room at the Inn," I said as we waited in the car waiting for the huge Highland cow to move from her position plonked in the middle of the twisty single-tracked road that led to the village.

The Plockton Inn and I had history of the embarrassing kind. We'd stayed there last year, me deciding the voice that called out 'room service' was Jack surprising me. Indeed a surprise for the teenager Jack had asked to deliver champagne when the woman who opened the door to him had no clothes on.

Too much to hope that the traumatised teen kept his mouth shut afterwards. No, no… ordering dinner later, he and the bartender, burst out laughing when the waiter made a joke about the dish of the day.

"Dressed crab," he'd smirked. "From a recipe by Jamie Oliver—y'know, the one they call the Naked Chef."

Jack joined them. The disloyalty!

The cow lumbered to her feet, and Jack took off the hand brake. "No," he said, grinning at me, as he turned right before the village, heading up a hill that overlooked the harbour with its fringing of palm trees that always looked incongruous in Scotland. A boat was returning to the jetty —one of the seal tours that took place every day in the summer, its occupants wrapped up well against the cold.

The car turned into a sweeping driveway, turrets ahead of me. "Is that…?" I twisted in my seat to face him.

He nodded. "Yup. If you're gonnae skive off work might as will do it properly, eh?"

I clapped my hands. "But isn't it expensive?"

"Ma lady is worth it. But in this case, I got a discount because I've recommended the place over the years to tourists."

By now, we'd arrived. Duncraig Castle wasn't old by Scottish castle standards. It had been built in the 1860s and even had its own tiny railway station. It had been extensively refurbished over the years, Jack told me as we made our way to the reception, and we had the remainder of the afternoon to explore the grounds and woods around us.

"Sod that," I said, once we got to the room. Not one but two free-standing copper baths in the ensuite and a bed so vast and sumptuous it screamed at me to jump on it. "A bath, room service and bed. Not necessarily in that order."

Jack dropped our bags where he stood. "Okay then. Good job I thought ahead and packed bubble bath. Shall we try them out?"

Later, the bath and bed activities satisfactorily concluded, I lay in Jack's arms as he scanned the room service menu. "All

I want is a sandwich," he grumbled. "And not a smoked salmon one either. Cheese and pickle or ham and mustard will be fine."

He wriggled his arm free and stood up, the light in the room, picking out the red gold of the hair on his head and chest. "Two rounds do you, Gaby?"

I propped myself up on my elbows. "As long as that's for me alone, and order two lots of chips too. I expect they won't mind what you order seeing as it's so expensive anyway."

Order phoned down to reception, he threw me one of the pristine white bathrobes. "Best put that on so we look respectable when the food arrives."

Like all bathrobes you get in hotels, they'd erred on the ginormous size. As everything else felt tight these days, I revelled in putting something on that wrapped around me effortlessly. The waiter who brought our food—sandwiches and chips covered in large pewter domes and wheeled in on a wood-panelled and tempered glass trolley cart—didn't bat an eye when he saw us.

The room included a massive, cream coloured sofa and coffee table. Jack pushed the trolley next to it and sat down beside me.

"I don't s'pose there will be any more opportunities to do this," I said. Jack kissed the top of my head and replied, "Exactly."

"Our lives are about to be ruin—I mean, changed. Forever."

He put his pint down "Sure. They are already, though, aren't they?"

Too right. Both of us working crazy hours having agreed to jobs that wouldn't have made sense even when I wasn't pregnant, never mind now. Jack had snatched my phone off me as soon as we'd booked in, promising me everything could wait until tomorrow. I knew I'd switch that thing on in the morning and find my inbox full to bursting, countless WhatsApp messages, and numerous texts, voice-mails and missed calls.

Then, there was the baby prep work I meant to do. When the little blue line showed up in the test, I'd bought one of those books, *Your Beautiful Pregnancy; The Yummy Mummy Guide*. Its recommenders included Kirsty—yes, that Kirsty, Jack's ex, and the Dating Guru herself. She wasn't, as far as I knew, pregnant herself, so her expertise in the preg-nancy area was debatable. But self-styled gurus rarely both-ered with qualifications. All you needed to do was sound super knowledgeable.

The beautiful pregnancy guide included chapters on what happened to your body and the developing foetus week by week and advice such as standing naked in front of mirrors, repeating, *'You're Beautiful, Fecund, Fertile and Amaz-ing'* twice a day. I hadn't bothered, imagining Katya and Mhari reading the advice out loud and snorting with laughter.

Perhaps if I had followed the advice of an expert, instead of worrying too much about what two women who'd never been pregnant thought, I wouldn't be feeling like this right now.

The panic I had experienced earlier in the day kicked in once more.

"Jack, I'm-I'm-I'm no-no-t ready! I'll do things like leaving it in Jamal's shop. Or, what if I don't love our child as much as Mildred!"

My husband's lips twitched. I scowled at him, and he altered his expression back to serious.

"On the other hand," I added, "I'm also worried I will

love our little one more than Mildred. Poor Mildred! She didn't sign up for this!"

Jack stroked my face, fingers sweeping from my temples past the cheeks to my jaw and back again. He said nothing but those dark eyes fixated on mine. If I had to take a guess at reading his mind, did his thoughts run along the lines, *Please, don't worry? Also, you're talking nonsense.*

The panic attack entered full throttle.

"I don't even call the baby him or her. It's an it, IT, Jack! Not even a 'they/them' so I can be woke and yet neutral at the same time. What if the baby isn't as good as Tamar? Everyone says he's marvellous. Ours might be much, much worse. We'll never get a full night's sleep again for a hundred years, and as for having fun, or even—"

A hand gently shoved a sandwich in my mouth. "Shush. And eat that. If you leave the baby in Jamal's shop, he or Enisa will look after him, her, it, them. They've got four weans themselves, so they know what they're doing. Seeing as you love Mildred a lot, if you love our baby say three-quarters as much as you love her, that will be fine. We're not going to live another hundred years, so the chances of getting a brilliant night's sleep before the 22nd century kicks in are not that bad."

I took another mouthful of my super-late lunch. Low blood sugars triggered mood swings, didn't they? A giant helping of bread would cheer me up.

"Call whatever is inside you whatever you want," Jack continued, tips of his fingers brushing my nose. "No-one cares. And finally, my mum, your mum, your Nanna Cooper if she ever gets the chance, Jolene and Stewart, maybe even Katya and Dexter will all queue up to offer overnight babysitting, so we get to... y'know."

There was too much pickle in my sandwich, a mistake

I'd pay for with indigestion half an hour from now. Nevertheless, I ate it all anyway. "What, McAllan? Make brothers and sisters for baba number one? You are not getting anywhere near me ever again unless you've had a vasectomy *and* are covered by two condoms!"

He glanced at his crotch. "If you say so, Gaby. Though I think a vasectomy usually does the job thoroughly enough. Now, is there any chance I can get some of those chips before you polish them all off…?"

He should have known better. I ate them in record quick time, stuffing them into my mouth and doing my best hamster impression. The carb overload worked its magic, sending me straight to the land of nod half an hour later, my head in his lap as we watched an old film.

When I did wake hours later in the sumptuous big bed I did not remember climbing into, I prodded myself. *Better, Gaby? Okay about being a mum very, very soon? I think so, yes…*

The space next to me was unoccupied. I surfaced groggily—where was Jack? As my eyes adjusted, I made him out stood at the bay window, bathrobe on and staring out at the darkness.

"Jack?" I padded my way over. "Are you okay?"

For a half-second, I didn't recognise him when he turned to face me. I flashed back to the first time I met him —Mr Pissed Off because I'd turned up two hours late for a key handover. Eyes bleak, face rigid and tiny tic pulsing at his jaw.

"Jack?"

"Couldn't sleep." His expression relaxed, and he extended an arm. I snuggled in. Lights illuminated the grounds—flower beds, shrubs and even a sundial. Jack pointed at something—a fox, its silhouette picked out as it ran from one side of the garden to the other.

Another one appeared and then another—two smaller foxes that trotted over to join the first one. They must be her cubs. "Oh!" I exclaimed. "That must mean something. A good omen, don't you think?"

He waited far too long before answering me. "Gaby, I'm…"

"What? The best-looking man I've ever been fortunate enough to sleep with? An incredibly talented hotel manager? The man about to be the best father in the world."

At that, he shifted so that we stood facing each other. "D'ye think? My mum telt me years ago my father changed when I came along. He'd always been a drinker, but he got violent after I was born. She didnae ken why. What if… what if…"

"No!" The force startled us both. "No! No! No!"

I clasped both his hands in mine, nails digging into his skin hard enough to make him wince.

"See? I'm the violent one in this relationship!"

A stupid joke, but I took heart when he smiled.

"You are not," I said, "and never have been, your father. Look at how you are with Mildred!"

Admittedly, not as sappy as me. Jack didn't resort to speaking to Mildred in a silly voice where he told her she was his bestest, loveliest littly-piddly doodley dumpling girl. But he encouraged her to sleep on our bed, searching for her when she didn't materialise there in the evenings. He loved to swoop her up for a cuddle too—Mildred wasn't quite as keen—and he ordered her toys from Pets At Home all the time.

"Maybe I won't love her/him/it/them as much as Mildred."

My own words.

"And if you do two-thirds as much that will be perfectly okay."

He smiled again. But briefly. "I don't want him anywhere near our child, Gaby."

"No problem. We'll manag—"

"I'm serious. I know you thought he was okay when you met him in Oban the other week but—"

"Shush," I said, standing on tiptoe so I could peck him on the lips. "We'll do whatever you want. Ranald's your real father. Come back to bed."

He followed me, seemingly falling asleep quickly when his head sank back onto the pillow.

But I was awake once more, back to fretting. All the things to worry about list. Longer than ever.

Chapter Twenty

"I'm stocking up on baby milk, so I'm ready for when McAllan Junior puts in an appearance," Jamal said, pointing at my belly.

He held up a tin of follow-on milk, shaking it from side to side. Where on earth would he put his baby products? As it was, every shelf in the place groaned and sagged, surfaces packed with goods. It was mid-day Saturday, and I'd spent the morning catching up with the work I'd missed out on Thursday and Friday thanks to the hospital visit and unscheduled skive off work.

"You're entitled to the time off," Jack grumbled when I told him what I planned that morning. True, but when we'd returned early on Friday morning, he dumped me back home and hurried off to the Lochside Welcome terrified the place might have exploded in his absence.

Friday passed in a blur. Ditto Saturday morning. I picked up the phone to call my mum late on Friday afternoon—*right, Mother! My birth. Dylan's. Every gritty detail. Do not hold back!* So far, no mothers I knew had seen fit to enlighten me on what childbirth was really like. Time, I decided to prepare myself for what lay ahead.

Dexter phoned at that precise second. "Super-amazing designs for the exfoliating pads, Gaby! You are, like, a genius!"

My heart sank.

"And I had this, like, wild idea. What if you…"

Five frustrating hours later, Dexter decided his wild idea was a no-goer. One, Logan said to me in a private bitchy message, I should have had the good sense to tell him myself. Further proof of how truly rubbish a boss I was. I added that worry—*why am I in charge, I hate it and I'm useless at it*—to the ever-growing list of things to keep me awake at night. Likewise, I was no further forward equipping myself with the knowledge of childbirth that would dissipate my fears. Or not. Ignorance, I told myself, insisted in fact, was bliss.

In the shop, I dumped my basket on the counter on tops of the newspapers. "Ah, no need to stock up, Jamal," I said, "because I'm planning to… um, y'know."

Oh, this was ridiculous. I'd developed a modesty issue which meant I was unable to say the word bre-bre-bre—see? Totally stupid, compounded when I ended up pointing at mine anyway, today covered by a shirt, the buttons straining. Jamal glanced there, the two of us meeting eyes when he did so and hastily looking away. Awks.

"Good, good!" He compensated with too much enthusiasm. "Excellent for the wean. If ye ask Enisa, she can gie you some tips."

Jamal and Enisa had four kids, ranging in age from nine to 19. All lively and noisy. Feeding tips maybe. I'd look elsewhere for parenting advice.

Jamal's expression changed—the narrowing of eyes and

biting of his top lip, making him look calculating. He ducked out under the counter and emerged with a small bag of baby bibs. "Enisa said you could have these. D'ye want the pink ones or the blue ones, Gaby?"

Nice try. I gave him my sweetest smile. "The white ones will do us nicely, thanks Jamal."

I left the shop and made my way to the pharmacy where Mhari worked. I might have managed to deflect Jamal's less-than-subtle attempts to worm the baby's gender out of me. Mhari was a different matter entirely. Sure enough, when I bought my pregnancy vitamins, she asked if the scan pic showed that the baby was the spit of Jack waiting for me to say, yes, he/she is or isn't.

"The baby," I said, "is a perfect blend of Jack and me."

Katya caught up with me as I left the shop. The High Street was busy. The English school holidays were well underway, which had led to a flood of visitors. Many people came for the walking, others for the remote location. I spotted minibuses—the Highland Tours one outside the Lochside Welcome once more, and a group dressed in waterproofs piling out and into the hotel. Unfortunately, three coaches had parked in the Royal George's car park, no doubt attracted by the smell of fish and chips coming from the van that was part of the hotel.

"How did the scan go on Thursday?" she asked, taking my bag from me. I attempted a half-hearted wrestle of it back. All I had in there was a packet of ham and a loaf of bread. She took it anyway.

"Fine. Although we got a bit of a shock because I hadn't got the dates right, so I'm now coming up for 24 weeks, not 22. Other than that, everything is progressing as it should."

"What did the baby look like?"

About to leap in with the answer, I stopped and folded my arms. "I know what you're doing!"

Katya widened her eyes. "What am I doing?"

"You're trying to trip me up, so I say, 'he looks like' or 'she looks like'. I got a similar question from Mhari. Are you a tag team or what?"

"You didn't give it away to her, did you?" Katya demanded. "We've got a bet on. The first to get the sex out of you wins the right to decide what we watch on Netflix for a week."

Sneaky of them too, thinking they would trick me into revealing all with one innocent-sounding question. Everyone was at it—even if it was a pointless exercise.

I thumped Katya's arm lightly. "We told the sonographer not to tell us, Jack and I genuinely don't know if we're having a boy or a girl, so there's no point to these trick questions."

"Fair enough," Katya said. "Can I buy you lunch?"

"Bored of the billionaire and her inability to see exactly what is in front of her?" I asked, and she nodded.

"Absolutely. I'm half-way through writing the book and have no idea how I'm going to stretch this out for another ten chapters. Let's drop your shopping off and go and get something to eat."

Katya surprised me by turning right when we left our house instead of left.

"Where are we going?" I squawked, hurrying after her as she strode towards the Royal George, its entrance an enormous wrought iron gate that opened into a car park and a colonnaded front.

"What does it look like?" She stopped, gesturing towards the van which was parked around the front affording those sitting at the tables and chairs the best view of the loch. Today, I'd woken up to sunshine and (almost) cloud-free skies, Jack watching the view hopeful but wary. Glorious sunshine did miraculous things—bringing tourists to Lochalshie in their hundreds.

"We're off to check the opposition so we can report back to Jack and try to find out what Miles is up to," Katya announced.

"Oh? That's what we're doing. Not popping in here just because Zac is back in Lochalshie?"

She had the grace to look shamefaced. "Well, maybe a bit. But it will be useful. And aren't you curious? Come on."

I ducked behind the parked coaches so no-one would be able to see me from the street. If we were seen going into the Royal George, someone would report it to Jack straight away. My name would be muck. Much better to tell him when we'd had our lunch, *and* I had useful info at my fingertips.

Katya pointed at a table at the far side of the garden in front of the Royal George. A large parasol advertised an expensive brand of craft gin, and she opened it to shelter us from the sunshine, the canvas unfurling stiffly—a rare day— one in the Highlands where you squinted thanks to too bright sunshine. Parasols in beer gardens got little use in these parts, and the one she opened sprayed out welcome droplets of cold rainwater. She sat down, moving her bench out from under its shade and sitting down, eyes closed as she soaked in the sun.

I did the same underneath the parasol. Two-plus years in the Highlands had turned me Scottish in my weather outlook. Any temperature of more than 20 degrees made me mutter about global warming, and how hot I was.

The man in the fish and chip van stuck his head out, clocking Katya right away. He froze there, the small group at the hatch having to repeat their order for deep-fried calamari and chips. (Yes, it was *that* kind of fish and chips place.) Katya's eyes opened, her face twisting, so she and Zac stared at each other. You could almost see the line that joined one set of eyeballs to the other. His eyes dropped, taking every bit of her in.

Adorned by silver threads, her flared sleeves green top stopped under her bust, Pilates-toned tummy on view. (*One day, Gaby,* I promised myself, *I'll be back wearing that kind of stuff again.*) The matching skirt fell to mid-calf, feet shod in silver platform sandals and her hair pulled back in a messy bun.

No wonder Zac stared.

I stood up. "Shall I get the fish and chips? Just the chips for you, Katya seeing as you are plant-based most of the time? Mushy peas and tonnes of vinegar, right? Gosh, I'm hungry. I want the fish too. As you know, it's supposed to be good for your baby's brain. This better be as amazing as it smells! I'll just head over there now before the queue gets too long and—"

Wittering. Works like a magic power to distract someone when you're terrified that they are about to make a colossal mistake, such as reigniting a spark that I thought had been extinguished some time ago.

Did I say works like magic? I meant, not at all. Katya marched off, and I collapsed back on the bench and fanned my flushed face with a menu.

A waiter appeared, dressed in the Hammerstone Hotels green and gold colours, the T-shirt showing sweat circles under the arms. Heat and having to do far too much running around.

He stopped at my table, took one look at me, and about turned.

"Hey!"

He shuffled back, face hangdog. "Gaby, you'll no' say anything to anyone will ye?"

The waiter was one of Mhari's many cousins and also related to Ashley.

I shook my head wearily. "No, I'll keep it zipped."

I didn't blame him. Hammerstone Hotels offered its staff the chance to move around. Start in Lochalshie, end up in Glasgow, London, Cornwall. Or, the gold prize, New York.

"Can I get you a drink?" he asked.

"Yes please. A pint of tap water with ice and lemon, ta."

No point in asking for anything else, the prices here would be astronomical. He brought me a sparkling water anyway as a reward for my discretion.

I'd finished the glass by the time Katya returned bearing welcome gifts of fish and chips in cones made of fake newspaper. She took the seat opposite mine, allowing her a direct eye line to Zac. His eyes seemed to bore through my back straight at her. I risked a quick look behind me. Yup, chatting and laughing with those people queuing but attention firmly on my friend, eyes landing all too frequently on Katya's cleavage.

She broke off a bit of battered fish, ignoring my remark about it not fitting the vegan diet model in any shape or form, dunked it in tartare sauce, bit down hard, chewed slowly, and licked her lips.

"D'you mind?" I said. "I'd rather not witness food

flirting while I eat. I'm still suffering from nausea most days. Don't make me want to throw up again."

She glared at me. "I'm *not* flirting."

"If you say so. Looks that way too—"

"Gaby! Lovely to see you here. And congratulations, by the way. Bet you and Jack are excited."

Too late. The man himself slid next to me, positioning himself, so he was knee to knee with Katya, big blue eyes wide and sparkling with mischief His hands, I was willing to bet, itched to slide Katya's sleeves off her shoulders as his lips moved down her neck.

Slowly.

I fanned myself with the menu once more.

"We are, thank you Z—"

"What do you think of the fish and chips, Katya?" he cut across me and grinned at her. "You promised me a blistering review."

Said with all the cocky confidence of a man who knows his food is sublime. And it was. Katya had stopped eating, but I dug in wolfing flaky, light fish and super-crisp batter all doused with malt vinegar so strong it made you suck in your cheeks.

Katya broke off another bit of her fish, scooped up the tartare sauce with her finger and pushed both into her mouth. I squirmed. Me, the spare part and no further forward in our original mission—the one where we found out how he knew Miles and what they were up to.

"The batter could do with more time in the fryer. It's a little too anaemic for me," Katya said, making Zac's grin widen. "And if you'd made the tartare sauce with homemade mayonnaise instead of bought stuff, I'd have given you ten out of ten. As it is… seven and a half."

Blimey. Praise and a half. Katya never gave anything

more than a six. Too many good reviews, she said, made people complacent. Zac recognised it for the compliment it was as well, a genuine smile replacing the cocky grin. Once upon a time, he'd worked in a Michelin-starred restaurant. Katya's praise obviously outdid any professional critic.

As I appeared to be superfluous to proceedings, I glanced around me. Not good at all. Yes, the last time I'd been in the Lochside Welcome it too had been jam-packed. But nothing like this. The three luxury coaches in the car park at the George had stickers advertising the origins of the visitors they'd dropped off—France, Germany and Japan.

Every table outside was taken. The George's lounge bar also looked out onto the loch, and it was packed to capacity. A team of waiters glided silently among the tables, delivering food and drinks, and whisking away empty glasses and dirty plates.

Tourists chatted, laughed and took loads of selfies of themselves in front of glorious views, Maggie Broon' Boobs in the background. If I checked the George's Instagram account, it would be chocka. Loads of photos and stories, all hashtagged #RoyalGeorge #TrueScotland #Highland-Escapes.

The Royal George advertised heavily. As it was part of a chain, the hotel was able to spend lavish money on making sure it appeared in the right places. And it was on all those hotel discount sites where you got a bargain price for a two-day break in a five-star hotel. As we lived so near the George, Jack saw the coaches and crowded car park every day. I watched him when he left the house every day, his head turning left, face tightening as he counted the cars and coaches.

I cleared my throat. "So how do you know Miles, Zac?"

Zac blinked, breaking off from exchanging flirty banter with Katya. She did too. Suddenly remembering that she was someone else's girlfriend? They shifted positions. If I ducked under the table now to check, I suspected I would find knees no longer nestled so closely together.

"He's…"

"What, Zac?" Katya asked. "One of your chums from public school?"

He shook his head. "Someone I know through someone else. Small world and all that."

Hmm. Zac looked distinctly uncomfortable. I thought back to Miles' remark when Mhari asked him why he and Tindra were in the village. A friend had recommended it as a lovely place to visit.

"Busy in here," Katya said, tilting her head towards the crowds of people surrounding us.

"A wedding," Zac muttered, "tomorrow. A lot of the guests decided to make the most of it and come today. Some travel guy on Instagram visited the other week and recommended us."

Huh. And another blasted wedding. I bet he thought the Royal George was doing tonnes better than the Lochside Welcome under Jack.

"You know Miles has spoken to us about pitching an idea to Netflix?" I said, finishing off the last of my chips. (Whisper it—they might have been better than those the Lochside Welcome offered… Gaby McAllan, wash your mouth out.)

"It's a docu-series about brilliant pubs in the UK, ones at the heart of the community. The Lochside Welcome is to feature. Heavily," injecting the tone with a tonne of confidence. Unseen by Zac, Katya shook her head, putting her index finger to her lips. I shot her a 'what?' look, the head-shaking intensified.

"How amazing," Zac said, arms folded on the table. Sarcasm or insincerity? Possibly both. What I didn't detect was envy, which set alarm bells ringing. Why wasn't he bothered by the mega dose of free publicity that might be coming the Lochside Welcome's way?

"I wouldn't hold my breath, though," he continued. "TV companies look at lots of different options before they make their mind up. They'll tell you how amazing you are, be all over you for a month or so and then vanish without a trace."

Oftentimes I had to remind myself that I'd reached a stage in life where I was supposed to leave childish things behind, the temptation to blow a huge raspberry in his smug face now, for example. It was time to get out of here. The longer I sat at the table, the more disloyal I felt. As if the Royal George were attaching invisible strings to me that would prevent me from moving from its grounds.

"I'm off," I said. "Thanks for buying me the food, Katya. She's right, though." I stood up and looked Zac in the eye. Katya might think his blue eyes twinkly. I considered them deeply suss, the eyes of a practised liar. Brown eyes are much better.

"The batter was far too anaemic. Best you keep practising."

The dramatic exit was hindered when Katya didn't follow me, waving aside my request that she accompany me to the "much, much nicer Lochalshie pub".

If we hadn't been surrounded by so many people, I

might have dragged her out. I made do with telepathy. *Do NOT fall for this terrible git again!*

Stewart spotted me coming out of the car park, Scottie bolting towards me tail wagging from side to side. Tamar was strapped to his chest once more and greeted me with coos.

"What were ye daein' in there?" Stewart asked, shooting the hotel filthy looks. Stewart had never set foot in the place, mainly because of how much it charged rather than any nobler reasons. When you drank as much as Stewart had done in his alcohol-soaked days, you needed your local to be as cheap as possible.

"Checking out the opposition," I said. "Dirty tactics."

Scottie backed me up on that one, choosing to poop prodigiously just inside the gate to the car park. Finished— me breathing through my mouth to avoid the smell—he wagged his stumpy white tail furiously.

"Stewart," I said, as the two of us scuttled away before anyone saw us, "responsible pet ownership is a fine thing but if you leave that there this one time, I won't tell anyone."

He nodded. "Aye, fine. Good dog, Scottie. Are ye off to the Lochside Welcome? Ma Jolene's there this afternoon. Could mebbe do wi' a hand as that agency waiter didnae show up."

I stopped to stare at him, incredulous. Did the bump not give away my non-suitability as a barmaid?

"What don't you help her out?"

He shook his head. "Naw, Gaby. I've got Tamar wi' me. And it would be too triggerin' for me. I'd be suppin' folks' pints at the same time as delivering them."

No arguing with that, was there? We set off, him treating me to a minute-by-minute account of his day so far and all the words young Tamar was now able to say. None of which Tamar managed to demonstrate, mouth remaining pursed shut when Stewart told him to repeat various things.

Someone—Jolene—I suspected, had tidied up the window boxes and plant pots around the Lochside Welcome, filling them with seasonal plants and flowers. A riot of pink and purple clematis and busy Lizzies that made the white of the painted stone walls stand out. Call me biased, but on a sunny day, the Royal George's grandeur faded next to the pure cosiness of the Lochside Welcome.

The public bar was noisy. It was nowhere near as busy as the George, but its smaller space packed in people who all grinned at each other and chattered loudly. From the snatches of conversations I caught, I gathered most of them were part of a hillwalking group from Glasgow who'd looked at the weather forecast this morning, circled the loch and descended on the village. They'd booked every room and were now desperate to knock back pints, pizzas, cake and whiskies.

Jack stood at the bar, fixed smile in place as two of the walkers their status marked by lightweight cagoules and sturdy boots, exclaimed at his resemblance to Jamie Fraser.

"'Mon, 'mon!" they cried. "We want a selfie wi' you!"

He pushed up the serving hatch, gamely putting an arm around each woman. I watched one of them—a woman who had to be twice Jack's age—let her hand linger far too close to his bottom as she and her friend cuddled up either side of him. A third one took hundreds of pictures.

"Gaby!" His greeting sounded relieved. "Maureen, Louisa—this is Gaby, my wife."

Emphasis on wife. Maureen made no move to drop her hand.

"That right, hen? You're an awfy lucky girl," she

beamed at me. "Mind, when ma daughter was up the duff last year, by the time she got to the nine-month mark, she went right off the bed bit. Me and ma friend here would be happy to help youse out. We could take yer man up they stairs and exhaust him so much, he'll no' touch ye for months."

My jaw dropped, as did Jack's though his expression was 100 percent pure fear. Behind the bar, there were snorts of laughter. Jolene and Xavier listening in and doing nothing to help us out. As soon as I got home, I was going to design a poster for the bar. One that made it clear in gigantic capital letters that the Lochside Welcome did not tolerate abusive, sexist behaviour towards its staff.

"An extremely kind offer," I replied, nodding at them both graciously. "Luckily, I am only at the five-and-a half-month mark."

Maureen's turn to stare. "Are ye haein' twins?"

The 100 percent fear face went full-on terror. While Jack and I agreed, two was a lovely number, having two kids at the same time did not appeal at all. Anyway, the scan I'd just had shown one baby only—as Jack well knew.

"No. Just the one," my words addressed as much to Jack as Maureen. He didn't need to know I'd gone home after the scan appointment and googled hidden twins on ultrasound. Rare, but possible according to the worldwide web.

Maureen let go of Jack, pinching his bicep. "Aye, well. Youse'll hae a bonny bairn, especially if it takes after its daddy. Fancy another bottle o' Prosecco, Louisa?"

Louisa nodded. Xavier uncorked the wine, the soft pfft of it raising a cheer from Maureen and Louisa's companions and handed it over. The women took it and headed back to their table, reminding Jack with a cackle that their offer still stood.

He pulled me in for a hug, the smell of pizza, chips and spilt whisky clinging to him. Underneath, I detected the faint trace of sweat. It had been another early start. "Myself," he whispered, words caressing my ear. "Will be over the moon if the wean looks exactly like its mum."

"Aye, aye Jack, met this yin comin' out of the Royal George."

Stewart, the man for whom the words 'impeccable timing' had been invented. Scottie had dived under the tables nearest the bar, his favourite spot for rich pickings. My other half stiffened, and I sensed rather than heard collective boos from the regulars at the bar.

"Katya said we should check out the opposition and report back," I protested.

Terry nodded. "Aye. Good idea. What price is a pint in that place, Gaby?"

"Fifteen pounds."

He and his buddies exchanged horrified glances demanding Xavier pour them two pints at once. Worried, I guessed, that Jack might get ideas and hike his prices up too. I hadn't noticed how much a pint cost. But no harm starting a rumour they were out of this world expensive. And making sure the hillwalkers heard me.

"So," Jack folded his arms. Pretend outrage. "What else did you find out?"

"Weeeellll… I didn't see anyone I recognised there."

Apart from the dastardly Zac, and the waiter who bought my silence with a free sparkling water.

"Was it busy?"

Katya always told me I was a rotten liar. My face almost always gave me away. I concentrated, desperate to spare Jack.

"A tiny bit. But it's a Saturday, right? Any hotel in this

part of the world is rammed with people at this time of year. Especially at the weekends and at lunchtime. Everyone wants fried haggis and chips. A true taste of the Highlands!"

Xavier appeared to be writing something down. Would the next iteration of Quebec Poutine feature chips, crumbled haggis, gravy and a fat dollop of melted cheese? Yes, if the Gods had anything to do with it.

Jack sighed, eyes closing briefly. *The over-cheeriness, Gaby*, I told myself. *Gave it all away.* How many of tomorrow's wedding guests had booked for tomorrow night as well? And had the coach parties all booked in too? Who among them had opted for the glamping?

(Yes, you could pay through the nose for a posh tent allowing you to kid yourself you were at one with the elements. The Royal George's grounds included tents with a loch view, heating and bottles of champagne in ice buckets. It tripled the number of 'beds' the hotel was able to offer. Today's warmth and sunshine made those tents much more attractive.)

Hammerstone Hotels must be raking in money this weekend. The Royal George had far more staff, tempting offers, better facilities and entertainment far more sophisticated than a weekly pub quiz... How could Jack compete? The shadows under his eyes tore at me, as did the crop of spots that had broken out on his forehead. Nothing to deter cougar-like hillwalkers, but stress-related for sure.

Xavier hovered nearby. "Ah, Jacques? We're getting a beet busy?"

(Bizeee... Why, why, why didn't that French accent do it for Mhari alone?)

I smiled at Jack—a 'see? There are tonnes of people in here too!' reassurance that I wasn't sure hit the mark. Jolene hurried past, summoned to the tables outside where people wanted to order. She shook her head when I asked if she needed my help. Fair enough. Jolene was smart enough to know I'd be more of a hindrance.

"What about if I do the washing up?" I tried as Jack ducked beneath the serving hatch once more. But the shouts from the hillwalkers at the other end of the bar drowned out my offer. Oh well. Fresh air and the beer garden beckoned. There, I wouldn't be under anyone's feet.

The planters were out here too, yesterday's rain and today's sunshine making the colours pop. I blinked. Most of the tables were occupied, but I spotted Mhari at the one nearest the loch, squinting at her phone. My mother-in-law often warned that staring at your mobile too often damaged your eyesight. At this rate, Mhari would be blind by the time she got to her 30th birthday.

"Mind if I join you?"

A shrug. Mhari's idea of a warm welcome.

"Hyun-Ki's havin' a fantastic time in LA," she sniffed, showing me the pictures and stories he'd posted to his Instagram account. I doubted they were representative. Given his workload, when did he have time to hang around all the city's coolest places firing off pictures left, right and centre? I made her pause, though, on the one where he visited a cat cafe and managed to get a picture of himself with five cats sitting at his feet. A more successful cat cafe visit than the one we'd had in London last year then.

(An unfortunate allergic reaction; one cat's bid for freedom.)

Xavier appeared, pizzas in each hand. He delivered them to the people at the next table, all three of them exclaiming in wonder at the size and smell. Hopefully, all of them would jump on TripAdvisor afterwards. *"We were served by a gorgeous guy! Almost—but not—quite as awesome as the pizzas he gave us!"* Or Instagram and counter all those Royal George hashtags with the far better ones, #LochsideWelcome4eva (I'd invented it. So far, it was yet to gain traction.)

Maureen and Louisa had followed Xavier out. Maureen's eyes honed on his bottom when he bent over to place the pizzas on the table. They took the table one down from us, Maureen's gawking something she didn't bother to hide when I glared at her.

Oblivious, Xavier wandered over to our table. As the not-so-much-in-charge person, under-eye circles and spots didn't trouble his complexion. Five weeks into being pregnant, my sense of smell had heightened disproportionately. Now it was my superpower. From Xavier, I detected wafts of freshly baked bread, basil and garlic. The cologne he wore—cedar? Mandarin?—underneath.

"Can I get you anything? A Chocolate Decadent dessert, Mah-ree?"

Even the way he said decadent made you want to fan yourself. Mah-ree, on the other hand, did not bother looking up from her phone. "No, ta. I've got tae get back to the chemist for the afternoon shift. It's goin' like a fair today."

"It is?" I asked, doing my best to imagine the pharmacy as busy. Impossible. Whenever I went in there, I was always the only customer. And everything on the shelf wore a dust overcoat. When I'd taken my mum there, she exclaimed at the make-up.

"They've got Miners' stuff, Gaby!"

I was the none the wiser.

"When I was a thirteen-year-old," she continued, deep down the nostalgia path, "Miners made this bright orange mascara I used to love. Amazing."

If you say so, Mum.

"What about if—" eef—"I give you a slice to take away with you?" Xavier asked Mhari, whose eyes remained firmly down. "Keep your energy levels up for the afternoon?"

And a free chocolate cake. What did the poor guy have to do to make Mhari sit up and pant as any other sane, straight, single woman would? I tried hinting at his fantastic potential, ducking my face, so I appeared in her sightline and jerking my forehead at him. She stared at me; top lip curled up puzzled.

"Gie it to Gaby."

Then, just in case I mistook that for a general softening in her attitude towards me, "Mind, dinnae add extra ice-cream. She's already wobbling aw' over the place."

I stuck my tongue out at her. Added two middle fingers stuck in the air in front of her face. Xavier smirked and disappeared back into the throng. He reappeared a minute later with a bowl of cake and two spoons.

"Where's Mah-ree?"

"Gone back to work," I said. "She was so sorry to miss you!"

Tiny, well total, exaggeration seeing as she'd said nothing of the sort. Another note to self—stop the hints and ask Mhari outright why she wasn't interested. If I weren't a happily hooked-up wife, I'd be asking Xavier out myself.

Just as I was tucking into my third ginormous spoonful of cake smothered in ganache, Katya waved at me from the doorway. I beckoned her over, anxious to know how the last of the encounter with Zac had gone. And that Katya hadn't made a colossal mistake. I checked her over. No sign of clothes hastily reapplied, or lipstick smeared across her face.

"You've just missed Mhari," I said as she sat down, dumping her bag and sunglasses on the table.

"That was deliberate. I saw her talking to you and

decided to wait. Otherwise, it would be all over Lochalshie that I'd dumped Dexter, declared undying love to Zac, and the two of us had run off to set up our own hotel in the Caribbean."

"Ha! Oh—er, that is a joke, isn't it?"

She plucked the fork from my hand and treated me to one of those stares I knew so well, having been the recipient of them for many years. Rough interpretation? *Duh, Gaby.* I pushed the plate towards her. Mhari's wobbling comment had not been kind (and yet another reason why she would never win the Supportive Friend of the Year award), but I missed my old skinny self even if I hadn't appreciated her at the time.

Katya dug in.

"Did you manage to get anything useful out of Zac?"

Cake finished in record time, she sat back face turned up to catch the sun (and to hide her face from me?). The rays caught her hair, making it shimmer.

"He did his best to convince me once more he is a trustworthy chap who means no harm to Lochalshie. I didn't buy it. But as I was leaving—"

Eyes closed or not, some sixth sense must have kicked in as Jack had appeared, that earlier frazzled air he'd worn intensified.

"I'm so sorry to ask, but would you mind helping me out, Katya? We're flat out, and we've run out of clean glasses and plates."

Katya leapt to her feet. "No worries. Though I'll take my payment in free beers. Gaby, come and sit in the kitchen with me? You won't need to do anything."

Jack thanked her profusely, reiterating that I should do nothing. He squeezed my hand as we moved past him. In the kitchen, stacked pint glasses and plates covered every surface, the problem exacerbated because one of the dish-washers was out of action. Katya pulled out a chair for me and handed over a dish towel, asking if I would be able to manage the odd plate.

"No problem!"

There was a knock on the door. Tindra stuck her head in. I hadn't realised she was back in the village. "Hey, d'you need a hand? Jack spotted me and suggested this would be the best way to find out what it's like running a hotel."

"Yes please!" replied Katya.

Tindra proved to be an excellent dishwasher, filling the one working dishwasher in record time and donning an apron so she could hand-wash the rest of the stuff. Katya took another dish towel, and they worked in harmony, clean plates soon outnumbering dirty ones. Jack looked in ten minutes later and blew us all kisses. I pretended not to notice when Tindra fluttered her eyelashes back at him.

We took a break after an hour; a lull thanks to it being 4pm and most people having finished lunch. Katya and Tindra joined me at the table in the middle of the room, Katya throwing down sopping wet dish towels on the table.

"You forget, don't you," she said, inspecting her finger-tips, the skin there white and wrinkled. "How exhausting this kind of menial work is."

Tindra nodded. "Reminds me of chalet work," the remark making Katya lift her head and roll her eyes at me. Chalet work. *Of course.* Posh girls' work, allowing them to ski in their time off.

"This will come in handy for the film, won't it?" I asked. "You've now got inside knowledge of how hard Jack and his team work, and what an important part of the community the Lochside Welcome is."

Tindra nodded and then looked dismayed. "Oh! I wish

Nina had been here. She could have filmed it. D'you think it will get this busy again?"

"Hopefully," I said, Katya butting in to ask if Netflix had given the go-ahead for the docu-series featuring the Lochside Welcome. She emphasised the name of the hotel.

"I don't know," Tindra shrugged. "There's a final meeting about it next week, so we'll know then. I'm, like, super-keen for us to make an amazing docu-series about a local pub. If Netflix says yes, Miles will need to take me on permanently as a researcher."

"Aren't you a researcher already?" I asked, mindful of the hours she'd spent in the Lochside Welcome (supposedly) finding out about the pub and its essential place in the local community.

"No, I'm only an intern," Tindra replied. "Miles can't afford to pay me at the moment."

Luckily for Tindra, she didn't notice the scowl Katya sent her way. Mine was directed at Miles. Unpaid labour just so you could put the experience on your CV. Unscrupulous businesses that took advantage of young people in a fiercely competitive labour market. How on earth did she manage without money?

Tindra must have sensed our question. "Um… my mum and dad set up a trust fund for my education years ago, and it included a gap year. I'm using that."

A double (silent) hiss from Katya and me, two people who'd needed to take the crappy jobs all the way through university and college and then leap into the first offers we got post-graduation thanks to not being born to wealthy parents.

Jack entered, his face showing how he was relieved to find clean glasses and plates. Would Katya and Tindra mind hanging on for another hour or so just in case…?

Tindra nodded eagerly. I tried not to mind her tongue practically hanging out whenever she looked at Jack. Later, as we all headed home, Tindra bidding us goodbye when she reached the door to the Airbnb next to Jamal's shop, Katya waited until she was out of earshot.

"Zac told me something when I was in the George earlier."

"Oh?"

"When he said Miles was someone he knew through other people. He meant Lois and Angeline."

Oh dear. Owners of Hammerstone Hotels. Drivers of too fast moss-green Jaguars. All-round schemers and evil witches.

"And when we overheard him with Miles talking about a meeting, that's who he meant. They're meeting with him on Monday. He promised me he didn't know what the meeting was about, but it's not hard to work out, is it?"

No. Not at all. And yet another spanner in the Lochside Welcome works.

Chapter Twenty-One

Sunday was a day off for both of us. Well, half a day. Xavier had come up with the idea of Sunday brunch at the Lochside Welcome—bacon, maple syrup and waffles for the cosmopolitan-minded, a fry-up for everyone else. Jolene was off, so Xavier needed help, especially because Lucas had promised he would drop off Highland Tour attendees at the hotel yet again.

Square sausage, tattie scones, haggis, bacon and eggs were, Jack told me, were the foods that had built Scotland. Was it not also responsible for the country's high incidence of heart attacks and strokes? I stifled the comment, kissed him goodbye and urged him to hurry home as soon as, so we could...

What? Chat about a meeting that was going ahead with Miles and the Hammerstone Hotels bosses next week and wonder what that meant. Talk about Jack's father who had since left several messages on the answering machine at the Lochside Welcome, calls unreturned? Discuss the baby and how utterly unprepared we were?

I spent the morning catching up on family phone calls then Mildred and I watched an episode of the Outlander series 5, Mildred agreeing with me that Jack was ten times better looking than Sam Heughan.

I read a few more chapters of *Your Beautiful Pregnancy; The Yummy Mummy Guide.* This stuff might be mumbo-jumbo, but maybe it worked. It was something small I could do to make myself feel better about everything.

Tomorrow morning, I promised myself, I will get up before work, stand naked in front of the mirror and tell myself how stunningly awesome I am. Maybe it would rub off on my work persona, and I'd finally manage to make Marty stop sliding into work three hours after everyone else.

The latest chapter in *Your Beautiful Pregnancy* told me by this stage in my pregnancy, I should add drops of Frankincense oils to my moisturiser to "ease any anxieties about childbirth". We had none of that in the house. And olive oil to—

I reread it. Yes, apply directly to your labia to aid with flexibility as you attempted to push a too gigantic thing out through a tiny hole. That sounded more of a solid tip than the Frankincense one. I flattened the book and squinted at the diagram, but labia massage looked complicated. You didn't just stick your fingers in the oil and wipe it down there. A massage meant...

Oh, a euphemism, then.

Did we have any olive oil? I checked the cupboards in the kitchen. Some months ago, Jack signed up for monthly deliveries of organic, artisan products made by ancient shepherds high in the Naples hills. (Or something.) I opened the door to the cupboard above the sink. Bingo—extra virgin cold-pressed, triple grade-rated, gold standard awarded extra virgin olive oil. Just the thing Yummy Mummies used for labia flexibility.

Mildred yowled at the back door. I let her out, armed myself with the olive oil and got ready for some solo fun.

"Caroline! I wasn't expecting—"

Key, Gaby, for once and for all take it off her! Please, please do not let her have seen that book…

Too late, I registered she wasn't alone. Behind her, book in one hand and Tamar strapped to her front was Jolene. She glanced up, spotted the bottle of olive oil and grinned.

"Good job we didn't arrive a few minutes later, eh?"

Caroline took the book off her. "Awfy waste of good olive oil. Didn't you try it, Jolene? Did it work?"

"No? I 'massaged' my labia for weeks before Tamar made his appearance and I ended up with a big rip and stitches anyway? I couldn't sit down without wincing for weeks."

No apologies for bursting in. I asked if either of them wanted a cup of tea and retreated to the kitchen. The fridge blasted out freezing air—all the better to cool down flaming cheeks. By the time I returned, Jolene had picked up the book and was reading bits of it out loud. Caroline called most of it 'stuff and nonsense' and wondered aloud who'd written this mumbo-jumbo.

"When's Jack home?" she asked. "I need tae tell him something about the Highland Games."

"Lunchtime, hopefully."

"Och. I'm away before then. Mind, mebbe you should get him to dae that lab—"

Universe almighty, save me!

"No, no! As Jolene says, it doesn't work."

Jolene unfastened the baby carrier on her front and handed Tamar to Caroline. She squinted at the room and began tidying it up, shifting the small coffee table to the side, picking up Mildred's toys, whisking wires out of sight and closing the kitchen door firmly.

Free cleaning was a welcome development, seeing as Jack and I were so rubbish at it, but I didn't remember asking Jolene or Caroline to turn up at the house and do it.

About to tell her where we kept the vacuum cleaner and mop so she could do the job thoroughly, I shut up when she handed me a huge tote bag filled with clothing.

"I hope you have a fantastic time with him," she said, casting a critical eye over the living room. "You'll need to keep this room hazard-free, eh?"

Wait, what? Then, the creeping realisation that a month ago, Jolene had said she and Stewart were planning a night away in July to celebrate the anniversary of when they'd first met. My words at the time, "Can I look after Tamar at some point? Whenever you want a night out?"

True. As I'd mentioned before—no previous experience of pregnancy and babies. But, but… those lovely things I'd planned for this afternoon when, for once, my husband and I would be not working at the same time… Even if that just meant setting up deckchairs in the garden, eating lunch outside and falling asleep afterwards, which was the most likely scenario.

"Amaze balls!" I said, clapping my hands and overdoing the enthusiasm to make up for any look of blind panic that might have passed over my face.

Caroline put Tamar on the newly cleared floor. He crawled over to me, grabbing hold of my legs and hoisting himself up. Jolene beamed, proof she said, of her offspring's precocity. He was doing everything well in advance of when the books said he should.

"He needs his lunch at 12pm. Keep the kitchen door

closed otherwise he'll crawl over to the cat litter tray and pick up anything that's in it. He usually has a sleep at 2pm for a coupla hours. Dinner's at six, and he goes to bed at 7pm. Usually sleeps through till seven. When do you start work on a Monday morning?"

"Er… eight am?"

"Okay, well we'll be back at midday. Jack can look after him in the morning."

Could he? I suspected not. Deliveries often arrived on a Monday morning, and Jolene wouldn't be working either. But before I could say anything else, she got up and bounced out—the prospect of a kid-free day and night far too exciting. Tamar watched his mother go, tiny bottom lip wobbling. He heard the door shut and began to wail. If Jolene heard him through the door, she gave no sign, disappearing in record time.

"Tamar!" I said, picking him up. "Your mummy's gone for the day, but you're going to have a fabulous time with Auntie Gaby and Uncle Jack!"

Another heartfelt wail. My mother-in-law held out her arms. Tamar twisted away from me; little arms outstretched to meet hers. I handed him over. She bounced Tamar on her hip, cooing nonsense words to him. The wails stopped abruptly.

"Er… I'd forgotten all about my offer," and neglected to tell Jack. "Would you be able to—"

"Cannae," she shook her head. "Ranald and me are heading tae the Luss Highland Games. I'm booked in as Psychic Josie. You'll be fine. I looked after this yin a few weeks ago, and he was as good as gold. Awfy keen on crawling so mind you shift aw' the hazards. Bye, Gaby!"

And with that, she handed Tamar back and departed, shouting over her shoulder that she needed to talk to Jack urgently about the Lochalshie Highland Games, now three weeks away, emphasising that I mustn't forget to tell him, the way I forgot things most of the time these days.

Tamar reacted the way he had when Jolene left— wailing so loudly any passers-by would report me to Social Services. I copied what Caroline had done, shoogling him up and down on my hip. He wriggled, desperate to get away from me: astonishingly robust things, babies. Mildred appeared once more and Tamar stopped mid-scream, pointing at her, mouth in a wide 'oh'.

Thanks to Scottie, he was used to animals. I sat him on the floor, and he twisted onto all fours and set off after her, the speed startling me. Mildred allowed him to come within a metre of her, hissed furiously her back arching and her tail doubling in size, and took off. More wails.

This was going to be a long day.

By the time Jack returned at three, opening the door and apologising profusely as brunch at the hotel had segued into lunch, I was as tearful as Tamar. He took us in, puzzled.

Jolene and Stewart's offspring was on the floor, me down beside him trying to persuade him naptime was long over-due. Lunchtime hadn't gone smoothly either. Jolene's bag of tricks included little jars of organic baby food. I picked the carrots, apples and parsnips variety, convinced it would be a winner. Not so.

Every time I swirled the spoon in the air, telling Tamar to open his mouth for the plane, he pursed his lips and shook his head. I allowed him to take the spoon himself, and he flicked the food at me. As a result, my face and top were covered in dried smears of orange gunk. He must only have eaten a quarter of it. Did this count as starvation?

"What's going on?" Jack asked, taking in the scene.

Mildred miaowed at him from her position at the top of the bookshelf, a place she'd decided was safest, out of reach of small grabby hands. Another one who'd missed out on lunch, thanks to her decision to stay well out of the way. Come to think of it, I'd not had lunch either. No wonder I felt so weepy.

"Jolene and Stewart are away for the night," I muttered, wiping my hand across my eyes. "And I volunteered to Tamar sit a few weeks ago. Thought it would be good practise."

On cue, Tamar burst into fresh tears, the howls making Mildred flatten her ears. Everyone else had said Tamar was a joy to look after—placid, easy to feed and happy to nap.

Jack swooped down, plucking up Tamar and swinging him up in the air. The tears changed to giggles. Jack swung him up and down a few times more. He had to be a lot lighter than a caber, and my husband was Lochalshie's champion caber tosser. Who knew it would have other practical applications?

"Thank you thank you thank you," I said, using the sofa arm to pull myself up. "I'm glad one of us can do this parenting lark. I'm officially useless at it."

Tamar's giggles continued. Jack swung him some more, letting him hang high above him for several seconds, little feet dangling in the air. Cute as...

"It'll be different with your own, Gaby," Jack said. "Do you want me to take him out for a wee walk? See if I can get him to go to sleep."

"Yes please. If he does sleep, maybe we could too."

I meant that literally. Crawling around after Tamar trying to stop him bumping into sharp corners, yanking Mildred's tail and tipping out the contents of my handbag, with the aim of putting everything into his mouth, had exhausted me. Jack's eyes were bloodshot and his eyelids heavy; someone else longing to hit the sack.

As Jolene's baby carrier wouldn't fit over me, Jack put it on, Tamar facing outwards. He reminded me of those ancient Athena posters from the 90s where hunky bare-chested men held babies. As we stepped out and headed for the loch shores, plenty of other people seemed to have got that old 90s reference too. Strange women sidled up to us, all saying, "So sweet," their eyes fixed on Jack. Maybe I should jump up and down, waving my arms. "Hello? I'm here! And I'm his wife! Pregnant too. Hadn't you noticed?"

But the walk worked. Within half an hour of us strolling the shores, Tamar's little head drooped back against the carrier, and we were able to head home. "What about his lunch?" I said as Jack tucked him up in upstairs. Laney Haggerty had given us an old cot that had belonged to her sister for our baby. I handed Jack the soft, faded tartan blanket Jolene had packed in her tote bag.

"I guess he'll wake up when he's hungry," Jack said as Tamar snuffled and turned over. He sat down on the bed, falling back with the muffled thump. "Gaby, I'm…"

Too late. He was out for the count also. I climbed on the bed next to him, turned over and promptly fell fast asleep too.

———————

When I woke up, shrill screams yanking me out of weird dreams where I found myself in the Lochside Welcome and kept walking along corridors that led nowhere, Jack sat bolt upright too.

I fumbled my way out of bed and over to Tamar, his

face bright red and a disgusting smell I recognised as all too familiar, thanks to Mildred and her litter box.

"Um…?" I turned to Jack; his eyes as bleary as mine. "If I make us something to eat, would you…?"

Another groan from my beloved. "S'pose I'd better get the practice in."

He muttered curses, pushed back the covers, and swung his legs out. When his face appeared next to mine above the cot, the crying died down. Worry set in once more. Did babies magically sense how nervous they made me? Jack got his phone out and asked Siri for nappy changing instructions, YouTube presenting him with ten different videos. ScottishDaDa sounded like the best bet. He wouldn't call them diapers for a start, and his channel had tens of thousands of subscribers.

I left them to it, Jack kneeling on the floor while Tamar rolled around the changing mat and did his best to wriggle out of Jack's grasp. If I stayed in the room any longer, I'd end up throwing up again. Just when I thought the nausea had disappeared for good too.

Downstairs, Mildred yowled. Her lunch was well overdue too. I breathed in as I emptied a packet of cat food into her dish and promised her everything would be okay. But it wouldn't, would it? If this was what Mildred thought of a tiny temporary guest, what was she going to make of a permanent one? Note to self—start doing Katya's recommendations to prep a cat for a baby ASAP.

Jack, Tamar in his arms freshly changed and giggly, came down as I was putting the finishing touches to doorstep peanut butter sandwiches. I held up two jars of baby food—one shepherd's pie and the other chicken casserole. What did he think Tamar would prefer?

"Is something wrong with your eye?" I asked, looking at him closely. His left eye beamed an angry red colour.

He set Tamar on the living room floor, the baby making an immediate beeline for the small stock of toys I'd left near the sofa.

"He peed while I was changing him. Got me right in the eye. And the mouth."

Eww… double eww… I'll say this for Mildred. She might throw up on the living room carpet occasionally, but she drew the line at peeing in our faces.

"Do not laugh."

"I'm not!" Well, only a teeny bit.

He gave in anyway, face cracking into a grin. "Pretty impressive aim, actually. When Lachlan and I were wee boys, we used to have peeing matches whenever it snowed. First prize for whoever could get it the furthest away. Tamar seems to be limbering up for the same competition."

Tamar's face split into a smile. Then, the small matter of us starving him hit home and his face crumpled. He turned his nose up at the jar of baby shepherd's pie, so I tried him with the chicken casserole. A big fat no to that too. Jack took over, employing the open your mouth for the big plane coming in bribery technique. Tamar clamped his lips shut and shook his head fiercely.

"Please eat, Tamar!" I begged, battling a rising tide of hysterical thoughts. *"OMG. This is dreadful. We're NOT ready at all. Should have taken Katya's stance and vowed to save the planet with the child-free choice!"*

Naturally, I did my best to stifle that one.

"Ask Siri! How do you force your baby to eat!"

I slammed my hand to my mouth. Jack and I trading worried frowns. Word choice, Gaby! Tempting better than forcing, surely. I amended myself, and Jack hastily barked the words at his phone.

"ScottishDaDa says you shouldn't worry too much if your baby refuses to eat. Just keep trying because they'll get hungry eventually."

I snatched the phone from him. Who was giving out this duff advice? The Children Catcher in that old musical, Chitty Chitty Bang Bang? But ScottishDaDa not only had a thriving YouTube channel with comments along the lines of 'you saved my sanity!' but a website with tonnes of tips and cute pics too.

Tamar, the wailing still in evidence, began hiccoughing. I walked into the kitchen and opened out cupboards and the fridge. Bland stuff, right? Nothing with any salt or sugar in it. At the back of the cupboard was a packet of quick-cook oats. "Stewart," I muttered to myself. "You might have been right all along."

Porridge made and cooled with two spoons of apple sauce stirred in, I took it through. Jack was on the floor, trying to coax Tamar away from all the sharp edges in our home. He whisked him up in the air, triggering off more baby giggles as baba decided he'd much rather be swung up and down than eat.

Five hundred or so swings later ('felt like', Jack said), he put Tamar down and took the bowl and plastic spoon from me.

"Are you sure?" I asked, wondering how on earth we were going to clean the resultant muck off the carpet.

"Aye. ScottishDaDa says babies Tamar's age are much happier feeding themselves."

Tamar stuck the spoon in the bowl and scooped up a helping. Most of it went down his front, but some of landed in his mouth. He tried again, then flung the spoon at me hitting me bang on the middle of my forehead.

"So much for that idiot's—"

"Ssh. Look at him."

Who needed a spoon when fingers would do just as well? Tamar dipped them into the porridge and shoved his little fist into his mouth, sucking happily. Had his hands been clean before he started? Jack had washed him post changing his nappy, but he had crawled about our floor picking up heaven only knew what.

"He's eating though," Jack said when I pointed it out. "And don't weans need exposure to a wee bit o' dirt and germs to build their immune systems up?"

Not this much though. Mildred wandered all over this carpet post using the litter box. I decided not to share all aspects of the Tamar feeding experience with Jolene, though Stewart would be over the moon about the porridge success. Proof, if you needed it, of the McMillan genes shining through.

Fed Tamar was much more cheerful, heading once more for his toys and engrossing himself in another game of smashing toy trains together.

"See?" Jack said, picking up one of the doorstep sandwiches I feared must have gone stale by now. "You're a natural. Motherhood will be a—"

"Do not say breeze. Or walk in the park. Or even natural. The only natural nurturer I am is one of cats. End of."

He bit off half the sandwich, jaw working furiously. Mouthful finished, he reached for another one. "Okay then. Why not get Katya to use you as a test case as she writes the world's first book or blog—*Raising Your Kids the Cat Way*. Bound to be a huge hit."

The silly joke cheered me up instantly. Tamar joined in the laughter, abandoning his trains and clapping along enthusiastically.

"If you say so." I bent over and stroked Tamar's little head, hair coal-black and silky smooth. Luckily for him, he'd inherited 90 percent of Jolene's genes and 10 percent of Stewart's by appearance and the limited bits of personality you get in a baby of that age.

From then on, feeding Tamar and getting him to sleep was easy. Ish. Jack swung him up and down in the air plenty of times and took him for another walk, the two of us attracting the same attention as before where women walked up to him, eyes blind to me.

By eight o'clock that evening, we collapsed on the sofa, Tamar asleep between us, and Mildred next to him. She liked him much better now he was silent and immobile. "A taste of things to come," I murmured, Jack grunting agreement.

"Can you order us something to eat from the hotel?" I suggested, reluctant to expend any energy whatsoever. "I'll pick it up."

"Don't worry about it. I'll do it."

He wriggled away from Tamar's side slowly, doing his best not to wake him. I knew I'd have to transfer him upstairs eventually, but the peace and quiet were too blissful to disturb. "Get us whatever's on the specials. So long as it isn't prawns or pate."

"Spot on."

He tip-toed out, the door shutting quietly behind him. Neither Tamar nor Mildred moved. Tamar had reached a tiny fist out, a bunch of Mildred's fur grasped tightly within. Miraculously, she didn't seem to mind. Perhaps the introduction of Mildred to the new baby thing wouldn't be too stressful after all.

I leant back, allowing my head to rest against the back of the chair. "Resting my eyes," I told myself, repeating another well-known Nanna Cooper saying. "That's all I'm doing."

Half-an-hour later, my phone vibrated, startling me awake.

"Sorry, sorry, sorry—got dragged into helping out. Busy down here."

The words I uttered were not baby-friendly. Just as well Tamar was still fast asleep. I knew I should have fetched the food. No-one would have been able to ask me to stay and help. Blasted Xavier! Couldn't he have managed for once? Dinner would have to be toast. Again.

Jack returned at nine o'clock just as I'd managed to get Tamar upstairs and into the cot without waking—congratulating myself as I did so on my newly learned baby care skills. More profuse apologies but at least he'd returned armed with food, Xavier having decided to try a French/Canadian/Scottish mash-up of haggis mixed with minced pork and covered in pastry.

"Tourtiere," Jack said, cutting us both large, steaming slices and adding a liberal helping of gravy. "And a French/Canadian staple."

Food finished, I sighed, wondering how on earth I was going to manage to drag my beached whale body up the stairs. Jack whisked away the plates and hovered in the doorway. I knew what was coming.

"You're heading back there, aren't you?"

He shifted from foot to foot.

"Yes. Sorry. It's so busy, and I cannae leave Xavier there

without me or Jolene. Those agency guys are okay, but they're new. They don't know the place that well."

"Promise, promise, promise me it's not going to be like this when the baby is born? What if I go mad, develop post-natal depression and end up stabbing you as you sleep?"

Caroline had warned me of the perils of post-natal depression. Midwives looked out for it. I pictured the scene. Me sitting in front of a torn-faced woman, her lips pinched and clipboard in hand, ticking off all the points on the baby care list I'd failed.

Jack flashed me the tiny hint of a smile.

"I don't think women with postnatal depression typically stab their partners to death."

"Maybe I'll be the first. And I'll plead insanity in the courts and be let off with a suspended sentence; left a merry widow to bring up our child alone."

Another smile. "And a fine job you'll make of it too. But no, cross my heart and hope to die, my paternity leave from the Lochside Welcome is set in stone."

The childlike vow made me smile too. For a second anyway. The doorbell rang, and I stuck a cushion in front of my face. "Tell them to go away, Jack! I'm too knackered. And if whoever has woken Tamar..." I broke off. Silence upstairs. Thank the heavens and every star up there. "Well, whatever. Just open the door, say you're off out and tell whoever to fu—"

"A lovely thing to say to your best friend. The door was open, by the way? Didn't you realise?"

Katya. Jack took advantage of the diversion, muttered a hasty 'goodbye!' and slipped out.

Katya sat down next to me. "How did you find your day, Tamar-sitting? The time I did it made me doubly glad I'm never having kids. Too late for you, though."

I glared at her. "You've been living with Mhari too long. Both of you are competing for the Least Supportive Friend of the Year prize. The competition is currently neck and neck."

She held her hands up. "Sorry! I was aiming for light-hearted jokiness. No offence. I was out for a walk just now, and I spotted Miles. Do you remember that Tindra told us he was back in London for a meeting with the Netflix commissioners?"

I nodded.

"And he was heading for the Royal George, where a moss-green Jaguar is currently sitting in the car park."

Dear, oh dear, oh dear.

"Sorry, did I wake you? Or Tamar?"

I was upstairs in bed when I heard the door open softly downstairs. Jack crawled in the bed next to me, having ripped off his clothes in record time—a situation I might have found highly charged in other circumstances if we weren't both bone-weary and me about to deliver the not-so-good news about where Miles had been spotted.

I snuggled up under his arm. "No. This is early for you, isn't it?"

Eleven o'clock on a Sunday night. Noise from the Royal George drifted over. Scottish licensing laws meant that drinks were not supposed to be served outside after 10pm in deference to the locals, but if the odd inebriated person stood outdoor for a smoke and was then joined by a few others, we heard their conversations. Primarily because alcohol altered most people's volume control. Tonight's smokers shrieked with laughter as someone told rubbish jokes.

"Xavier's handling it," he said. "Lucas brought in a French party, and they were thrilled to find someone who spoke their language. What did Katya want, by the way? I havenae thanked her properly for all the cleaning up she did yesterday."

Cue the conversation…I repeated what Katya had said, finally remembering to pass on that we had spotted Miles and Zac together the week before.

"Katya reckons they are planning to film the George too —maybe show us as rival hotels in the one village, which might not be that bad. If I saw the two hotels on screen and everyone having terrific fun in the Lochside Welcome, I know what one I would choose to visit."

A sigh. Heartfelt. "At this moment in time, I couldn't care less. And if they do some filming at the George, they won't be under my feet all the time. Now, please, please, please can we go to sleep?"

"Just one more thing. Tomorrow morning. Are you still okay to look after—"

Too late. He'd crashed out straight away.

Chapter Twenty-Two

Tamar woke us early the next day. I pitched from early morning dreams—more anxiety-ridden ones, where you're naked in public, hated by everyone you know or in charge of a cat or baby you've abandoned in a dangerous place—to full panic. What, where, who, why...

I bolted from the bed to the crib, clutched the rail and leant in. "Tamar!"

He stared up at me, changing suddenly from tearful disgruntlement to contented coos. When I lifted him up, he clung to me, chubby little arms wrapping around my neck and dark eyes blinking. "Look!" I said, whirling the two of us around to face Jack. Tamar giggled. "He likes me! I've got this mothering thing, after all!"

"Course you have," Jack said, squinting at the old school alarm clock we kept in the bedroom. "Does that say ten past six, by the way?"

"Yes."

"Oh god... I was hoping he'd let us sleep until eight. Nine or ten o'clock, even."

"Go back to sleep," I said, bouncing Tamar on my hip. "I'll change and feed him."

I was as good at my word, whipping off Tamar's nappy in double-quick time, letting myself out of the room and creeping downstairs, Mildred tagging along. She must have slept in the spare room.

The two of them fed—Tamar once more on self-service porridge mixed with chopped egg, food Mildred showed interest too once she'd scoffed her Whiskas—I fired up my iMac. I'd deposited Tamar on the floor along with all his toys—various brightly coloured things, most of which made loud noises. Mildred fled back upstairs, where she'd find a warm and much more peaceful haven curled up next to Jack.

Caitlin had promised me Blissful Beauty were a fabulously modern, female-friendly company. One then that would not mind if its head designer had to keep one eye on a baby this morning. Late on Friday, Trish had sent me some mock-ups for a social media campaign featuring influential YouTubers using the pharmaceutical range. What did I think of them?

Tamar had crawled off, heading for the kitchen with its litter tray danger. Yet again, I'd forgotten to shut it. I leapt out of my chair and scooped him up just as he got to it, slamming the door loudly enough to set him off howling and stir movement in the bedroom above me. We'd woken Jack too.

"Darling!" I jiggled Tamar on my hip once more, trying to summon up the earlier maternal magic. "You don't want to touch that, I promise!"

Tamar wasn't convinced. The crying continued, now a low rumbling gurgle the opposite of content. Jack stuck his head around the door, hair tousled, and bare-legged. He took in my wild-eyed look and held out his arms. "Let me try."

I handed Tamar over, and he shut up immediately, cooing cutely one more.

"Jack, I can't..." furious with myself, I dashed away tears with the back of my hand. Oh, this was ridiculous. What if I didn't have 'it' the mystery quality that made some women natural, fantastic mothers? Our own kid might take one look at me and start screaming.

Jack, Tamar by now back to giggly sweetness, moved to where I sat and ruffled my hair. "Gaby-sketch, d'you want me to take this wee one up the stairs with me? We could play wi' Thomas the Tank Engine if you hand him up?"

I sent him a watery smile. "Please!" Train with a face located and passed over, Jack winked at me and headed back upstairs, singing nonsense to Tamar as he went—"Oh Tamar o' Scotland, when will we see your like again? Who fought and died for, your wee bit New Zealand gen?" Hallelujah. One of us would be able to cope with Baby McAllan whenever he/she/it/they finally made an appearance.

Back to the immediate concerns; being Blissful Beauty's UK head designer. I'd decided against using my mother-in-law to offer fake psychic advice where she communed with Marty's dead grandmother and expressed profound disappointment about his attitude to timekeeping/work attendance.

A pity. "Ma receptionist is the model employee these days," Caroline often expounded. "Terrified her granny watches over her, shaking her head in disapproval when she's late or is spending too much time reading celebrity gossip on her phone when she should be sending out flu jag reminders to folks."

Knuckles rattled against our door, making me jump. Unbelievably, it was gone eight o'clock already, which made this a borderline acceptable time for people to pop around.

Speak of the devil... Caroline. Key-free as I'd confiscated the spare one yesterday, which didn't mean she now thought an invite to come in was how ordinary people behaved. She barged past me, firing questions in my direction. Had the ginger worked? Where was wee Tamar? What did we think, post our weekend looking after him? Oh, and there was this Highland Games thingy, nothing for us tae worry about but a bittie important...

I hurried her through to the living room and into the kitchen. Our bedroom was above the living room. Anything 'nothing for us tae worry about' might be overheard in there. I flicked on the kettle switch to make doubly sure.

"Jack's upstairs with Tamar," I said, pointing upstairs and miming shush. "If you need to talk to us about the games, we're not on the committee this year. Remember?"

"Aye never mind no' being on the committee," Caroline said. "Busy two days there for me, Gaby, at the Luss Games! I've been run off my feet. I could murder—"

My face must have made it clear any further words along this vein would be unwise. "I'll get maself a cup o' tea."

Suitably refreshed—having made tea 'properly' in a china cup and saucer—she told me her news. One of the Lochalshie Highland Games' major sponsors, a nearby whisky distillery owned by one of the big drinks companies, had pulled out.

"Why?" I said, gulping when Caroline told me how much money the sponsorship was worth. Highland Games were not cheap to run.

She shrugged. "They didnae see fit to enlighten me.

Mumbled some nonsense about re-thinks on the number o' things they sponsor. I heard they're sponsorin' Braemar this year—ye ken, the one the Royal family go to. Obviously, dinnae see us as big or important enough anymore."

"But, but, but…"

The implications for Jack were clear. He was relying on the Highland Games to bring in tonnes of visitors as it usually did—people who'd want to spend plenty of money on the bar, on food and booking overnights in the hotel. Already, he'd told me bookings for that weekend—just under three weeks from now—were worryingly down.

He had his fingers and toes crossed for last-minuters, the spontaneous arrivals who decided on a whim to visit Lochalshie, see the Games, drink too much and need to stay the night to sleep it off. If the Games didn't have money to cover everything planned, the committee would need to scale it right back. And that would make the Games and the village less likely to bring many people in.

"What are you going to do?" I put on some eggs to boil, a vague inclination that I should eat more protein to help the baby's brain development. Mine too if I were to come up with fantastic design ideas.

Caroline put her cup down on the counter, the cup clattering against the saucer. "Well, Laney Haggerty offered a bit o' money from the riding school. And Big Donnie volunteered some from his antique shop."

Bless. It wouldn't come close to touching the whisky money.

"We'll need to hae a wee think about it. I was hoping…" Her eyes gleamed—one of those speculative looks I knew so well. I quaked in my fleecy slippers. "You ken aw' these fancy folks in the cities, don't ye? Mebbe you could reach out tae them? Investment bankers and the likes, spending their filthy lucre on yachts and restaurants where a bottle o' wine costs more than a thousand pounds."

Someday, I was going to persuade Caroline that my hometown of Great Yarmouth was not a gleaming metropolis, rather its streets unpaved with gold and its inhabitants generally as dirt poor as the rest of us.

"… and persuade them they need tae ease their consciences by pouring their money into a community-minded initiative. Or," she paused, "even tell them they could dae it as a tax dodge?"

"I don't know anyone like that!"

"No? That's an awfy pity."

Indeed. I flipped my way through my contacts list in my head, scrabbling to find someone who might have a connection to a wealthy banker desperate to appease his or her conscience. There was always my ex, commonly known to Katya and me as Ryan the douche bag. His family were affluent.

"Hey, Ryan! How are you? Recovered from the way I publicly humiliated you when we split up? Wanna demonstrate the car industry's corporate social responsibility by bunging a community initiative in the north of Scotland a load of money? No? Ah well."

Caroline stood up, resting her hand on top of my head. "Aye, sorry to bring my troubles to your door, Gaby. You and Jack bein' so busy and all. Be an awfy shame, though, if the Highland Games fizzles out."

She left me on that bombshell. When Jack made his way downstairs later, Tamar bright-eyed and happy, I chickened out of sharing the news. It could wait until the evening. Tamar planted on the floor where he decided his toys held more appeal than yet another attempt to get into the kitchen and the cat litter tray, I took in Jack's wet hair, water dripping down his face.

A man showered because he was about to go to work. He caught my look—face half dismayed, half guilty—the forgotten promise he would look after Tamar in the morning while I carried on with the serious business of pretending to be a boss.

"Crap. I'm so sorry, but the brewery phoned me yesterday and said they wanted to deliver first thing. I'd forgotten all about it. And Xavier's not in until later."

"Go," I said, "Jolene and Stewart are due back at midday. We'll cope, won't we, Tamar?"

"Ai," he said, nodding solemnly. Jack and I exchanged delighted whoops, high fiving each other. "I'll take that," I said. "Proof being taken care of by Gaby and Jack helps develop a baby's understanding."

"Too right," Jack pulled me in close and let his hand rest on my belly, fingers spread over the bump. "You're going to ace being a mum, Gaby-sketch."

The little speech left me tearful once more, eyes watering as Tamar and I waved him goodbye from the living room window, Jack turning back just before he moved out of sight to blow us both a kiss. I jiggled Tamar up and down a few times. "Darling boy, d'you think you can entertain yourself for an hour or so?" No repeat of the 'Ai' but I took the solemnness in his expression as an indication he understood. I lowered him to the ground, and he zoomed in on the play mat and the toys.

The Monday morning catch-up with Blissful Beauty's (my) design team was due to start in ten minutes. I positioned my iMac so the camera wouldn't show the floor. Tamar was engaged in a noisy game of trains, bashing Thomas into all his friends and screeching with delight. Plan B then… a quick google search and I found what I wanted.

"Take this, Tamar," I said, handing him my phone. I'd found a baby app that reviewers praised to the skies for its diversion powers. "Keeps my little princess occupied for ages!" one said. The gurus of baby care would not approve but desperate times… "Now, if you could just be quiet as a mouse for the next forty-five minutes, I'd be incredibly grateful."

Marty was late for the Monday morning catch-up yet again. A quick check online showed him in a nearby coffee shop. Honestly, when I'd been a lowly junior designer some years ago, I'd known the basics. If you're going to skive, do it discreetly and don't put the evidence online.

It did mean I'd need to face up to him, instead of meekly nodding when he reeled off his excuses—emergency dental appointments, hospital visits to the sick granny post her 75th birthday, etc. I added a 'looking forward to seeing you this morning for work chat'; comment to his post, then chickened out and softened it by inserting smiley face, coffee cup and cake emojis as well. Too late, I realised I'd accidentally added an angry face—one where I looked as if I had steam coming out of my ears. Oh well. Maybe that would scare him.

Fifteen minutes into the meeting, it seemed my 'I'm watching you, fella!' hint hadn't fazed him at all. He'd since added another (admittedly super cute) film of a dog in the coffee shop to his stories. No sign of him and no reply to my comment.

Tamar's face had taken on a transfixed expression as he stared at the baby app. Again, best not to reveal that tactic to his mum and dad.

Unlike Marty, Trish proved her worth in gold—coming up with several amazing ideas for web pages and social media graphics we could use to help launch the super-strength skincare products in the UK. When I told her to do me some mock-ups, she beamed.

This was what managing people was all about, I told myself, finding their talents and making the most of them.

"Wah!" Tamar bellowed, making Trish and Ali jump. "Have you got a baby with you?" Trish asked, screwing her nose up. Admittedly they weren't that much younger than me—four years tops—but the look on their faces was me at the same age. *"Babies?! Bleurgh…"*

I shifted the screen and moved out of sight. "No, no! It's one of those baby toys the NHS provide you with so you can practise your parenting skills."

"Wah!"

"Super realistic!" Trish exclaimed.

"Isn't it?"

Out of sight of the webcam, I took my phone off Tamar. Ah, the app had frozen because… oh honestly, he had used up all the free sample that was available, and if I wanted to continue to keep him quiet, I'd need to upgrade to the paid version. "The babies are programmed to wake up all through the night, and they scream during the day if you don't look after them."

App rapidly purchased and Tamar happy once more, I returned to my seat in front of the iMac. Marty drifted in just as I was about to hang up. Apology-free. I made a point of looking at my wrist, the gesture spoiled because I wasn't wearing a watch. He sat down, announcing those well-worn words, "Tube strike."

Blimey. All I needed to do was check Twitter to call him on that one. Trish's eyes flashed. The model employee irritated that lousy behaviour didn't get corrected.

Did I hold up my phone and the evidence of his coffee

shop stop? Accuse him of being a liar outright? Mutter, "Fine. Let me know next time, right?" instead?

Cursing myself for being so wet, I went for the latter. And vowed that Psychic Josie and Marty's dead, great grandmother *would* be the surprise attendees at next week's team talk.

A window flashed on the screen. Trish and Ali had stood up but sat down instantly when they saw who was calling, mouths rounded in surprise.

"Is that…?" Trish asked, and I nodded. Say hello, team, to the big boss.

I clicked on the flashing green button. "Caitlin! We were busy discussing the latest plans for your new range."

"Gaby, hi!!!!!!"

What time was it in LA—the city was eight hours behind London? One o'clock in the morning? Caitlin looked as if she was in a gym. Her mansion if I remembered rightly, had its own gym, a cinema room and games room. Did being a reality TV star with so many plates spinning in the air mean you needed to get up at sparrow's fart to cram a work-out into your schedule? Judging by what she was wearing, it must do.

"Hey, can you 'n me talk about something, like urgently? Just a super-quick chat?"

She sketched a wave at Trish, Logan, Ali and Marty, all of them awe-struck. An idea came to me.

"Certainly, Caitlin. We're just finishing up our weekly team meeting. Hey, how about your drop in on one of those meetings next week? If it fits your schedule?"

"That would be amazing," Caitlin replied. "I love

getting behind-the-scene insights into the work of creatives. What time does it start?"

She nodded when I told her the time, me making it an hour earlier than usual to spite Marty. "Sure. I'm in Paris next week, and I'll have a half-hour break between my morning personal training session and my sunrise yoga. That's ideal. I can't wait to see you guys in action!!!!!"

Gaby one, Marty zero. Now, he'd have to turn up early. It was one thing ignoring me and drifting into work whenever he wanted. Another thing entirely if you did it to Caitlin Cartier.

I waved goodbye to the team, trying my best not to smile too smugly in Marty's direction. Or make my expression look too much 'Gotcha!' like.

"So, this urgent thing?" I said once we were alone. "Yeah, super-important. I need to ask for your advice about Donal's birthday. Do you have time?"

No. Not really. The Monday to-do list increased every week. Caitlin 'super-quick' chats never matched their description. What choice did I have? I nodded.

"How are you—and how is your little baba?" Caitlin pointed at my stomach. During one of our previous private chats, she'd admitted that with everything she had going on these days, she wouldn't have time for a pregnancy until she was 45 at the earliest.

"Fine," I said, twisting the screen so she could see Tamar. "Practising." Caitlin wouldn't mind evidence of my less-than-professional-boss behaviour. She never phoned for a chat about work, after all.

"How cute," she said, blowing him kisses—all of which were ignored thanks to the baby app. "So, here's why I'm calling you, yeah? I wanted to ask your opinion on a birthday present for Donal. I had some ideas, but I kinda feel they might be too over the top. What do you think?"

Ha! This, I would pass on to Katya—the very scene I'd suggested she include in her female billionaire romance book. Congratulating myself on my ability to work out the 'problems' of billionaires, I mulled over Caitlin's question.

As she'd grown up in a fantastically wealthy family—even before she made her own fortune with Blissful Beauty—way over the top gifts were de rigueur in the Cartier family. They loved their bling. When Caitlin passed her driving test at 16, her mum gave her a gift-wrapped dark red Ferrari. Teenage boys (and a fair few adults) around the world wept. Presents ordinary people gave each other were something she had no knowledge of and thus needed to call on my expertise. Donal got antsy about over-the-top spending, mainly as he was determined not to plough his way through Caitlin's money. Unlike her sisters' husbands and boyfriends.

"Shares in Manchester United? They're his favourite football team?"

"How much do they cost?" She named the figure, and I shook my head. Far too much.

"This suit—it's Tom Ford. That's like, loads cheaper than Dolce and Gabbana."

She pasted a link to Tom Ford's website. 'Cheap' was a relative term, specially where the Cartiers were concerned.

When I gave her a thumbs-down for the suit, she tried another tack. As an Irishman, Donal loved whisky. Why didn't she get him a case of their 30-year single malt, and request they supply it with personalised labels? I clicked on the link she posted and drew back tutting.

"The people who make that whisky have just pulled out

of sponsoring this year's Lochalshie Highland Games. Please don't give them any of your money."

Behind Caitlin, a woman entered the gym, yoga mat strapped to her back. Caitlin held up a couple of fingers to her, and the woman nodded. That schedule was non-stop. Imagine doing yoga at one in the morning.

"How much is the sponsorship?" Caitlin asked. In for a penny, in for a lot of pounds, I told myself and doubled the figure Caroline had given me. If a superior being hovers above us all, judging by the lies we tell this one wouldn't count, would it? Money from a woman so rich, she sent out for takeaway bagels when she was hungry rather than walking to her fully stocked fridge and making one herself. Then, there was Caroline's point. "Don't companies often offset their corporation taxes with charity sponsorship thingies?"

"Yeah, I guess I could put that on the website—how Blissful Beauty believes in giving back to communities. And the Highland Games is where I first launched the company. Do you remember that day, Gaby?"

Remember it? It was etched on my brain, not least for me having to leap in with a blanket to cover up the naked Caitlin. But yes, the day when Jack and I first got together, right?

"Donal would love that. It's such a super awesome idea, Gaby!!!!!!!! I'll tell him I've bought him sponsorship of the Highland Games for his birthday. He gets no present at all, and he won't mind if I spend tonnes of money on it!"

"Buy him socks," I pitched in quickly, anxious that poor Donal should have something to open. "But only if they are from Marks and Spencer. Not those 100 percent cashmere, hand-knitted ones."

Hard not to, but I punched the air once we disconnected, delighted that the Lochalshie Highland Games now had twice its original budget in return for us putting up a few signs mentioning the company on the day.

Not a bad day's work for a Monday morning, and only another two hours until Jolene and Stewart picked up their son, who remained, miraculously, alive and unharmed.

I returned to my iMac, determined to make up the time I'd wasted in meetings. A new email message popped up in the corner of my screen, and I clicked on it automatically (Katya tip—effective leaders are not slaves to their emails; they check only once or twice a day) and then hit my hand to my forehead.

Dexter with a long list of instructions for changes to the designs the team and I had created for the pharmaceutical skincare launch. I got half-way through it and lost the will to live. It would be easier to phone him.

"Dexter!" Fake cheerfulness. I wanted to strangle him.

"Gaby, hi! Your team's ideas are super amazing. I was stoked when I saw them."

Ordinary people did not say super-amazing or stoked and then tell you to change everything. He couldn't see me or the rude gestures I made. We went through every one of his nit-picky alterations, and I promised to send him the new work the next day.

"Caitlin's promised Blissful Beauty sponsors the Highland Games in a few weeks, by the way. Do you think we could offer people freebies?" I dropped in. Doubtless, he'd want some input there too.

"Whaaatttttt?"

Oops. Not best pleased, then. A string of colourful Texan curses followed. Tamar glanced up, and I sent him an apologetic smile and hoped he didn't understand any of it.

"… but y'know what, Gaby? We could use this to our advantage. Say if we offered…"

Terrific. Yes, all his ideas for marketing Blissful Beauty's sponsorship of the Highland Games would bring in punters in their thousands. They also meant a tonne of work for me —posters, banners, graphics, landing pages, Instagram posts and stories. Dexter was putting his new marketing assistant, Alex, in charge of the sponsorship deal. I was to liaise closely with him.

"D'you think I work too hard, Gaby?"

The question caught me by surprise. The usual Dexter hyper-enthusiasm had dialled down several notches. He sounded… glum.

"Katya sent me this long email about our relationship. Y'know how amazing she is with words. It kinda made me think. Wonder if we have a future, or if it would be fairer to split."

No, no, no, no! Much as my best friend was more circumspect with the details of her personal life, breaking up with Dexter wasn't her plan. I was sure of it. *What about that excessive interest in Zac*, my mind whispered. Again, no, no, no…

"You do work quite hard, Dexter," I said. A massive understatement. "But goodness me!" Now overdoing the chirpiness. "What a fantastic couple you are! The sizzle! The matching interests! How you can make Katya orga—"

Shoot! Did I say my best friend was circumspect? She was, most of the time. But she let slip once that Dexter could get her to—y'know—through what he did with his mouth to her neck and nipples alone…

"—make Katya so organised in her working life! She would be devastated if you split up. You just need some quality time together, right? A mini-break or a holiday or something? Yolo, remember? What if you went phone-free too? That would *really* impress her."

"I dunno. I think it's better if we—"

"No, no! You are meant to be together. Goodness me, yes."

The Gaby pep talk; works every time. A long silence his end.

"Don't tell her I told you about the email, will you?" he asked eventually, and I swore on my grandfather's grave not to. I tried not to be too offended when he said he would prefer it if I swore on Jack and Mildred's lives seeing as discretion and I weren't bosom buddies.

Solemn declaration made, I hung up. *Your first loyalty, Gabrielle Amelia McAllan*, I reminded myself, *is to the friend you made at North Denes Primary School in Great Yarmouth 20 years ago, remember?*

Voice number two decided to pipe up. *But you swore on Jack and Mildred's lives to keep your trap shut!*

No harm, though, I decided, if I dropped lots of heavy hints about Dexter's general excellence compared to Zac's general untrustworthiness and how Katya might want to remember it.

Chapter Twenty-Three

"Tindra—wait!"

Katya and I spotted her leaving Jamal's shop two days later, Katya was insistent that a daily walk—more like a route march led by a shouty sergeant major—would make childbirth easier for me to deal with.

Tindra spun around. I tried to work out what her expression conveyed and decided it was resignation. "I bought some ice-creams," she said, holding her bag up. "And I need to talk to you anyway. Shall we eat them over there?"

She pointed at the picnic bench on the far side of the road. The last few days had been warm and sunny—the temperature evidently hot enough even for a Londoner.

"Okay, then," I said, more than happy to give up the walk. "By the way, Blissful Beauty is sponsoring the Highland Games in a few weeks, and the Lochside Welcome is the official provider of the Games' beer tent. Should provide you with lots of fabulous footage for your series."

She waited until we'd all sat down, distributing white chocolate Magnums to Katya and me.

"Yeah. About that."

Katya unwrapped her ice-cream, expertly lobbing the foil into the nearby litter bin. "You're going to be filming the Royal George as well, aren't you? Pitching the two places against each other to make the documentary more exciting?"

She bit off a large chunk of her ice-cream. Mysteries of the world; some people can bite off chocolate-covered ice-creams neatly without bits of chocolate flaking off and scattering everywhere. I was not one of them.

Tindra squirmed, her ice-cream untouched. "The Lochside Welcome is my favourite pub in Lochalshie for sure. Nina and I got some awesome footage of the place. It's such a friendly place. Everyone knows who you are, and Jack and Xavier are so, like, super-hot. You should see the film I got of him when he was behind the bar."

She handed me her phone. I gave it back. A) I saw the super-hot guy in real life every day, and B) I recognised stalling when I heard it.

Katya had finished her ice-cream. "Well?" she asked, managing to sound far more intimidating than me.

The woman opposite me coloured, her cheeks turning a delicate pink. "We won't be filming the Lochside Welcome at all."

Katya treated her to some of the English language's finest Anglo-Saxon swear words. And a few choice Polish ones too. Tindra's cheeks reddened further.

"What happened?" I asked. "Why did Miles change his mind? He seemed dead keen."

She let out a huge sigh. "Miles and Zac are old friends. They met up at some big party in one of the London

Hammerstone Hotels last year. Zac told him he'd been working in Scotland for a while. That's what gave Miles the idea to film a documentary about a local pub. We came here originally because Miles wanted to look at the Royal George and suss it out."

"And Miles sent you ahead of him to research the possibilities?" Katya asked. She took Tindra's own Magnum off her. Tindra didn't object. I would have done. That one was the almond version with caramel in it.

"Yes, and I thought the Lochside Welcome would make the much better story. Miles came up to see it, and he agreed. But when Ashley was rushed to the hospital, we didn't know what would happen to the hotel so Miles decided we should stick to his original plan and film the George instead."

"And then I told you Jack was going to take over management of the Lochside Welcome," I added, and Tindra nodded.

"But Lois and Angeline heard about it. They met with Miles and persuaded him he'd be better of filming the Royal George," Katya finished. "Am I right?"

Another nod. "I'd come up with some amazing ideas of what we could do, and I told Miles the Lochside Welcome would be far more interesting for viewers."

Pointless. Why would he listen to an unpaid intern?

Tindra twisted the ring on her thumb. "I do love it here! The Lochside Welcome is much, much nicer than the Royal George, and Jack and Xavier are lovely… gorgeous, kind, principled…"

"Ahem." Much as I agreed with her, a reminder that she was talking about my husband needed inserting into the conversation. She'd gone dreamy-eyed.

"I'm sorry. I know the publicity would have been useful."

Understatement. Try life-changing as people flocked to that place 'offa the telly' partly to gawp at Jack and Xavier, partly to try out the pizzas and Quebec Poutine. The injustice of it.

"Has the series been commissioned?" Katya asked. Good point. If Netflix (and no-one else) wasn't interested, then no harm done. The Lochside Welcome didn't get its place in the spotlight, and neither did its rival.

Tindra nodded, repeating the by now familiar phrase. "So sorry you guys!"

"Girls," Katya growled, the generic term for people bugged her.

"Girls. Netflix loved the idea. They told Zac there's a terrific demand for heart-warming, people-centred documentaries about small towns and businesses. They saw the footage of the Royal George and how busy it was and loved it."

Worse and worse and worse… How had Lois and Angeline managed to convince Miles (and him in his turn the programme commissioners) that the Royal George was a) a heart-warming place and b) a small business? Hammerstone Hotels was nowhere near the Hilton or Premier Inn scale, but it dwarfed the Lochside Welcome.

"When does filming start?" Katya asked.

"Next week."

Tindra got to her feet. "I better go. Miles wants me to…" She trailed off, realising that whatever Miles wanted her to do it wouldn't benefit the Lochside Welcome or us.

"Thanks for telling us," I called out as she set off in the direction of the Royal George. She sent me a grateful smile.

"I hate them," I said, "rotten, lousy, horrible cows! And as for that lying, murderous, smarmy—"

"He's not," Katya interrupted, making me stare at her in disbelief. "Murderous or smarmy. Or that much of a liar.

"Anyway, I did some thinking while Tindra was talking, and I've come up with an idea. A way you can publicise the Lochside Welcome without Kudos Media. Better than a Netflix series even. D'you want to hear it?"

Jack returned at eight o'clock. I was steeling myself to give him the lowdown about Miles and his double-dealing. At least I'd managed to cheer him up on Monday when I'd told him about Blissful Beauty's sponsorship of the Highland Games. The sum of money I'd managed to get out of Caitlin made him smile and ruffle my hair.

"Just as well I married someone with brains and beauty, eh?"

"What do you want to do this evening?" I asked. He collapsed on the sofa, sticking his legs out in front of him and tipping his head back against the headrest. "A film. One that doesnae need me to think. You cuddled up next to me. A big bag o' crisps."

Easy enough. Jack didn't share my passion for pickled onion monster munch, but we did have one of those industrial-sized packets of hot chilli tortillas and a tub of sour cream and chive dip in the fridge. I didn't even bother decanting them into a bowl waiting for him to scoff half the packet before imparting the news that Kudos Media would not, after all, be making my husband the next reality TV star.

He let out a high sigh and closed his eyes.

"Thank God."

"But all that publicity!"

"Mebbe, but I dinnae like seeing myself in photos and on film."

"What?!"

The man next to me put many a Hollywood leading man to shame. Caroline and Jack senior's genes had mingled, creating the perfect mix of bone structure, height, hair colour and eyes, Jack adding to the effects with hard physical labour that created a muscular torso and limbs. Biased I might be but look at everyone else's reaction to him too. Tindra, Maureen and Louisa the hillwalkers, the women drooling over him and Tamar, and all those other tourists who stayed far too long at the bar whenever Jack was serving.

"It makes me look awfy full o' myself."

Ah. The ultimate Scottish crime. He wasn't going to like the idea Katya had come up with then…

"Do you remember when Mhari filmed you catching those plates? The time my mum and Nanna Cooper visited? When she showed it to me, I thought it was amazing. Like something a professional would do. I guess she's learned a lot on that course she's been doing."

One eye opened, and he squinted at me. "And?"

"Why bother with Netflix, Katya says, when you can do it yourself. A channel on YouTube. We start it straight away, so we're miles ahead of the Royal George by the time the programme goes out on Netflix. You show off how amazing Lochalshie is, what fantastic food you get there and how much visitors and the locals love the Lochside Welcome."

Jack put a hand in front of his face and let out a muffled groan. Hand removed, he eyed me beadily. "Do I have to?"

"Yes," I said, my fingers tracing their way down his

throat to his collar bone. "But why not make Xavier the star instead of you? Mhari might want to film making his pizzas —throwing the dough up in the air. Talking about how much he loves his adopted home?"

Jack's expression changed; the dismay replaced as he mulled over the suggestion. "Who's going to film, edit and upload this stuff?"

"Mhari and Katya. It's good practice for Mhari. And Katya says editing films is not that different from editing books. You need to work out what's needed and what isn't. And working on the films would give her a welcome break from writing about the love lives of female billionaires. I'll do some cool graphics for the channel. Ones that make people remember the brand."

"And I get the final say over what goes on YouTube."

"Yes," I said, hoping that was true.

"S'pose it wouldn't do any harm." He pointed the remote at the TV; my signal to shut up. *An excellent week's work, Gabrielle Amelia McAllan,* I told myself thanking Katya too for her input. A YouTube channel in the pipeline *and* the Highland Games sponsorship secured. Just three tonnes of work to do for that, thanks to Dexter, the thought of which had sent my poor, frazzled brain into overdrive.

Chapter Twenty-Four

Two weeks later

"Out Instagram account has gone mad," Alex said, me by now all too familiar with his face thanks to our three-times daily FaceTime chats. The games were two days away.

"… which is awesome. I've spoken to DPD, and they say you can expect the delivery at 11am."

Dexter's idea for marketing to take advantage of the opportunity offered by Blissful Beauty's sponsorship of the Highland Games was to provide advance samples of a product kept under wraps until now. His marketing assistant was fresh out of university and desperate to make his mark. No detail was too trivial for him. When he'd phoned me the first time—five minutes post my conversation with his boss —he asked for Google maps of Lochalshie, the full programme of events for the Highland Games, the location of the nearest bus stop, train station and airport, and a complete breakdown for where the Blissful Beauty logo would appear.

Now signposted ahead of Saturday's games, a visitor to the village might be forgiven for thinking its name was Blissful Beauty and not Lochalshie.

"Brilliant, Alex. I'll let you get on."

Like Dexter and Caitlin, Alex was an American yet to work out British speak, even though 'I'll let you get on' was the phrase I used all the time with him. I spotted Katya, making her way towards the house. She'd promised to help when the delivery arrived. Alex hung up on—too much to hope that he wouldn't phone another four times today—I opened the door to her.

"Can you believe this weather?" she asked, the two of us taking in blue skies unsullied by clouds.

The last fortnight had seen record temperatures hit the UK, and particularly this part of the world where it hadn't rained in SIXTEEN DAYS. We'd experienced temperatures of over 22 degrees day after day. One day, it even hit the heady heights of 29.

Jamal's shop had sold out of sunhats and the sunscreen that sat on his shelves year after year. Lager supplies at the Lochside Welcome had run out on the peak heatwave day. "God knows how many customers I lost that day," Jack had groaned later. "Never mind," I said, the two of us padding through the waters of the loch attempting to cool down. "You did a roaring trade up until then."

A discussion about the weather marks you out as British, though moans about the rain were far more common than grumbles about sunshine. Unused to so much sweating, most Lochalshie inhabitants whinged.

"Scotland isn't set up for sunny weather," Jolene had explained to me on Wednesday evening when I'd wandered down to the Lochside Welcome for a break after 11 solid hours working on graphics. Jolene's Māori genes had propelled her outdoors to soak up the rays, and she sat on the low stone dyke in front of the loch, face tipped upwards. "No air con?" she said. "Your shitty little fridges don't have ice-makers as standard and most of your houses face south to try and capture the sun."

Fair enough. But the two weeks had seen weird things; the grass is turning from a luxuriant verdant green to brown and crinkly. People sitting outside in their gardens, night after night. Mass dipping in the loch most sensible people usually body-swerved thanks to its arctic temperature. And everyone I knew sported a red-tipped nose or ears, scarlet toes or on the back of a neck, angry red patches where they had forgotten to apply sunscreen.

Katya pointed to her left. "There's your delivery."

A DPD van pulled up, and its driver leapt out, opening the back door to his trademarked red and white van. He unloaded five boxes onto a sack truck, wheeled it up to the front door and stopped in front of us.

"Gaby McAllan?"

"That's me."

"Got a few boxes for you." He looked me up and down, taking in the stomach that now entered a room five minutes before I did, and sighed.

"I s'pose you're no' able to help me wi' the unloading."

He supposed right. I took pity on him. Jack was working. There were others I could call on. Stewart. Angus. And Katya, even, who I'd once seen deadlift twice her own body weight, and who was here anyway.

Ten minutes later, my team in place with only minimal grumbling, the serious business of offloading began. As the overseer, my role was to supply instructions and water. Only the latter received any appreciation.

By the time the four of them had decamped all the

boxes, the air in my living room stank of sweat. I did my best to disguise the urge to gag. When my nine-month sentence was served, the thing I looked forward to the most was my sense of smell reverting to normal rather than hyper-sensitive. Katya had spotted it too, her head jerking towards the three men as we tried to work out who was the guilty party. Angus? Stewart? The driver? All three?

The driver, damp patches on his T-shirt under his arms and on his back, handed me his hand-held proof of delivery device to sign.

"What's in they boxes?"

"Make-up and skincare," I said, "for next week's Highland Games."

He screwed up his nose. "For Highland Games? What, do the competitors need tae pretty themselves up afore they toss their cabers? I'm fae Luss originally. We dinnae hae make-up and skincare at *our* Highland Games."

Besides me, three people bristled. I did too, all of us outraged at this slur on the highlight of the Lochalshie calendar.

"No?" Katya said. "How backwards of you. Ours is a *very* modern event."

The 'ours' made me smile. Part-time resident, she might be, but we allowed no-one to slag off this village unless they'd lived here.

Driver suitably chastened and off to deliver 300 or so Amazon packages, we surveyed the sea of boxes. Stewart slit the taping on one of them and pulled out a small brown bottle with its distinctive pink and silver labelling.

"What's this stuff for, Gaby?"

About to answer him, Angus jumped in ahead of me. "Retinol." He took the bottle from him and squinted at the label. "10 percent."

When I'd told Caroline the Blissful Beauty sponsorship package included skincare freebies not yet on general release, I said I was worried that all those extra visitors would only turn up for the retinol.

"In the skincare world, a free sample like this is gold dust. People won't balk at driving hundreds of miles to pick it up. Then, they'll just turn around and go home again."

Caroline shook her head, eyes gleaming. "No, they will-nae, Gaby. First, because we're only goin' to gie away the freebie bags to folks who buy a ticket to the Games. Second, Lochalshie is in the middle o' nowhere. They'll get here, take in the beauty o' the place and stay.

"But just in case they don't, I'm gonnae bump up the ticket price this year to £15."

One huge rugby-playing hand dwarfing the tiny bottle I knew would retail at upwards of £80, Angus gazed at me sheepishly.

"Eh… d'ye think I could hae this, Gaby? Retinol's meant tae work miracles on wrinkles."

Not that miraculous. Angus was a few years older than me, but an outdoor life and years of playing as a scrum-half had made him screw his face up all the time, the expression lines now carved profoundly and permanently onto his face.

But I'd googled retinol. Incredibly effective, according to experts. Not for pregnant or breast-feeding women though. "Why not? Katya? Stewart?"

They needed no further encouragement, diving into the boxes to retrieve their own bottle. Though I shook my head when Stewart tried to take a handful of them. They'd end up advertised at twice the price on eBay.

The guys departed, Katya taking her laptop out and telling me the change of scenery might inspire her to dream up more words for the billionaire romance.

"What are we meant to do with all this stuff?" Jack asked when he returned home at four o'clock, squeezing past boxes.

"Put together a limited number of freebie bags to give away on the day," I said, holding up an empty pink and gauze one. My team and I had spent the last two weeks designing graphics for a social media campaign promoting Retinol10. The Blissful Beauty website, Instagram, Pinterest and Facebook accounts had been flooded with inquiries.

"Where can we get this? When? When? When?"

Katya, her laptop so far unopened, sat on the floor, a sheet of paper in front of her as she tried to work out the best way to create an assembly line.

"Alex got us to start an unsubstantiated rumour that we're giving away samples of retinol so strong you can only usually get it on prescription," she said. "That will bring in the punters in their thousands!"

"Who planted that rumour?" Jack asked, picking up another empty bag. We had 500 of them to fill.

"Who knows…?" I said. "Did I take delivery of several cardboard boxes labelled top secret today? Did I accidentally mention to Mhari that our house was now the storage vault for what counts as gold in the skincare world?"

No-one controls Mhari. Maybe she wandered her way to our house on her lunch break, spotted the cardboard boxes as soon as I let her in and was unable to resist ripping the tape off… Out spilt beautifully packaged bottles and boxes that she set up on a table, her newly-educated photographic brain taking over.

Snap, snap, uploaded on Instagram, and set up with a song on Tik Tok as Mhari lip-synced to that old James Blunt song, *You're Beautiful*. Anyone who then googled 'has Blissful Beauty launched its retinol product?' landed on an obscure

Facebook page—the one for the Lochalshie Highland Games, the banner proudly declaring 'Sponsored by Blissful Beauty'.

An ambiguous post that said the organisers of the Games were very much looking forward to the new and free exciting products they had to giveaway, courtesy of the sponsors…

"Have they included sunscreen?" Jack asked, inspecting the products. Mildred was in her element. We had emptied out several of the boxes, supplying her with an instant playground with endless boxes to scratch and jump in and out of.

I scanned the list I held and shook my head. "When Alex asked me two weeks ago what they should include in the freebie bags, I laughed when he suggested sunscreen."

My exact words: "Oh no! We don't get the sun here—or not for awfully long. That will make the Highland Games even more appealing for beauty pundits, right? No need to worry about skincare enemy number one."

There was nothing in the freebie bags people could use to protect themselves. When Jamal took his regular weekly trip to the wholesaler nearby, he told me he'd never seen that aisle of the store so busy and so depleted. He'd managed to find some Factor 50 tucked away at the back and stocked up. Scenarios you never thought possible Scotland—that the one bottle of sunscreen you purchased way, way, way back would run out in two weeks.

Katya put the boxes in order so we could move along them adding retinol, heavy-duty moisturiser, lip balm and mascara to each bag. Packing them took us ages, though as Katya pointed out if we'd stuck rigidly to her assembly line system, we might have shaved off a good ten minutes. Jack left at six, telling me he had promised Xavier help.

"Have you spoken to Dexter today?" I asked Katya as I fetched her a cold drink. She sat back on her haunches, drinking most of the can's contents in one. "No. He's working stupid hours. As flipping usual."

Oh dear.

I reached out my hand and patted her shoulder. "But you two! The sizzle! The mutual interests! The clever things he does with his tongue!"

"Gaby." My name came out as a growl. "You've said that every day to me for the last two weeks."

Oh. I thought I'd been subtle about it. Some days, I said chemistry instead of sizzle.

She stood up. "Anyway, I better go. If I don't make it home before Mhari, she'll rummage through my drawers."

I hugged her at the door. But when I watched her from the living room window, I spotted her change direction, walk back the way she had come and head straight for the Royal George.

Blast it.

Chapter Twenty-Five

The bags hung around in the living room for the next two days, gathering dust and rousing Mildred's curiosity. Yanking back the curtains to the by-normal dazzling sunshine on the day of the Games, I breathed a sigh of relief. At last, we were going to get rid of them.

They were to be distributed just before the Highland Games started. The Games were traditionally launched by the local pipe band marching down the High Street into the park. I'd need to make sure they were handed out in time. Lochalshie wasn't big enough for a band to squeeze past hundreds maybe even thousands of fanatical skincare fans waiting for their free samples.

Jamal would pop by later with his white van. We'd load it up with the freebies and park in just inside the field where the Highland Games were taking place.

"Do you need a hand with those bags?" Jack said as he got out of bed.

I shook my head. "I've got my squad ready. Katya,

Stewart, Mhari and Angus." The latter probably hoping to filch another bottle of Retinol10. "Off you go!"

I wished him luck knowing he hadn't slept properly in two days, sick with worry about the Games. Always a money-spinner for the village, would it prove to be so today? And if it were, would he cope with it? Were all contingencies covered? Would five members of staff be enough to deal with the hoards…

Hoards. Fingers crossed.

"It'll be fine."

Famous last words of every single person in the world ahead of some event where everything turns out to be a disaster. I plastered the smile on anyway. My role in our marriage had always been that of the cheerer upper. Often misguidedly but it's a yin yang thing, right? For every pessimist, there must be an optimist.

"This Highland Games," I said, holding out my hand so Jack could grab it. "Will be the best Lochalshie has ever witnessed. The food and drink they have in the Lochside Welcome will blow their socks off!"

Feet planted, he stood up fast enough to make me gasp. Someone too used to slow movement these days. Arms encircled me, hands resting on my belly, soft voice in my ear. "The best thing about you—and there are lots of them, Gaby-sketch—is your endless optimism. Sometimes, I even believe it myself."

He kissed my ear. "Today, I definitely do."

I tilted my head, resting my forehead against his shoulder. "Good. Go out there and make this Highland Games the best there's ever been. I know it will be!"

Freshly showered, Jack resembled the man I'd first met some years ago. His red hair gleamed, and his skin shone, the dark eyes glittered, a combination of mischief and a secret—the kind of dirty secret a girl wanted to beg to know. In short, the Jack I hadn't seen for a while, him hidden under a veneer of care-worn over-responsibility.

"What are you going to wear today?" I asked. Pregnancy did this to a woman, made her a voyeur who turned men into sex objects. "Please, please make it your kilt."

"If ma lady insists!" Dark eyes focussed on mine. The reverse striptease, if you've ever had the luck to experience can often be sexier than the other one. A man, tall, strapping and muscular, stood in front of me. Gloriously naked, skin freckled across the arms and face. Muscles that rippled as he moved. He rolled on socks, black thickly ribbed ones that stopped just under his knees. Added the tiny dagger once a vital weapon now a decoration, Jack's topped with a miniature jewel. The kilt wrapped around his waist, a length of plaid that appears far too long when you see it unworn but fits perfectly, thanks to the tailoring. The sporran dangling suggestively over a man's best bits. Next a shirt he buttoned to the top before I shook my head, leave it... Much better to leave the collar bone and the hint of chest hair on show.

He side-glanced me, a wink and a smirk. "D'ye approve?"

Oh yes... So, would all those visitors to the Highland Games, those who wouldn't usually dream of going to something so lame but had been attracted by the promise of advance samples of the pharmaceutical range all the beauty journalists and influencers were raving about. Luckily, I wasn't the jealous sort. Well, not much. I'd adapted to the pregnancy invisibility, ironic given the size of me... but sometime soon, I looked forward to a) attracting my own second glances (hopefully) and b) baring my teeth at all predators who advanced on my husband and telling them to back off.

"Off you go and win customers!" I said, blowing him a kiss and waiting until I heard the front door shut before dropping the smile.

Fulltime optimism was hard work.

"Aye, so," Mhari said when she arrived half an hour later, "I cannae help you put this stuff in Jamal's van. I'm the official camerawoman, mind?"

Handy, huh? The last time I'd looked at Mhari's profile on Instagram, I spotted she'd added photographer extraordinaire to her bio. Nothing like a bit of belief in your abilities, eh?

She and Katya had already uploaded two five-minute films about the Lochside Welcome. In the first one, Jack and Xavier were pictured laughing and joking behind the bar watched by adoring tourists. In the second. Xavier put the finishing touches to pizzas while he talked about his new-found passion for Scotland. I checked the views and likes every day. They were not substantial. "These things take time," Katya said when I asked her, waving her hand airily. "Um, I don't think Jack would approve of that first film," I added, mindful of my promise to him he got final approval. He hadn't seen that one.

"Too bad," Katya said. "It's for the greater good."

"Shouldn't you be at the Lochside Welcome, then?" I asked Mhari now, "so you can film Jack and Xavier as they deal with thousands of customers?"

"No," said Katya, who'd arrived in sync with Jamal's van. I glanced out at it and did a double-take. On the side was a giant logo, Blissful Beauty, followed by the tagline, Make-up and skincare so good you won't need to cover up! Jamal walked into the house, rubbing his hands together. "I negotiated a deal," he said, beaming at me. "Where a company pays you a bittie o' money to put their logo on your motor and drive around various places."

My understanding of that kind of deal—something I'd once investigated as a debt-ridden student—was that the company logged where you drove. It was meant to be through traffic/population-dense areas. Would Jamal waving at a few sheep in a field as he sailed past in his van, the only vehicle for miles, count?

But the deal explained his enthusiasm for filling his van with the freebies. It would be parked just inside the field, ready for the excited Blissful Beauty superfans to grab their bags.

"No, what Katya?" I said, "what are you two doing about filming? My husband's in his best kilt. He'll be awesome on YouTube."

"This is part of the excitement of the new channel," Katya said, gathering up the bags in her arms. "Mhari has lots of footage of Jack and Xavier in the Lochside Welcome already. She's filming the goodie bag grab to add colour and intrigue. I'm the director, by the way. In charge of the overall look and feel of the films."

Mhari pointed out that only folks who didnae have the talents to work a camera called themselves a director. The real skill, she said, lay in filming. Katya flicked two fingers at her.

"Anyway," Mhari said, "Gaby, pick up one o' those bags, open it up and look awfy surprised. Take the retinol bottle out at the same time."

Katya nodded when I pulled my 'must I?' face. Acting

has never been my strong point. As Katya and Mhari hurried to tell me after my first attempt.

"That's no' surprise!" Mhari complained. "Mair like constipation, which at your stage o' pregnancy is likely. Have you been to the loo this morning?"

"Shut up," I told her, sending dagger glares in Jamal's direction too when he nodded in agreement, telling us that during one pregnancy, Enisa had not taken a dump in a week. Honestly. Why did my pregnancy have to be everyone in this village's business?

I tried again, making myself gasp when I took out the retinol and exclaimed that the product was so in demand, stocks had sold out way ahead of its official launch. "Just think!" I said. "How brilliant it must be for wrinkles!"

"Will that do?" Mhari said, putting down the professional camera she'd borrowed. Katya nodded. "Yes. Maybe cut the speech out though."

Outside, Jamal's van was boxed in. It was only ten past ten, but news of the freebies must have travelled fast. Both sides of the High Street were lined with cars, and strangers milled about—many of them younger than your usual Highland Games attendees.

"Mhari," I said, suspicion growing. "Did you tell people Caitlin was coming?"

She pointed the camera in the direction of the loch shores. Gareth's ice-cream van was doing a roaring trade already, people crowded around his hatch as he dispensed Mr Whippys in record-quick time. They were far enough away for her not to need to ask their permission.

"Mebbe. No' my fault people are too ready to believe fake news, is it?"

Oh well. With any luck, they'd deal with their disappointment at Caitlin's non-appearance by drowning their sorrows at the Lochside Welcome's bar.

Anyway, the van not being able to move worked in my favour. If I stayed here with Katya, we could hand out the freebies when the Games opened and I'd be close to our house, able to access a clean, private loo readily enough. The thought of a chemical toilet made me heave.

The bags deposited in the van and its door shut and padlocked, Mhari headed off to the Lochside Welcome and Jamal to his shop desperate to cash in on all the visitors milling around.

I put my hand up to shield my face from the sun. The Royal George's banners advertised Zac's pop-up fish and chip van, declaring them voted the best fish and chips in Scotland on TripAdvisor. A free glass of Prosecco for everyone who opted for the dish. Another sign offered a half-price deal on a five-course taster menu later that evening. No wonder their car park was full yet again.

Already, they had the advantage. Those enticing offers trounced by the fact that the hotel was located just next to the field where the Games took place. Where were hungry and thirsty tourists going to walk into first?

"Have you talked to him again?" I asked Katya, tipping my head in the direction of the pop-up van parked in front of the loch.

"No." A tiny pause before she said it. "Well, I did go for a drink there the other night."

"Katya, you didn't!" I'd seen it myself, hadn't I? "And how come you managed to sneak that past Mhari?"

"She was at her mum and dad's house."

"What did you speak to Zac about?"

"Weddings."

"Whhhaaatttt? Getting married? Who, you and Dexter?

But not in the Royal George, surely? That would be desperately disloyal of you both." I grabbed her arm, an unwelcome thought jumping into my head and taking up residence there.

"OMG! Has Zac proposed? You're so fed up of Dexter and his workaholic tendencies, you'll marry Zac to spite Dexter, who will then see the error of his ways, promise you sincerely he has changed forever and for the better. At that point, you get a quickie divorce from Zac, marry Dexter, and you and him live happily ever after?"

Kata planted her feet and folded her arms. "Gaby, has the sun gone to your head? That's the stupidest thing I have ever heard. You know what I think of marriage—a sorry institution that props up the patriarchy. No, I went to the George because I saw something the other week and wanted to ask Zac about it. I'll tell you later."

Too hot and bothered to question her any further (it wasn't even eleven o'clock. What was it going to be like once it got to midday?) I nodded. "Okay. What are you going to do now?"

She looked beyond the Royal George to the field. "Help Psychic Josie set up."

My mother-in-law's side hustle. Part of being psychic was advertising your attendance at events weeks in advance and telling people they needed to book up quickly to avoid disappointment. Name submitted, my mother-in-law and her trusty helper—usually me, excused this year on account of the pregnancy—could search for people online and find out everything she needed to know from their Facebook, Instagram, Twitter and Snapchat feeds.

"And you?"

"Sleep," I said. "Stockpile a few hours, so I last beyond 5pm this afternoon."

Katya hugged me and headed off. I watched her go and turned to let myself back into the house. Upstairs, I had a pair of noise-cancelling headphones. I'd taught myself how to sleep in them. They worked a treat too; I dropped off within three minutes of climbing on top of the bed, Mildred only too happy to join me.

My phone rang an hour later, the shrill ring tone jerking me into consciousness at once.

Jack.

"Hey! Is everything okay?"

"No. Got an emergency here. Gaby, I hate to ask but would you mind…"

"The lorry hasn't turned up," Jack told me, panic-stricken when I arrived at the Lochside Welcome minutes after he called me.

"Oh!" My hand flew to my mouth. Ideally, the lorry delivering all those barrels of Tennents should have been here yesterday. But thanks to the heatwave hitting Scotland, the nation's pubs were doing well. Plenty of people wanted lager to slake their thirst. "We'll deliver tomorrow first thing!" the brewery promised.

An hour after the allotted slot went by, then another and still no sign of it. Jack rang the brewery. No answer. He tried again and eventually got through to a hassled-sounding receptionist who told him the lorry had set out that morning. She made a few phone calls, got hold of the driver who phoned Jack and said, Aye, aye he had delivered his load tae Lochalshie, the hotel at the end o' the High Street.

"What end?" Jack asked.

"Far end," the driver replied, a new man to the job and area. Just as the instructions said.

A driver who has been working in the heatwave non-stop to deliver lager to thirsty punters sometimes cuts corners. Such as double-checking an address. Or relying on the man who stood outside a hotel when he produced his barrels to answer appropriately when asked his name.

"Didn't he notice the signs outside the hotel?" I asked, unable to believe the man's stupidity.

"Nope."

"What are you going to do?"

Dear, oh dear, oh dear. My husband and Zac Cavanagh did not have a happy history. Once upon a time, Jack had punched him and broke his nose. Debate the rights and wrongs of that move all you like, but for obvious reasons, I didn't want them being anywhere near each other.

He let out one of those sighs where the lungs emptied of air altogether. "Go up there and demand my lager back. With any luck, they haven't unloaded the whole lot yet."

"Jack, please…"

He cupped my face and kissed the tip of my nose. "I won't lose my temper, I promise. If the worst comes to the worst, I'll drive to Oban and pick up as much as I can from the micro-brewery there."

That would cost a fortune and take an age.

"Do you want me to come with you?" I asked. The Lochside Welcome wasn't too busy as most people were buying ice-creams and not yet at the lunch/pint stage.

He shook his head. "Can you stay here? Xavier and Jolene are setting up the beer tent in the field. I need you in the hotel with Tina and Russell, the agency staff."

"Fine," I said and watched him head up the street. Miles and Tindra were going to get their wish for drama. Filming a fight scene would add lots of local colour to their stupid Netflix docu-series. I'd spotted Tindra earlier outside the George. She pretended she hadn't seen me.

A large group of women came into the pub just as Jack left. "Was that Sam Heughan?" one of them asked me, her eyes rounded in wonder. Her accent was pure Birmingham, as were the others. Seekers of Retinol10 I guessed.

"Yes," I said. It wouldn't do the Lochside Welcome any harm if people thought Sam Heughan could be found here. "He's from Lochalshie originally. Likes to spend time here in his favourite pub."

The woman screwed her face up. "I thought he came from New Galloway?"

Darn it. Sam Heughan fans rabid in their devotion. They knew a lot about him. "That's right! But he used to work here. His gran is a local resident."

Lie accepted, the group demanded three bottles of Prosecco and disappeared outside to soak up the sun. I shouted warnings after them, "Remember to put sunscreen on!" Another sentence dusty, thanks to infrequent use in this part of the world.

Half an hour later, the women's conversation had increased 100 percent in volume, but we had no other customers. Where was Jack? My one big task of the day was to give out Blissful Beauty freebies, and the hands-on the clock edged ever nearer to one o'clock.

"Are you okay if I pop up to the Royal George, Tina?"

She nodded, drying yet more glasses ready for the (soon-to-come, hopefully) rush. "That's fine. If we run out of lager, though…"

Quite. The beer tent needed most of it, but there would also be customers in the Lochside Welcome later all desperate for a drink.

I set off, noting that fresh cracks in the tarmac had appeared. The earth in the half-empty whisky barrels used as planters was bone-dry and the flowers wilted. Mhari, a huge wide-brimmed sunhat over her head, joined me. Too much to hope that she hadn't heard about the missing lager.

"Ten to one, he's punched Zac. That's what the WhatsApp group reckon."

"Do they," I snapped. "How helpful of them. And why are you here?"

As if I needed to ask. "I'm gonnae film it," Mhari replied. "Katya says you need lots o' excitement to make people watch things on YouTube. Cannae get more exciting than two fit guys wi' their fists flying."

Oh well. She would come in handy if I needed help pulling my husband off Zac.

We passed the fish and chips signs and the tourists that packed the car park and grounds of the hotel and made for the small courtyard at the far side.

"No, I didn't!" Raised voices. That one was posh, plummy English.

"No? You're tellin' me the lorry came in, the driver asked if your name was Jack and this was the Lochside Welcome, and you said, 'Aye, that's me?' and didnae notice his mistake?"

Mhari darted around the corner, closely followed by me, dreading what I might find there. The courtyard at the George was cobbled over old horse troughs along the side of the wall marking its long-ago status as a coaching inn. I bumped into Nina, busy filming the action while Tindra egged her on. I glared at her. She shrugged.

Jack faced our nemesis across one of them. They looked up when we clattered in, returning instantly to the stand-off. Both were dripping wet.

"What happened?" I whispered.

Tindra turned to me. "Jack threw him in the trough as soon as he got here. Zac pulled him in with him. We got it all on film!"

Eeks. Mhari had her phone out too, zigzagging it between the two of them—both faces flint hard.

"Ever noticed how similar our names sound, mate?" Sarcastic emphasis on the 'mate'. "Zac and Jack? I heard him say the name and assumed he meant me. He gave me the papers and drove off. I didn't look at them."

Zac threw an arm behind him. "Unlike your shit hotel, it's terribly busy in here. I had other things to worry about. But when I rechecked the papers, I realised the driver had made a mistake, and I was about to call you."

Much as I trusted Zac as far as I could throw him, his words had the ring of truth.

"Then, you storm in here, shouting your head off and don't bother waiting for an explanation."

I shifted uncomfortably. If Nina was getting all this on film, Jack wasn't going to come out of it well.

"He's right. I was here," a voice piped up. I turned startled. Katya, wearing cut-offs and a red camisole top. Very flattering. But different from the outfit she'd worn earlier this morning when she'd helped Mhari, and I load Jamal's van. She refused to look in our direction. Helping Psychic Josie, my backside! Mhari's camera moved straight in front of her.

"I heard him," Katya continued, "the driver. He mumbled the name. And Zac...had things to do."

Argghhhhh. Mhari dug her elbow into my side. "Wee turn-up for the books," she said. "Unfinished business, eh? You always need tae scratch that itch."

Argh, again. No, you didn't. Particularly, when you were

meant to be blissfully happy with your hot, talented, kind American boyfriend, also my line manager. I blinked, half-hoping that if I kept doing so, the image in front of me would fade away—no such luck.

Jack's eyes met mine. Katya as Zac's alibi might make me squirm, but if she was telling us something that made her look bad, then it must be the truth.

Jack ran a hand through his hair—a gesture I recognised well. "Sorry, mate. Been a stressful few months. No' sure how you manage hotel management as well as you do."

Zac eyed him warily. Trying to work out if what he said was genuine, I supposed. He must have decided it was.

"No harm done. And the cold water was a relief."

The edges of Jack's mouth tilted upwards. "Too right."

He reached forward hand extended. Zac shook it.

"We've not put the barrels in the cellar yet. You're free to take them."

A solution, but how on earth were we going to get so many barrels of lager across the field to the beer tent, and down to the Lochside Welcome, on the hottest day of the year so far?

It was half-past twelve. The Games were due to start at half-past one. More importantly than that, though, were the Blissful Beauty goodie bags, expected to be distributed before then. From the chants nearby, *Why are we waiting, why are we waiting*, the retinol seekers wanted those goodies in their hot little hands, like, yesterday.

The last time I checked, Alex had sent me ten (unread) messages, all of which would demand to know was I ready and had the goodie bags distribution begun.

What were we going to do?

Chapter Twenty-Six

Jack turned to Zac. "Can I borrow some of your team?"

"Sure," Zac replied, roping in three staff members including the sheepish waiter who was one of Ashley and Mhari's cousins. They loaded barrels onto trollies and pushed them down the street to the Lochside Welcome. The ones for the beer tent, Jack, Angus, Lachlan and Katya (refusing to meet my eye), rolled over the grass to the beer tent where Xavier met them, sighing in relief. What good was a beer tent with no beer?

For that matter, what good was the promise of freebie skincare at one pm when it was now less than 15 minutes away?

Beer tent and pub fully stocked once more. Jack thanked everyone. They scattered, work requirements elsewhere, leaving him, me, Zac and Katya. She fiddled with her hair, the back of it suspiciously mussed up. No film cameras—the professional or the amateur—still on-site, thank everything in the universe.

"I, ah, jumped to the wrong conclusion," Jack said.

Most of the time, Zac wore a permanent smirk. I put it down to a man thinking he was better than the rest of us. Or entertaining filthy fantasies about any nearby woman. Any time he looked at Katya, for instance. His face cleared now; the smile rueful rather than knowing.

"Don't blame you, mate. I don't think Kudos Media was honest with you or me. Miles promised me from the start he wanted to film the Royal George. Then, he decided the Lochside Welcome was the better story before Lois and Angeline sweetened the deal with the promise of investment in his company."

That conversation Katya and I had overheard that night, where Zac talked to Miles about money.

He shrugged. "I know the Lochside Welcome needs the publicity far more than Hammerstone Hotels do. Though I think Katya's idea for a YouTube channel for you will work much better anyway."

She'd told him about it! Katya met my eyes at last. What message was she trying to send me?

Jack nodded and held his hand out. Zac shook it. "So long as I'm not on it too much. But thanks again." He dashed off, saying he needed to check the beer tent, leaving Katya, Zac and I in the courtyard.

The chant, *why are we waiting*, had started up again. "Um, I'd better…" I gestured behind me.

"There's something else, Gaby," Katya said. "Tell her, Zac."

"I don't think…"

"Tell her, Zac."

"The weddings," he said. "Did Ashley ever wonder why they'd dropped away or say anything to you about it?"

I shook my head, expression puzzled. Was this the wedding chat she had mentioned two days ago?

"Hammerstone Hotels has a huge advertising budget. The advertising agency they use was able to run ads on all the social media platforms. We ran a package that was cheap enough for people to change their booking to the Royal George. The overall cost took into account the non-refundable deposit they'd put down at the Lochside Welcome. Because the George can handle more people, it seemed like a great offer."

He and Katya glanced at each other. "The way Lois and Angeline work… sometimes it makes me uncomfortable. But they're my employers. What can I do?" He turned in my direction, blue eyes wide and face open. "I think the Lochside Welcome is brilliant. And I'm so—no, he'll have to tell you himself."

Who? What? But on that cryptic note, he disappeared inside. There were too many punters milling about to ignore.

"I must help your mother-in-law," Katya muttered and fled. I sent her a telepathic message—*you, me, this evening, big discussion about your love life.* My opinion of Zac might have increased ten-fold given the latest revelations, but I didn't he think he was Katya life partner material. Team Dexter all the way for me even if he was a hyper-picky pain in the butt.

Jamal appeared, keys dangling in his hand. "Gaby? Mhari said you needed help moving the van?"

"Yes please," I pounced on the offer. Jamal was eager that his van escaped intact. The decals on the vehicle made it clear where the stocks of goodie bags could be found, and a crowd had gathered around it outside our house, fists thumping on the sides.

Angus appeared seconds later, putting his years of part-time bouncer work to good use to clear us a path to the van doors. "Step aside, lassies. There is plenty for everyone!"

Was there? The crowd wasn't 500-people sized but what about the people milling about the loch shores, in the Royal George and the Lochside Welcome and wandering around the stalls in the field?

We weren't going to get the van past them. Might as well give those goodie bags out here as per my original plan. I retrieved the foldaway table from our house and set it up at the back of the van. Angus held back the slathering hordes, and Jamal opened the doors, pulling out the bags and setting them on the table.

Carnage. A scrum started up straight away as hands darted everywhere, trying to snaffle a bag. Angus ended up with his back to everyone, body hunched over the table to protect the bags. Several of the women tried illegal Rugby scrum moves on him that would have got them blacklisted from the game. He put up with it for a few minutes before straightening up and bellowing, "Oi! Stop that!"

Angus was six foot five and twice the width of me. The yell worked, the crowd of women retreating, expressions cowed.

He folded his arms. "Now, every one of ye is gonnae queue nicely, show us your ticket tae the games and say 'thank ye very much' when Gaby and Jamal here hand ower the bags. Agreed?"

Fervent nods from the crowd.

"Anyone who doesnae," he growled, "will be thrown in the loch."

Two women looked far too delighted at the prospect of a dookin'. "Does that mean you would put us over your shoulder?" one asked, her smile gleeful.

"And," her friend threw in, "spank our bottoms?"

"No!"

But the threat worked. From then on, the distribution of Blissful Beauty's legendary Retinol10 went smoothly. Angus buoyed up on adoration from the women who loved the idea of him throwing them over his shoulders, settled into a flirt mode and helped Jamal and I give out the bags.

"You're a lucky, lucky girl!" he told one. The 'girl'—a woman old enough to be my mother—simpered. "Ten percent retinol," she said, peering into the bag. "That's why I came here today. From Newcastle."

More than four hours away. Good grief.

Angus batted his eyelashes back. "You don't need retinol, hen. Dewy-soft your skin is!"

I gritted my teeth. But the mega charm dose from Lochalshie's least likely Galahad was doing its best to mollify the women. We were 40 minutes later than advertised distributing the bags.

The Brummies I'd served earlier in the Lochside Welcome arrived, many of them pink-faced and shouldered thanks to the sunshine. "Serve me next, big boy!" one of them called out. Angus winked at her and flexed his muscles. Honestly.

Bags finally gone, Jamal locked up his van once more. It was still boxed in. "I better go, Gaby," he said. "Enisa is on her own in the shop, and we've had loads o' customers today."

Angus took the table in for me. He needed to head off too. The actual Highland Games started at half-past one, and he was down for the caber toss, hammer throw and farmer's walk. All activities that needed a thorough warm-up and stretches beforehand. The two women who'd gone through paroxysms of joy at the thought of being hurled into the loch by a huge, kilted Scotsman after a little light spanking followed him.

My front door swung open—an invitation. *"Gaby,"* it said to me. *"Come in, come in. Put your feet up. Shut the door and sit outside in the back garden with Mildred where you can fall asleep for a while…"*

Oh house. Thou art temptation too much.

Despite the noise all around me—the pipes had started up in earnest and chatter and laughter from such a large gathering drifted over—I knew I would sit in the deckchair in the back garden and be snoring in seconds.

(Pregnancy side effect. Remember?)

But today had thrown up too many things I needed to check. Had Jack managed to get the barrels in place in the beer tent in time? Did my mother-in-law need further assistance, seeing as Katya had been diverted by Zac? Talking of which, was she okay? Should I corner her, force her to speak to me about Dexter and Zac? Did I need to pop into the Lochside Welcome and ask Tina and Russell if they were managing? Or what about—

"Awright, Gaby?"

Mhari. Ginormous sunhat, big enough to protect her shoulders, still in place. "Ye'll never guess who I spotted in the beer tent just now. Only Jack's faither… and him wi' a beer in his hand too."

Argh. That trounced everything else I'd just worried about. With a last, despairing glance back at the house, I surrendered my nap fantasy and set off for the field, imagination buckling at what I might find.

The Lochside Welcome was the traditional supplier of drinks for the Highland Games via a beer tent in the field. Although the hotel was the Games' official drinks partner, I clocked the Royal George's attempt to muscle in as Mhari as I strode towards the Lochside Welcome's beer tent.

Women crowded around the George's gin and Prosecco pop-up, most of them holding the Blissful Beauty freebies.

"We should have done more," I told myself. "Said they only got their freebie bags if they bought a ticket to the Highland Games AND went to the beer tent afterwards."

I followed Mhari, who knew the way far better than I did. She weaved expertly around people, ducking under elbows, squeezing past stalls where visitors waited for venison burgers, pulled pork in brioche buns and deep-fried haggis pakora.

Thanks to the fearsome heat, the interior of the beer tent had to be ten degrees warmer than outside. The punters crowded in any way, desperate for an ice-cold lager. Lachlan stood behind the makeshift bar, he and Jolene both sweaty and frazzled looking.

Xavier, Mhari told me, had returned to the Lochside Welcome to cover demand for pizzas. (Fingers crossed that market existed—today's visitors not enticed by the Royal George's fish and chip signs.)

"Where's Jack?" I asked Lachlan as he expertly uncapped five bottles of Punk IPA and poured them into plastic glasses.

He handed over the glasses and cleared his throat. "When his dad turned up ten minutes ago, pint o' lager in hand. Jack hit the roof, ordered him to leave the tent and stormed out after him. I woulda gone after him, Gaby, but…"

A few years ago, Lachlan had beaten up Jack's father

following his assault on Caroline. But the man I'd bumped into in Oban with Mum and Nanna Cooper had seemed so sincere in his promise that he didn't drink any more. What did I know? Years of experience showed my powers of judgement, except in the matter of life mate choices and then only latterly, were rubbish.

"I better find them," I said, sketching a wave at Jolene. "Mhari!" Lachlan called out, "we need your help at the bar."

"Oh, but—"

"Now!" he snapped at her, and I shot him a grateful smile.

Outside, I welcomed the contrast in temperature even if it was unnaturally warm for Scotland.

The Games were in full swing, and the sponsorship gamble had paid off. The truth of Caroline's prediction was all around me—the field a mass of people. On a stage to the left, dancers stood, their purple and green velvet jackets making them stand out. Every stall had a queue in place, the demand highest for anyone selling sunny weather goods —handcrafted hats, cold drinks and ice-creams.

A lot of the freebie women stood outside Caroline's tent. A huge sign at the entrance to the Games declared Psychic Josie open for consultation, complete with the claim—As Used by Caitlin Cartier, and a one-sentence review. *"Like, super awesome advice!!!!!!!!"*

Next to the George, a roped off area was filled with giant rubber tyres, logs, hammers and markers ready for the competitors. Angus twisted from side to side warming up his spine ahead of the caber toss. Three women, their tongues hanging out, watched him, eyes widening further when he started flexing his biceps.

Honestly. Weren't people shallow? Katya's laughter in

my head. *"Richardson! You spent your first month in Lochalshie mooing over Jack because of what he looked like. Admit it!"*

Angus caught my eye, tipping his head towards the Royal George. Oh heck, had Jack's drunken father wandered in, followed by Jack and were now in the middle of a full-scale row in front of the customers while being filmed by Nina and Tindra?

On a day like today, no-one would sit inside. I ducked out of sight, around the front of the hotel and garden that sat right on the loch shores. As busy as ever, the air shimmered, scented with coconut sun cream and fish and chips. Sure enough, there were Nina and Tindra who darted among the guests, film camera held high out of the way.

Handing out free Proseccos to those eating his fish and chips, Zac spotted me. He pointed beyond the garden, and I nodded my thanks.

There they were, Jack and his father, sitting on the stone wall. Jack had taken off his socks and boots, bare feet and legs dangling in the water. The plastic glass next to his father was empty. I gulped.

"Jack!"

He turned, frown disappearing in a smile, and beckoned me over. I studied them both, no sign of animosity. His father leapt up. "Sit down, sit down, Gaby! D'ye want to take your shoes aff too?"

Too right I did. The shock of cold water made me groan in pleasure. I closed my eyes, enjoying the contrast of warm sun on my face and feet slowly turning numb.

"Is everything okay?" I opened an eye and squinted at Jack.

He took my hand, pressing it down on the wall between us. "Dad's on the no-alcohol lager. I jumped to the wrong conclusion. I seem to be making a habit of it today."

His dad stared out over the loch, its surface glass-smooth thanks to the lack of wind. "You cannae blame him, Gaby. He went through a lot as a wee boy."

The fingers on my hand pressed down firmly. I squeezed back.

"I have nae excuses for what I did. But I havenae touched a drink in three years now. Never will again."

He cleared his throat. "And I've done a lot o' work on anger management tae try to get over my issues. A year o' counselling to make me see the error of ma ways."

More pressure on my fingers. I knew what Jack was doing—indicating he was willing to give his dad a chance but letting me know that the final decision lay with me.

"I very much hope I can be a better grandfather than a father. But I know it's a lot tae ask of both of ye."

A lot, yes. And not a decision for today when there was so much going on. Jack and I needed to be alone, undisturbed by the demands of hotel management and graphic design jobs.

"We'll think about it," I said, touched when Jack Senior's face lit up. He dropped down beside me, sandwiching me, the current incubator of the next generation, between McAllan father and son. It would make a fantastic painting.

Jack's dad pointed at Gareth's ice-cream van. "Can I get youse two an ice-cream?"

We nodded, me asking him to add a can of something fizzy taken from the iciest part of the fridge. He wandered off.

I leant on Jack's shoulder. "What a day," I said. "I feel as if we've been fire-fighting non-stop."

"Mmm."

"Have you got time for this?" I asked, kicking my legs

gently, so water splashed Jack's knees. "The beer tent's super busy."

"They'll cope." He swung his body around, resting his head in my lap, ear pressed up against my belly. I stroked the hair from his face and marvelled at how the freckles had multiplied over the past few weeks.

"I'm taking a much-needed break wi' ma wife. The Lochside Welcome can manage without me for a wee while."

Chapter Twenty-Seven

Jack fell asleep for a while. Jack Senior returned with two ice-creams, and I indicated the head on my lap, shaking my own. He turned away to open the can of Fanta quietly, and I took it from him, mouthing thank you.

"I'll find some folks tae gie these ice-creams to," he whispered, and I nodded gratefully. This opportunity felt far too precious—a tiny oasis of calm after months of madness. Behind us, laughter and chatter rang out, and the pipes played Flower of Scotland for what felt like the 100th time. Didn't matter. I watched the water and the terns as they dived in on the hunt for food.

The Lochside Welcome was sited directly across from where we sat. A distant figure—Xavier? —moved around delivering pizzas. Most of the tables were occupied. But it was nowhere near as busy as the George behind us. Perhaps once the Games were over, it would fill up with people who didn't want to spend £15 on a pint (I must start spreading that rumour again.)

A large group of women stood outside the door, and I

caught the flash of pink and silver bags. *"Go in!"* I willed them silently. *"The Prosecco's much cheaper than that stupid pop-up in the park."* It worked—one of them pushed open the door and the rest crowded in behind her. Fingers crossed Xavier, and his team could cope with them all.

My stomach wobbled—a weird fluttering that was internal and then a… oh! A kick! A proper, proper little leg (or arm, who knew?) hitting out against its confines.

I stared at my abdomen, awe-struck. Really, truly, finally, proof that what was inside me wasn't too many helpings of pizza and chips. Even the scan hadn't convinced me the way this did. What if, say, the screen showed the results of what was inside the patient before me? Jack flicked one eye open, orb meeting mine. We grinned at each other—the wonder of it all, an ordinary, every-day experience that happened to billions of people world-wide overwhelming and joyous to us.

"Clever you," he said.

"Clever you," I replied.

He pressed his head closer to my stomach—another flutter and then a distinct prod-like movement. We exchanged delighted smiles once more.

"Don't go back," I said, threading my fingers through his hair. It was filthy; sweat making it greasy and the locks stick to my fingers. "Let's run off and join the circus."

Hormones rendered me giddy, irresponsible, not a good sign when you're three months off motherhood.

"Aye? If I'm the flame swallower, what are you going to be?"

"The lion tamer, obvs. Look at how brilliant I am with Mildred. I can handle her big cousins. Then, when our baby comes along, we'll enlist the services of the Great

Supremo and turn him/her/it/them into the greatest trapeze artist the world has ever seen."

"Course we will."

Jack shut his eyes once more.

The Blissful Beauty sample women were now out of the beer garden and by the shores of the loch. I cursed them. They were meant to stay in the Lochside Welcome and order food and drink. Whatever. I returned to stroking my husband's hair, letting the tips of my fingers gently push against his scalp.

"Jack!"

He groaned and turned his head, burying his face in my stomach. "Yes?"

His dad back again, face creased in anxiety. "Ower there!" He pointed at the Lochside Welcome, where the group of women by the loch shores seemed to have doubled in numbers. Are they fighting over those free samples? Too bad. Let them sort it out themselves.

I frowned. "Can't it wait? Jack's taking a break."

Jack Senior shook his head. "Eh... I think they're mebbe trying to cool down."

Jack sat up and swung his legs around, both of us trying to make out the scene opposite us. One woman ran for the loch, cheered on by everyone else. The move encouraged the others, who all began to strip off as the few people who were in the beer garden egged them on.

"Have they taken off their underwear?" I asked my eyesight not up to the challenge of working it out.

"Yup," Jack said, his face grim. "And that bit o' the loch shore counts as Lochside Welcome property. I better sort this out."

Naturally, I had to accompany him. Trust-worthy as he was, I had no faith in that many drunken buck-naked women. They'd eat him alive.

As we hurried down the street drawing our own small crowd, expressions gleeful. The prospect of so many women in their birthday suits far more exciting than tree-trunk thighed men hurling hammers and tossing cabers.

"Aye, they've all been downing Proseccos like there's no tomorrow," someone said, "lowers your inhibitions, doesn't it? Makes ye think it's a fine idea tae jump in the loch."

Katya and Mhari appeared at my side, the latter camera in hand. "You can't film this!" I said. "They might not care now, but once they sober up, no-one is going to want their naked body displayed to all and sundry on YouTube."

"I'll pixelate their faces oot. Naebody will ken."

Ahead of us, Jack took off. By the time Katya, Mhari and I had reached the Lochside Welcome, my breath coming ragged gasps.

"Come on," Katya grabbed my hand. A bottleneck had formed at the front of the hotel as people tried to enter and get to the beer garden. The house next to the Lochside Welcome—an ultra-modern des-res I'd lived in when I first moved to Lochalshie—had a concealed gate in the shrubbery that surrounded it. These days, the house was an Airbnb property, let out for those wanting a Highland hideaway. We let ourselves through it and made for the back of the house, and the enormous garden that backed onto the loch, throwing 'sorry's!' over our shoulders at the bemused couple sat in deckchairs as we passed them.

Beyond the six-foot-high bushes at the back garden was a low brick wall. Katya stepped over it, keeping her grip on my hand. Mhari followed us.

Twelve women in various stages of undress—four of

them wearing nothing at all and seemingly unbothered—huddled together. Jack and Xavier were with them, both men in the clasp of a woman either side. They faced the loch, pointing at a head that bobbed up and down some twenty metres away. Someone had gotten into difficulties, underestimating how strong the loch currents were.

The woman at the end of the row wearing only her pants suddenly bolted, running into the water.

"Come back, Kylie!" her friend screamed at her. Kylie carried on oblivious, but by the time she was waist-deep, she started wailing herself. Two weeks of sunshine had warmed the loch, but this was not the Mediterranean. Deep waters carried rapid bone chill factor all year round.

"Don't do it!" I yelled. Kylie's friend ignored me and ran in too, reaching her friend seconds later and adding her own shrieks to the cacophony. I'd once rescued Stewart's dog from the loch. I put my bag down and took off my shoes.

Katya read my mind. "No way. You're not going in there."

"But I was a Norfolk champion swimmer years ago!"

All those early morning sessions in the swimming pool day after day... Jack peeled away from the group. "No, Gaby."

"I used to work as a lifeguard in ze local leisure centre," Xavier said, peeling off his jeans and T-shirt, accompanied by cheers from the women left on the shore. He waded in.

Jack folded his arms. "I should help too," he said, eyes glued to Xavier whose powerful front crawl had taken him to the farthest away woman. "But... I havenae got anythin' on under the kilt."

Ah. Kilts are heavy things. That plaid weighs a tonne when wet. While it is often a (lovely) myth that true

Scotsmen wear nothing under their kilts, most of them choose to protect the Crown Jewels with a pair of boxers. Today's ultra-warm weather had persuaded Jack to leave his off.

"I don't think you're needed," I said, tipping my head towards Xavier returning to the shores much more slowly this time, one woman in tow. Kylie and her friend clung to each other, screaming about the cold and what was underneath their feet. Arms outstretched; their friends yelled at them to return.

"Blankets," I said to Jack. "I think our swimmers might need them."

He nodded and disappeared inside. He kept a store of blankets in the lounge area to give to punters who wanted to sit outside in the evenings. Katya had found bottles of water and was dispensing them to the rest of the group.

I picked up clothing and cleared my throat. "Er... maybe it might be an idea to get dressed? You don't want sunburn in delicate places. do you?"

A widespread agreement, thank goodness. T-shirts, crop tops, skirts and jeans vanished in a flurry of arms, as nine women made themselves respectable once more.

I might as well make myself useful. Everyone would need hot drinks.

"OMG! Look!" Katya had turned away from the group, her hand sheltering her eyes. The women beside her paused too, T-shirts and tops half-pulled on. Tongues hung out; a picture-perfect moment—clear blue skies, the sun hanging above Maggie Broon's Boobs and the shining white of the building behind us.

Two half-naked men torsos dripping—one swarthy French-Canadian and the red-headed Scot whose rippled abdomen and muscular biceps I knew so well—accompanied by three half-naked women emerged from the loch, the moment freeze-framed for its super-appreciative audience.

"Why did you need to go in?" I asked. We'd borrowed the towels from the bedrooms upstairs. Coffees made and distributed to the women recovering from the shock of the loch's cold waters, we sat away from everyone else. The Lochside Welcome's beer garden included a cutely named Love Seat, where a gazebo threaded with ivy, honeysuckle and blue-flowered clematis offered shelter and privacy. Fat bees buzzed around it their tiny feelers dotted with pollen.

The near-drowning excitement hadn't detracted too much from the Highland Games. To my right, the pipes played on, and cheers sounded out—applause for those competing in either the strong man stuff or the Highland dancing.

Xavier was surrounded by women, cooing over his bravery and fighting over who had the privilege of sitting next to him. He shot me one of those 'get me out of here' looks. I shrugged. Katya had donned a black apron, expertly weaving in and out of tables as she took food and drink orders, the afternoon's excitement hunger-inducing.

Jack, towelling his hair dry, paused. "Kylie and her friend," he said. "It happened so quickly I think I was the only one who saw it. The two of them toppled over and went under."

My hand went to my mouth, the scene playing out in slow motion in front of me.

"There are unpredictable currents in the loch," he continued, "and I didnae want to hae to deal with the publicity where folk read about a wee hotel in the Highlands where two women drowned after drinkin' too much Prosecco in there."

A rueful smile. It summed up, I guessed, thirty seconds of blind panic where worst-case scenarios played out in Jack's mind one after another, and he took responsibility for the end of each one. I kissed the tips of my fingers and pressed them onto his nose.

"They drank too much Prosecco in the pop-up too," I pointed out. "Not just in the Lochside Welcome."

"Even so."

"Take this." The scalding hot coffee I handed over was black, no sugar. Just the way I liked it too. Or did when I wasn't protecting my unborn child from caffeine. I inhaled it anyway as I passed it over. "I'm terribly glad, though, that you managed to find a pair of boxers before you plunged in. Some things are for my eyes only."

A mischievous grin. "Aye? When I ditched the kilt inside, I gathered a wee audience, all cheering along as I unwrapped myself."

That deserved a mock punch. Duly delivered. "Oh, you!"

We snuggled up, the gazebo working its magic. People mocked love seats, but they did what they set out to do on the tin, forcing persons one and two to cuddle up and be at peace. The absence of Wi-Fi in this exact spot might have played a part too.

"Mhari filmed the whole rescue thing too," I added. "Katya says we must upload it on YouTube soon as. She says it's like a guy version of that Botticelli painting, *The Birth of Venus*, and three hundred times better publicity than a stupid Netflix docu-series for sure."

Jack grimaced. "Only if you pixelate my face out. Concentrate on Xavier. He's batting them off like flies."

True. Kylie and her friend were now stuck to him, limpet-like, Mhari gimlet-eyed as she took them in. Maybe it might open her eyes to what was right in front of her, younger man or no.

When she'd handed me her phone with the order, "Keep this, I've got things to do," I'd stopped myself. No asking, 'what, are you off to stake claim to the sexy Canadian at last?' If she and Xavier weren't an item by the end of the day, I'd eat her oversized sunhat. But she'd headed off in the opposite direction. Oh well.

I waved Mhari's phone in the air. "Do you want to see what she recorded?" I asked Jack. He shook his head, shuddering.

"Aye, aye, Jack. Awfy lot of excitement here this afternoon."

I whipped around, the familiar voice startling me.

"Ashley!"

The man didn't match the voice. The Lochside Welcome owner I'd always known was a big man in height and girth. The guy in front of me was about half the size, the weight loss emphasising his towering height. His skin had changed too—the greyness gone and a tan in place. If I squinted, he might qualify as a man in his 30s, not late 50s.

But in the last update he sent us he said he was heading for Tenerife and planning to stay there until November. What was he doing here?

He smiled at me. "Gaby! You've reached the glowing stage. You look much better than the last time I saw you."

"Thank you," I accepted the comment with a gracious nod. Three years in Lochalshie and I'd grown used to back-handed compliments.

He squeezed himself next to us on the Love Seat, face

tipped up towards the sun and eyes closed. "I left Costa Adeje on Thursday. It wasnae much warmer than this."

Jack edged forward, tilting his head to the side so he could catch my eye. Why was he here? Why now?

More cheers in the background from the Highland Games; the pipes started up. Highland Cathedral—the traditional end to the day's festivities.

"Can I get you a drink, Ashley?"

"Aye, please Gaby. A Diet Coke. I'm on that low-carb diet for the diabetes. I've lost three stone, and my blood sugar results are much better."

He certainly looked the picture of health, especially if you compared it to the memory of the man months ago—grey, overweight and exhausted. I made a note to myself, google low-carb diets for post-pregnancy weight loss potential.

No sign of that limp either. I glanced at Ashley's leg, he picked his foot up and waggled it from side to side. "Touch and go, Gaby, whether I would keep ma foot or no'. But it's healed up alright."

Diet Coke fetched and handed over Ashley drank its contents in one go.

"I've been doin' a lot o' thinking these past few months."

Jack shifted in his seat eyes fixed on Ashley, who seemed to be doing his best not to look at him.

"And the thing is… I cannae work in the hotel business anymore. Mair than 20 years I've been here working long hours and just aboot every day o' the week. I'm thinking of… selling up."

Silence as we both tried to figure out what that meant. Jack's management of the Lochside Welcome was always intended to be temporary. He'd take over Highland Tours once more—the eight months on/four months off cycle I'd grown used to. Perhaps Xavier might want to stay in Lochalshie. He might consider working for Highland Tours again too, so my husband got to ease off the crazy working hours and help play a more significant part in our baby's upbringing.

"I've been made a generous offer."

Oh. The selling up bit was further ahead than indicated. Maybe there was an affluent Indian software developer who suddenly hankered for a hotel in Scotland he could descend on from time to time. Hands-off management. That kind of thing.

"I dinnae think anyone can beat it. The hotel's no' done as well as it used to, and it's only gonnae get worse. Folks dinnae go out that much these days. They'd rather stay in with their cheap wine or beer fae the supermarket and binge watch Netflix."

I opened my mouth to protest. Then closed it. It was true. In the last few months, Jack had told me all the things he'd love to do to the Lochside Welcome if he had the money to make it far more enticing to the boxset-loving, supermarket drinkers. That big 'if'. We had nowhere near the capital.

I clasped his hand. The Indian software developer might want to keep the temporary manager and his team on. He —maybe she—would have plenty of money, and be terrifically open to Jack's ideas, encouraging him to develop them to bring the punters in. Thanks to all that cash I imagined swirling around, there would be enough money for more members of staff too, easing the burden on the current lot.

"They're no' my first choice, obviously. But they know the area. Love the peace and quiet o' the place. Think if they buy the hotel, add it to their existing—"

"Hammerstone Hotels," Jack said, his voice flat. I thought back to what Zac had said earlier in the day. *No, he needs to tell you himself…* the who 'he' was answered for me.

"Aye." Ashley leant forward, hands resting on newly slimmed knees. "I know they're no' everyone's cup o' tea."

Putting it mildly. Not mine for sure. When they'd snapped up the Royal George, they told the village no-one had anything to worry about. Not a threat, no, no! And then proceeded to greedily hoover up as many passing visitors as possible. Plus, there were the dirty tricks wedding tactics Zac had told me about.

"What are they going to do with the Lochside Welcome?" I butted in.

Ashley's right hand moved from his knee, fingers raking through what was left of his hair. "Lodges," he said eventually. "Fantastic location and all that."

True. The Lochside Welcome at the top end of the village was closer to the loch and its views more picturesque than those from the Royal George. Plenty of people would queue up for rural escapism, their shiny clean 4x4s jammed full of food, supermarket booze and their Netflix account sign-ins in hand.

"Chips!" I said, my voice oddly squeaky. Jack and Ashley stared at me.

"Where will I get my chips?"

Not my finest argument. A company concerned only with profit hovered on the brink of seizing the Lochside Welcome, a Lochalshie institution since… forever. They would raze it to the ground and plonk kit lodges there instead, off-limits to the villagers, who would no longer be able to sit and watch the sunset in a beer garden where the sun's rays dimpled. Laser beams that blazed through the clouds and spotted the ground with dazzling circles of light.

Granted—current heatwave situation aside—sunny days were rare.

Or gather in there on Friday nights for the pub quiz, where they cheated by sneaking in their phones and googled everything. Met their friends there, those who valued the odd night out when their Outlander/Games of Thrones/Stranger Things viewing schedules allowed.

Almost every meaningful date on the Gaby-Jack time-line happened in the Lochside Welcome. If they dug it up, they'd mash my history into the ground. What happened to the time, 50 years from now, where Jack and I celebrated our golden wedding anniversary there? (If, of course, the universe spared us.) Or even just our tenth?

That's what my chips question *really* meant.

Jack shuffled, edging closer to me. He got it too. My husband had attachments to the Lochside Welcome that ran deeper than mine. The eight-year-old taken there one night while his about-to-be stepdad flirted with his mother, signalling the beginning of a much happier life for child-hood Jack. The 18-year-old playing pool with his best friend Lachlan watched by women who suddenly found themselves fascinated by the sport, as they watched the light above the table catch the gleam of his auburn hair and highlight the planes of his face. (I didn't dwell too much on what happened next in that scenario. Winner taking the spoils, etc.)

The 22-year-old made redundant from the Forestry Commission coming in one night, perching on a stool at the bar, putting his head in his hands and asking everyone, "What am I going to do?"

To this day, he was hazy whose idea Highland Tours was. Ashley's? Terry and the rest of the regulars at the bar? Stewart, even? But one person piped up, "Why no' start wee tours o' the Highlands? Ye ken the area well. Lots o' folks like signing up for a minibus day oot."

And lo, a business was born.

The Lochside Welcome wasn't a building to us—it had taken hold of our hearts and crushed them tight.

When the bulldozers came to flatten the place, I'd lie in front of them.

Chapter Twenty-Eight

Two days later, the weather broke. I greeted the rain like a long-lost friend, opening our bedroom window so we could listen to its familiar pitter-patter.

"Skiving off work then?" I asked as I got back into bed, and Jack shook his head. "I promised I'd go in this afternoon. Jolene, Tina and Russell are on breakfast duty for the overnight guests. I'm no' needed."

He wiped his face. Men don't cry in Scotland—or not over anything important. If their team loses at football or wins the Scottish Cup fair enough. At the thought that their village is about to change forever, not at all.

He flicked his hand at his eyes once again.

No, men don't cry.

Ashley's announcement hadn't been that surprising. Who else was going to buy this hotel and keep it on as it was? But when Jack argued the case against Hammerstone Hotels' takeover and what they would do with the place, Ashley came up with another proposal.

"Can ye match the offer?"

We'd stared at him, aghast. Match the money a conglomerate had? Of course not. Jack was a sensible fellow though, Ashley said. One who might be able to convince a bank to lend us the money because he knew all about budgets.

I clasped Jack's hand in mine. "We'll try," I promised him. "Put together a business plan and see what we can do."

Ashley had to get back to Hammerstone Hotels by mid-September so they could begin the process of planning applications. The local council, Jack told me as we lay in bed, would find the idea attractive because the proposal would mean local jobs. Builders, electricians, plumbers.

"For the short-term!" I said, rolling over so I could prop myself up on my elbow all the better to study his face. "The Lochside Welcome offers long-term employment."

"Not if no-one goes there, Gaby." He shook his head sadly. "I tried, but…"

I pushed me and my bump up against him. "You did. Your ideas for what might bring in business are brilliant. Blasted, blasted, blasted Hammerstone Hotels."

The Lochside Welcome… gone, it's spacious garden, the bar I'd loved right from when I first moved here, reduced to rubble diggers will scoop up and drive away. The bricks in its walls appeared to move of their own accord, crumbling into piles of dusty masonry in front of me.

I banished gloomy Gaby for the Blissful Beauty team meeting half an hour later. Whisper it… Gabrielle Amelia McAllan did like some bits of being the boss. Caitlin promising to turn up for our meeting worked a treat on Malingering Marty. When I turned on Zoom the Monday before the Highland Games, there he was. Since then, I'd had no problems with his attendance, and he'd come up with some brilliant ideas for what we did on Instagram.

As I'd suspected, him, Trish, Ali and Logan were all far better designers than I was. But I'd found a way to make the team gel. The additional money was welcome. Meeting concluded—everyone agreeing that we were on schedule for the official Retinol10 launch mid-September—I decided to do some skiving of my own, googling how to write a business plan.

The internet presented me with not only guides on how to do so but templates. Result. I printed them off, pen poised on a practice one. No harm setting out some ideas Jack and I could finalise later.

Half an hour into it and I gave up. Katya would be able to help me. She knew how to write business-speak. Mildred, sat on her usual spot next to my monitor where she could take advantage of its heat, swished her tail. An agreement, I reckoned.

Besides, apart from a few WhatsApp messages where I asked all the questions, and Katya replied with one-word answers, I still didn't know for sure what had happened between her and Zac. Time to find out.

"Is Ashley selling up then?"

Too much to hope for that the news would not yet have spread. Jamal bagged up the sandwiches and crisps I'd earmarked for the lunch hour I planned to spend with Katya.

"Might be," I said. No point in lying.

"To Hammerstone Hotels?"

Wasn't everyone well informed?

I took my canvas tote and hitched it to one arm. "I don't know." A truth of sorts.

"Well, that's okay," Jamal said, taking me by surprise. "That's what these big companies do, isn't it? They buy up the wee companies, let them keep their own brand. They get the Lochside Welcome and add it to their boutique hotel business, and folks think—aw, this is nice. Two totally different hotels in Lochalshie. But they're the same thing. Aw the money goes intae the one big pocket."

"Yes," I swiped my card. Let Jamal believe that benign scenario for now.

Katya must have been watching for me out of the window as the flat door opened, before I'd even knocked on it, my hair frizzing around my head thanks to the persistent drizzle.

"What kind of sandwiches are they? I'm back doing strict plant-based," she said as she took the bag off me.

"Hummus and watercress," I said. "Jamal got them in 'specially when you moved back to Lochalshie. Though they are not that old, obviously. I've got the business plan templates with me, but first, we need to disc—"

"Katya!"

Her head, buried in my bag as she inspected my other purchases (Doritos, no animals whatsoever harmed in the production of said 'food' item), whipped up. As mine did. There, on the other side of the street, stood Dexter, phone in one hand and face fizzing with fury.

He must have flown up from London to Glasgow on the red-eye this morning. Hadn't I suggested he whisk Katya away on a surprise minibreak? Only it wasn't meant to start with one person looking like he might explode any minute now.

"Did you sleep with him, you fu—"

Ah. Whoops. The rest of that sentence was none too complimentary. Let's just say the last cut off word there ended up being one of the milder insults Dexter hurled at my best friend—that liquid chocolate voice of his turned up to decibel-blasting volume.

Behind us, curtains twitched. A bleary-eyed Mhari poked her head out of the top window. "Wazz goin' on?" She must have been in bed. I gestured to her to go away, unsure of what I should do myself. I was 99 percent sure Dexter wasn't violent, but these were extreme circumstances. Safe to say he knew about Zac.

"Katya? Are you okay? Shall I call the police?" My best friend appeared frozen in place; the bag of food still held in front of her.

Dexter hadn't broken the law, I was reasonably sure, but best to be on the safe side. I said it loud enough for him to hear.

She shook her head. "No, I... but..." She glanced upwards.

I dashed up the stairs and burst into Mhari's room. "Come on," I said, throwing open the chest of drawers in her room and flinging underwear and clothes on her bed. "You're coming to mine for the afternoon."

Bless her. She only grumbled a little bit, dressing hastily and grabbing her phone before we headed back downstairs.

But it didn't matter anyway. Katya and Dexter were nowhere to be seen—the bag of food abandoned on the doorstep. If Dexter had flown into Glasgow this morning, he would have needed a hire car to travel to Lochalshie. They must be in that.

"D'ye think he'll kill her?" Mhari asked, helping herself to one of the sandwiches. Concern for a friend did nothing to affect her appetite.

"No!" At least I hoped not. My phone pinged—a message from Katya.

"I'm okay. We've gone somewhere to talk."

Hardly reassuring. But what could I do? I handed Mhari the rest of the food and set off for home.

"So, what happened?" Jack asked later as we tried to figure out the business plan by ourselves, Katya's help not forthcoming for understandable reasons. I'd sent her a message in reply—'call me as soon as' and spent the afternoon checking my phone in case I missed a message from her—no such luck.

"How did Dexter find out about it?"

"Ah… well. Hyun-Ki, for his sins, never left the Lochalshie WhatsApp group and he saw all the messages on Saturday flying back and forth."

Mhari's phone had died overnight—something that frequently happened thanks to constant use. Once she'd charged it up again, it repeatedly beeped, WhatsApp, Facebook, Instagram, text and voicemail all signalling messages from her one-time boyfriend now racked with guilt.

"Given that Dexter was the one who gave him a job at Blissful Beauty," I told Jack, "he's 100 percent loyal to him. He had one Goju shot too many last night and phoned Dexter just as he was stepping onto the plane in London. Said he owed it to him."

As a young guy who'd never been in a proper relationship—the Mhari one didn't count—Hyun-Ki viewed these things in black and white. You had a long-term partner. You didn't sleep with anyone else. End of.

Which most people would agree with. But perhaps

Katya should have been left to deal with the whole mucky situation by herself…?

"Other people's love lives. Complicated, hmm?" I said, parking all thoughts of Katya (worried though I was about her) to one side.

"Whereas we only need to worry about…"

Coming up with a business plan so mind-blowing it convinced banks to finance us. Easy-peasy, right?

Jack studied the screen in front of me where I'd typed in his plans for how we would expand what the Lochside Welcome offered to visitors. So far, all we'd come up with was establishing more partnerships with local tour companies, those running Outlander-themed expeditions. Excellent for the tourists to wander into the pub and see a Jamie Fraser lookalike, right?

The next week disproved easy-peasy in two days. Jack made an appointment with the local Scottish Enterprise office in Oban to ask their advice. Then, he traipsed around the banks, asking for the money.

They all said no. This wasn't the heady days of the 1990s and the early noughties when banks threw money at businesses left, right and centre. No, this was post-recession cautious, post-Brexit Britain. No-one wanted to invest. I looked out of our living room window every morning, eyes glancing right first to the Royal George and then left to the Lochside Welcome, trying to work out what the village would look like with log cabin lodges at the far end instead of a white brick building.

Besides nothing from Katya. Even though I sent her endless messages. I knew she might not want to talk, so I kept them brief. "Are you okay?" That morphed into, "Are you alive?!" "Earth calling Katya, come in!"

"The thing is," I told my bump, "little one, you're going

to need Auntie Katya in your life. I'll do my best to be an excellent mummy, but Katya's a better bet for common sense and solid life advice."

I sent that as a caption on a picture to Katya too. A smiley-faced emoji came back. Alive then, thank heavens.

The news about the Royal George was now common knowledge—villagers shaking their heads when they talked to us but no-one able to come up with any ideas. They knew too that the banks had all refused us money. Laney Haggerty sidled up to me one day and said she had a couple of thousand she could spare. Would that help…?

Bless. And no.

The summer was ending—the rain, wind and shivery temperatures back in full force even though it was only late August. Was there much point in the hotel limping on any longer?

Chapter Twenty-Nine

Tuesday night and I thought I'd have dinner in the Lochside Welcome, my workday too energy-sapping for me to muster up cooking, or really, heating up skills. The High Street had that battened up look to it already—the one it got once the tourism season was over. Doors closed, deserted of cars and only one brave soul out walking a dog. I drew my coat tighter around me and shivered.

The regulars in the Lochside Welcome had awarded me special status on account of the pregnancy. One of them always shifted off his stool as soon as I came in. Mind you, they were high stools and getting up on them these days was tricky.

"D'ye need a hand, Gaby?" Terry asked.

"Please." I held out my hand. His friend put a foot on the base of the stool to steady it, and Terry yanked me up. I landed on the cushion with a loud thump.

"Quiet in here tonight," I said.

"Aye," Terry said, "the English schools are back. Makes

an awfy difference. We like it better. Dinnae have tae wait too long for a pint."

Apart from the four regulars at the bar, the only other people in there were a group of three tucking into pizzas with a great deal of enthusiasm. Xavier and Jolene were behind the bar, the latter polishing glasses and trying to stifle yawns.

All those packed out times I'd been in here over the summer were an illusion. Come the end of September, Monday to Friday would be like this—the hotel not bringing in nearly enough money to sustain a business.

"Earth calling Gaby!"

"Katya!"

There may not have been many people in the hotel, but all of them looked up sharply. News of that screaming match was common knowledge, and all the chatter stopped; everyone waiting on an update straight from the horse's mouth.

Katya, I could tell, knew this. She nabbed the stool next to me. "I was waving at you for ages! You were miles away."

"Where have you been?" I dropped my voice to a whisper. "And is everything…?"

Tickety boo? Had she and Dexter had split up? Or were they still together? My messages and texts had all been ignored. I clocked the absence of red eyes, pallor or hair badly in need of a wash. Evidence whatever had happened in the last few days hadn't made her unhappy?

Katya shuffled on her stool, taking her coat off and shaking out her hair. Stalling. Did this mean she was now with Zac, planning a permanent move back to Lochalshie where she would spend all her time writing billionaire romances? At the same time, he turned the Royal George into the most successful Highland hotel there has ever been, people queuing up to eat there, those rat-race escapees in the lodges built on the ruins of the Lochside Welcome all flocking there in the evenings. However, we locals never got to eat or drink there because the astronomical prices made it way beyond our reach...

"Hey, Gaby!"

That would be a 'no' to the 'now with Zac' thing then. Dexter draped an arm around Katya's shoulders—the two of them exchanging a small smile. More mumblings from the locals and Jolene exchanging raised eyebrows with me. I sighed, relieved.

"We're here to celebrate," Katya said. "Guess what?"

"You're engaged," I burst out. "Brilliant! I promise I'll organise you the best hen party in the world ever. Pity you won't be able to marry here, but I'm sure we can all travel to Great Yarmouth, take Jack's minibus perhaps and have a wonderful time there, and then—"

"Get a grip," Katya said. "We're not engaged. I told you before. Marriage is a sorry institution that props up the patriarchy. Why on earth would any sane woman enter into it willingly?"

"Right enough, hen," Terry cackled. "Ma wife says the same." He finished off the remains of his pint. "What is the patriarchy, by the way?"

"We are gonna put some money into a property together, though," Dexter said, the tops of his fingers resting on Katya's breast, and she leant back into him. I don't think they realised they did it—an unconscious gesture of intimacy. I was right about the sizzle. Did chemistry make a guy overlook anything? I remembered Jack's words on the subject. "Gaby—no-one knows what goes on in a relationship apart from the couple themselves."

"And if that doesn't say permanent commitment, I don't

know what does," he added, he and Katya giving each other another of those complicit smiles.

"Oh, where?" I knew these two made serious money together, but London was bonkers expensive. Did they mean to buy here—in which case, hooray! I loved the idea of Katya being in the village permanently, especially now I'd worked out it would not be with Zac.

"Wherever," Katya said, waving a hand about. Deliberate vagueness, I decided. "But I'm also celebrating because LeAnna and Daniel have just kissed for the first time. I managed to make it go on for three pages and then I typed THE END in capital letters. Best feeling in the world. *High Heels and Pink Glitter* is now finished, thank the stars. Jolene, have you got any champagne?"

Jolene ducked under the counter, resurfacing with a dusty bottle, vintage, by virtue of its age. Who drank champagne these days when Prosecco was so much cheaper? My best friend must have decided she was worth it.

"Make it two bottles, no three! And get yourself a glass." The thrill of finishing that book had made her giddy. "Chaps," she called out to Terry and co. "Would you like one too?"

"Naw, naw," Terry said. "Makes me hiccough."

The other three accepted, though. Never look a gift drink in the mouth as the saying didn't go.

"Champagne, eh?" Mhari. The woman who possessed an uncanny ability to materialise whenever there was gossip, free food and drink on the go. "How're, Katya? Kissed and made up wi' Dexter then despite you... you know."

She waggled her eyebrows and mouthed 'Zac'. Subtle, it wasn't.

The pub fell silent, everyone awaiting the reply.

Dexter, I noticed, tightened his grip on Katya. Something must have happened, but they'd worked it out.

"I'm fine, Mhari. How delightful to see you!" Heavy on the sarcasm. "I've cancelled my Netflix account, by the way."

"But I'm only half-way through Tiger K—whatever. I'll hae one o' those glasses of champagne, though."

Xavier appeared with the champagne in an ice bucket. Jolene joined us at the other side of the bar. Katya poured champagne into flutes and gave them out, holding the last one out of Mhari's reach.

"What for? Nosiness? Spreading rumours? Qualifying as the worst friend a girl could have? And don't forget, I enlisted your help with that book. The only thing you told me to do was write about flower petals opening and flag-poles sliding into them full tilt. Plus, you haven't washed the dishes in the flat for weeks."

"The noise o' the washing up would have disturbed you. Stopped you thinkin'. And when I read the third last chapter, there were roses aw ower the bedroom. Was that no' a hint LeAnna and Daniel have been humpin' like mad?"

"Humping? Shagging?" Xavier raised an eyebrow, pointy triangle style. "You Brits. So many romantic ways to say making love."

Mhari pushed two fingers into her mouth. "Making love? Urgh. That phrase gies me the dry boak."

A nod from Jolene.

Katya grinned at Xavier, taking a glass from him. "If someone with a French accent says it, it's hot. Or a Texan one," Dexter took a sip of champagne and pecked her on the lips. "Then, and only then."

Later this evening, I promised myself, I'd test this theory out. Get Jack to tell me he wanted to make love to me in a

French accent. Then in his typical accent and see what it did for my libido. I would, however, keep the results of my little experiment to myself.

We toasted Katya, me on Appletise. Jack appeared, the two of us giving each other small, wistful smiles that were nothing to do with French-accented requests and more sadness about the end of an era. "Ah well," Jolene said, "I might see if there any other classroom assistant jobs going."

Xavier nodded, murmuring that it might be time to return to Canada. "But what about—" I burst out and then shut up. Mhari? What had she done since the loch emerging incident as we now called it? (10k + views on YouTube and about as many thumbs up.)

Not a thing. When I remarked loudly and frequently about Xavier's beauty, she stared at me and asked if Jack knew about my 'wild and uncontrollable lust' and what he thought about it. Jolene put it more bluntly, leaning across the bar and hissing at her. "For heavens' sake, you thicko. She means, why haven't you asked—begged—him to go out with you?"

At that, our nosey friend—the one who spent all her time wheedling secrets out of everyone else—clammed up. Jolene asked her again, and she shrugged. "Look, I'm busy bein' a career woman. Concentratin' on my photography and filming. Hyun-Ki's been mentalling me in his spare time."

"Mentalling?" I screwed my face up.

"Aye, mentalling. Where someone takes an interest in your career development and coaches ye."

"Oh. Mentoring. Right."

A fascinating development there: Hyun-Ki and Mhari back in touch. If they'd ever broken off contact in the first place.

"What are you celebrating?" Jack's father.

Jack glanced up sharply, the words setting off alarm bells. A teetotaller Jack Snr might be these days, but the last time he'd been in this pub had not ended well. The regulars must remember it too, their heads swinging up in unison and their expressions wary.

"My friend has just finished writing a book," I said, determined to head off any sign of trouble. Katya elbowed me lightly. The infamous Jack McAllan Snr here in person and her first sighting of him. In the two weeks since the Highland Games, he and Jack had met up the once—a long stroll on the shores of the loch, me leaving them to it. (Heroic action on my part if you ask me. Mhari wasn't the only nosey person in Lochalshie.)

They'd talked about Jack's childhood—what had happened after Caroline, and he left Jack Senior. There were a lot of years Jack Senior had missed out on. He wanted to know everything.

"Do you want to join us with an Appletise?"

He smiled. "No thanks, Gaby hen. I hope you're keepin' well. I wanted a word wi' your husband if that's okay wi' the both of you?"

Jack nodded, first at me and then at his father. He opened the hatch and stepped out, telling us he wouldn't be long. Wouldn't matter anyway, given how few customers were in. They set off for the beer garden.

I stuck my hand out to the side automatically, preventing Mhari from heading after them. "Don't you dare."

"Oh, but—"

"No."

It was remarkable how similar they looked, Jack and his father. I did my best not to stare at them out the window, their backs to everyone as they sat at one of the picnic benches and facing the loch. Not warm, but it was dry, their backs hunched the same way, heads held at identical angles —one topped by vivid red hair, the other more faded.

"Anyway," I said, holding up my flute of Appletise. "Here's to you, Katya! Congratulations on finishing your first novel."

"Don't congratulate me. It's the worst book that ever had the misfortune to be written."

"I'm sure it isn't. But, if you don't want to toast that, what about this mystery property you and Dexter have bought together?"

Two sly smiles from them both. Katya tapped her nose. "All in good time. Anyway, Xavier! Why not sit this side of the bar right next to my friend Mhari here who is too shy to ask you out and has begged me to—"

"Hey! Shut your big gob you nosey, interfering—"

"Kettle, pot, black. Take those three words, Colquhoun, and rearrange them into a popular phrase!"

"Youse are all barking up the wrong tree, anyway!" Mhari said, nodding towards Xavier.

Behind us, the door opened again. Lucas. Xavier's face broke into a wide smile.

Lucas took the last available stool at the bar. Xavier leant across and kissed him.

Clink! Clink! Clink! The sound of pennies dropping as Jolene, Katya and I met eyes and exchanged, 'Ah, now we understand!' nods.

"Xavier's my BFG," Mhari said, waving towards the happy couple, "ye ken? My gay best friend?"

A heroic effort on my part as I struggled with the effort not to correct her on which way round the initials should go. The Xavier-Lucas thing explained a lot, such as why Lucas kept dropping off guests from the Highland Tours at the hotel. I thought he'd been helping Jack, but sneaking visits to Xavier had been his ulterior motive.

"Hooray!" I clapped my hands. "This calls for more champagne! Shall I find some behind the…"

Jack, his face dazed, let himself back in. He hooked an arm around my shoulder. "Got something to discuss with you. Shall we go?"

I was off the stool straightaway. "Of course. Goodnight everyone."

Chapter Thirty

"So, they've all clubbed together to help us?" I asked, dazed myself.

Jack handed me a cup of tea. A proper one. Pregnant or not, I needed the caffeine to focus correctly.

"Seems like it. We only told a few people what was going to happen but—well, you've lived here three years, Gaby. You know what it's like."

He shut the curtains and shoved the footstool closer to the sofa to allow me to put my feet up. Me comfortably settled, he stretched out, his head in my lap. What a difference half an hour made... My fingers traced the planes of his face, working lightly from his forehead to the cheekbones then along the jaw. When was the last time I'd seen him so relaxed? Months ago. I loved his face frown-free.

"And will there be enough?"

"Yes. If I sell Highland Tours to Lucas, and I think he'll be glad to take it on as bookings were up again this year—"

I had to interrupt. "Did you know he and Xavier were an item?"

Jack stared at me. "Aye? Wasn't it obvious?"

Men, eh? They notice something incredibly significant and promptly forget all about it.

"Oh, I s'pose. So, you sell Highland Tours."

"And put my savings in along with the others, we'll be partners in the business."

"My savings too."

The head in my lap stirred, dark eyes meeting mine. "No, Gaby."

"Yes, Jack." I resumed face stroking. "What did Dexter say earlier? No stronger proof of commitment than buying a property together and my name isn't on the title deeds for this house."

"I'll sort that. I meant to do it when we got married but this year…"

Ran away with us. No, my savings were going into the partnership too. Impulsive decisions were my speciality, but this one went to the core of me. It was the right thing to do, no question.

Caroline, Ranald and Lachlan had conferred at the weekend—all of them as attached to the Lochside Welcome as Jack was. What if, Lachlan suggested, we partner up? Ranald was due to retire. He and Caroline wanted to downgrade to a small house closer to the village. He planned to sell the farm and put his money into what he called his retirement fund. Caroline had savings a-plenty thanks to the Psychic Josie stuff. Lachlan had… well, a lot of money squirrelled away in a lot of different pots.

Partners one, two, three, four, five—now six. Caroline had rung Jack McAllan Senior two days earlier. "Were ye lookin' for something special you could dae for your son and grandchild's future?" she asked. Too right he was.

Jack senior's sober years had been kind to him. A

chance investment in a Highland fish farm start-up had yielded healthy returns by the time it sold up to a far superior Norwegian firm. He was loaded. Partner number six was able to invest far more than anyone else.

"How do you feel about that?" I asked. Our baby appeared to want to know too, delivering a gentle kick to his head that made us both smile.

"Okay," he said. "We discussed it. He's awfy anxious I shouldnae feel obliged. But he listened to my ideas for what I might change and said he knew his money was a long-term investment. Nae pressure, except where I prove to him what a fantastic entrepreneur I am."

"And is your mum okay about it?" As Jack Senior's punchbag in his younger years, her opinion mattered to Jack far more than his father's did.

"She spoke to us while we were out there."

She had? Wow. I hadn't spotted her in the pub. She must have used the same hidden pathway in the house next to the Lochside Welcome. Apparently, Jack told me, his father had sought his mother out months ago, desperate to apologise for what he had done. Caroline, a successful GP, fake psychic and all-round decent sort, accepted it. Ranald, Jack added, was far warier but content to go along with whatever Caroline chose to do.

I bent over to kiss Jack—the movement much trickier now, thanks to the baby. When I hovered in mid-air, stuck by the bump, he reached up, and we exchanged a clumsy bump of lips.

"You will be an utterly brilliant hotel owner stroke manager. With business ideas, I'm dead happy to sink my savings into."

Serious face from Jack. The frown returned, a furrow

between the brows as two large, almost black-irised eyes lasered in on mine.

"Sure?"

"Surer than I've ever been."

Chapter Thirty-One

"... so, all's well that ends well!"

At the other end of the phone, Katya snorted. She was back in London and speaking to me from the Blissful Beauty flat. "As much as I adore your grandmother, Gaby, it's my sacred duty as your best friend to ensure you don't turn into her. That was 100 percent Nanna Cooper. Please never say it again."

I poked my tongue out. A wasted gesture as we were doing old-school phone time—i.e. on an actual landline. It might deprive you of seeing someone as you spoke to them, but they did sound so much clearer, especially in a village where mobile phone signals were never as brilliant as the company website promised.

"I'm thrilled those two witches didn't get their hands on the Lochside Welcome," Katya said, and I nodded, forgetting yet again she couldn't see me. Ashley had been more than happy to accept our partnership offer, once the details had hastily been finalised by Ranald's solicitor—making us all sign a contract that appeared to bind us together for centuries. Jack asked me repeatedly, "Are you sure?" He repeated the question to Katya and Dexter, worried that two such worldly, glamorous people had unrealistic expectations of what shares in a small hotel might bring them. They dismissed his fears.

"Don't worry, man," Dexter said. "Katya's kinda attached to the hotel. It's where we first... y'know." At that, he cleared his throat. I hadn't always thought Dexter capable of anything less than self-assurance. His eyes flickered above—the ceiling below the main bedroom. Reliving that night, I decided.

As you might expect of a best friend, I had tried to get her on her own and make her swear to me she was okay. "Yes," she said and left it at that.

Deal done and dusted, I suggested to Jack we ask Ashley if we could be there when he told Hammerstone Hotels where to stuff their rotten offer. He smirked at that. "Oh, yes."

And so we were there... Ashley met us outside the Royal George. I aimed a kick at the moss-green Jaguar in the car park, and we entered the hotel. The receptionist directed us to the office behind her, where Lois and Angeline waited, the latter with bare feet on the desk.

Lois raised her eyebrows when Jack and I followed Ashley in, congratulating me insincerely on the pregnancy.

Ashley refused to sit down, offering me the only remaining seat.

"An awfy generous offer, ladies," he began, "and I'm that grateful to you—"

Lois pushed a sheaf of papers towards him. "Fabulous! Those lodges will bring so many tourists to the area and offer fantastic local employment opportunities."

She squinted at Jack. "Perhaps you might consider moving into construction, young man?"

Jack nodded. "I might."

Ashley took the pen she handed him and scribbled on the dotted line, giving the papers back to Lois. He turned to the door. I got up, and Jack and I made to leave too.

"Whaaattttt!"

Ashley stopped, hand on the door handle.

She stared at the paper, the words 'away and bile your heids!' sprawled along the bottom.

"I've had a much better offer," Ashley said. "But a pleasure doin' business wi' you, ladies. Cheerio!"

And the three of us fled, giggling like schoolchildren. On the way out, I spotted Zac who waved and grinned. I grinned back.

Wednesday 6 September. We signed the paperwork, and the Lochside Welcome was now ours—a village pub and hotel more than it had ever been. I swung from elation to terror most days. Jack did too. "But it will be okay," he told me, the two of us lying in bed at night facing at each other. Mine was usually the optimist role. "It'll take time, but we'll put new ideas in place and take it one day at a time."

I repeated the phrase to myself now—*one day at a time*. I threw in a cliché of my own. *It's better to try and fail than not try at all.* Mildred jumped up beside me, poking me with her paw—the gesture she always used when she wanted a person to stretch their legs out and allow her to sit on them. I did so.

"Ouch!"

"Are you okay? Gaby? Are you?" Katya's voice staccato-ed, the urgency emphasised by the loud, are you. As this was 'our' first pregnancy—me and my best friend's experience of what happened to a woman over the nine months

326

of growing a baby process—Katya had taken on the excessive worrying part for me. Exceedingly kind of her.

"Fine," I replied. "Mildred just dug her claws into my legs."

"Right. Have you started the Mildred adaptation programme for the baby?"

The answer, no. Tomorrow, I promised myself. Yummy-mummy organic, paraben-free baby lotion to purchase then rub on my hands that I then let her sniff.

"I can't believe Lachlan had that much money," Katya mused.

I could. "Is the money, er, clean?" I'd asked when Jack told me how much money Lachlan was willing to invest. I never bothered querying the small details of what Ranald's nephew did.

Jack grinned. "It is now. He's awfy good at playin' the stock market."

Nevertheless, I made him look up money laundering laws trying to work out what might be taken off him if he was found guilty of trying to wash dirty cash through the hotel. A bridge to cross when we came to it. (I was wise enough to keep that thought to myself, rather than risking accusations of Nanna Cooper-isms from Katya once more.)

"And Ranald and Jack's father being partners too!"

"I know." I stroked Mildred's head and flinched as she resumed the clawing. "Ranald says he'll be the silent partner. A job he was made for."

True. My sort of father-in-law was a man of few words. He preferred conversations with his cows and sheep. The ones he was about to say farewell to, as he sold up the farm and downsized.

"And Xavier's going to take over general management?"

"Yes, thankfully. It should mean a few less late nights.

Anyway, the tourism season is over. The hotel has quietened down a lot."

The baby kicked me. The internal football games were brutal these days, reminding me of what was coming and how unprepared we were. Had Jack and I really made a baby, the question surfacing all too often. I stared at myself these days, the unfamiliar reflection disconcerting. "Who are you?" I asked the mirror, "and what have you done with Gabrielle Amelia McAllan?"

Not ready, not ready, not ready…

Distraction needed, I thought up a question for Katya. "How are the edits on the book going?" At the other end of the phone, she snorted. Yesterday, Katya had returned from a meeting with the publishers and phoned me straight afterwards.

"OMG, Gaby! You won't believe what they have ordered me to do. I've got to make it 'sizzle' more apparently. When I pointed out that it's awfully challenging to sizzle when the billionaire can't even kiss the chauffeur/handyman until right at the end, I got no sympathy. 'Use your imagination,' they said. 'Make them exchange hundreds of meaningful looks.' And every blasted meaningful look must be described differently. You've no idea how rotten difficult that is!"

"His eyes undressed her?" I'd suggested and been shot down. "No. If only. That's too rude. No hints whatsoever of stripping in this wretched, stupid, terrible book. If I ever, Gaby and I mean this with all my heart, sign up for another writing gig like this, shoot me."

I'd held back from pointing out this was the first in a three-book deal. Maybe by the end of book two, the billionaire got to place her hand on the chauffeur/handyman's bare chest. And once book three was over and done with, she was permitted to pat his bottom. Only if he consented of course.

Katya blew a raspberry now. "Not well. I keep getting Dexter to stand in front of me so he and I can do the 'meaningful looks' thing to see if I can find a fresh way of describing it but every time we try, I start to giggle, or he does. No use whatsoever."

There. I had my opening.

"So, are you and Dexter…?"

As awkward scenes went, the one where Dexter screamed the question, did you sleep with him you dot dot dot was up there in the top ten of all time.

Another raspberry. "Dexter will never change."

Oh dear. I wanted my best friend to be happy and loved up, mainly for selfish reasons, so I didn't need to worry about her. Even better. She changed her mind about marriage, so I could add that event to my about-to-end entirely social calendar. Imagine if they got married in the Lochside Welcome! Fabulous photos, a social media campaign orchestrated by the finest two minds in PR and marketing. Fantastic publicity. Unlikely to happen by the sound of things.

"I won't either," she sounded remarkably cheerful. "We might as well accept it. Dexter is a functional workaholic—functional in that he also passes as a human being from time to time. I'm someone who finds other guys attractive. So we compromise. He works a bit less. I ease off the flirting. Perfect, right?"

"Um, if you say so."

Other people's relationships… so complicated. I sent her good wishes through the phone line and the universe. *Be happy, my friend. Let you and Dexter work yourselves out.*

"You'll be back for the party, though, won't you?" I

asked. "Where we make our official status as the new Lochside Welcome owners known?"

A solemn promise that she would drag Dexter from his desk kicking and screaming to attend, and we said our goodbyes. My mobile buzzed. Hyun-Ki. He'd phoned me the other day to rave on about the brilliant work me and my team had done on Retinol10 and the rest of the pharmaceutical range.

"Gabs!"

"Hyun-Ki! Tell me you are returning to the UK super-duper soon where I can hand over all boss-like responsibilities to you and go back to being merely the 1,005th best graphic designer in the world."

Ominous pause.

"Ah. That's what I'm phoning you about. Blissful Beauty has offered me…"

Chapter Thirty-Two

Ten weeks later

Trish's face flashed up on my screen, and I waved enthusiastically. Wednesday lunchtimes were my favourite part of the working week. It was the day I got to hand over to Trish as part of the job share arrangement we had figured out between us.

Hyun-Ki's appointment as creative director for Blissful Beauty's operation in South Korea hadn't been that surprising. Why on earth wouldn't he want to return to his home after four years away from it? And that elevated position had placated his super-hard to please parents. They took in the title, the responsibility, the number of people he'd have underneath him and finally agreed their son had done well.

Not excellently or amazingly for one so young but well; maybe South Koreans had more in common with the Scots than previously thought. My Lochalshie friends did not believe in excessive—sometimes any—compliments either.

But when he had first told me about his promotion, I

panicked. Yes, yes, the boss bit had been more enjoyable than I'd expected. But the punishing hours took everything out of me. In desperation, I suggested Trish should be the boss instead. The perfect solution, right? She was in London for a start, and even though she was new, she had excelled herself.

Hyun-Ki, who had read tonnes of leadership and management in the 21st-century guides, came up with a suggestion. Why didn't Trish take over the head designer role while I was on maternity leave but in the meantime, we could do the UK head designer role as a job share with a view to making that arrangement permanent once I came back from maternity leave…?

Trish was only part-time anyway. She leapt at the chance. As did I. Still a boss, but only a part-time one. Trish was so desperate to prove herself, she bent over backwards to adjust to us sharing information and handing over to each other every week.

I did Monday to Wednesday lunchtime, and she worked Wednesday afternoon to Friday, leaving me free to do the odd bit of work at the Lochside Welcome if necessary. (Not so far. Jack always shook his head when I offered. Perhaps remembering my reputation with plates and glasses.)

"How's Marty been this week?" Trish asked. We both found him a challenge—issues handling women bosses, Katya said—but we were able to share ideas for how to manage him. I confessed to Trish that I'd once considered using my mother-in-law's Psychic Josie persona to persuade him his great-grandmother was watching and disapproved. "Not that bad an idea," she said.

"No problems yet," I said, "and I raved on about how wonderful I thought his social media graphics were for the

Christmas range. He bombarded me with loads of ideas after that."

The doorbell went behind me. "Hang on a sec."

Getting off the sofa these days required five-minutes advance notice. I harrumphed, remembering too late I had to keep noisemaking to a minimum if I wanted to avoid those 'are you going into labour' queries. Sure enough, the phone, dangling over the sofa edge, squawked. "Are you…"

"Fine, fine!" I shouted my reply, lumbering awkwardly to the hallway.

By the time I got to the door, puffing and panting post-marathon run style, I could see the postie heading off. Dressed in shorts even though it was late October and the wind chill factor had ramped up. They bred hardy types up here.

"Hey!" I called out, just as he opened the gate.

"Alright, Gaby? When's the wean due?"

Gavin was a nice enough chap. Mhari's cousin's boyfriend, but like everyone else these days, his conversation opener lacked originality.

"Early December. Have you got a parcel for us?"

He shook his head, opening the enormous sack slung across his torso. "Naw, naw. One o' they sign-for letters. Jack's no' back in front of the sheriff court for punching folks, is he?"

Did I say Gavin was a nice chap? Pregnancy hormones have gone wonky. He, on the other hand, found his own joke hilarious, guffawing as he rummaged around in his sack trying to locate the signed-for envelope.

"Here ye go!"

He handed me a thick envelope, embossed paper with a logo I didn't recognise on the address label. Having scrawled my name (a set of squiggles, mainly) on his proof of delivery device, I made to shut the door.

"Aren't you goin' tae open it?"

He might not share genes with the Colquhoun family (yet), but Gavin had already inherited that all-important nosey family trait. He stood in front of me, an air of expectancy buzzing about him.

"No?"

"But it's awfy important. Mebbe the police changed their mind, and they're gonnae charge Jack after all, and yon letter is an emergency summons to the court on Monday."

Ninety-five percent of me was sure this was not how the criminal justice system worked seeing as that time Jack had punched Zac was now more than 11 months ago. But the five percent gave in and ripped the envelope open, Gavin doing his best to read the letter I took out, his head tipped over the page so he could see it.

"Wow!" he exclaimed.

Wow indeed, and news I couldn't wait to share. Gavin started to talk about how these events were such a big deal. I shut the door hurrying as fast as my bulk would let me in the direction of the Lochside Welcome. "Aye, aye, ye'll never guess what…" Gavin was already on his phone. That gave me approximately six minutes until our news was general knowledge.

It was only when I got to the Lochside Welcome I remembered I'd left Trish on the end of the phone.

Message fired off to Trish apologising for leaving her hanging, I searched the small sea of faces for Jack. As it was just after 12 o'clock, a queue of people stood at the bar ordering lunch, all of them faces I recognised.

The news of the local partnership take-over had increased business at the hotel. I knew it was likely to be temporary in support of what we were trying to do, but hopefully, it might last. Lucas was there too, by now a semi-permanent fixture now the tours had finished for the year.

Laney Haggerty sat at one of the tables, her dogs lying at her feet. Her face tilted upwards, eyes widening in alarm.

"Awright, Gaby? Are you in—"

"No, no! Where's Jack?"

"Through the back."

I lifted the bar hatch, nodding a 'hello' in Jolene's direction. She was the only person left in the village these days who didn't enquire after my health. When she'd been in her third trimester, I, along with everyone else, asked her every time I caught sight of her. Never again, I promised myself. Any eight-month pregnant woman in my nearby vicinity would be asked no questions whatsoever on the state of her cervix.

Jolene stood aside and elbowed the door to the kitchen open for me. Jack and Xavier both glanced up as I came in, Jack's forehead creasing in alarm.

Xavier leapt forward. "Oh! Gaby, are you—"

"No, nothing like that. Please don't give my husband a heart attack. Read this!"

I handed over the letter to Jack, watching gleefully as his expression changed, a massive beam of delight taking up space there. He punched the air.

"Yes!"

"'Ave you won ze Lottery?" Xavier asked.

Jack pulled me to him, his arm around my back and his

hand resting on top of my stomach. "Mate, I won that when Gaby decided to move to Lochalshie."

My eyes, all too ready to spill over these days, prickled.

"Vom!" Jolene exclaimed; the noise attracted her to the kitchen. She pulled the door shut behind her, muscular arm shutting out the outside world. "You've been together, like forever? Time to stop the soppy stuff? And by the way, two people have just ordered four-cheese pizzas so better not keep them waiting?"

Xavier took a handful of dough out of the bowl on the side and began to stretch it with his hands, tossing it around until his knuckles showed through the thin disc. He and Jack had perfected their routine by now; Jack placing the stone they used in the wood-fired oven on the table and putting out the tomato sauce and the tubs of grated and crumbled cheese. Two bases made, he spread them with sauce and topped them with the cheese. Into the oven for seven to eight minutes, the fearsome heat of it, making us all sweaty and red-faced.

Jack took his place by my side once again, and I nudged him, me struggling to hold back tears. He didn't bother with the soppy stuff most of the time so that when he did, each word was a diamond to cherish. He squeezed my hand. I returned it with interest.

"Read this." He handed the letter to Xavier, who skimmed it quickly and looked up, eyes bright too. Jolene snatched it out of his hands.

"Sweet as! That date, though. It's in two weeks', isn't it? Anyway, I'd better get back out there."

I took the letter back. "So, it is! We won't be able to…"

"Yes, we will," Jack said. "We're going—you, me, Xavier and Jolene. There's no way I'm missing this."

"Is everything okay?"

Caroline dressed in her GP 'uniform'—a smart jumper over a mid-length tweed skirt and sensible shoes. She looked as if she'd run here, and her eyes ran up and down me.

She put a hand to her chest. "Stewart spotted you running to the Lochside Welcome so him and that daft dog o' his burst into the surgery and telt me I'd better find ye quickly before you went into premature labour."

Honestly.

"I'm fine, Caroline. Gavin the postie delivered a letter I needed to share with Jack. It's from UK's Best Restaurants and VisitScotland. We're up for an award for best original marketing campaign thanks to the YouTube channel."

"What?"

I handed over the by-now much-creased letter.

"But that's in two weeks'!"

"Mmm-hmm," Jack said, taking the pizzas out of the oven. Tomato, cheese and garlic smells took over the kitchen. Jolene reappeared, winked at me, expertly balanced two of the pizzas on their plates on her arm and headed back out again.

"And we're all going. Two nights. The last chance for Gaby and me to have a night out before the wean comes along and ruins our social life for the next 18 years."

He smiled at me as he said it. I wouldn't be the first woman who said, "My life won't change when the baby comes along!" only to be proved spectacularly wrong. But when you live in a small village where your friends and neighbours queue up to babysit, and a lot of socialising goes on in everyone's houses maybe we didn't have too much to fear…?

"Aye, alright then," Caroline said, getting her phone out. "I'll just phone Ranald and tell him. D'ye want me tae book us a hotel in Edinburgh for the two nights? I'm awfy good at finding bargains on they hotel sites?"

From the way Jack stared at her, I guessed he hadn't intended sharing our triumph with his mum and Ranald. But then weren't they sleeping partner in our operation? And if they came, shouldn't Lachlan be one of our guests too? Mhari too, for the part she'd played in making the hotel well-known. Katya and Dexter. They'd helped us with a lot of marketing and publicity ideas for the hotel, which had brought in plenty of guests over the last few months. Two nights. One of them at the awards—the other where Jack and I wandered off and cherished our time alone.

"Thanks, Mum. That would be great."

The kiss that he dropped on my head asked for understanding.

"So," I said, plastering on my best 'this will be brilliant' smile. "Party on the thirtieth. Everyone invited. Amazing."

Chapter Thirty-Three

"Ouch!" I detangled hair from where it had caught in the zip at the back of my dress.

Jack, embroiled in the complicated process of wrapping a kilt around himself, glanced up, alarmed.

"Are you okay? Are you going into labour? Do you need me to call an ambulance?"

Funnily enough, those three questions were ones everyone asked me all the time now whenever I made any kind of noise. Jack, first thing this morning when I stubbed my toe on the table leg. Jamal at eleven o'clock when I dumped my basket onto his counter with too much of an "Oof!" Stewart when blasted Scottie ran circles around me and tied up my legs with his extendable lead. Life was a non-stop round of reassuring (disappointing) people that no, the baby wasn't about to make a sudden appearance, and they wouldn't need to shout, 'Fetch me hot water and towels!'.

"No, I'm fine. The midwife told me the other day the baby still hasn't dropped. My hair's caught."

Jack wandered over anyway, moving my hands and gently lifting my hair up and away from danger. Caroline had been as good as her word. She was a dab hand at nabbing a bargain on a hotel site. We were in Edinburgh's Caledonian Hotel on Princes Street. "I thought I'd get you a wee treat," Caroline told us when we arrived earlier that day, everyone giddy with excitement. Jack drove us down in his minibus, the mood far too raucous by the time we arrived in Scotland's capital, thanks to the prodigious amounts of alcohol our friends in the back drank. (Three exceptions to that rule.)

My mother-in-law had booked us into the honeymoon suite—the space larger than our entire house, I calculated when the porter opened the door. It incorporated a bedroom, a living room and an ensuite, bigger than any bathroom I'd ever seen. My feet sank into the super-spongey carpet, thick walls muffled all the street sounds, and the windows looked out directly onto the castle. I spent 10 minutes investigating every luxury on offer. "Molton Brown toiletries, Jack!" He was none the wiser. "Chocolates on the pillows!" I scoffed them immediately. "A gym and a sauna!" We didn't bother.

He rested his chin on my shoulder now as we stood in front of the full-length mirror. My one upon a time skinny figure a dim and distant memory, I'd moaned about having nothing to wear for the awards night. Once we'd booked in, Jack had taken me to Harvey Nicks and presented me with a voucher—£500 and a session with a personal shopper. Wasn't he the greatest?

Or perhaps it was Cheryl the stylist, who took a quick look at a person as they stood before her in their underwear and dashed out returning ten minutes later arms bulging with tops, skirts, trousers and dresses. I'd never tried on so many items in one session, but by the end, the vision in the mirror in front of me looked unrecognisable. A vintage 70s print dress in bold blue, green and pink colours, with an adjustable waist which meant I could wear it post-pregnancy. Paired with thigh-high boots, I would strut into any event as if I belonged there.

"D'you know what going into labour will feel like?" Jack asked me now.

"Nope," I said. "My best bet is that I'm suddenly struck by hideous pain and scream my head off."

I shifted from foot to foot, the 15-kilos plus by now super awkward to carry around. My back was killing me too. At least this evening, we'd be spending most of the night sitting down.

Jack's hands moved to my stomach, cradling the weight of it. The tips of his fingers burned an imprint there. "I'm no' impressed by humans," he said. "Awfy inefficient when you compare childbirth to the coos. They moo a lot, dump their wee calf on the ground, and that's that. Easy-peasy."

"Thank you for the cow comparison."

A joke, he hastened to add, dropping butterfly kisses on my neck and collar bone.

"Are you ready?" Caroline's voice and a knock on the door.

"C'mon then," Jack said as we clasped hands. "We've got prizes to win."

The UK's Best Restaurants and VisitScotland's awards night was taking place at The Hub, a venue at the top of the Royal Mile. It being November, darkness had set in hours ago, but the area was lit up, VisitScotland's distinctive thistle logo sharing space with the knife and fork one the UK's Best Restaurants used.

A piper struck up as we walked in. Not nearly as talented, Caroline said once we were (thankfully) out of earshot, as any of the village's pipe band players. "The food better be excellent," I said to Jack. At an awards evening celebrating tourism and Scotland's finest eating establishments, how could it be anything else?

We were a large party. Ten to fill a table, and we were more than that; Jack and me, Caroline and Ranald, Mhari, Xavier and Lucas, Jolene and Stewart, Jack's father and Lachlan. Dexter and Katya joined us too, having taken the train up from London. I hugged my friend, noticing how pale she was. Spotty too, which was unusual as Katya's diet, exercise and skincare regime courtesy of all those Blissful Beauty freebies gave her glowing skin most of the time. "Are you okay?" I whispered, noting the pause. "Sort of. Tell you later."

"Gaby, love!" My mum and Nanna Cooper. When we'd compiled our list of attendees, I had felt my side was not as well represented as Jack's, so I'd invited them too. I ordered them to get a bus, rather than have me worrying myself silly over them driving to Edinburgh. They were staying in an Airbnb with Jolene, Stewart, Mhari, Xavier and Lucas, and excellent it was too, my mum said. "The owner left orange juice and croissants for us, Gaby! How kind of her."

The noise in the entry hall, its ceilings bedecked with banners and bunting, made it hard to hear anyone— hundreds of conversations competing with background music. Naturally, there were canapes. I made our party take the trays from the waiters who were taking far too much time to circulate for me.

Ranald, never a fan of crowds, picked up a canape and

frowned. "These things aren't very big, are they?" My nanna gave him hers. Rich food, she announced, did not agree with her. It made her appendix grumble.

My mother-in-law, the in-house medical expert, regarded her curiously. "Grumbling appendix? I'm no' sure that's a thing, Lillian. D'ye mean it gies you flatulence?"

My mum, by now already on her third glass of Cava, burst out laughing. "Yes! For the love of God, don't let her near anything that has pate or cream in it."

My nanna glared at them both and handed Ranald more of the canapes. He wolfed them down—someone, presumably, whose digestion did not mind rich food. Or he couldn't care less if he broke wind in front of everyone.

Katya, Jolene and Mhari wandered over to join me, the latter eyeing my stomach nervously.

"That thing's no' gonnae attack me again, is it?"

"No, Mhari."

Last week, McAllan Junior got restless during the quiz. As I was sitting so close to Mhari, she felt the kicks. Claimed the experience freaked her out. When I'd shown her the stretch marks on my stomach, she screwed her face up in disgust and told me pregnancy was for mugs.

"Nice dress, by the way."

Woah. Praise indeed. Katya nodded too, saying that she thought it was even better than the one we had borrowed from the boutique in London the day of Hyun-Ki's leaving party. "Have you spoken to Hyun-Ki lately, Mhari?" I asked, my tone sly.

She held her phone out, where a grinning Hyun-Ki sat in a cat café in Seoul. "She's coming over for Christmas," he told me. "So I can check up on her progress as a camera-woman and film director."

Good grief.

"Who's looking after Tamar?" Katya asked Jolene, who had the giddy air of someone on a free pass. "Laney," Jolene said, draining her second glass of fizz. "For two nights too. Tomorrow, I'm gonna drink latte in a coffee shop, hit every shop in this city, climb Arthur's Seat and visit the castle. And all without Stewart!"

We laughed. It was a joke, I think.

A gong sounded, and people began to move, drifting towards the dining room. We'd be able to sit down, at last, allowing me some relief from the ache at the small of my back. Our table was near the rear, three extra seats crammed in. It was going to be very cosy. Adjustments made to allow us all to fit around, I sat down and realised I needed the loo. Toilet trips currently averaged three an hour, but I ought to go before they started the presentations.

Katya stood up too. "C'mon then," she said, holding her hand out. "I'd better make sure you don't go into labour while you're in there."

Amazingly, we had the bathroom to ourselves—its interior decorated in warm amber marble and dark panelling. Super-soft toilet paper as well all the better to... ah. ARGH. I let a minute tick by, working out my options. A, B or C? B, I decided.

Outside, I admired myself in the mirror. Did anything look different? Apart from my reflection showing Glamorous Gaby, the creature I'd forgotten all about, no. Katya ran a brush through her hair and peered at her complexion.

"Are my spots very noticeable?"

"No, no!" Yes. "Are you a bit run-down?"

Her eyes met mine in the mirror before darting to the door. Beyond it, we heard applause and cheering. The awards must have started.

"Blast it," I said. "We'll need to sneak back and—"

"I have to tell you something!"

"Yes, of course."

I turned to face her, troubled by her tone—worry, fear, panic.

"I'm pregnant."

Most of the time, my mouth works before my brain. It gets me into a lot of trouble. This time, however, I managed to stop it before the words, "Oh wow, congratulations, that's brilliant, we'll have kids the same age, and they can be besties just like us, isn't that amazing!" popped out.

If Katya thought it remarkable, she wouldn't look so unhappy.

"Well, er, you don't need to—"

"No, it's not that," she shook her head. "It's… don't judge me, please… I, I don't know who the father is."

Ah. And whoops. My best friend. Always the super organised one. A woman far too smart to forget about contraception the one time never mind two. The Highland Games 11 weeks ago. The applause continued. We would need to return to our table before it became too noticeable.

I did what all best friends should do and flung my arms around her. "I will support you whatever you choose. And I won't tell a single soul."

No, not even Jack. This time, I owed my first loyalty to Katya.

She gave me a watery smile. "What about Mhari? She's got superpowers when it comes to finding anything out."

"Not that super," I said, though I mentally crossed my fingers as I did so. "Um, does Dexter know you're pregnant?"

She nodded. "I didn't want to tell him until I worked out what… well, whatever. But he's not that stupid. He noticed things, and he's over the moon. Thanks me all the time for changing my mind about how I feel about children."

More applause and the introduction of tonight's host —a Scottish film star who had made his name in Hollywood; the organisers' budget for the event must be enormous.

I squeezed Katya's hand. "Thanks for telling me, but we better go back. Phone me tomorrow, yeah?"

She returned the pressure. "Yeah."

We sneaked back in, managing not to draw attention to ourselves as the table was near the doors. I sat next to Jack. "Okay?" he asked, and I nodded, mind buzzing. Things I never expected in a million years—and something so big it was almost enough to distract me.

Almost. When I'd gone to the toilet there, my waters had broken. At first, I hadn't been sure. First pregnancy, remember? My stomach had been bothering me all afternoon—an uncomfortable tight, full feeling that made me pace the floor. The baby size, I told myself. I'd sat down on the loo, felt something 'pop' and water trickle down my legs. My first—mad—thought was, 'Thank goodness I'm on the loo! Otherwise, this gorgeous dress would be ruined!' The second? 'Labour takes forever, right? I've got a few hours... enough to see Jack win his award and then we can make a mad dash to the hospital.'

The third... IN THE NAME OF XXXX, I'M THREE WEEKS EARLY!!!!!!!!

I thought of Andy, my midwife (midhusband?). He was the Highlands first male midwife. The pressure of being the only guy made him super-keen to impress. "My Mrs has had two weans, Gaby," he told me when we met. "I've made her describe childbirth to me hunners o' times. And I've helped plenty o' women. When you go intae labour, I'll be wi' you every step o' the way! Any drug you want, I'll get it for you!"

I believed in him. But he wasn't going to be here, was he? And if the baby made its appearance in Edinburgh, did that mean he or she wouldn't be a Highlander? Oh no...

Back at the table, I gave thanks for the subdued lighting. It hid my expression. Waters breaking aside and the slight sense of relief it had given me, I had none of the other signs of labour Andy had warned me about. No urge to push, for instance. If the baby could just hold off for two hours...

The film star finished his speech—one in which he waxed lyrical about how much he loved Scotland. "Not enough to live here, though!" Jack whispered to me. Should I tell him? Yes, he deserved to know. No, I wasn't in labour yet (well, I didn't think I was...) and if I told him, he would insist we leave straight away and then everyone else would get involved.

No, then.

I smiled at Katya, Dexter's hand around her shoulder. Now that I knew, I spotted those too-frequent glances at her stomach. Better hope Mhari didn't. Always a giveaway. Stewart was in conversation with Jack's dad, the two of them discussing the benefits of the alcohol-free life. Next to Stewart, his girlfriend poured herself a large glass of wine and knocked it back. Caroline removed the bottle in front of Ranald before he poured himself another one. My nanna muttered about the food. It was way beyond her six pm dinner time deadline. The thought of food made me want to heave. Was that a sign of going into labour?

On stage, the film star continued to read out nominations for this award, that award. The small of my back ached, and the tightness in my stomach had intensified. Cramping, I decided—period pains on steroids.

"Are you okay?" Jack again. He must have noticed my wriggling.

"Fine," I said, discreetly checking the time on my watch, "and isn't it—

But the film star had started speaking again.

"And now, ladies and gentlemen! Our final award! The most innovative use of social media to promote Scottish tourism businesses and the nominees are…

The screen behind him lit up. We were first up—the Lochside Welcome's YouTube channel. The film they'd chosen? Take a guess… Two half-naked men emerged from the loch, droplets of water clinging to torsos as they walked towards the shore. A huge cheer sounded, wolf whistles all around us. Jack put his head in his hands.

"Oh god…"

The tables all around us quickly worked out who we were. Heads turned to stare at us, and fingers pointed to Jack and Xavier. I heard whispers, "Is that Sam Hingie fae Outlander? Cannae be, surely?"

The other nominations flashed up; a gift shop in Speyside that had run an Instagram campaign that increased their online business by 200 percent; a Glasgow pub that created an app offering discount deals on food that punters could only download within 500m of a Wetherspoon's the chain pub, boosting its business so much, they'd had to open another premises.

"And the winner is…"

I checked my phone. Forty-five seconds again. The last one four minutes ago. Okkkkaaaaayyy… Around me, everyone else's faces were glued to the front of the room and the film star about to announce who'd won the award.

I closed my eyes and dropped my head. *Hurry up hurry up hurry up…*

The actor followed the award night cliché by pausing far too long as he opened the gold envelope, managing to lose his cool by dropping it to the groans of the audience.

Jack slipped his hand around mine. Fingers encircled my forefinger and pinkie. He turned to face me, alarm setting in.

"You're in labour, aren't you?"

"Yeeesss?" First pregnancy. Maybe this was the fabled Braxton Hicks. More tightening. No, it wasn't.

"The—

I got to my feet and dashed out, closely followed by Jack and the shouts of our friends echoing after us. It drowned out the film star as he announced the winner. By which point, I was beyond caring.

Epilogue

One way to get punters into your pub when you're competing with the temptation of Netflix is to... offer them Netflix or at least TV entertainment they can watch in there.

The sign outside the pub said, "Lochalshie Premiere! Free glass of fizz with any main course and two for one on Chocolate Decadent desert!"

"That, darling girl, was your mother's idea," I patted the warm bundle strapped to my torso and pointed at it. "And a genius one if I may say so myself. What do you think?"

Evelyn ('Evie' for short) let out a huge sigh, shifting to twist her head, so she faced right instead of left. I liked to think she agreed with me. But even if she didn't, who cared? I dropped a kiss on her head, the dark red of her hair soft and sweet-smelling.

Honestly, if she hadn't come out of my body no-one would know I was her mother. She was McAllan through

350

and through—Jack's dark eyes, his auburn hair and the shape of her face, baby round now, showed the signs of taking on her father's excellent bone structure in later years.

"Lucky old you!" I told her frequently. Again, I was probably not the first woman to think her first-born the most beautiful, advanced, genetically perfect generally brilliant child ever to have emerged into the world.

But. It *was* true. And another truth I discovered along the way? Labour. There were good reasons mothers didn't tell those who'd never given birth just how... visceral the whole experience was. When I went through it, I did everything the squeamish before-birth Gaby had shuddered at.

I crapped myself. By that point, I didn't care. The pain had me screaming my head off, the opposite of a Scientologist wife. When the midwife told me it was too late for an epidural—*Andy* would have done it for me!—as I begged her for one, I swore so much I must have offended every single person in the hospital.

Finally, when I was wheeled in for the emergency Caesarean, thanks to Evie taking far too long to move from womb to cervix, Jack gowned up and white-faced beside me, I started listing all my belongings, making Jack promise he'd distribute them as per my as yet unwritten last will and testament because yes, I was going to die.

"Mildred, Mildred," I said, anxiety making me desperate to convey what I wanted. "You MUST look after her. She needs three meals a day, plus snacks. Don't starve her, Jack. Promise.

"Katya. Give her all my Blissful Beauty freebies. Tell her to make me a character in the next Billionaire clean romance. I can be the designer who comes to the billionaire's house and does her a website for her business. One that makes her a multi-billionaire or something."

At that point, I almost told him about Katya being pregnant and not knowing her baby's paternity. Some miracle made me keep my trap shut.

"My mum and my nanna! Phone them a lot."

None of this, he promised me, would come about. Because you, Gabrielle Amelia nee Richardson now McAllan—tightening his hand around my fingers as he said each syllable—are going to survive.

You feel the cut of the knife. It wasn't painful as by this time the anaesthetic had kicked in, but the wrench as skin ripped and my insides were opened was the strangest thing I'd ever experienced. My eyes blurred over as they lifted her out of me, a tiny, red squalling, caul-covered thing that I didn't immediately recognise as a baby.

Then it happened. Time slowed, even though the clock in the theatre showed only a minute had passed. My vision cleared, almost as if the baby were pixelating in front of me; her tiny form outlined and sharp, and the tears ran down my cheeks.

"Jack, Jack…" I turned my head to look up at him, his gaze fixated on her, and his eyes glassy.

"Oh, Gaby…"

Six months ago. Remember me saying, "Our lives won't change?" Tell that to the universe, and it guffaws. But not maliciously. Our lives were turned upside down, the tiny Evelyn a bulldozer who cheerfully ran us over and obliterated everything we were before. My mum was as good as her word. She and Nanna Cooper had decamped to Lochalshie for a month when Evie arrived. Just as well. Jack and I spent the first two weeks in a shell-shocked daze.

Much to my surprise, I found I didn't mind. What had Jack and I talked about before Evelyn came along? And those disturbed nights where I dragged myself out of flat-out exhausted sleep to feed or try to persuade her she really wanted to sleep herself? Even they had a sparkling, magical quality to them—the sense of achievement when Evelyn did drop off. I stared at the dark stillness of the night when she and I were all alone in the world, me feeding her and singing soft, silly songs.

(Checking Twitter and Instagram too. C'mon. Instagram is the saviour of we midnight breast-feeders, right?)

As I predicted, babysitting offers flooded in. The presents we received—new stuff, perfectly good condition old stuff—had been numerous, I was yet to get around to writing thank you letters. Not that I remembered who'd given us what. Baby brain *is* a real thing.

"Is it okay if I just say thanks, do you think?" I asked Katya when we FaceTimed each other. She was my go-to guide for modern-day etiquette. "No!" she said sternly, then relented when she saw my expression. "Oh, everyone will understand. Just don't do a group thank you on Facebook or anything ghastly like that."

Darn it. That was precisely what I'd planned.

"How is everything?" I said, carefully watching her face.

That question covered a lot of bases. Katya was due to give birth any day. She rang me often, asking anxiously every time, "Can you speak?" She meant, was anyone else there who might hear when she went into full-blown panic.

The next question was always, "What if the baby looks exactly like Zac? What am I going to do?"

"You," I said, "are going to be such an amazing mum! And Dexter is going to be a fantastic father. End of."

Guess what? Dexter, the workaholic, had already eased off the hours he put in at Blissful Beauty. He read how to be a father books, determined he would do the most exceptional job possible. A small part of me thought the baby's paternity wouldn't matter to him that much.

"If you insist," Katya smiled. "Hold Evie up so I can blow her a kiss."

Mhari appeared beside me now, trailing behind Xavier who was unloading the van parked outside the Lochside Welcome, and interrupting my thoughts.

"Can I have a wee cuddle?" She stretched her arms out. Life surprised me all the time, but this development possibly more than most. Mhari adored Evie. She was top of the queue for Lochalshie villagers on the desperate to babysit list.

Evie blinked at her, face widening into a smile and tiny hand reaching out. My eyes flickered to Xavier, remembering the time I'd scared him by talking about how newcomers came to the village and made babies. He'd paused, crate in hand, expression indulgent. Perhaps he and Lucas might consider an arrangement with Mhari where she carried a baby for them? Ooh, I should suggest that... *No, Gaby. Leave people alone.*

"I thought you were 'elping me, Mhari?"

"Aye, well. You'll manage fine," Mhari said. I'd unbuckled the carrier and handed Evie over. Mhari balanced her on one hip and shoogled her up and down, my daughter laughing delightedly. (See? I told you she was the best, most advanced child the world has ever had the luck to see.)

Xavier did one of those exaggerated sighs I always thought of as impeccably French and walked past us. "Jacques!"

Sometimes, I called my husband that when we were in bed, attempting to add those sighed-out syllables. Debatable whether it worked or not.

The back door opened, and Jack poked his head out, his face lighting up when he spotted me. More probably Evie.

"You're early!" he said, and I grinned. "Nothing better to do."

"Does that mean you're looking for work?"

If I'd ever imagined owning shares in a hotel made me high-powered and glamorous, I was sadly mistaken.

Xavier, fresh out of delivering one crates-worth of goods, dumped one in my arms. "Thee store cupboard, Gaby. You know where eet is?"

Later, we all sat down in the pub lounge. Mhari still had hold of Evie, who by this point had decided sleep was her best bet. Earlier, her tiny hands at plucked at Mhari's top. Jolene and I smirked as we watched Mhari's expression, eyes widening as she figured it out.

"Is she tryin' to…"

"Yup," I said, snatching my daughter back. "'Fraid so. Get your own one."

She threw her hands up in horror. "No! Yuck. Absolutely disgusting."

Evie latched on—it's incredible how discreetly you can do that in public places. Caroline and Ranald joined our table, the former dressed in her Psychic Josie costume of tiny-mirror-covered velvet skirt, peasant blouse and a Hermes scarf tied around her hair.

"Who've you been advising?" I asked.

"Caitlin Cartier," she announced, the grandeur so over the top, me, Jolene and Mhari all snorted, making her narrow her eyes.

"I was, ye ken! She likes to commune with the spirits on Skype, so I dress the part."

Ranald took a massive swig of his pint. His eyes met mine in a ghost of a wink.

"She wanted my advice on when is the best time fae her to get pregnant. I telt her when the stars align—"

"Doesn't it depend on her managing to be in the same place as her hubby for more than ten minutes at a time?" Jolene asked.

An excellent point. Hard to get pregnant when the physical means to do so were on a different continent.

"The sun is in Jupiter next week," Caroline said, "and I said that would provide fertile conditions if she and her man decided tae—"

It was far too much for all of us. Jolene started, Mhari joined in, and I gave up holding back also, the three of us sniggering way too obviously. Evie broke off from suckling me, her eyes accusatory. She preferred fewer distractions when feeding.

When Evie was born, my mother-in-law had offered to draw me up a comprehensive chart for her. Part of me wavered, tempted to see what the future offered my daughter. Then I remembered that I thought astrology was a crock. Just because you happened to be born on a specific day, it made no difference to what the fates offered you.

"And you, little Evie," as I told her all the time, "can be whatever you want. Me and your daddy will do our best to give you the best start in life we can."

Jack moved from behind the bar where he'd just finished serving Laney Haggerty and her extended family—gin drinkers one and all. The jukebox went quiet, but the noise hadn't penetrated the loud chatter anyway. He took himself to the back, where the roller held a large screen—one he'd spent considerable money on.

Most of the time it was used for the Champions League, the unmissable Scottish Premiere games and the Six Nations, and whatever was drama everyone was raving about. Tonight, he had another use in mind, and so far, it looked as if he'd pulled it off. Villagers who might otherwise have watched the first episode in their homes had ventured out. Xavier was flat out behind the bar pouring Prosecco into flutes—the freebie we'd offered as further temptation. I'd given Mhari mine, seeing as Evie objected to grape-flavoured breast milk.

Jack stood back from the screen, remote in hand. The movement made his biceps ripple subtly, and as he lifted his arm, I admired his triceps in turn. The Lochside Welcome now had a uniform, courtesy of me. I'd designed the logo and T-shirts. He and Xavier wore theirs with cargo pants in the winter and black kilts in the summer. Black worked for them both—setting off Jack's dark red hair and suited to Xavier's swarthier skin. Recent reviews of the pub all mentioned him and Jack, their warm welcome, charm and their attractiveness."

"Aye," Mhari had said, reading one out to me from her phone. "See what it says here. 'I couldn't make up my mind which yin I wanted tae sleep wi' the most.' Some lassies are awfy forward, aren't they?"

The screen flickered into life, raising a cheer and then several "Ssh!s" We were taking part in a pub-based version of Channel 4's Goggle Box. The people of Lochalshie's reaction to a brand-new series: *The Local*, tag line *The UK's community-based pubs laid bare*. Episode one, The Royal George, Lochalshie.

The music started up at the same time as the chat,

people recognising the scenes on the screen that was part of the introduction, and snorts of derision as Zac was pictured standing outside, arms folded and arrogant grin in place.

"Tosser!" someone yelled, several others nodding in agreement. Still, I thought the insult sounded half-hearted. The Lochside Welcome had not won the best use of social media award for our YouTube channel, the Glasgow pub with its app download idea pipping us to the post.

But YouTube views had made it so popular, we got plenty of visitors. People often drove up here from Scotland's central belt at the weekend and left us rave reviews.

"Can I get a pint of the Punk IPA please?"

Oooooh! Silence as Xavier hastily froze the programme, and everyone turned to stare.

The man himself on screen and now in front of us. He hadn't been in Lochalshie for a while, disappearing at the end of the year to work elsewhere. His hair was much shorter than when he'd been filmed for the series and his skin deeply tanned. Somewhere hot then.

It took some chutzpah to walk into the Lochside Welcome on a night like tonight, didn't it? Chutzpah or maybe something else. He couldn't take his eyes off Evie and me.

Jack shrugged. "Course."

"And one of your pizzas? The four-cheese one?"

Xavier nodded and vanished into the kitchen.

Pint poured, he hesitated a second or so before walking to our table. "Mind if I join you?"

I shook my head. "No, no! Please sit down."

No-one had restarted the programme, Zac's appearance far too intriguing. The secret Katya and I kept made me overcompensate with friendliness. I struggled with its magnitude most of the time, but I'd kept schtum. Goodness me, so lovely to see him! Where had he been working these last few months? Barbados? Gosh, how amazing…

"Didn't ye want to watch the show in your own place?" Mhari asked.

"No," Zac said. "I thought it would be more fun to watch it here."

Someone cheered. "Too right, pal!" and Zac grinned, raising his pint in a toast. Jolene pointed the remote towards the big screen, and the music started up once more. Zac's eyes flicked towards it and away again. "Don't think I'll ever work with a TV company again. It's too much hassle."

Debatable too, whether the hassle had been worth it. Netflix decided at the last minute that they didn't want to commission the series. Because he had so many hours of footage and a storyboard worked out already, Miles tried other streaming services before eventually selling the show to BBC One Scotland, its audience tiny compared to Netflix. Rumour had it, Miles had returned to shows about A&E and women in labour. Tindra had left and found a proper, paid job. She was a big fan of our YouTube channel and shared it with her thousands of followers on every social media channel.

Jack joined us, also holding a pint of Punk IPA. "Are you back for the summer then?"

Zac nodded. "Yeah. Lois and Angeline wanted me here in case the business increases thanks to the programme. If we get too many extra guests, I'll send them your way."

"Thanks. And ditto." My husband clinked his glass against Zac's.

Life is much easier when everyone is friendly, I reflected, wondering at the same time about how problematic that secret would be to keep if Zac took up part-time residency once more.

As if he had read my mind, he studied Evie. "How's Katya?" the words said softly enough for no-one else to hear.

"Fine," I said, "blooming, I mean blinking marvellous. Fantastically happy."

He must know she was pregnant. Katya didn't post that much about herself online, but like all of us, she got tagged in others' pictures a lot. Easy enough to tell he wanted to ask more.

"Busy writing the next instalment in Caitlin's billionaire romance series," I wittered. "Amazing how tricky it is to find love when you are hyper-rich. Takes these billionaires a whole book to move from trading secretive smiles to tongues, ha ha ha!"

Evie, her ears protected by baby headphones, chose that moment to wake up and yell her head off, much to my relief. I got up, muttering apologies that everyone told me were unnecessary. Outside in the beer garden, a few people had chosen to take advantage of the light evening. The love seat was unoccupied, however, and Evie and I parked ourselves there.

"Room for another one?"

I handed my daughter to her father. As ever, it worked like magic, Evie's cries stopping immediately. I rested my head on his shoulder, and we watched the gulls as they swooped and dived on the loch seeking fish.

My phone vibrated. Katya. "We're at the hospital. Wish me luck."

Tonnes of it, my friend… I sent her my best wishes. Let it all work out for her, whatever happened. At least she wouldn't miss the chance to get an epidural. Last week, she'd sent me through her birth plan. It was five pages long with every eventuality covered.

"Any more thoughts on running away to join the circus?" Jack asked, and I smiled.

"Maybe next year. You the flame thrower, me the lion tamer and Evie... well, people just turn up to see her because she is amazing in general. She doesn't need to do anything."

"Nothing at all," he replied, peering at the little face which gazed up adoringly at him. "Shall we leave everyone to it?" He tipped his head behind, indicating the bar where we could hear chat, laughter and the TV.

"Mmm-hmm," I stood up. Much as the Lochside Welcome was a warm and friendly place, tonight I wanted the comfort of shutting the door on everyone. Jack, Evie, me. Mildred too, now that she had finally come round to Evie being a permanent fixture.

How heavenly.

I slipped my hand in his, and we set off for home.

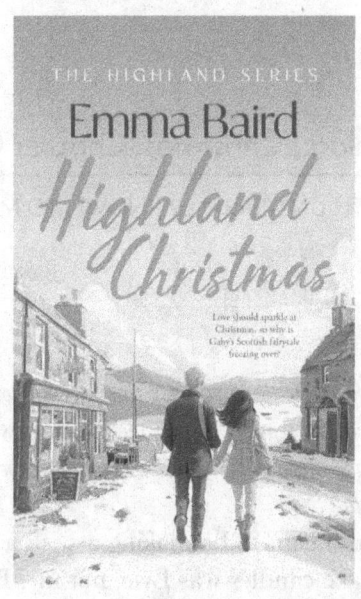

vinci-books.com/HighlandChristmas

Tinsel, tantrums, and a Christmas no one saw coming...

Gaby and Jack are ready for a quiet family holiday—until
meddling mums, surprise secrets, and village drama turn festive
cheer into chaos. Can they unwrap a peaceful Christmas before it
all falls apart?

Turn the page for a free preview...

Highland Christmas: Chapter One

THE TRUTH UNIVERSALLY KNOWN TO MOTHERS

Dear Santa, I appreciate this is a busy time of year for you, but if you could see your way to sending a few more customers to the Lochside Welcome and make this the best family Christmas we've ever had, I'd be eternally grateful…

The person meant to be making a wish as she blew out her birthday cake candles was Evie, not me. But as this was her first birthday, I thought she wouldn't mind me appropriating her request. And boy, did we need those customers… Today, however, I would not be dwelling on non-existent punters. I pursed my lips. "Blow, Evie! Like this, one, two, three!"

Ah. Too late. The village's second-youngest resident, Tamar McMillan, a year and a half older than Evie, sneaked up underneath the table, stuck his head up, blew with all his might and ducked back under again.

"Tamar!" The little scamp's mother barked at him. He ran from her, giggling. Evie wriggled in my arms, desperate to go after him. Evie loved Tamar. Her feelings weren't reciprocated. The last time Jolene and I took them swimming together, he did his best to duck her head under the water and keep it there.

"It's a phase he's going through," Jolene had said, "at least I hope so?"

I put Evie down, and she scooted off on all fours—Tamar far more enticing than the prospect of cake.

As Evie was Lochalshie's youngest resident, everyone had assumed they were invited to her birthday celebration. Our house wouldn't have handled the numbers, so we hit on holding it in the Lochside Welcome, the hotel we part-owned with six others.

Jack had strewn the bar with the pink, silver and white bunting I had designed and helium balloons. The tables had been cleared away to make enough space for party games.

Xavier, the hotel's manager and head chef, had gone to town on the food. Brought up in Canada, he was unfamiliar with traditional British party food staples. Most of it made him shudder. But he'd stumbled on an old Nancy Spain cookbook from the 1960s. "Look at zees, Gaby! You slice cucumber up very thin and put it on ze whole salmon, so people think it is scales! Shall I do zis?"

When I pointed out children weren't always the biggest fans of salmon and many people in Lochalshie promised fish "gies me the dry boak" despite fish having been a natural part of the Scots diet for centuries, he pouted. Then cheered up when he read about the hedgehog—half of a grapefruit studded with cubes of cheese and pickled onions on cocktails sticks. I'd already worked my way through far too many of them, consoling myself that the pickled onions must count as one of your five a day.

The Lochside Welcome's signature pudding was a chocolate decadence dessert. Xavier had made the dessert Evie's birthday cake, levelling up the luxury with gold leaf—

the gleam of it caught in the flickering flames of the candles.

He reappeared, knife in hand, and sliced the cake into as many pieces as there were people. Tricky given the numbers, but job done, he, Jack and I handed the plates round.

Mhari, taking a break from her semi-official role as party photographer, sat down next to me and filched my cake.

"Hey!"

"Well, my slice was titchy. Cannae expect me to survive the rest of the afternoon on just a wee bittie o' cake."

"Can I see the pictures?"

"No. I need tae touch them up. 'Specially the ones of you."

Mhari, my Lochalshie self-described best friend, was an acquired taste.

"I got a cracking shot of Jack, though. Look."

Oh, wow. That one was going on our website for sure. A tough job being the wife of a man as delectable as Jack McAllan, but someone had to do it, right? Mhari had captured him as Xavier placed the cake in front of Evie— the candle flames illuminating the planes of his face, casting exaggerated shadows that only emphasised the similarity to the ancient statues of Greek gods. She must be using an enhanced colour filter too as the red of his hair stood out in sharp relief.

"I took some o' the outside of the hotel too," she added, showing them to me. "Looks awfy Christmassy, eh?"

The lights outside the hotel were OTT, though we'd yet to get around to decorating the hotel's interior. In the garden, a reindeer pulled a sleigh at the front next to an enormous tree dotted with star lights and a gobo that projected holly leaves and berries on the white walls of the hotel. The electricity bills had soared.

"It's Christmas made camper," I'd said when we'd set them up a few days before. Jack raised an eyebrow. "Can you make Christmas camper?"

Probably not, but with any luck, the Lochside Welcome's Christmas lights would be one of those displays people drove to from miles around to see, dropping in for a drink or some food while they were in the area.

My phone buzzed as it had been doing all day—people reacting to my pictures on Instagram or phoning to wish Evie a Happy Birthday.

The screen showed my mum calling again. She'd already phoned early this morning in tears because she couldn't be here for her only grandchild's first birthday. Great Yarmouth was too far away to make visits easy, and Mum's budget too limited for her to able to afford a trip here for Evie's birthday *and* Christmas.

"Mum, hello!" I switched the phone to FaceTime mode and showed her the birthday girl now sat on the floor tearing up birthday gift wrap.

"Your brother," she replied, "wants to apologise for not having posted Evie's birthday present and card on time."

Does it count as an apology when you overhear your mum standing behind your brother, hiss-whispering that he needs to say sorry, forgetting that a mobile phone makes all background noise clear as a bell? If Dylan had remembered Evie's birthday or it crossed his mind that as her uncle, he should buy her a card and a present, I'd eat my Christmas cracker hat.

Mum came back on the line. "I'm so looking forward to Christmas! What a wonderful celebration it will be this year when we are all together."

"Me too!" We blew each other kisses and hung up. Yes, Christmas shimmered on the horizon in all its glittery glory. But that familiar prickle of worry, whenever I thought about the future started up. Money worries took the shine off somewhat.

This year's summer had been a stinker. Lochalshie's weather gods had lulled me into a false sense of security since I'd upped and moved sticks to the north of Scotland. Warm, dry-ish summers, the odd autumn storm and cold but dry winters. This year rain started mid-May, stopped for a day or two in June, and then continued into the autumn when it turned sheet-like and icy. The weather deterred everyone. We'd put up with endless cancellations and days on end when the numbers in the bar didn't surpass those working in the hotel.

Evie scuttled towards the fire, Jack swooping in to whisk her up as everyone cooed in admiration and remarked yet again on how similar they looked. It's a truth universally known to mothers... All a dad needs to do is hold his baby, jiggle her up and down a bit, and he qualifies as father of the year. Meanwhile, we women stir ourselves from sleep three hours earlier than we would like, spend our days running around after our tiny tyrants, juggling a job at the same time, and dealing with our extended family, before flopping into bed at 10pm, exhausted.

Two women sharing a bottle of wine watched him, transfixed. They nudged each other, open-mouthed. Snatches of their whispered conversation drifted over. "OMG! He can father my baby any day!" "Yeah! My ovaries have just exploded!"

Just as well I'd grown accustomed to such reactions. If Jack had been a sex god before Evie appeared on the scene, nowadays he was Zeus at the top of Olympus. Women tailed him, tongues hanging out. Even if I stood next to him, waving my left hand in the air. "Ring, fourth finger, placed on said hand by the gent you're ogling!"

"Mind and take plenty o' pics," Caroline, my mother-in-law, called out to Mhari. Jack, Evie balanced on his right hip, screwed up his face. Posing for photographs topped the list of things he hated.

Caroline joined me, waving a glass of wine at Evie, now pestering one of Laney Haggerty's ginormous Alsatians. Laney's dogs tolerated Evie to a remarkable extent, putting up with her tugging their tails and pulling their ears.

"It's good tae have a relaxed approach to parenting," Caroline said. "Evie will build up a good immune system, wi' all the exposure she has tae filthy animals. She gets that wi' Mildred too, doesn't she?"

Mildred, our ancient moggie, had yet to forgive me for Evie's usurping her rightful place as Queen of Our House.

"How are the Christmas bookings coming on?" she asked. Caroline and her husband Ranald were part of the consortium that owned the hotel.

"Three reservations for lunch," I told Caroline. "And only two of the hotel's rooms booked. Any chance you might ask the spirits to intervene and persuade people to come?"

As a sideline, my mother-in-law doubled up as a psychic. Jack and I regarded Caroline's hobby as a load of old rubbish, but any help we could get with the hotel's success, we would take. Best to cover all bases.

"I'll ask them the next time we commune," Caroline said. She'd been faking the sideline so long she'd started to believe she honestly had powers beyond the limits of rationality and logic. What harm could it do if she put forward a sincere request?

"Would you and Ranald mind having my mum and Nanna to stay on the 27th?" I asked. Our own celebrations would take place two days after Christmas once all the hotel guests had left. Last year's Christmas had been muted, thanks to Jack and I's zombie-like state as we adjusted to life as new parents. This year, I wanted the family party to be epic.

"How long for?"

The abruptness startled me. Caroline never objected to hosting my mother and Nanna. The house where Jack and I lived only had two bedrooms. Too much of a squeeze for us to fit anyone else in there.

"Um… seven days? That way they can see in the New Year with us too?"

"I'll have tae ask Ranald," she replied. "He likes his privacy, mind. I'm gonnae get a bit more food and drink."

She had a point. Much as I loved them, inflicting Mum and Nanna on anyone for seven days was a big ask. If the worst came to the worst, there was a caravan park on the other side of the loch. It closed from October to April, but the owner let out caravans to people on the proviso they kept quiet about it.

Caroline stood up and made her way toward the buffet table, its legs groaning with the effort of holding up so much food. We'd barely scratched the surface.

Evie had fallen asleep snuggled into the Alsatian's stomach, the dog curled around her. Babies were lucky that way —able, like animals, to drop off whatever noise went on around them when they were tired enough.

Mhari crept over to take her photograph. She limited her insults to me. If I died tomorrow, I knew she would leap at the chance of being Evie's guardian.

Dring! The phone again. I hit the green answer button.

"Katya! How are you? I tried to get you earlier."

My best friend's voice sounded muffled. In the background, I heard wailing—her six-month-old. "I know. I've been a bit… busy. Sorry."

"Is something wrong?" The flatness in her tone rang alarm bells in my head.

"No, no!" Fake cheery. "Is Evie there so I can say happy birthday?"

"Fast asleep, I'm afraid. But the party has been lovely. I wish you and Dexter had been here. And your little one."

"Next year, I promise. And I'll try to make it up to Lochalshie soon. Maybe for Christmas. It would be nice to escape London. The capital's hell at this time of year."

The wailing started up in earnest. Katya let out a sigh. Often, we phoned each other late at night to swap tips on childcare. More often, they ended up as mini counselling sessions, both of us reassuring each other we were not as crap at motherhood as we suspected.

"You wanted Evie, though," Katya would say. "I didn't wan—oh, it's pointless to moan. And I do love the little wretch, really."

A lot of the time she sounded as if she was trying to reassure herself, rather than me.

"I better go," she said now. "I'll be in touch soon, okay? M'wah!"

I m'wahed back and hung up, placing my phone on the table. I'll try to make it up to Lochalshie, not we'll try to make it up. "Promise you'll tell me if anything is wrong?" I fired off the message and clapped my hands.

"Anyone for musical statues?"

One hour—and a lot of cheating—later, people gathered their coats. Outside, a downpour had the rain rattling off the windows. Thickly padded coats over multiple layers, woolly hats, scarves and gloves were the only way to muddle through the winter months here. Above the smell of pizzas cooking—another Lochside Welcome speciality—I caught the distinctive aroma of damp wool.

Caroline got to her feet, her movements unsteady. A believer in strict adherence to public health guidelines on safe drinking levels, she limited herself to one glass of wine most of the time. I'd spotted her necking a second one earlier.

"I better find Ranald and head home, Gaby," she told me, indicating vaguely behind her.

The party guests streamed out, everyone calling out cheery goodbyes. The door opening and closing let in brief blasts of icy air, forcing me out of the booth where I'd taken a seat to one nearer the fire. Jack scooped up the empty plates. Evie was still slumped on Laney's dog.

"I need to wake her, up or she'll never sleep tonight," I said. Jack nodded, moving off to the kitchen, pausing next to the dog to gaze in raptures at his daughter.

Mhari, official photographer role finished for the day, took the seat opposite me.

"Something wrong wi' Katya?" she asked her attention half on me, the rest on her phone.

"Nothing at all!"

Mhari hadn't seen Katya, her erstwhile flatmate, for months. Katya made a point of never posting pictures of her child online. Mhari had cajoled, threatened and sucked up to me, desperate for me to share any photos I had. So far, I'd held out—mostly because Katya threatened to kill me if I did.

"Didnae sound like nothing to me. D'ye ken what I thought? That bairn of hers—"

The phone rang again—my mum. She must be terribly upset about missing Evie's birthday.

"Hello, you!" I said, "I was just about to send you this gorgeous pic of Evie. She's curled up asleep on—"

"Gaby, love!" my mum burst out. "Your Nanna's in hospital! You need to come down here as soon as you can!"

Highland Christmas: Chapter Two

THE HAVE A GO GRANNY

Jack materialised by my side, mouthing the words, 'What's wrong' I pointed at the phone and said 'Nanna', making my way through to the deserted conservatory, him following me.

"What happened?" I asked as Mum hiccoughed her way through an explanation, I jolted enough to worry that the all the pickled onion and chocolate cake I'd eaten might reappear.

Kathleen Millar, Nanna Cooper's oldest friend, had phoned my mum in a panic an hour earlier. She'd called around to Nanna's small, terraced house in Norwich, so the two of them could go to their weekly Tai Chi lesson and hadn't received an answer at the door. Phone calls hadn't worked either.

Kathleen knew where Nanna Cooper kept her spare key —in the plant pot at her front door. (And yes, Mum and I nagged her about the riskiness of keeping the key in the first place a potential thief would check.) On this occasion, though, the crystal-clear hiding place came in handy. Kathleen let herself in and discovered my nanna lying on the floor. She'd fallen and been unable to get up.

"She was so lucky, Gaby," Mum told me. "If Kathleen had got there any later, imagine what might have happened! Your poor gran, lying there, unable to feed herself or get to the toilet! We don't know yet if she's broken her hip. I've read the stats, Gaby! Elderly women who break their hips often end up dying after a year!"

She burst into tears, me joining in. Jack, able to hear everything, put his arm around me, dropping a kiss on the top of my head.

Elderly women. A descriptor that now applied to my nanna. The woman who'd only recently thumped a man who tried to rob her at a cashpoint, earning herself the headlines 'Have a go granny hammers hooligan' on the website of the local TV news programme.

"What have the doctors said?" I asked. Nanna was currently in Norfolk and Norwich University Hospital.

"They want to keep her in for an X-ray," my mum said, "and observation. But you should see her, Gaby! All hooked up to these machines beeping away. She's so thin too. I can't bear it."

Jack held his phone in front of me, the screen showing flight availability to Norwich. The airport wasn't a major one and flights from Edinburgh infrequent. However, there was one tomorrow at 11.15am, which would get me to Norwich an hour later.

"I'll be down as soon as I can, Mum."

And with that, I hung up and fell into Jack's arms. "Gaby, I'd come wi' you, but Monday's gonnae be full-on."

Late November wasn't a busy time in the hospitality industry. Still, we'd managed to persuade one of the local council departments to hold its annual community prize-giving event in the hotel.

Several local lollypop persons, care workers, and charity representatives were very much looking forward to the afternoon. They would eat their bodyweight in pizza and drink prodigious amounts before making their wobbly way to the front of the function room. That is where they would receive their medals and be photographed for an honorary appearance on the council's Facebook page and in the local press.

He squeezed my shoulder. "I'm sorry. I should be wi' you."

I gave him a watery smile. "Well, we knew what we were taking on when we bought a share in this place, didn't we?"

Words I said all the time to myself. Even though I'd stopped believing them a long time ago. Knew what we were doing my backside! The sheer relentlessness of hotel work threatened to grind me down all the time. And I wasn't even the person who spent the most time in here.

Nestled in the Highlands, the hotel and other local businesses relied on tourism through April to October when visitors flocked here to experience the countryside. Behind the village, the peaks of two hills, affectionately christened Maggie Broon's Boobs by the locals, offered views for miles around. The peace appealed to those who spent most of their lives crammed into the UK's overcrowded cities.

Running a small hotel in the middle of nowhere was a rollercoaster of highs and lows, where we lurched from one crisis to the next, never sure if the income from one month would keep us going another.

After a terrible summer, we needed Christmas to be mega. And to come up with a long-term plan that would keep the hotel viable in challenging times.

I blew my nose. "We better get back to the party."

Jack nodded. "Gaby, you're no' to worry about anything else except Nanna Cooper, d'ye hear me?"

Dark eyes searched mine. I nodded. "Message received and understood."

Back at the bar, everyone expressed sympathy.

"I'll babysit," Jolene volunteered. "Tamar will be so happy if Evie comes to stay with us!"

Tamar was busy plunging Evie's favourite teddy bear in and out of the giant bowl of non-alcoholic punch. What did that say for my daughter's chances of survival should she stay with them?

"Thanks, Jolene, but I'm going to bring her with me. Evie might be what Mum and Nanna Cooper need. And if I don't take her, my mum will never speak to me again."

Another unwanted thought surfaced later when Jack, Evie and I made our way home.

"If Nanna's broken her hip," I said, "she won't be able to come here for Christmas!"

"You don't know that yet," Jack pointed out.

"No, but…"

This was Evie's first Christmas. (Sort of.) I'd planned every aspect of the day. From when Evie woke up, to the nibbles we'd eat at Caroline's house where we opened the presents and the later riotous Christmas dinner eaten in the hotel with all our family and friends. The perfect Lochalshie celebration—the thought of which had cheered me up considerably in the last few weeks.

If Nanna couldn't make it, then it wasn't fair for me to expect Mum to come on her own. And if Jack, Evie and I went to Great Yarmouth instead, we'd miss celebrating with all our family and friends here, too awful a prospect to bear…

Highland Christmas: Chapter Three

INSULTING ENCOUNTERS

Eighteen hours later, I was in Edinburgh trying to stop my mind flashing up hideous images where I got to the hospital too late.

"Well, Evie. This is an adventure, isn't it?"

Solemn-eyed, my daughter took in her surroundings. Edinburgh Airport buzzed with travellers seeking a week of winter sun in the Canary Islands and suited business fliers. A family ahead of us wore sunhats, flip-flops, shorts and jaunty print T-shirts, dressed as if they were in Tenerife already. As the resident of a tiny village, Evie must find the sheer number of humans in one place unsettling.

Travel with a one-year-old brought its own challenges. What you carried on a flight. What you didn't. The pain in the butt liquid rules where anything over 100mls needed to be checked in. So far, Evie and I had made it through security. All I had to cope with now was taking her on her second flight ever and hoping her little ears could cope with the pressure in the cabinet as the plane took off and landed.

The first flight, when she was four months younger,

hadn't gone well. When we stumbled off the plane at Stansted, every other passenger hurried past, muttering about the 'worst flight ever'. Even the flight attendants' goodbyes, employees schooled in fake sincerity, rang hollow.

In the queue behind me waiting to board Flight EC9674 to Norwich, I heard muttering. "Oh God, there's a bloody baby on the flight. I'll never get tae sleep!"

About to turn around and give whoever a piece of my mind—*How dare you call my child bloody!*—I changed my mind, recalling her first flight. Until only a year ago I would have thought the same. Though I might not have said it out loud.

Evie and I made our way down the tunnel that led to the plane, her big brown eyes gazing around her in wonder. The air stewards beamed at us. "Oh my God!" one of them said, chucking Evie under the chin. "I can't believe the colour of her hair. What a lucky girl."

Seat located near the front I placed my rucksack in the overhead locker checking I had everything I needed for the flight. The Gaby flying no children version had only needed her phone, a trashy magazine and a drink. Babies required so many more 'just in case' items. Fingers crossed, toes too, that she wouldn't need her nappy changed. The prospect of doing such a thing in a tiny toilet while people queued outside appalled me.

Jack had insisted on splashing out for an upgrade for the flight, though an 'upgrade' on a bargain bucket airline meant little. All I got to do was book a specific seat and have about 10 centimetres more legroom, but I got to settle down before the rest of the passengers made their slow way onto the plane. As I fiddled with my rucksack trying to work out everything I needed to take out and what could be shoved up into the overhead lockers, I sent Jack grateful thanks.

When I finally sat down, Evie gurgling away on my lap, a man stopped in the aisle, checking his phone and the number on the row. What rotten luck. I'd ended up in the same row of seats as Mr 'I'll Never Get to Sleep on the Plane'. He looked just as dismayed, eyes lingering far too long on Evie as if he hoped glaring at her would stop her screaming her way through the entire flight.

(Mate. You've clearly never had children.)

He turned to the air steward, busy shoving handbags and carry-on suitcases in the locker. "Can I change seats?"

She took his boarding pass from him. "Sorry, Sir. You've paid for a specific seat and this is it."

He muttered a rude comment about FlyMe upgrades and how they ought to come with warnings about who you would be sitting next to.

He stretched up to put his bag in the locker, affording me a too-close glimpse of a tattoo that covered half of his torso and sat on the aisle seat. Another woman shuffled up the aisle, halting beside us. He shifted next to me.

Evie whimpered. I had one option up my sleeve for soothing her when the plane took off. But much as giving birth and motherhood had toughened me up to what embarrassed me and what didn't—tends to happen when you've had eight different people peering up your doodah—I hadn't envisaged having to sit next to a hostile man while doing it.

Great.

Evie's whimpers grew louder. The man let out an exaggerated sigh and sat down, rummaging through his bag. He took out a pair of headphones and jammed them pointedly over his ears. I recognised the brand—quality ones, but not noise-cancelling. The last time we'd flown, Evie had proved herself capable of industrial level decibel piercing.

"Look, I'm sorry, I—"

The words met empty air. The man stared fixedly at the seat in front of him. I settled for visiting all kinds of silent curses on him. May your girlfriend or boyfriend dump you. May your credit card be refused the next time you try to pay for a designer shirt (he was wearing a poplin slim fit shirt that smacked of too much money). And, my favourite one, may you step on Lego in your bare feet.

The air steward began her demo of the safety briefing. I paid attention, shivering at the bit where she instructed passengers to put on their own oxygen masks before attending to children.

"Not going to happen, Evie," I whispered to her. "I promise!"

At least her whimpering had settled down, my daughter too entranced by the slow movement of the plane along the runway as it began take-off.

The quiet didn't last. As the plane sped up, Evie opened her mouth wide and screwed her face up, shaking her little head. The screams started. Next to me, Mr Designer Shirt pulled his headphones down. Oh-oh. Emergency measures needed.

Breast-feeding, Jolene had told me beforehand, would soothe her. She should know. At nine months, young Tamar had embarked on his first flight. To visit his New Zealand maternal grandparents no less. "The sucking motion," Jolene promised me, "will ease the pressure on her ears. The flight will be a breeze!"

I was wearing a Lochside Welcome branded hoodie over a shirt. Straightforward enough to unzip, open the buttons and pop her in inconspicuously. She settled down, baby-shampoo scented soft hair brushing my skin and dark eyes meeting mine. The plane rose in the air, and she gave a little start of alarm before relaxing once more and carrying on.

I glanced sideways at my neighbour, who stared at me in horror. I glared back. What a Neanderthal creep—the type who thought women should breast-feed in the toilets. He removed his headphones. "How old is she?" his tone incredulous.

"Two," I said, betting that he had no idea what a one-year-old baby looked like. "Saves me a fortune in baby food. Not that it's any of your business. Think yourself lucky she's stopped screaming."

That said, I turned to stare out of the window, making a point of not looking at him for the rest of the flight.

Grab your copy...
vinci-books.com/HighlandChristmas